Cancelled

THE THRESHOLD

THE
THRESHOLD

MARLYS MILLHISER

G. P. PUTNAM'S SONS / NEW YORK

Library of Congress Cataloging in Publication Data

Millhiser, Marlys.
  The threshold.

  I. Title.
PS3563.I4225T5   1984   813'.54   84-8355
ISBN 0-399-13012-8

PRINTED IN THE UNITED STATES OF AMERICA

Second Impression

I am particularly indebted to the published works and careful research of Roger Neville Williams of Telluride, Dr. Duane A. Smith of Fort Lewis College, and David Lavender, whose reminiscences and thoughtful studies of the mining life in the Rockies are gold mines in themselves. I am indebted to Dr. Gene M. Gressley of the University of Wyoming, his *Bostonians and Bullion* and the marvelous archival material he safeguards in Laramie. To Frank A. Crampton's *Deep Enough; A Working Stiff in the Western Mine Camps*. To Suzanne and Dick Fetter for their *Telluride; From Pick to Powder* and for allowing me use of their extensive notes. To Karl Horn, hard-rock miner, and his daughter Wanda Apodaca, who spent her first school year in the little schoolhouse in Alta. To Elvira Wunderlich, a native of Telluride, for helping to check up on some stray and little-known facts. To Arlene Reid and her San Miguel County Muscum. To David Millhiser, consummate photographer. To the reference librarians at the Boulder Public Library, who stand ready to find answers to any and all crazy questions. And especially to my agent, Roberta Kent, who would not let this tale rest until it had gone "deep enough."

Any errors in fact in this tale of fancy are due to the dictates of the story or to a fallible author rather than to the talented and generous people listed above.

To Kathy and Dick Ralston
for introducing me
to the wonders of Telluride

THE DEEP, BLACK STOPE

Click—click—click, boys, down in the deep, black stope.
  The babies are sleeping, the stars are keeping, vigils
    on those above.

Strike—strike—strike, boys, for this is the only hope,
  to sweeten the life, of the faithful wife, who gave the
    world for your love.

It is not so hard to labor, boys, it is not so hard to wait,
  till sturdy, honest, and faithful, we lay by a little store.
It is not so hard to struggle, till the generous smile of fate,
  shall shed its lustre, on those who cluster, inside the
    miner's door.

But down in the awful blackness, in every tunnel and raise,
  at every shaft and station, about each timber and rope,
The angel of death is lurking, while the faithful mother prays,
  for him who sings, as his hammer rings, down in the deep,
    black stope.

Clean out the holes and load, boys, tend to your business well.
  This is a ticklish matter, where brains with danger cope.
Handle the powder with care, boys, that yellow quintessence
  of hell.
On every level, you're facing the devil, down in the deep,
  black stope.

Tramp—tramp—tramp, boys, to the toll of the old church bell,
  marching in solemn order, out to the barren slope,
Out to the dead man's city, his ghastly ranks to swell,
  for another soul signed death's pay roll, down in the deep,
    black stope.

—*Miners' Magazine,*
February 1900

PROLOGUE

THE first time Aletha Kingman met Callie O'Connell, Aletha was sketching the disintegration of a miner's shack in the ghost town of Alta, Colorado. Callie O'Connell looked like a real child, alive even to the slight sheen of moisture across her brow, to either side of a pert nose, and above the bow formed by her lips.

Aletha had been sitting cross-legged on the littered floor of an extinct building with the sketchbook on her knee and staring across the dirt road without premonition. The shack was of rough-sawn pine boards so weathered that some of the harder grain and all of the knots protruded, the softer material around them etched away by winter gales and high-altitude sun. The protrusions marked intriguing shadows too slight for her pencil to capture.

A marmot sunned in the crumbling door frame. Another stretched along a windowsill vacant of window.

A soft bur of wind in the pine tops heightened the silence. Insect wings whispered on the thin air—flies in the sun shafts, bees among wild yellow blossoms that thrust between fallen boards or crowded long-dead tree stumps. The water drooling out of the dark mouth of the mine tunnel in the mountainside above cascaded over the ledges of wreckage behind her with a muted babble. The air was cleansed of all but the faint and gentle smells—earth and dust, tree bark and weeds, rot too old to be offensive. Even the tang of pine needles seemed subdued this afternoon.

Aletha was trying to portray the mood of the black blankness behind the door frame which had no door, impatient with her lack of skill, when the girl appeared as though through a tear in nothing to stand on the road before her. The tear widened and that part of the road within it narrowed to a track. The tear shaped to an oval with blurry edges.

Aletha was too startled to react, not only by the girl but by the pounding roar that intruded with her, the accompanying shaking of the floor. A choking odor of sulfur seared Aletha's eyes and throat, the tender linings of her nose. She could see the shack behind and to the girl's right. One marmot still sunned in the doorway, unconcerned by the blurred edge of the tear just inches away. The window had emptied of the other marmot and had filled with glass panes. Below the window a platformed porch ended abruptly in the blur. A section of sheet iron was in place on a roof that looked sturdier and newer. And all the trees around the shack were gone or had become waist-high stumps. The lovely forest looked ravaged as if by war as far as the tear permitted sight.

The girl stared back, sun gleaming off rich brown sausage curls going limp and stringy where they touched her neck. Tight sleeves buttoned to the wrist, her skirt hitting some inches below the knee, and dark stockings covered her legs to the scruffy leather shoes. She seemed more surprised than frightened. Finally she smiled and Aletha had a sudden memory picture of the head and shoulders of a child with just such curls and dimples, plump and innocent and framed in an oval of entwined flowers on the lid of an antique cigar box her mother had given her.

This child stepped forward and spoke words that lost themselves in the din. She walked directly up to the concrete foundation on earth that was lower than outside the tear.

"How'd you get in there?" she yelled to Aletha.

"Callie, what are you doing?" A woman with skirts brushing the dust swirled into the oval. "I asked you to help with the washing," she shouted, and grabbed the child's hand, turning them both away, and the oval was gone.

The fat, furry marmot again reclined on a windowsill with no glass. The pine forest crowded up to the shack once more and the panel of sheet iron sagged sadly from its roof. Aletha Kingman reached into her jacket pocket for a tissue to wipe away the sulfur from her eyes. She gulped in clean air. The experience had taken but a moment, and had not bothered the marmots in the least. But now Aletha had time to react, and she shook, instead of the floor. Sweat seemed to prick out of every pore on her face and her fingers ached from the stranglehold she had on her pencil. Her knees threatened to cramp and she had to uncurl them with her hands. Stretching her legs out over the edge of the foundation floor, she reached for her sketchbook. She couldn't find it.

The marmots scurried into the blankness inside the shack when she stood up. Her legs worked pretty well and suggested she head for her car and away from this place, while a stubborn little thing in her mind demanded to know the whereabouts of her sketchbook. She made a thorough search of the weeds at the base of the foundation, the floor on top—knowing there was no place for the damn thing to go.

The sun, the quiet, the forest, the clean air—everything was normal and trying to convince her that nothing had happened. The sound of an engine grated up from the hillside below. Grated on her tingly nerve ends, until a jeep packed with people and a dog appeared around a curve. Aletha scurried, like the marmots, into the blankness behind the doorway of the shack across the road. She needed a little time to sort out her thoughts and calm the adrenaline still coursing through her body.

And all over the dead town the marmots began to whistle, each taking up the cry and passing it on.

PART ONE
ALTA

1

"B ut, Ma'am, didn't you see the lady sitting in the hole in the mill?" Callie turned for a quick glance to be sure the lady was really gone.

"Well, there's nothing now." Luella, who'd felt distinctly peculiar for a moment back there, looked over her shoulder again. She hurried her daughter around the cabin to the platform porch on the back, the tubs, and the scrub board.

"The lady was wearing pants," Callie insisted as she spread Bram's pants on a tree stump to dry.

"Then she was no lady." Luella handed Callie a pair of John O'Connell's overalls, washed but still reeking of burnt-powder smoke and damp tunnels deep in the earth. "Turn over the petticoats. They should be about done." Callie's mother dumped the soapy wash water out onto the porch and set to scrubbing the boards and steps with a broom. Part of her hair was coming down.

"The lady had a book on her lap. It fell off in the dirt—"

"Callie!" Luella leaned the broom handle against her bosom and fastened her hair up into place with side combs. "That is the last I wish to hear of your imaginary lady. Now, go peel the potatoes."

The cook stove overheated the tiny kitchen and Callie gazed longingly out the paned window. But shadows already stretched across the road and the stove's warmth would soon be welcome. And the lady's book still lay up against the concrete foundation of the mill. The hole in which she'd sat had not returned.

Callie cut bad spots from potatoes that were old and rubbery and sliced them and three big onions while Ma'am pounded beefsteak with the edge of a thick plate. The table where they worked jumped with Luella's blows as she attacked the meat. She paused to take pinches of salt and pepper from the palm of her hand, sprinkle them across the steak, and pound them in. Callie tried to think of an excuse to nip over and get the book as she helped Ma'am layer pieces of steak, potato, and onion, all dotted with suet, into a greased pan. Luella poured in water and crumbled dried sage and bay leaves over it. Callie rolled out the thick pastry crust to put on top.

The fruit pie and flat cake came out of the small oven, the meat pie went in. They washed the cooking dishes, and Ma'am combed up her hair again and put on a clean apron. "We'll mix the biscuits and shell the peas later. I'm going over the hill to see if your Aunt Lilly has a cup of tea for me. You do your lessons."

Neither young minds nor young hands were meant to go idle, Luella had determined long ago. Idleness led to such imaginings as Callie had known this afternoon and to puzzlements that were worse. She glanced back at the child perched on her powder keg, bent obediently over the worn copy of *Barnes's Complete Geography*.

The table was an upended spool that had once held iron cable for the tram that carried the mill's concentrates two miles down the mountainside. It took up well over half the kitchen. The proper table Luella had brought with her from Central City graced the sitting room now, covered with a fringed cloth, upright books between bookends, her prized stained-glass lamp, family pictures, and the Bible. It was too small to service the gigantic meals the men required after a shift in the mine.

Luella was halfway to the mill when the change in the clamor— the clanging, thundering, screeching constant in her life—stopped her. The thundering eased and halted altogether. The screeching increased to a scream as if brakes had been set in motion and then it halted too. Silence shocked the world and rooted her to the spot. In the eight-odd months the O'Connells had lived in Alta, she had known the mill to shut down completely once and that had been for repairs too major to remedy while work was in progress. That shutdown had been announced well in advance. She heard the rush of Callie's shoes on the porch, braced herself as Callie bumped into her and clutched at her skirts. "Ma'am?"

"I don't know, Callie. Perhaps something has broken down." Luella realized she was shouting, as they'd all become accustomed to doing.

Young Mr. Ivorson came to a side door in the mill, a hulking frame building composed of a series of connected sheds each on a level higher than the one below and reaching up in giant steps to the mine that fed it. He began to retch with such violence the spasms drove him to his knees. Luella started toward him, dragging Callie with her, when the mine whistle shrieked its dread warning to everyone within miles. Not the summoning of a shift at this hour.

Men came running from the boardinghouse, some still pulling galluses over their long johns, others tucking in their shirttails. Decorum was no issue when the whistle shrieked out-of-hours. It did so only for accident, death, and destruction and it brought a shudder to the spine of every woman in the camp.

"They don't shut down the mill for a cave-in," someone said behind Luella, echoing her own relief. Cave-ins claimed the most souls and were thus the most feared. "Trouble must be in the mill."

When she realized Callie was no longer attached to her, Luella moved again toward the door and poor Mr. Ivorson. He hung out halfway to the ground and she could see over him to the gray-crusted table floor, the lowest floor of the mill. A gray-begrimed mill hand lowered something down a wooden-ladder stairs to another hand below. She recognized what passed between them at the same time as did the men to either side of her, and they all inhaled involuntarily more of the noxious fumes of the mill than they wanted. It was the naked arm and shoulder of a man. Bloodied stringy things dangled from where it should have been attached to the body. The lower portion that would have led to a wrist and hand was bruised and flattened. It reminded Luella of the raw beefsteak she'd tenderized for supper.

" 'Tis Haskell Gibson." Mr. Crowe, the shift foreman, leaned over young Mr. Ivorson and mercifully blocked their view. "Got 'is clothes caught in the workings, he did. Got pulled in. Would you find Ora, Mrs. O'Connell, and head her off before she gets here? She shouldn't see wot's left of the man."

Luella swallowed back gorge and pushed through the crowd that had formed behind her. As she turned up the road to intercept Ora Gibson, she saw Callie slip into the house.

Callie stared at the pencil pictures, trying to understand what she saw. Then she hid the lady's book under the mattress of Bram's cot that also served as sofa in the sitting room, feeling distinctly sly and secretive. Ma'am had warned her that no one liked little girls who were sly and secretive. She turned over the pants and overalls and brought the dry clothes in.

Ma'am still had not returned, so she pulled the book out and looked at the pictures again. Then she shelled the peas the vendor had brought up by wagon that morning, silence hanging strange and heavy all around her. A dog barked somewhere far away and Callie stopped to listen, realizing she hadn't heard that customary sound since coming to live by the mill.

When she'd finished everything else, she opened *Barnes's Complete Geography* and read aloud to ease the uneasy silence. " 'Within the torrid zone, where food and shelter are obtained with but little exertion, there are no powerful nations. In the North temperate zone, where extremes of climate demand the greatest skill and energy, are found the most perfect types of man.' " When Bram came home, Callie was back staring at the lady's drawing book and the cabin smelled of sage and onion.

"You had better not, Bram," she warned as he cut a hunk of cake and ate it in two bites.

"I'm a hard-rock stiff now, Callie child, and I need my food."

"You're just a nipper. Ma'am had to go to Mrs. Gibson."

"Hear poor old Haskell's spread in pieces from one end of the mill to the other." He reached for the cake again. Bram had smudges of dirt still streaking his face and hands, matting his once sandy hair. Fourteen years old and over six foot, he could out-eat all the rest of the family put together. It was obvious Bram didn't come from any torrid zone.

"You just keep away from that cake, Bram O'Connell."

"Don't get wrathy with me, little girl, or I'll tickle you." Callie squealed and tried to wiggle off the powder keg as he lunged with his favorite nasty leer. But he stopped, noticing the lady's book open on the table. "That's some fine drawing, Callie. Who did it?"

"A lady. She left it. Want to see our house?" She turned the page to the picture of their cabin, falling down and deserted, the porch gone, a whistle pig lying across the doorsill. "She only draws sad pictures."

"That can't be our house with the trees all grown up around it. But this sure looks like the boardinghouse gone to rack and ruin. Where's the mill? And the sheds at the portal, and the change-house?"

"I think this is the commissary all fallen in."

"Who *is* this lady?" His voice broke in anger. "Why would she draw everything destroyed and all the people gone?"

"She left before I could ask her. Maybe she's from Telluride. There's pictures of there too, and Ma'am says they have every kind of lady in Telluride."

Bram flushed and looked surly. But he kept turning pages. "Maybe you better set the table."

"Passed the hat for Ora and the baby. It'll not go easy for her with no insurance or family," John O'Connell said at supper. "Burying's in Telluride tomorrow."

"It's been an unsettling day altogether, what with poor Haskell . . ." Luella pushed the piece of steak she'd cut to the side of her plate and speared a potato slice instead. "And Bram eating half the cake and Callie seeing imaginary ladies and sneaking that book in here."

"She can't be imaginary if she can make pictures like this." John picked up the book and chewed some more on the tough meat. "But this lady sure has imagination. Lookee here. This is the Senate in Telluride and a tumble-bumble rendering of the Silver Bell. But this building across the street sure ain't the Gold Belt Dancehall. Why would she draw things that way? I'll show you tomorrow when we go to the funeral."

"You will not. No lady goes to that side of town, John O'Connell. And not to sketch pictures of it either. There's more pie, Bram."

"You keep feeding him up and he'll grow into his feet. Then where'll we be? Have to rent two houses." John ladled meat pie onto Bram's plate. "One for him and one for the rest of us."

When Ma'am wasn't looking, Callie slipped some meat scraps from the edge of her plate into the waxed bag on Bram's lap under the table. The bag had once held candy from the drugstore in Ophir but was now used to collect food for Charles.

"I wager you peek around corners when you go shopping to see what it is that's there on 'that side of town,' Mrs. O'Connell." John raised the book so he could slip some meat for Charles to Callie, and lowered it again. "And look at here, now, them's the cribs around the corner."

Luella put her hand to a flaming cheek and Callie leaned across Pa's arm. It smelled of muck and smoke. "What's a crib, Pa?"

"That's a wee house, hardly bigger than a baby's own crib." And John O'Connell laughed his big-bear laugh that shook the table and tickled something in Callie's middle. The lady had drawn a row of tiny houses with peaked roofs all crowded together. Two long windows and a door took up almost the whole of their fronts. John sobered at his wife's stunned look. "Well, now, Callie's all of ten years old and soon to be a woman." But he squirmed and couldn't meet Luella's eyes. "Can't keep her in the dark about everything . . . forever."

"What Callie doesn't know won't hurt her."

"Haskell Gibson didn't know better than to get too close to the workings," John O'Connell answered his wife in an ominous tone, and waggled a finger at them all, "and he was hurt mortal bad."

2

ALETHA Kingman stood inside the miner's shack and stared toward the exposed floor on which she'd sat while marmots whistled all over what was left of Alta. The rough wood of the door frame felt withery dry under her hand. Houses, like people, dry up when they get old. Was this where Callie had lived? Alta had not been abandoned until the 1940's. That's why so much of it was still intact. But that forest had taken more than forty years to grow back. Probably lots of people had lived here after Callie.

Daylight penetrated cracks between the bare boards of the outer wall. Whole swaths of cloth hung colorless, worn to a gossamer thinness. Wads of newspaper had the print drowned out by weather stain. Odd patches of sheet metal and even squashed tin cans with the ribbing bumps still running through the middle and pieces of shredding linoleum—all bore witness to the desperation of generations to stop the herculean winters from leaking in. A heavy beige paper had been applied throughout at one period, and more recently a series of once-gaudy wallpapers now aged to pastel and gray.

The marmots had quieted but Aletha could hear voices as the jeep travelers spread out to explore the ghost town. The dog's barking sounded harsh and unnatural where memories slept and life had died. The shack had one small room and one tiny one, with a narrow staircase against the wall of the former. The tiny room had been a kitchen with a hole in the ceiling for a stovepipe, a back door, and two miniature window holes. A shelf under one window contained a sink that must have drained into a pail, because there was no sign of pipes.

The larger room had a hole in the wall for a stovepipe, a front door, and two windows. Aletha turned her shoulders sideways to creep up the bowed stairs and wondered how a hearty miner had managed his shoulders in this space. The loft upstairs was so low no adult could hope to stand upright even under the center of the steeply pitched roof.

Aletha supposed the woman who had come to claim Callie was the girl's mother and she tried to imagine the two of them in this derelict place, unable to believe she was admitting that any of it had happened.

The mother didn't seem to have noticed Aletha, but she'd never really looked up. She'd swirled into the oval in a mild huff, bent to grasp the girl's hand, and turned away. Her eyes had been on Callie the whole time. The woman's hairdo was turn-of-the-century or before, done up in a big plop on top of her head with wispies coming down all around. She'd be long dead by now, probably Callie too. The little girl anyone would want to hug on sight had aged and withered and died already.

Aletha left the shack to perch against the foundation across the road in as close to the same spot as she could remember. She'd stood for a long while, not particularly wanting to repeat the experience, when a head with a face and a monstrous bulge on the back of it appeared in the darkness of the doorway to the miner's shack. Aletha gave a startled squeak. Eyes widened and met hers in a flash of anger. A man with a rolled sleeping bag on top of a full-framed backpack shifted and bent low to step out the door.

"Sorry." She tried to straighten the silly look off her face. "Guess I was expecting a ghost."

He forced a smile that didn't pretend to go past his lips. His stubbled chin was as scruffy as Callie's shoes. "Probably some around. Place like this."

He clomped off up the road in heavy boots. He'd broken the spell. Aletha brushed grit from the seat of her jeans, made another useless check for her sketchbook, and followed him. A slight chill reminded her of the lengthening shadows and shortening daylight. She wondered what this place did at night. The window holes of the boardinghouse were even now sinking into slanted shadow, like eye sockets in a weary face. Rows of eyes with formless silhouettes behind them, like memories or thoughts. Wraiths?

Two couples and the dog were loading into the jeep next to her car. They ground off on what Aletha's map showed to be Boomerang Road. The same map warned that her little Datsun would have to travel back the way it had come, which had been bumpy enough.

The man with the backpack was setting up a small tent on the leveled space in the midst of flattened buildings that once meant things to living people. He was unusually tall and she wondered how he could fit in the tent. Aletha slid into the Datsun, started the engine, and was about to close the door when the backpacker was suddenly there holding on to it. "Is there any way I could hitch a ride if you're going somewhere near Telluride? Maybe just to the highway? I'm out of everything except granola. I hate granola."

"Well, I . . . guess."

"Thanks. Just a minute and I'll get my tent."

Aletha thought seriously of taking off without him. She'd learned how dangerous it was to trust people. But if he'd meant to do her harm he could have yanked her out of the car when he held the door. No need to get neurotic over a poor man who needed a lift. She greeted him with an apologetic smile when he stuffed his gear into the backseat and slid in beside her. With him came the reek of wood smoke so thick she rolled her window down for air. His smile was reserved and tightened her back up a bit. "Aletha Kingman. I'm staying in Telluride. I'll take you on in."

"Cree Mackelwain. Thanks."

She backed and turned the Datsun on the road between the boardinghouse and the commissary, headed down the hill past Callie's house slowly because of the rocks and washouts.

He studied her and she sensed he was nervous riding with her. He had to be half again her size. "Do you live in Telluride?"

"Just staying there. For a while." Cree Mackelwain put his hand to the dashboard. "Will you please watch the road?"

"I've had a wild afternoon." She laughed and heard hysteria. Only a trace.

*　*　*

It was the time of day deer move out of cover toward water. But Cree didn't look into the forest at the roadsides. Twilight grayed the colors around them; not enough to make the headlights of any use, but enough to fuzz vision. The hard-sprung Datsun didn't take the unsurfaced road well and the woman seemed to aim for every chuckhole and rock in it at a speed to match her flaky laugh. He shouldn't complain; not many lone females would have picked up a camp-ripe backpacker.

He was struggling to think of something halfway pleasant to say when they rounded a curve where two trees and a wooden tower blocked their path. Cree hit the windshield when she hit the brakes, even though he was braced against the dash. Pebbles flew as the Datsun's rear skidded around and the front hung up over the far side of a drainage ditch, throwing him back against the seat.

"That's some reaction time, lady," he said when he realized they'd stalled.

She stared at her hands on the steering wheel. "It was the tear again."

"Tear in what?"

"The tear in what I'm seeing today."

Cree glanced out the side window. No tower, no trees blocked the road. "For just a moment . . . the road we're on wasn't there."

"You saw it too?" Her whisper croaked, "I thought it was just me." She drew a piece of ragged pink rock on the end of a chain out from under her sweatshirt and began to worry it with her fingers. Then she bit it.

Shoving his breathing back under control Cree stepped down into the ditch. The Datsun had hung up on a bank soft with dead red pine needles about six inches from a hard live tree trunk. "This kind of thing happen to you often?"

"I saw a little ghost named Callie by that shack this afternoon, but other than that I don't think I've done this before. I don't need any of this. I just got out of . . ." She grabbed three times for the door handle before she made contact and then disappeared into the ditch on the other side.

"Just got out of what?"

"It scared me." He took her arm and forced her to walk up and down the road. "If you saw it too," she said, "then maybe the tear *was* there. And what do I do with that?"

Cree had rarely met anyone who could talk so much and make so little sense. He wished she had a big nose or thick hips or something. But she was slight and . . . honey-colored. "That was a tram tower we saw. Tram used to go right along here." He walked into the trees, kicked an ancient wooden plank, took hold of a loop of rusted metal cable that stuck up stiffly from the soil. "This is part of what we saw. They shipped ore concentrates in buckets down to a railroad that used to run below."

"Just what is it you do for a living, Mr. Mackelwain?" she asked in total disregard of the conversation he thought they were having. Her hair seemed to catch what little light was left in the world.

"I'm unemployed." She was impossible to talk to. "So what do you do?"

"Same as you."

Cree offered to drive once they'd pushed the Datsun back onto the road, but she refused. "Let's just hope the road continues on into this year," she said.

Both kept quiet with their thoughts on the way into Telluride. Cree had thrown out about every explanation he could come up with for the roadblock that wasn't there. He'd even toyed with the idea this Aletha person had some kind of power to induce hallucinations in others. He threw that one out with a snort he tried to transform into a laugh when she glanced at him. He was bone weary after four days on the trail. That's why, when she'd parked the Datsun on the main street of Telluride's little business district, he was surprised to hear himself say, "Buy you a drink at the Sheridan in about an hour?"

She peered over the car roof at him and shrugged. "Sure."

Aletha hurried through the lobby of the New Sheridan Hotel, which was the oldest hotel in town and its lobby the tiniest, most unimposing lobby imaginable. It had an ornate cage for the registration clerk and a booth displaying souvenirs where she'd bought the little piece of quartz on a chain she wore around her neck. *Take a piece of Telluride home with you*, the sign above the booth read. She'd chosen that particular one because it had a pretty pinkish stain to it, whereas the others were more a milky white. They all had gold and silver glitters that flashed in the sunlight. She'd decided that it would bring her luck.

A narrow stairway led off the hall on the way to the dining room up to a landing where one turned abruptly onto a staircase that swept to the top of the building, with only a small level space as a step-off point to the second and third floors. Balustraded balconies allowed entrance to the rooms on both floors and looked down upon the illogical and abrupt ending of the staircase.

In her room Aletha switched on the light and took the antique cigar box out of her suitcase. She used it to keep stationery, letters, and stamps in, but she looked now with new interest at the little girl in the oval picture ringed with flowers on the cigar-box lid. This child had a velvet bonnet atop her sausage curls. It was tied under her chin with ribbons that seemed to blow in the wind. She too had a dimple in each plump cheek, heavy lashes, and eyes of delighted innocence. Aletha's mother collected old advertising posters. Many used representations of little girls with that look of guileless helplessness. "Establishment pornography of yesteryear," Helen announced often and with a certain glee. "Dirty old men always were and always will be."

Cree Mackelwain was waiting in the bar when Aletha arrived. The place had old smoky glass in the mirror behind the bottles, old photographs of a long-dead Telluride on the walls, and the requisite blare of new music. They sat at a table and had to shout. Cree Mackelwain looked dark even after an obvious scrubbing-up and a shave.

"So . . . have you talked yourself out of it yet?"

He grinned. "Just about."

"Don't worry, by tomorrow you'll have yourself convinced either nothing happened or somehow it was my doing." She described Callie to him, and the smell of sulfur. They fell into an uncomfortable silence. He was not a comfortable person. He rallied and tried to talk about his backpack trip but kept searching her face as if he doubted anything was getting through. Finally they sat and watched other people talk. He went to the bar to get himself another beer and a burgundy for her, lingered to speak to an eastern cowboy in an expensive western shirt.

"So . . . uh . . . you said you just got out?" Cree placed the burgundy before her. "Don't tell me. Let me guess. You had a nervous breakdown," he said gracelessly, "and you've just been released from the hospital and you are on a needed vacation, right?"

"Wrong." Aletha raised the glass of purple-red wine and looked him straight-on over the top of it. "I just got out of prison."

Cree sat perfectly still a moment, staring into his beer. Then he raised it to his lips and almost choked on a mouthful when he exploded into laughter. Three guys standing up to the massive bar cheered when Aletha slapped money down on the table and walked out.

3

THIS promised to be one of the finest days of Callie's young life. Luella and John O'Connell went to the funeral for Haskell Gibson in Telluride. And Callie had Bram and Charles to herself. With the Fourth of July and Christmas as the only scheduled holidays and a seven-day work week as standard, camps closed down for funerals, giving everyone a time to mourn the dead and ease life's tensions in town.

All but a few of the camp children had gone with their parents on down the winding Boomerang Road in a procession that had started before dawn. Many of the single miners rode the tram buckets to Ophir Loop and then took the train on into Telluride. Callie and Bram had been left behind to save on expenses.

She sat in the privy now, humming blissfully and contemplating a whole day to do with as she wished. A panicked fly buzzed his struggles in a web near the roof and a brown spider the size of a shooter marble watched from a crevice close by. Callie kicked the seat with the heel of her shoe, making a familiar hollow thud, thud, thud. The privy was already becoming sun-warmed and fragrant but Callie much preferred this place in summer. In winter there was ice on the seat. She cleaned herself with a square of newspaper and stepped out into the sun.

Bram sprawled across the porch stroking Charles, who reclined majestically on his chest. Charles lived in the warm places under their house. He'd been living there when the O'Connells moved in and had no intention of moving out just because Luella did not like cats. She often tried to chase him off but Charles would circle around her and slip under the house where the broom couldn't reach. Charles was not a clean cat as cats go, which was unfortunate, since he was all white. But living under the house and sometimes scrounging rodents or tidbits from dinner pails over at the mill, or scraps left out on the town garbage heap next to the O'Connells' cabin, had given him a distinctly blotchy appearance.

"Come here, Callie, and listen. You can hear Charles purr now that the mill's shut down."

Charles's purr sounded more like a rattle somewhere deep in his breathing. But the little sounds they didn't usually hear—like the drone of bees, the sad cry of the train whistle down at the Loop—made this golden day even more special. Callie could even hear Bram's stomach gurgle.

"Let's go see if Aunt Lilly's done her baking yet." He stood and draped the cat over his shoulder. Charles stiffened and his ears went back. His tail flapped this way and that across Bram's chest. Charles preferred always to do his own walking. The mill rose in tiers to one side, houses or cabins lined the other, and above these a row of homes that boasted such things as separate bedrooms, enclosed porches, and even pantries. The white schoolhouse sat shuttered. Bram crossed over and kicked the door. Charles leapt off and away from him.

"The new teacher will be here next week and you have to stop work and go to school," Callie taunted, and hiked herself atop the hitching rail.

"I'm old enough to earn a wage and we need the money." He gave the door another kick. "I'm a man and I want to work." Bram had gone through all the schoolbooks Ma'am had brought with her from Ohio as well as what education was offered him in their no-madic life. He could read anything in the Bible Ma'am asked him to. She hoped to locate in a big town with a high school in the next year or so.

Because of the heavy snows, school was usually in session in Alta from May to October, but a teacher had not been found until late this year and she'd promised to stay on through December. Callie couldn't wait. Lessons with Ma'am were not as much fun as being in a schoolroom with other children. Luella had taught in a one-room country school near her farm home in Ohio before she'd caught the eye of the big Irishman who was passing through. Married teachers were almost unheard of. Even though teachers were needed wherever they went, Luella never considered the job. Her big Irishman continued to call her Ma'am in gentle fun anyway, and Callie and Bram could think of her in no other way.

Callie and Bram walked on, past the commissary and the cookhouse, and stopped to give a few words of encouragement to Mary Jane, the blindfolded mule tethered to a stump on a patch of grass beside the road. Mary Jane had hauled ore cars on the five-hundred level for the last six months and the only light she'd seen had been from miners' candles and carbide lamps.

Aunt Lilly sat on her front step, her chin in her hands. She didn't look up when they stood before her. "Wonder what's ailing Aunt Lilly, Bram."

"She's fretting because she didn't get to go to Telluride."

Lilly gave a half-grimace, half-grin. "Cookies are cooling on the table."

"Callie, fetch the milk." Bram stepped around his aunt. "We'll have a party."

Callie ran to the spring behind the cabin, pushed aside two wooden planks, and drew out a small covered pail. Fresh milk was a luxury of summer, canned milk being the staple here. Bram had mugs and cookies waiting in front of the step. Lilly hadn't moved. They sat at her feet.

"Best cookies I ever ate."

"I could make them out of wood shavings and you'd say that, Mr. Brambaugh." But Lilly finally took her hand from beneath her chin to mess his hair. "You two are the only fun that ever happens in this place."

The cookies tasted of sweet and cinnamon and oatmeal. The milk smeared buttery slime on Callie's tongue. Mary Jane coughed and hacked across the strange stillness.

"Only thing ever happens around here is people get killed." Lilly's pretty face screwed into a pout. She didn't resemble her sister, Luella, except for certain expressions in her eyes. Lilly was the younger and had been married only a year. "I hope this will settle her down," Luella had said when she'd heard of the marriage to Uncle Henry. "She's always been so silly and flighty."

Aunt Lilly had become so settled that her light step had turned into a waddle, the lightness in her laughter had deepened to irony, and Uncle Henry had gone alone to Telluride this day. "Must be wonderful to be a man," she said, "have all that freedom."

That afternoon Callie and Bram walked into the little lakes not far from Alta, watched the ducks take off and land, skipped stones across the water. In places there were dams built up to trap water for ore processing, and before winter the O'Connells would catch fish from behind them to salt down in five-gallon crockery jars.

Bram had grown so pale since working in the mine his dark eyes stood out large and liquid. But his shirt was fuller, threatening to tear between the shoulders. Callie took his hand to jump across a section of bog and he let her hold it for a while. It was warm and bony and strong and she wished the day would not have to end.

"Why does Aunt Lilly call you Mr. Brambaugh?" She reverted to her little-sister voice.

"Because that's what was written on the note pinned to me. 'His name is Brambaugh. Please find a loving home for the babe.' " Would Callie never tire of this story? Bram wondered. "Look away. I'm going to swim."

"Why can't girls swim, Mr. Brambaugh?" Callie turned around and sat to take off her shoes and stockings.

"Because their behind part is so big they'd sink." Bram was trying to see the face of the woman who had left him on the step of Ma'am's schoolhouse in Ohio. Luella had told him the woman was probably very poor and couldn't keep him, had wanted to do the best thing for him because she loved him. But he couldn't see her. Ma'am's face kept getting in the way.

Callie hiked up her skirt and petticoat and waded in, hissing at the cold, stumbling on the greasy rocks. Long curls bounced on her shoulders. She looked at him then, her eyes growing soft and serious. "I love you and Charles best in all the world."

"Callie, you love everybody and everything." Bram slid out farther so she wouldn't spy his nakedness through the water.

In Telluride, Luella had almost finished her shopping before the long ride home. Her packages, wrapped in brown paper and tied with twine, held cloth, buttons, thread, and lace for Callie's school dress, material for a shirt for Bram, a whole chicken picked and ready for the pot, a bag of sticky candies. She needed only to visit the drugstore, buy fresh fruit, and she'd be ready to meet John. She averted her eyes as she passed a saloon with its doors open to the streets, but heard the rumble of men's voices, the flappety-click of a gambling wheel. Luella had seen few ladies on Colorado Avenue this afternoon. They seemed to scurry between stores and not linger on this street where vice and commerce mixed willy-nilly.

At the drugstore Luella purchased two large bottles of Wyeth's Wine of Coca, a prepared tonic she'd found indispensable for the treatment of sluggishness during her monthlies, the family's various aches and colds in winter, John's exhaustion after too long on the hammer, and just a general restorer when energies flagged. The clock on the wall told her she had time for a quick Coca-Cola at the marble soda fountain. It was a chance to get off her feet. The drink was cool, refreshing, exhilarating. In fact before she had it half-finished Luella felt better able to cope with John. His possible condition after some hours on the town had been a worry to her.

A large woman in black with a white lacy dust cap bustled in, made a hurried purchase, and gave Luella a curious glance as she passed. "I'll be going out the back way, Mr. Holder."

"Right you are, Mrs. Stollsteimer." The druggist nodded and turned to Luella. "You might want to do the same, missus. It's three o'clock and the girls from the line'll be up on the street to do their shopping. Most of the ladies make themselves scarce this time of the day."

"Oh . . . ohmygoodness!" Luella grabbed her packages and guzzled the last of her drink before she ran from the store.

"And what do you make of that now, huh?" John O'Connell stood in front of the Senate Saloon and Gambling Establishment, newly reopened. He pointed to the Silver Bell on the corner. "It looks to be more like the new Silver Bell than the old that burnt, does it not? Yet she's drawn the new building gone old and saggy."

"Beats me how a woman could draw so good to begin with," said an unsteady miner on John's right.

"Why'd she leave out all the hitching posts, I wonder," said the miner on John's left. The three had found themselves marching together in Haskell Gibson's funeral procession, and with the help of a few drinks had become fast friends.

"Maybe she wasn't done drawing yet." They stood swaying, shaking their heads, looking back and forth between the paper and the reality. The Silver Bell, the Senate, and McPherson's Boardinghouse had stood in a row until recently when an angry patron set fire to the Silver Bell and a whirly little wind came up to spread it along to the other two buildings. The Senate had reopened in the lower half of what had been the boardinghouse, the upper story gone, and fresh bright bricks ringed its top like a crown. That left a small vacant lot between the two rebuilt structures, which this artistic lady had dutifully included. But she'd filled it up with weeds when in fact it was burned clean of everything except the new building debris of its neighbors.

"Has me flimflammed," John said when the three had returned to the interior and stood to the bar. "Gives a man the need of a bracer, is what it does. Make it a Bright Eye this time, Mr. Jessup," he told the bartender. While Mr. Jessup poured a tiny packet of white powder into a shot of rye for him, John opened the lady's book one last time. "Lay you odds you'll not be knowing what that is."

"Ain't a trolley," said one of his companions, "nor a train engine. Not a buggy. Not a wagon."

The bartender craned around to stare at the Chevy Citation parked in front of a building they'd never seen. "Wonder what you'd pull it with. No place to hook anything up. Couldn't haul much in it."

When John O'Connell left the Senate with the lady's book under his arm, his eyes were indeed bright.

4

ALETHA Kingman put away the cigar box and tried to concentrate on something more important than Callie. She'd come to Telluride to rest her nerves after a harrowing year and to find a temporary job to tide her over through the winter.

Every third person in the world, it seemed, wanted to while away some time—ski, have shelter and minimal support in Telluride, Colorado—until they got themselves together. Pay was low, living costs extravagant. Aletha groaned and rolled over in the bed. Her feet and legs ached from her job search. She picked up the phone and called her mother in San Diego, collect.

"Is it because you were in prison?" Helen asked when she'd heard Aletha's troubles. "That conviction was reversed. You just tell them that."

"Nobody's asked about a criminal record, Mom. I haven't even gotten to the application-form stage. There is no work and there's going to be some sort of jazz festival held here soon and there won't be a room in town available. Including this one."

"I was hoping things would go right for you after . . . everything." Helen's sigh came tired across the miles. "I'll sell the Monks' Brewery sign and wire you the proceeds. Stay with it, honey."

When she'd hung up Aletha slugged the pillow in frustration. A little college, a little travel—her mother and Bertie had gone along with it all. But Helen's encouragement was sounding thin and Aletha couldn't blame her. There was no such thing as a "little" prison.

The phone rang at her end and startled her. "Aletha . . . ah . . . Kingman? This is Barry down at the Senate. I just now found out I got a waitress and two subs down with the flu and we open in an hour. Can you get over here?"

"I'm on my way."

"Yeah, listen, Aletha, we don't do uniforms. Wear your own stuff but dress it up a little, you know? No pants or Nikes, huh? We are a class establishment." He laughed as if the whole phone call were a joke on her. But he wasn't laughing when she arrived at the Senate teetering on high-heeled sandals and wearing her "little-piece-of-Telluride" pendant on the outside of her blouse to dress it up. "Bartender just called in sick. Can't get ahold of the busboy. We'll all have to take turns at the bar," he said to the two waitresses and one waiter marshaled before him. "Aletha, you start there."

"I don't know how to mix drinks."

Barry's striped sport shirt opened halfway down the front to show a silver chain and the dark curly hair tight to his chest. "Look, all you do is if a guy orders a martini, ask him what's in it and then make one." He tied a white dish towel around her waist. "Next time somebody orders a martini, you'll know."

Barry returned with a pan of ice to fit in one of the deep metal-lined cavities and a plate of lemon and orange slices and lime wedges.

"Not to worry. Regulars come in first. Mostly drink beer." He turned the wooden "Closed" sign around to "Open" and pulled back the glass door so customers could use the swinging ones. "Just don't pour it over ice."

The first customer was obliging enough to order a beer, but as more arrived and word of her inexperience spread, the orders grew a trifle exotic. She found a menu to determine the price of drinks and discovered that although the tone of the Senate was one of informality, the entrées ran to things like Boeuf Wellington, pheasant, and shrimp-stuffed sole, with prices to match. The menu also advertised "Elegant Intoxicants." Aletha started throwing in extra fruit.

A golden nude statuette hung from a central chandelier in a sort of swimming position over green-felted gambling tables around which drinkers loitered in captains' chairs. Victorian love seats grouped in corners and a potbellied stove hunkered along the far wall. Dusty stuffed critters and modern paintings of Victorian-era females hung amid old mining implements and a roulette wheel. "Notice any big rips in the scenery lately?" Cree Mackelwain settled on the last vacant stool at the bar. "Thought you were unemployed."

"No. And today I was unemployed. Tonight I'm working. Tomorrow I'm unemployed. And please don't order anything fancier than a beer."

"I'll have a beer. Plain Michelob."

"And I'll have an Amaretto Alexander, please, on the rocks with a twist," the guy on the next stool said.

Aletha ignored him and bent close to Cree with her hand cupped around one side of her mouth. "I'm sorry about last night. Please don't mention what I said."

"You're about as convincing an ex-con as I would be a ballerina," he whispered.

"Hey, fella, you got something going with my barkeep?" Barry grinned and slid behind the bar to untie Aletha's dish-towel apron. "Go out and earn yourself some tips. Tracy'll show you around."

In the various back rooms small tables sported linens and wine goblets. Deep florid wallpapers muted the light. Cree was gone when Aletha went out to the bar to order cocktails for her first customers. About nine-thirty he showed up at one of her tables with a woman he introduced as Renata Winslow. Renata had a tan like Aletha had not seen since the Caribbean, a model-slender figure, a luxury of dark hair that fell and swept in all the right directions, and only a perfect and simple way with clothes and make-up. Aletha resented her instantly.

"Aletha tears up scenery," Cree said by way of introduction. "Renata helps find people jobs."

Renata smiled perfectly too. She handed Aletha a business card, *Renata's Helpers. Quick Substitute Workers for All Kinds of Work. When Your Staff Can't Make It, Call Renata. Qualified Personnel Only.*

"You don't find rooms for your 'qualified personnel,' do you?"

"I'll ask if any of my helpers has need of a roommate."

"There's lots of beds where I'm staying at the Pick and Gad." Cree looked over his shoulder as if to see if anyone was listening. "But then, it's a whorehouse." They laughed at her and she served them bread, salad, shrimp-stuffed sole, wine, and coffee. Where Callie had dimples, Cree Mackelwain had deep vertical creases, and Renata Winslow reached across the table to trace one with a finger.

Aletha did not call on Miss Winslow the next day because she was offered another evening at the Senate. But she did the day after and got work cleaning bathrooms and changing sheets at the Tomboy Inn. "Where can I reach you? With the jazz festival in town, there'll be work."

"I'll call you." Aletha spent her first night out of the New Sheridan at Tracy's one-room apartment because Tracy's boyfriend was on a fishing trip. The next day she wore a bright orange vest and helped direct day visitors to the concert into the parking lot at the edge of town. Then she spent a long night, mostly awake trying to sleep, in her car on a side street. It was still better than prison.

"You slept in your car?" Renata said the next morning, and surprised her by adding, "Cree does have extra room. Oh, if you think you're up to it, there's work at the car wash today and the Senate tonight. I mentioned you, and Barry said to give you first chance."

Aletha was feeling worn when she arrived at the Senate after the car wash. She'd changed in the laundromat's bathroom.

"Haven't found a room yet, huh? I've been asking around." Tracy Ledbetter invariably wore dark skirts of flimsy, silky material that showed the panty seams in her panty hose and every gracious contour of her buttocks and hips. She topped these with thin lacy sweaters that revealed less than they promised. She sported the fried-hair hairstyle that brushed out all over, and dark purple lipstick. In sunlight she would look like a caricature of something but in the Senate's dim interior and against the dark wallpaper the whole effect worked somehow. An occasional lapse in her carefully controlled speech would produce things like "New Joizey." "It was a real shock to find almost everybody out here talked like Jane Pauley or Johnny Carson," she confided the night Aletha had stayed with her. "Coming into the country has been a real experience."

With the influx of visitors for the jazz concert, the Senate had a busy evening and only one busboy. So after closing time Aletha and Tracy were still carrying dirty dishes back to the kitchen. Aletha had volunteered for this extra duty to put off the time when she'd be forced to retire to her cold car. She was slightly ahead of Tracy, each of them carrying a heavy tray, when she entered a back room and was about to swing around toward the kitchen doorway when it happened again.

There was no smell of sulfur this time. Aletha could almost see the crack in the decor as a metal cabinet and a freezer parted and then disappeared and the oval widened outward. The bright light from the kitchen didn't penetrate the oval but glistened on the blurry edge of it to make it look aflame. Two women sat behind a table, facing her. The light from a wall sconce glinted on their hair and on golden flowers in deep red wallpaper. One of the women dropped her spoon and soup broth splattered on the bodice of her dress. Her empty hand remained in place. Her mouth hung open as if still expecting some soup. The other woman lifted a finger to point at Aletha, and Aletha stared into Callie's eyes once again.

She had no trouble recognizing the girl even though Callie had grown. The rich chestnut hair was drawn back at the temples now and tied with a bow at the crown. The rest of it tumbled down her back. Callie's cheeks were not so plump. "Aletha? Miss Heisinger took your book," she said all in a rush. "How is Charles? Do you still have him?"

Tracy gasped and dropped her tray. There was the sound of dishes and glassware breaking, the clatter of silverware. Aletha ignored the wet splatter across her shoes and legs. "Callie, what are you doing here?"

But the oval closed like the pupil-slit in a cat's eye. The freezer and cabinet moved in to sit innocently against the wall. And Herm the dishwasher stood in the doorway, arms folded, looking from the floor to Tracy and back again. "Nice."

Tracy took Aletha's tray and disappeared into the kitchen. She returned with a plastic garbage can and knelt to pick up greasy shards. "She was talking to you, this Callie." Her pallor made the dark lipstick look black. "Who's Charles?"

Aletha's legs stopped shaking when her knees hit the floor. She began separating whole dishes from the gooey junk. "I've seen Callie once before. I don't know who Charles is."

"Either the old Senate has suddenly become haunted or this was a trick, done with film or something. All kinds of practical jokers around here." Tracy threw broken plates at the garbage pail with a vengeance. "Thought you were a friend. Let you stay at my place. Never thought you'd stoop to a joke like that, scare a person to—"

"Some joke." Barry stood above them, kicked a broken wine goblet with his toe. "Aletha, that Mackelwain guy's out there. Wants to talk to you."

Her skirt, hose, and shoes were still spattered when she faced Cree across his beer. "You look like twenty years after the end of the world," he said, and when that got no response added, "Renata tells me you spent the night in your car."

"It happened again." Aletha slumped into a captain's chair. "The tear and Callie too. Right back there by the kitchen. Callie's going to be taller than I thought. And she knew my name. I didn't tell her my name, Cree."

He drained his beer and lifted her to her feet. "Let's go to my place."

"I'm too exhausted for a whorehouse."

"You don't have to work tonight."

5

CALLIE'S new school dress had a white collar and white lace ruffles sewn into the shoulder seams that looked fresh and pretty. But Miss Heisinger transcended all. Her skirt swept to the floor in a slim forest-green line and Callie could not discover one mended or shiny place on it. A waist-length jacket hung on a peg by the flag beneath a straw hat lavish with satin. Her blouse was snowier than a blizzard, with pleated sleeves that puffed out and a high neckline under an amber brooch pinned to a green ribbon.

Her straight form floated with such grace around the schoolroom that Callie wondered if this creature could be human. She'd caused a sensation yesterday at the boardinghouse when she'd stepped off the daily stage. And today off-shift miners kept peering in the windows, heads bobbing up to catch a glimpse.

Bram was painfully aware of the new teacher too but he felt the fool sitting in this schoolroom with the little ones. He should be deep in the stopes by now with the men. Because of his size and strength he would have been promoted from nipper to mucker if Ma'am hadn't insisted he go to school.

"Well, Mr. Brambaugh O'Connell, it appears from your previous records that it's going to be difficult to find work for you." Miss Heisinger stood close to his seat and bent down to show him a paper with little boxes all checked off in ink. "Seems you've been promoted out of nearly everything." Her smell was delicately sweet as if she kept a sachet in her trunk like Ma'am did. There was not a mole, not even a pox scar marring the milkiness of her complexion. Her eyes, when she turned them to him up close, were almost as pale a green as Charles's, with the same amber flecks deep inside.

"Yes, ma'am." He felt trapped by Miss Heisinger's closeness, her cool regard, and the helpless sweatiness that tried to stop his breathing.

"I expect I'll find something." When she smiled, her tiny teeth showed no uneven spaces between them.

Bram caught Callie watching them and hoped she couldn't see his trembling.

Shortly after Bram and Callie had settled into the school day, Luella put aside her washing and rushed over the hill to her sister's cabin. A neighbor of Lilly's had summoned her. Lilly's time had come. As the news spread, other matrons wandered in with food and stayed to encourage Lilly, to exclaim over the layette, and to chat with whoever had stopped by. Lilly didn't listen much to the encouragement. If the mill hadn't been thundering away her screams would have been heard clear down to the Loop.

"Try to relax, dear, you tense your body and make the pains worse." Luella couldn't hide her embarrassment over her sister's lack of control, but Mrs. Traub, the manager's wife, who'd brought a cake for Henry's supper and dinner pail, tried to make Luella comfortable. "It's harder on some than on others. She'll make a fine mother, I'm sure."

Mrs. Traub went on to exclaim about her new boarder. They'd stepped outside to hear each other over Lilly's screams while Mrs. McCall spelled Luella at the bedside. "She brought two trunks. Have you ever heard of such a thing? A schoolteacher with two trunks? And big ones too. She must have a change of clothes for every day of the week. And sleeping in with my Bertha that way, well the room's so full you can't move around in it. 'Mark my words, Mr. Traub,' I said, 'that young woman will be trouble here with a boardinghouse full of single men.' "

"And what did he say?"

"Said she was all they could find and the children must be taught. Such a fancy lady, Mrs. O'Connell, do you know she offered no help in putting the supper on last night and when we'd finished she sat at the table and talked to Mr. Traub and the little boys? Let Bertha and me do the dishes. Then, when I finally got all my work done and had a moment to sit in the parlor and visit, she gets up and goes off to Bertha's room to read. What do you think of a schoolmarm who talks only to men?"

Callie was amazed to hear that Jesus had brought Aunt Lilly and Uncle Henry a baby boy. "Did they see Jesus?"

"Callie, don't be silly."

How could he give them a baby in broad daylight without showing himself? Throw it at them out of a cloud? But she knew by Ma'am's tone better than to pursue the subject. Callie wondered why Jesus didn't deliver kittens too. She'd watched Bertha Traub's cat deliver its own. And a messy business that was. The strangest part was that of the five kittens, three looked so much like Charles.

After a cold and hastily prepared supper, Luella took Callie over to Aunt Lilly's to see the new baby. The new baby looked like a baby but the change in Aunt Lilly was astounding. Even under the bedclothes she looked as slim as the new teacher. And all the blood appeared to have washed out of her face. "Why are you in bed? Are you sick?"

"Callie!" Luella warned, and Uncle Henry laughed.

The next day when Callie had changed out of her school dress and put on her everyday dress, Ma'am sent her over the hill with a bottle of tonic because Aunt Lilly needed "toning." She also needed cheering, so Callie told her all about Miss Heisinger and the lady who'd left her book by the mill. The tonic seemed to work and Lilly soon sat up. "What's in that stuff?"

Callie took the bottle over to a window. " 'Wyeth's Wine of Coca. Body and brain strengthener. Sustains. Refreshes. Nourishes. Never causes constipation.' " She turned the bottle over and squinted at the tiny print on the back label. " 'Extracted from the leaves of the mysterious tree deep in the South American jungle, Erythro . . . Erythroxylon Coca.' Is that the same kind of coca that's in Coca-Cola?"

"I think so, but this tonic of Luella's makes you feel even better."

" 'For many years past it has been thoroughly tested,' " Callie continued, " 'and eminent physicians urgently recommend its use in the treatment of anemia, impurity of the blood, consumption, asthma, nervous debility, biliousness, dyspepsia, loss of appetite, and obesity. Especially beneficial to the convalescent and languorous infant. Very palatable and agreeable to take. If you wish to accomplish double the amount of work or are forced to undergo an unusual amount of hardship, always keep a bottle of Wyeth's Wine of Coca near you. Its sustaining powers are wonderful!' "

Aunt Lilly's hair tumbled across her shoulders. She looked delicate and pretty with the soft dark half-circles under her eyes. "Do you ever wonder, Callie, if all they say on them bottles is true?"

"Ma'am says she doesn't believe they could print it if it weren't." Callie helped herself to another piece of Mrs. Traub's cake. "Aunt Lilly, couldn't Jesus have put Bram on the schoolhouse steps? Then he'd be my real brother, wouldn't he?"

"Jesus? What's he . . . Oh . . . uh, no, honey, Bram was seven or eight months old when he came to us and uh . . . then there was the note. Jesus doesn't leave notes." Lilly picked up her sleeping son. "I wanted to name this little fellow Brambaugh, but Henry insists we name him Henry. He's up at the boardinghouse smoking cigars and playing poker with his friends. All new fathers do that, I'm told. Ladies do all the work, men congratulate themselves smoking cigars. And don't look at me that way, Callie question box, I don't know why either."

"Don't you like men, Aunt Lilly?"

"Take one of them pies home with you. We won't be able to eat all this food in a month of Sundays."

One day after school Callie and Bram went berry-picking along Boomerang Road. They'd not gone far when Bram stopped to listen, shushing Callie and pulling her to the side of the wagon road as the sound of shod hooves clicking on pebbles drew nearer.

"You promised we'd pick berries, Bram," Callie whispered, feeling somehow deserted as she did so often when he opted for boy things. "You never catch one anyway."

He put his hand across her mouth and gave her a stern look. The riderless horse came down the road at a trot, empty stirrups swinging out and in, the reins tied to the saddle horn. The horse saw them of course, they always did. Callie could tell by the way it swerved to the other edge of the road as it passed. Bram handed her his bucket and she was tempted to clash it against hers to startle the animal clear to Telluride, but followed Bram quietly instead.

They heard the horse chomping before they saw it browsing in a tiny roadside meadow. In winter rented horses headed straight back to the livery when their riders turned them loose, but in summer they'd stop to grab a bite along the way. Callie could tell the horse knew all about Bram sneaking up behind it by the way its ears twitched around to find the sound.

Bram made a sudden move for the stirrup with one foot and the saddle with both hands. The horse sidestepped on its back feet, leaving its head down to graze in the same spot. Bram fell on his face. Callie snickered behind her hand and crawled onto a stump. The horse snorted as if laughing too, and kept shying just out of Bram's reach while continuing to eat. Finally, tiring of the sport and the meadow, it broke for the road in the middle of a dodge, leaving a red-faced Bram throwing rocks after it, making frustrated sounds in his throat and behind his nose.

Giggles held Callie helpless until she realized her brother stood over her, fists clenching and unclenching on stiffened arms. The stump was a high one and her eyes were on a level with his throat, where the pulse of his blood threatened to break out of his skin. Bram held his teeth together, tight. His nostrils flared open. His eyes looked remote—as if someone other than Bram were behind them. He kept shaking his head back and forth. "God damn you, Callie girl, God damn . . ."

Callie's last giggle ended in a screech. She dropped the pails. His big hands enveloped her arms and shoulders. Bram shook her instead of his head. "Damn you, don't you laugh at . . ."

Callie heard snapping noises in her neck and little screams in her head before they came out of her mouth. Suddenly Bram stopped and blinked into her face. He stared at his hands as if neither belonged to him. "Oh, Callie," he whispered. He picked her up and sat on the stump with her on his lap and rocked them both from side to side. "Oh, no."

Callie cried tears into the coarse fabric of his shirt while she forgave him, while he blew warmth into her hair as he repeated her name.

6

"For the unemployed, you live pretty well." Aletha sat on a kitchen stool and watched Cree Mackelwain chop garlic cloves, plum tomatoes, and fresh parsley. He dumped the lot into spattering olive oil, added whole dried spices by the tablespoon.

"This place belongs to a friend." He poured white wine into the sauce and slid spaghetti noodles into boiling water. "He's . . . lending it to me for a while."

"This place" was one of several condominiums fashioned out of the interior of a brick building which was once a fancy house of ill repute. It had two bedrooms, two baths, a sunken living room, and a seven-foot Jacuzzi. Compared to the interior of a Datsun "this place" was Windsor Castle. Aletha lifted a long-handled spoon from a hook and stirred the spaghetti. "In prison, they didn't stir it enough. Parts of it would stick together in thick ropes."

"And you really stick with that story."

"It's not easy to forget." But the rumbling in her stomach ruined any chance for pathos. He grinned. The spaghetti lived up to its fabulous odors and Cree served it with wine and crusty bread. "Was the Senate a whorehouse too do you think," she asked him, "like the Pick and Gad?"

"The old advertising lists it as a drinking and gambling establishment."

"Well, it served meals. Callie and a woman were eating at a table."

"You ought to go up to the museum and see if they have much on the Senate. I do know this part of town was considered fit for only a certain kind of woman. There were trunks of clothes, paintings of the painted ladies, furniture, and junk left in this building that had to be moved out before renovation. Most of it went into private collections but some of it found its way to the museum."

"I hate to think of Callie on the wrong side of town. She's so sweet and vulnerable," Aletha said. "I'd been sketching up at Alta. After my . . . whatever happened, I couldn't find my sketchbook. Tonight she told me someone had taken my book and something about a guy named Charles. Do you think she found my sketchbook?"

"I think if your eyelids get any lower you're going to fall asleep at the table. You can have the extra bedroom and your own bath."

"Why are you doing this? Being so kind?"

"Why did you give me a ride from Alta?" He clasped his hands behind his head, stretched backward until she could hear the cracking in his shoulders. "Maybe I'm just kind."

He didn't look kind, she thought as she was about to fall asleep in the luxury of a real bed. Cree Mackelwain looked grim. Cree Mackelwain looked like someone she shouldn't trust. Of course, most of the people she'd found she really shouldn't have trusted had looked completely trustworthy. Aletha slipped into vulnerable sleep anyway and awoke in the morning to find Cree's door open, the rumpled bed empty. Aletha repacked her suitcase and left.

Cree stood on the road in front of Lone Tree Cemetery at the edge of town, puffing from a run to the end of the canyon and back. He still wasn't used to the altitude. Across the San Miguel River sprinklers whirled water drops across a huge drift of mill tailings.

An attempt had been made to plant something green over this refuse from inside the planet. The sun finally struggled to the top of notched mountain crests. It sparked the droplets from the sprinklers and caught up pieces of light in the river, casting a pink glow on steeply pitched roofs in town. A speck in the sky circled in a thermal, an eagle or a hang glider, and set off an excitement and a sense of recognition in him.

Telluride, at an elevation of 8,745 feet above sea level, still sits at the bottom of a great chasm. On three sides monstrous peaks of the San Juan range rear into the sky, as stunning as they are threatening. The wall of rock that boxes in the end of the canyon is scarred by snowslide and torture cracks and a silver water ribbon that plummets from a saddle some eight hundred feet to the valley floor. Cree tried to imagine what all this must look like from above.

Lone Tree Cemetery had more than a lone tree. He poked around among old tombstones and plaques, markers weathered bare of inscription, a mass grave for miners caught in a fire. Many marked the violent demise of young men, caught in their prime by accident, fate, and highly treacherous work. Telluride's union troubles had placed more men here. Pneumonia, silicosis, and gun fights over a slight or a whore had claimed many others, he knew.

Cree began looking for the name of "Callie" on a whim, and because it helped him forget a more recent tombstone, that of his partner and friend Dutch Massey. Dutch had led a dangerous life too. Cree found young women who'd died with their babies in childbirth, and many babies and children. He found names—Italian, Scandinavian, eastern European with their "ak" and "eck" endings. No Callie.

Cree had an amateur's interest in history that caused bits of fact and pieces of trivia to stick in his head. It made the odd events occurring around Aletha indelible and Telluride's history in general of more interest than it should be. He had work to do here that had nothing to do with history.

He, his father, and his brother had once stood in a graveyard such as this in Oregon. The boys just listened politely at first as the elder Mackelwain expounded upon the possible lives and deaths planted forever at their feet. But they soon began to see real people in strange clothing going about varied tasks unaware of the fate awaiting them here. Gregory Mackelwain had sold everything from cars to swimming pools and he'd sold the tingle of enchantment about the past to his sons as well. Cree's brother had gone on to become a professor of history but Cree found the dryness of its study like sand after the excitement of his father's reality. Something inside had already committed him to the sky.

"My, you're out early." A woman with wavy gray hair and pleasant features knelt beside a grave and set down a trowel and a basket of flowers. There weren't many people over forty in the town and this one lacked the driven look of the younger citizens. "Are you searching for someone special or just browsing?"

She probably sells real estate, he thought. "Just curious about a possible burial, someone named Callie. I don't know her last name."

"Callie, oh yes. Over there and up by the fence. There're many unmarked graves in that area. She's a small headstone set flat to the ground. Come, I'll show you." She led the way to an area Cree had thought vacant. "This is a section some friends and I have been trying to figure out. Hers is one of the few markers left. Most have grown over until they're buried. Callie, C-a-l-l-i-e, is that the right spelling? Most of the records have been lost, I'm afraid."

"I haven't seen it written." Cree looked down on a rectangle of stone. Callie, just Callie. No more information. "Have you lived in Telluride long?"

"About fifty years or so. Which makes me a true old-timer. I came as a bride. All but one son and three grandchildren are over there." Her trowel pointed back the way they'd come. "There are a few of us left who haven't sold out to the new wave yet." She smiled wrinkle lines deep into her face and started back toward her family. "Perhaps we've stayed to finish the history we all started and because it's so deathly beautiful here." The trowel waved at the looming peaks and she paused to stare up at them. "And then . . . it all seems to have gone so fast." She shook her head and the smile vanished. "Why were you looking for this Callie?"

"I have a friend who's been dreaming of her . . . no, not dreaming. More like haunted by her."

"That's interesting. I have a friend who has spoken of a Callie, but my friend is very old and much of what she says is impossible to understand." She laughed, short and melodic. "Tell your friend that my friend has not enjoyed being haunted by this Callie." The sun glinted on the bifocal curve in her glasses and hid any meaning her eyes might have held.

* * *

"I hope you didn't spend another night in your car." Renata wore tight designer jeans and a blue work shirt unbuttoned halfway down the front.

"Cree lent me a spare bed."

"Wonder what that man is up to," Renata said slowly and more to herself than to Aletha. "Always asking questions." She sat on the corner of her desk, chewed on the end of a ball-point without touching her lipstick to it. She giggled. "You don't suppose he's a narc, do you?" She stared through Aletha and then straightened. "Oh, I have a job for you today."

Aletha sank onto the long bench beside the door and tried to sound casual. "What makes you think Cree's a narcotics agent?"

"I was just making silly guesses. Some of our citizens and visitors have been busted over the last few years for dealing cocaine, and it's become a half-scandal, half-joke around town. I really doubt that Cree's a narc. He's too obvious. The Sheridan needs a maid today."

"How long have you known Cree?"

"Just the week or so he's been in town. He introduced himself right away. We had a mutual friend. Our friend is dead."

Renata's office was upstairs in an old store building that seemed to have kept its original dust. Traffic patterns had worn hollows in the wooden flooring and stairs. Wainscoting reached shoulder-high on the walls and the ceilings were lined with embossed tin. Footsteps echoed up the stairs from the street now, passed the doors of several other offices on this floor. A woman with a trowel and gardening gloves came to stand in Renata's doorway.

"Hi, Mrs. Lowell, been out to the cemetery?"

"Yes, and a fine morning for it too."

"Mrs. Lowell, this is one of my new helpers, Aletha Kingman. Mrs. Lowell was assistant to the county clerk at the courthouse before retiring, and before that she taught English at the school here. Now she's president of the San Miguel Historical Society."

"I'll bet you're really here for the skiing." Mrs. Lowell poked Aletha's arm playfully and turned back to Renata. "I think it's time Mildred had a good cleaning up again."

"I can get somebody over there tomorrow. Clean . . . Miss . . . Heisinger's," she repeated slowly as she wrote on a scratch pad. "How's she like the Meals on Wheels?"

"She won't say, but she's eating again anyway. I swear she'll outlive us all. Incredible woman."

Aletha hurried up the street to the New Sheridan Hotel, wondering why the name "Heisinger" should sound so familiar. It kept nagging at her as she stripped sheets off beds, scrubbed down sinks and toilet bowls. She was sitting on the staircase waiting for some late risers to pack up and check out and staring at the life-size portrait on the wall where the stairs ended when it came to her. She'd seen the portrait before, but now the woman in it looked familiar.

The portrait was done in oil on a dark background that suggested either a dim red sunset all but overpowered by swiftly encroaching night or the faint fires of hell abroil behind the powers of darkness. The nude in the center foreground was about twenty pounds overweight, pear-shaped, with long kinky hair flying out behind her. Her pose in midair suggested she might be running, one arm thrown up as if in panic, the other crooked so she could place the back of her hand on her brow to show deep distress. Amidst this drama her expression was surprisingly composed, if not a trifle bored. She'd shaved her underarms and pubic hair but there was a suspicious suggestion of darkness on her lower legs. A swath of gauze with tiny stars peppered all over it swirled about her loins, concealing much of nothing. And all this was enclosed in an ornate gold frame.

Aletha had dismissed it as a cornball tourist-grabber until now. Now she recognized the face as that of the woman who had been eating with Callie at the Senate when the oval had replaced the freezer and the cabinet. The woman who'd dropped her spoon and spattered her soup and . . . that's when Aletha had heard the name "Heisinger." That's when Callie had said a Miss Heisinger had taken Aletha's sketchbook. She left the pillowcase stuffed with dirty sheets on the stairs and raced down to the pay phone in the odd little room under the staircase that connected the lobby and the bar. She called Renata Winslow. "Is this Miss Heisinger you're going to have cleaned tomorrow a native of Telluride?"

"Well, I don't know if she was born here, but nobody around can remember when she didn't live here. Doris Lowell thinks she's over a hundred. And still staying through the winters. Can you imagine? Why are you so interested in old Mildred Heisinger?"

"Renata, I want that job tomorrow, the Heisinger job."

Renata laughed. "You make it sound like a bank holdup. Listen, Aletha, I got a call from Norwood, little town about thirty miles from here, for a job you'll like better—fry cook. It pays much more."

"Please give me the Heisinger job. It's important. Please?"

"Oh . . . all right. I'll scare up somebody else for Norwood. I honestly do not understand you. Hers is the little Victorian across Pine Street from the Pick and Gad and down a lot length."

Aletha was hoping to get back to the dirty sheets before they were discovered, when the girl in the registration cage in the lobby called to her. "Hey, if you're still looking for a bed, there's one in the women's dormer tonight. Cheap by Telluride standards."

"I'll take it. Do you know anything about the naked lady on second?"

"There's a naked lady on second?"

"In the painting at the end of the staircase."

"Oh yeah. She's supposed to be some kind of legend. I take all legends with a grain of salt and a bourbon-and-Seven myself. You can probably find out about her up at the museum."

But Aletha didn't make it to the museum because Renata sent her to baby-sit three children in a pseudo-Victorian condominium for the rest of the day and into the night. When she did crawl into the dorm bed at the Sheridan, she had ambivalent feelings. She wished she could tell Cree Mackelwain about the nude in the painting. But she was relieved not to be sleeping in with a possible narc. Mostly she was excited about meeting Miss Heisinger in the morning.

7

MILDRED Heisinger wore her black gathered skirt with a satin cummerbund, snowy blouse, and a black ribbon around her throat. This was her second post. Mildred was eighteen. Things had not gone well in her first position for reasons she still did not understand. She'd not been asked to return and came here without recommendation. Knowing she must succeed in Alta set a feathery, cold sensation to crawling in her stomach. It also caused her to withdraw, giving her the appearance of an icy composure far from her true state.

Her students ranged from four to fourteen, the usual mix of bright, willing, obstreperous, and disinterested. Mildred believed she'd pretty well won them over. Except for one. Brambaugh O'Connell, the oldest, who stood much taller than she, who had to sit sideways with his legs in the aisle, who never spoke unless spoken to and never missed a word while reading aloud or in composition.

She'd taken to seating him in her own chair when working with him, and standing herself so he'd be more comfortable and she'd feel more in control. He had a dignity she knew to be part resentment at being forced to attend her school and part attraction to her. Sometimes he was a little boy in an oversized body, sometimes his eyes held a maturity that made her drop her own.

Mildred found herself engaged in small fantasies concerning her oldest pupil: She would surprise him with some sudden bit of knowledge that would light up the sullen expression. Or she would see him as a grown man returned to find his teacher whom he'd never been able to forget. She stood behind him now and watched his large hand make small, perfect ciphers on his tablet. She could almost feel the power growing in the restless shoulders, was tempted to touch him carelessly as she did the other children. But of course she did not.

Johann Peterson reached around Callie O'Connell and stuffed something down the back of Mable Fisherdicks' dress. Mable wiggled and screamed. Miss Heisinger tapped Johann on the head and pointed to his destination in the corner. She asked Callie to accompany Mable to the cloakroom and help remove whatever forced her to squirm so. No one ever teased Callie with her brother in the room.

Sudden thunder from the sky displaced the thunder of the mill, shook the earth beneath the school, rolled in on gusts of wind that rattled in the rafters. Raindrops splayed across window glass and lightning dazzled the room. This was the third day in a row a thunderstorm had flared shortly before the school day was to end. Yesterday she'd kept her students late to let it pass.

"That was a wise decision, Miss Heisinger," Timothy Traub, the Alta mine manager and her host, had said at dinner. "The ground was fairly crackling with electricity this afternoon. It's a wonder nothing was struck here on the hill. Or, God forbid, the current from the plant below should arc and shut down the mill."

The entire area had been electrified even before many large cities by mining interests who'd denuded mountain slopes of timber to fuel steam boilers and who needed cheaper power than coal to continue operations. This was the first time Mildred had actually lived with electric power and she'd been amazed to find a light bulb on a long movable cord available in every room of the manager's house. There were two stationary bulbs in the schoolhouse. She switched these on now to brighten the storm gloom and calm the children.

Just as Callie and Mable scurried back and Mildred Heisinger was about to order her students to put their heads down on their desks—a proven method of restoring calm and order in an unsettled class-room—a particularly sharp lightning crack followed by a thud jarred the floorboards. Callie O'Connell headed for the arms of her brother instead of her seat. The littlest girls squealed and one began to cry. Even the boys were struck round-eyed and still. The two light bulbs flickered out. And the thunder of the mill silenced.

An onrush of wind-driven rain pushed in on great peals of thunder that carried much more of a clamor without the steadying of the mill throb in the background. Lightning snaps ignited all around them. Charges of electricity sizzled down the stovepipe and crackled and danced on the potbellied stove. It seemed to Mildred as if she and her students were isolated innocents caught on a battleground under cannon siege. She tried to fight some authority into her voice. "Callie and Johann, return to your seats and everyone put his head down upon his desk. This will pass very soon, as have the others. Callie, will you please—"

It was a small still breath while the weather tamped and reloaded, and into it came Brambaugh O'Connell's voice—level, low, and relaxed. "She's afraid and she'll stay right here."

The burnout from the storm lasted only two days before the mill thundered once more and the people of the mining camp breathed easier. When the mine and mill did not prosper, neither did they. The next thunder Callie heard was in her father's voice. "Payday! The first in a while, wouldn't you say? And it's in scrip. All because of the shutdowns at the mill, says they. And me looking for a little time off to prospect." He pounded on the cable-spool table and that thundered too. "What do you think of that, Ma'am, huh?"

Callie saw her mother cringe but continue to ladle soup. "The supper's ready, John." Her tone was steady like Bram's had been when Miss Heisinger had called Callie back to her seat and Bram had held her so she couldn't go. "There's much that we need we can't buy at the commissary, but scrip will pay the rent. Bram, will you offer the Lord's thanks, please?"

Halfway through the meal the thunder was still on John O'Connell's face. "Sure, it's no wonder the union men been hanging about so much of late."

Their one light bulb hung above the table, its braided wires draped over a hook. There was another hook in the sitting room where they could move the light after supper was cleaned up and all could read under it in comfort. This was the first Callie had lived with electricity too and she much preferred it to oil lamps. But now the miraculous bulb, of clear glass with a worm-like filament ablaze inside it, cast shadows across her father's features. Odd shadows, unfamiliar, threatening. She looked away and dribbled a crisscross of stripes in dark syrup on her cornbread.

"I hope they don't start trouble here. They've caused so much bloodshed and heartache elsewhere." Ma'am's face sagged, as did her shoulders. She'd been spelling her sister on night watch over the cradle of a sick baby Henry. Even the wonderful tonic did not seem to restore Luella. One bottle was already empty, the other over at Lilly's was more than half gone. And this was the tonic that was to have lasted through a winter not yet arrived. Shadows played across her face and Callie looked up to see if the bulb was swinging. But it was still.

"All they're asking is a day's wage for a day's work and a day that's not so long as to kill a man. And conditions safe for a man to work under." Payday came once a month. John would hand his pay—usually in silver and gold coin—over to Luella, keeping back a tenth. He would then go down to Ophir or sometimes into Telluride and squander it on masculine pursuits, missing a day or so of work in the bargain but ready to take on another month of grueling seven-day weeks when he returned. Single miners often returned to the boardinghouse in the same amount of time with a month's pay gone. At three dollars a day they out-earned most laboring men.

But as a popular saying went, "The miner mines the mines and the 'line' mines the miner."

Most miners' wives had an ongoing fantasy of reforming their men to more righteous ways, and rarely did a woman marry a man she didn't plan to change. Luella was no exception. Men in mining camps dreamed their own fantasies. It was only a matter of time before they stumbled across their strike. This would happen, of course, on one of the few days they could afford to devote to prospecting.

"Well, if they don't pay in coin, they pay in other ways then, do they not?" John reached to lift a large chunk of rock from the pocket of his coat and laid it on the table. A milk-white rock on the top and one side with specks of silver and specks of gold glinting back at the electrical light bulb. "What is this white stuff here, lad?"

"Quartz," Bram answered.

"And the little speckles of silver and gold?"

"Mica and pyrite."

"And this here, Bram?" He turned the rock over. Luella and Bram hissed in on their breaths. Callie thought the other side was prettier. This one was almost solid with a dull and dirty yellow. "What would you call it, now?"

"That's highgrade, Pa." Bram looked confused. "You're high-grading."

"How do you steal from a thief? Tell me that." John O'Connell's hair had grown ever thinner and farther back on the top of his head. He ran his hand over it now, as they had seen him do so often when agitated. "Paying in scrip is thievery. And taking it all back in rent and at the company commissary is slavery."

Luella stared hard at Callie and Bram. "You're not ever to breathe a word of this to anyone."

Callie knew of two other such rocks hidden under the house. She'd helped bury them. Those two were a secret among herself, her father, and Charles. "Taking me a little walk down to Ophir tonight," John said. "Be back tomorrow with some real money."

When he'd left, Luella sighed and stretched her back up and then her shoulders. "Callie, you'll have to do the dishes alone. And, Bram, don't look at me that way. John O'Connell is an honest man who can be pushed too far. Did you know that when he was working the Molly Deal the owners in Boston closed the mine owing the men three months' pay? How do you think we survived that?"

"If you'd let me work like I should, there'd be two earning a wage and he wouldn't have to steal." Bram's voice seldom broke now. It was taking on a low rumble.

"You're not happy at school, are you, Bram? I'd think with such a pretty young teacher you'd—"

"You've already taught me more than she can. And she's not a good woman. Not like you."

"Miss Heisinger? She's hardly more than a girl. What do you mean by 'not good'?"

"She's different. She looks at me . . . different."

"I like her," Callie said, pouring boiling water from the teakettle onto soap shavings in the dishpan. "Just because she's pretty doesn't mean she's bad." She dipped cold water from the five-gallon oil can into the hot water and stirred with her finger until the water turned milky-colored. "Everybody looks at you, Bram, because you're too big to not see." She turned to find Bram's color rising and her mother studying them both.

"Too big not to be seen," Luella corrected distantly, as if she were concentrating on something else.

"I never lied to you, Ma'am," he whispered. "You know that."

"I do know that." Luella stood behind him and put a hand on each shoulder. "And I couldn't love you more if you'd been born to us. I don't know how I'd have lived through the loss of the first two, if we hadn't had you with us. I will think on this, Bram, I promise. Now, help Callie finish up and then both sit to your lessons. I'd best go back to Aunt Lilly's."

"Callie, why must you keep looking out the window?" Bram asked when they had books spread out on the table.

"To see if the lady has come back to the hole in the wall." There were enough lights on the mill to see her even at night.

"There couldn't have been any hole. It would've had to have been boarded up and that'd left a mark too." He'd patiently explained all this before, but it was no help to Callie because she knew what she'd seen.

"I just want to give her book back to her. She must be missing all those fine drawings. And I'll ask her how she made the hole and then tell you." It gave her a good feeling that there were some things even Bram didn't know about

John O'Connell did not return until the next evening, and late enough that Callie and Bram had finished their studies. They were allowing Charles a little sniff around the kitchen, thinking it was safe enough because Luella had left long ago for Aunt Lilly's house. When they heard the first footfall on the porch they thought she'd returned early. Callie grabbed for Charles and missed. Bram sat up from a reclining position on the floor so suddenly he hit his head on the undersurface of the spool table.

But it was John and not Luella who stood in the doorway, staring back at them a little uncertainly. "Walked down to the Loop and took a tram bucket up," he explained, and began to nod his head as if agreeing with himself. "Brought your Ma'am some of her tonic. S'pose she'll be at Lillian's again." He set the wrapped bottle on the table rather hard. He smelled of cool mountain night, alcohol, and snouse. Soon the whole kitchen did. "And I brought a bag of something sweet for Callie and a bag of something sweet for Bram and I even brought a wee something for the kiddy. Whadaya think of that?"

Charles was already rubbing one side of himself on John's pants leg. Callie and Bram opened the waxed bags and selected a choice candy each. John stumbled the few steps across the kitchen to hang up his coat on a peg and didn't notice when it promptly fell to the floor. He knelt, untied the string on a tiny package, and spread out a paper with bits of bloody meat on it.

"Shopped liver," John said with a conspiratorial wink and still nodding agreement with himself, "made me a special friend at the butcher's, I did." The four managed to take up all the available floor space in the kitchen and together they held the edges of the paper flat so the cat could lick up the last lingering flavors, and laughed at the silly creature who was usually so self-collected.

That's why they didn't hear the footfalls on the front porch. Charles was the first to notice Luella standing above them. He backed into Callie with a hiss. She held him against his struggles and held her breath too. Luella stood for long uncomfortable moments staring at her family and at Charles, her hair hanging down on all sides, her face and eyes reddened. She had never looked so wild.

"Ma'am?" This time Bram's voice did break.

Luella put her hand against the wall for support. "Mrs. Traub says she has some poison that'll rid us of that filthy creature." Her voice held no expression. "I turn my back and you bring it into my kitchen. Knowing full well how my feelings run about the animal. That's the thanks I receive for all I do."

John O'Connell stretched his arms toward her. His head shook from side to side, this time in disagreement. "Oh now, Ma'am, you'll not be thinking—"

"And you, Mr. O'Connell, you with three sheets in the wind. And baby Henry." Callie had never heard her mother's voice go so low and so flat. "I came to fetch my sewing basket. The babe is dead."

When Callie tripped on her father's coat on her way to the back door Charles scratched her throat but she held tight to him.

"We gave him some tonic," Luella was saying with a touch of disbelief. "Label said it was recommended for languorous infants, and he certainly was that. But even tonic did no good." John was "tut-tut-tutting" and "now there, there-ing" and stroking the top of his head. But it was Bram who held Luella against his chest as finally she wept.

Callie sat in the dark of the back porch and cried too while Charles perched on a stump and washed liver and blood from his whiskers with the side of a wet-licked paw. She cried for baby Henry and Aunt Lilly and Ma'am. But most of all she cried for Charles.

8

ALETHA stepped through a gate rusted open and stoppered by vegetation. Miss Heisinger's house sat on a large lot with trees along one border and three crumbling outbuildings lined up behind it. A low iron fence, elaborate with spikes and curlicues, surrounded the property. The fence sat black in patches, rusted in others against an exuberance of vibrant green and yellow weeds— many with blossoms gone to gauzy seed. The weeds pushed right up to the front door with just a hint of footpath worn between the door and the gate.

The house itself was far more worn. The paint on the wooden siding had weathered away long ago, the boards rippling or bulging or sagging. The bricks at the top of the chimney were blackened. Yellowing curtains drooped at high narrow windows under a peaked roof of metal gray and of more recent vintage. Broken gingerbread filigree traced the eaves. An odd cupola perched above the door, with one window in its center that faced the Pick and Gad. The house was small, almost dwarfed by its outbuildings. Their sides seemed to be sliding slowly into oblivion, as if a giant stood within and pushed outward. Their windows gaped, empty of glass and dark. All the buildings looked shabby-gray and cold amidst the brightness of sun and weeds and the spectacular backdrop of rearing mountainside.

Easily spooky, if one were so inclined, but Aletha's shiver was more that of expectancy. Doris Lowell answered her knock. "Are you from Renata? Oh yes, I met you yesterday . . . Alice?"

"Aletha." She stepped into a tiny entryway on linoleum so worn that small ovals of wooden flooring showed through. She saw pieces of herself and Mrs. Lowell in round mirrors, oval mirrors, rectangular mirrors that were small and beveled and grainy, all in ornate frames, some with knickknack shelves attached, all crowded in on each other to make room. Doris motioned her into a narrow kitchen with more depression-era linoleum scrubbed almost clean of color and pattern.

"Mildred, this is Aletha. She's come to clean your house for you." Doris raised her voice, spoke distinctly and slowly. "She's from Renata."

A tiny, withered person sitting at a table turned to look at Aletha. "Renata's a slut." Her S's sounded slushy because she had no teeth.

"Now, Mildred, you don't know anything about Renata Winslow."

Miss Heisinger walked with halting steps to stand almost under Aletha's nose. And Aletha looked down into the palest of green eyes. They reminded her of those seedless grapes called white but really green. They were magnified out of proportion to the little face by eyeglasses with clear plastic rims. They studied Aletha until she squirmed.

"You're a snoop," the old lady said, and walked out of the room.

Aletha, brimming with questions about a possible connection to Callie, realized that's just what she'd come to do—snoop. "Does she live alone?"

"Some of us around town look in on her, take her to the beauty shop, bring in groceries, drive her to the doctor—that kind of thing.

She has no family. But except for the noon meal brought in by Meals on Wheels, she does her own cooking and washing, even a few repairs. It's amazing how well she manages."

"She's lucky in her friends."

"I'm afraid she doesn't think so. She resents our trying to get her to remember about the old days. Says we nag her. But so much history will be gone if we don't urge these old ones to talk and remember before they're gone too." Doris Lowell showed Aletha a combination pantry-broom closet situated in a windowless lean-to on the back of the house. Two other rooms in the lean-to provided space for a furnace room and a bathroom. One bedroom opened off the bathroom, and off that a "parlor" where Mildred Heisinger sat in front of a color television that blared so loudly conversation was out of the question.

After Doris left Aletha started in the kitchen, feeling like a rat because she couldn't help but examine every item as she came to it even if she had to go out of her way to come to it. She found exactly what she'd expect to find in the home of someone this aged. One good set of china that looked as if it had never been used, a set of pottery made up of odds and ends that was well-used, lots of depression glass and canned soups. The hot-water heater sat in the bathroom next to the shortest, deepest bathtub Aletha had ever seen. It stood on its own feet, each shaped like the slender foot and ankle of a young woman. The bedroom had a dark four-poster that was all knobs. Aletha did not stoop to going through drawers but she did inspect each item she dusted. Porcelain figurines, paintings of demure women with men in greased-down hair gazing adoringly— regular old-lady stuff. But no photographs of family, children, friends, houses once lived in.

By the time Aletha worked her way to the parlor, Miss Heisinger's meal arrived and she put her teeth in to eat it. That made a startling change in her appearance, filling out the wizened face to more recognizable proportions. Aletha had hoped to start the woman talking, but Mildred ate and then nodded off with the television still blasting. The parlor had a piano sporting yellowed keys, layers of wallpaper coming loose in the corners, a cut-glass chandelier, bookcases, more figurines, and dotty paintings. No photos of when life was young. The house smelled musty, almost vacant, as if Miss Heisinger couldn't use up enough of it to make a difference.

Aletha didn't want to run the elderly vacuum on the parlor floor while Mildred dozed, so she dusted the multitude of mirror frames in the entry hall. They extended from above her head almost to the level of her knees. A porcelain doorknob protruded from between two of them and Aletha noticed a vertical crack between rows of mirrors. Well . . . any snoop exposed to a rip in the fabric of time could hardly be expected to . . . She *had* been asked to clean the *whole* house. . . .

She turned the knob and a door full of cloudy mirrors opened toward her, exposing stairs as narrow as those in Callie's shack in Alta. There was much dust but not many stairs, and at the top a window overlooking the Pick and Gad through the trees. The cupola had about enough room to stand in and turn around. It also had a door leading to a room full of boxes, stacks of aging books, various covered shapes, and a tiny round window. Against a wall under the peaked roof stood a painting in oil of a beautiful woman with blond hair piled on top of her head and a white blouse with a cameo pinned to a ribbon around her throat and the pale green eyes of Mildred Heisinger.

"Done snooping yet?" Mildred asked when Aletha turned on the vacuum in the parlor to wake her up.

"I'm almost done cleaning, Miss Heisinger," Aletha shouted.

"Good. I'll make us some coffee." When they sat at the kitchen table over weak coffee and a Sara Lee carrot cake, Mildred said, "None of it matters any longer, all that Doris Lowell wants to know. Why do they want to know so bad?" She jutted a trembly head forward, squinted. "Where have I seen you?"

"We haven't met, Miss Heisinger, but I did come here with some questions. I've sort of been . . . seeing this little girl, Callie. She mentioned you and I—"

"Callie O'Connell? She's no little girl."

"I saw her first in Alta and—"

"Alta, yes . . . stinking place. Full of noise and stupid people. Taught school there. Stay away from Alta. Hard on young women. I should know."

"But Callie . . . she's bugging me so."

"Now they're messing in Alta's history too? Not with my help they're not." Mildred took out her dentures and refused to speak again. The sunken face and faded eyes looked completely mad.

* * *

"Cree, I want to go to Alta and spend the night." Aletha stood at the door of his condo. She'd come straight from Mildred Heisinger's.

"I'm a real sucker for a subtle proposition." He led her to the table, poured them both a cup of strong coffee. "But there's an embarrassment of beds here."

"I don't mean to sleep or to . . . I mean to camp. I'm afraid to go alone, and you're the only one who knows what's going on."

He slid some papers into a manila folder. "Just what is going on?"

"I have to warn Callie not to come to Telluride. Or this part of it anyway."

"You mean the line. That's what they used to call these streets of vice." He took the folder into the bedroom and spoke from there. "I talked to Tracy at the Senate. She wouldn't open up about the experience you two had until I told her about the vanishing roadblock." He came back without the folder, put his hands on the table, and leaned over her. "If what she said is true, Callie has already visited the line. You can't change history."

"How do you know? Would you have believed any of this could happen to begin with? That we could even be seeing this . . . history?" He was massive standing over her like that and she began to doubt the wisdom of all this trust she kept putting in him without thinking it through first. "Do you know who lives across the street from you? Callie's old teacher. And I mean old." She slid out of the chair and went to the window to point out Miss Heisinger's cupola and to get away from him. "I'm sure it's the Miss Heisinger Callie told me about at the Senate."

"Tracy and I have about decided you're the catalyst that's making all this happen. There aren't even any old rumors of such a thing going on before Aletha Kingman came to town. Have to admit I'm curious."

"Maybe I shouldn't have bothered you about tonight." Now that he showed interest in going, she'd almost decided she didn't want to be up there alone with him. On the other hand, she didn't want to be up there with no one, either. "I was just excited and I didn't know what I'd do if I met up with a bear or a ghost or two." Her laugh sounded thin even to her.

"I'm no protection against ghosts." He pulled a couple of rolled sleeping bags off the shelf of the coat closet. "Not a real hotshot when it comes to bears either, but I'm a great camp cook. You choose the menu. Any flavor you want." Cree separated packets of freeze-dried food from a cardboard box into different piles. Stroganoff, spaghetti and meatballs, pork chops, stew, peas, and more. "Now, this group tastes like glue. This bunch tastes like old tires. And these all taste like kitty litter." Cree had noticed the thinness in Aletha's laugh too. "But once the sun goes down and the chill comes up and there's not a thing to do but eat, even dirty rocks taste good."

"We could just sit in the car all night and talk and keep watch."

"Anybody who works as hard as you do needs her rest. But first . . ." He took her by the shoulders and marched her over to one of the couches. He tried not to notice the instant alarm in her eyes at his touch, the smooth little rear which was about cut in half by her jeans. One minute she looked like everybody's kid sister—vulnerable and luscious—and the next, hard and bitter. He didn't know much about schizophrenia but her behavior certainly called that word to mind. "I want to know all about this prison business you keep spicing up the conversation with. You haven't really spent time in a prison."

She put the vulnerable and luscious face on, which made it hard to concentrate, but he held on to her arm because the rest of her looked poised for escape. Her eyes grew wider, as if ready to fill with tears. "Do you know one of the worst things was the smell? Even when I got used to it, it smelled bad. Like old urine and disinfectants, steam-table food, and that vomitlike smell you get when locked in with slowly evaporating plastics. . . ."

9

ALETHA paced the condo with her arms folded as if she were cold. She'd been in a jail in New Orleans for three months before her trial came up and then in a federal penitentiary in Fort Worth. And all because, she claimed, she'd grown tired of attending the University in Albuquerque and had gone to work for a man there named Harry Sloane. Harry ran a dive shop and training center for scuba divers. Aletha took the training, received her certification, and helped arrange group tours to the island of Roatan off the coast of Honduras, where Harry had another dive shop and an understanding with a resort.

"People could get group airline rates, a Caribbean vacation, scuba training and certification, and glorious underwater reefs all in one package from good old Harry. And for his staff it was work that was more fun than work. It was kind of like postponing adulthood."

Cree could see what was coming and wished he couldn't, wished this slight, bouncy girl weren't involved in the same nasty game that had ruined him and Dutch.

"And then one day after about three years of all this fun I was coming back through customs in New Orleans with Bobby, another of Harry's dupes. We were bringing back some tanks for repair from the Roatan shop. I'd done it dozens of times. But this time my whole life changed in just one minute."

"They found drugs in your scuba tanks."

"Cocaine. Several million dollars' worth." She turned on him with a movement that made the hair tucked behind her ears fall forward across her face, leaving one intense, accusing eye staring at him. "Are you a narc? Renata says you're a narc."

"No, I'm not a narc. But I've read enough to know that scuba tanks are about the worst bet there is for smuggling. They've been used so often they practically flag suspicion on sight."

"Apparently Harry had been getting away with it for years. When Bobby and I got caught, he disappeared. But somehow they found Harry. And when they did he bragged that he'd used his staff as mules from the beginning and not a one knew about it until Bobby and I were caught."

"Lots of killing goes on in Harry's trade. You were lucky he wasn't murdered before he cleared you."

"I didn't believe it when they let me out of Fort Worth. I thought it was a trick. And then it took more months to get the conviction reversed. My mother and Bertie did all they could to help me, but I'll always feel guilty and dirty. Because I was in prison for something I didn't even know I'd done." Her eyes remained empty. "The sentence was thirty years. If I'd served the whole time I'd have been older than my mother is now when I got out. I wanted you to ask me about it. That's why I kept dropping dumb hints. If I'd just keep my mouth shut no one would know. I'm an ex-convict."

As she drove up the grumpy road to Alta, Aletha imagined that he looked at her differently now. "Maybe I can change history. Maybe I can keep Callie from that one awful moment that could change her life forever."

"Slow down, will ya? In case we meet another roadblock." He braced against the dashboard as he had the last time they'd traversed this road. "Were you . . . abused in prison? Sexually?"

"Subtlety is just not your main talent, is it?" But it was her fault for opening herself up to this sort of thing.

"You're right. Sorry."

"Renata says you're asking questions all the time. But that you're too obvious to be a professional investigator of any kind." That last was an attempt to hurt him back. "You're too tense to be on vacation. You're looking for something, Cree Mackelwain. What?"

"I don't have your penchant for confession." No roadblocks interrupted their journey and soon the Datsun bucked over a washout, rounded a curve, and Alta came into view above them. "That big chunk of concrete you see there was probably the base for the tram house," Cree said. "Bottom thing on the hill. Mine at the top, then the mill, then the tram—perfect setup."

Aletha parked by the tram base and they walked up to Callie's house.

"Looks like Callie lived next to the town dump." Cree hunkered on an embankment of rust-colored bedsprings and cooking stoves, jagged hunks of linoleum, five-gallon cans lacy with bullet holes. There were lumps of thick white plate pieces. Aletha kicked over a knuckle bone that must have come from an ox. Cree motioned between trees where white bones were scattered on down the slope as far as the eye could see. It looked like a tormented burial ground. "Used to eat lots of meat in the old days. Let's set up camp by the commissary and gather some firewood before it's too dark. Then we can prowl around."

Aletha had just opened the car door when someone at her elbow said, "Tap 'er light, John." And someone, either inside the car or on the other side of it, answered in a gravelly voice, "Aye, tap 'er light."

Aletha spun away as if the car were blistering hot, and collided with Cree. He stared upward. She hung on to him and looked over her shoulder. She saw nothing. She heard now the pounding, clanging sounds she'd heard before when here, but not so close as to drown out a repeated clickety-clack in the sky. "Tram buckets," Cree whispered, "going over wheels or cogs on the tram towers, like a ski tow."

"But there's nothing there now," she said, glad she'd not come alone after all. As soon as she'd said it the sound wasn't there either. "I heard someone in the car."

He gave her an unnecessary squeeze and crushed the piece of quartz on the souvenir necklace into her skin. He bent to look in the Datsun.

"And someone standing right here said, 'Tap her light, John.' "

"I heard them too, Aletha." They waited, eyes searching the air. Gray twilight descended, making everything colorless, putting the day sounds to bed, not yet waking the night sounds. Just the furry wind high in the trees.

Finally they drove up the hill to what a Forest Service sign assured them had once been a commissary. While he fought an interesting combination of slender poles and line, she hunted for sticks and "squaw wood," the brittle twigs at the ends of dead branches on the lower trunks of pine trees that snapped off and hurt her hands. "Even Indians were sexist," she grumbled when he'd pointed out this source of kindling.

"Everybody was sexist. Natural way of things. Still is in most places," he said. "Notice you didn't bring a woman up here with you."

Aletha didn't bother to answer. She didn't wander too far from him either. An old bank safe lay on its side next to a flattened building. It had feet and four iron wheels rusted immobile. The outer door was gone, the inner door stood open. The sky was a fading purple-pink over a distant mountain range that had an absurd phallic protuberance standing alone as if it had erected away from the mountains around it. The guidebooks called it Lizard Head. Aletha could see no resemblance to a lizard.

Cree pumped away at a small circle of metal as she deposited her pitiful offering for a fire. "Camp stove," he answered her look, "upon which I shall prepare your evening kitty litter."

The tent, blue-and-yellow nylon-awful, hunkered in the weeds—

graceless, small, cozy. She should have come alone, stayed in the car. What were ghosts and bears against an automobile? It took forever to boil the water to rehydrate the packet meal, and shadows deepened into darkness with just enough glow on everything to make it impossible to ignore the boardinghouse across the road staring at them with vacant windows. The wind came down out of the trees to flutter weeds. It hummed in the dead boards of buildings still standing. Night things rustled just out of sight. Cree poured something steamy into plastic cups and handed her a spoon. The food, part crunch and mostly mush, tasted of seasonings only but felt warm and good going down. The cup warmed her hands. Aletha watched the Lizard Head disappear into gloom through the window holes of a roofless commissary. "What do you suppose 'tap her light' means?"

"Could be an old mining term. Or maybe a drinking term." He formed a little tepee of twigs inside a circle of rocks and grinned. "Might even be dirty man-talk."

They had coffee and Hershey bars around the tiny fire. They waited and listened, started every time a stick cracked somewhere off in the forest, listening to the wind whisper and rush, sigh and grow still. Stars came out and the sky grew brighter as the earth grew darker and lights appeared on the side of the boardinghouse. The Datsun split slowly in two and disappeared. Outside lights on poles reflected in the glass of the boardinghouse windows. And then one by one those windows lit up from behind. The boardinghouse had grown a porch. Drifts of snow mounded up to partially cover it and the windows on the lower floor. The thundering sound of this place was almost overcome by the screaming of a shrill whistle. Men's voices shouted above it. Figures still slipping into coat sleeves came off the boardinghouse's new porch on the run.

"You can't have a fire there, man." A man came up from behind and ran off toward the lights. "What're you thinking of?" Aletha reached for Cree as another form hurtled out of the dark and collided with the tent. Making cursing sounds in another language, he struggled free and rushed past with a mere glance for them. "Must be a cave-in!"

The panic in his voice pulled Aletha forward, tugging Cree with her. The light chill in the evening had turned to biting cold. Her tennis shoes crackled on icy snow. The drift under them grew higher as they moved away from the tent, and put them on a level with the eaves of the commissary roof as they rounded a corner of it. They faced a lighted area filled with people and buildings. A long low snowshed ran down from the mouth of the mine and disappeared into a large building at the edge of the blur. Smaller sheds sat drunkenly amidst drifted snow.

"We'll freeze to death here," Cree said in a steam drift from his mouth. "We have to go back. What if we can't?"

Women in ankle-length coats wore shawls draped over their heads as in old pictures of Ellis Island immigrants. Some turned to put their heads on the shoulder of the woman next to them, were embraced and patted. Some had small children standing close at their sides. The men yelled at each other what sounded like commands but looked like puffs of cloud above pinched faces. They passed long-handled tools over peoples' heads and gradually disappeared into a door in the side of the snowshed.

One small figure turned away from the edge of the crowd not far from the commissary. It doubled over as if sick, then straightened, took a few steps toward Aletha and Cree and stopped. Cree was trying to pull her backward but hesitated when Aletha shouted, "Callie?"

The figure moved closer, a white nightgown billowed beneath a jacket far too large. Callie wore a shawl hooded over her head too. "It's Bram," she said, terror rasping her voice. "Bram! He's in there." The little girl stretched a mittened hand toward Cree in a curious gesture. "What can I do?"

"Callie, listen to me. Don't go to Telluride. Callie, do you hear?" Aletha could see the edges of things moving together out of the corners of her eyes. "Callie," she screamed to a landscape suddenly empty of buildings and lights and crowd and snow. She dropped to the level of weeds and against the corner of a rotting commissary. There was moonlight now. The wind had risen from a sigh to a dirgelike moan. Her hands and feet were numb. Her ears and even her teeth ached with a cold that no longer existed. Only the pendant seemed warm between her breasts.

10

Aunt Lilly did not recover her strength as she should have after the death of baby Henry. Finally her husband and her sister took her down to Telluride and found her a room in the home of a widow. The widow would do her cooking and laundry and all Lilly need do was rest and convalesce with doctor, hospital, and drugstore nearby. Back in Alta the O'Connells made room for Uncle Henry at their supper table. Luella was rummaging through disorderly stacks of work pants and overalls in the commissary one day when Mrs. Traub, the manager's wife, bustled in, a purpose in her eye. They exchanged pleasantries and then, "What's this I hear about our new teacher and your boy, Bram?"

Luella's mother had always said that suspicion once planted could grow its own evil, and Luella knew that to be true. "She's his teacher, hardly more than a girl herself. What could—"

"Old enough to turn a boy's head. And my Bertha says her color rises every time he so much as passes her desk. That's not a good influence on the other children either, if you ask me. But Mr. Traub says to let it be. It's either Mildred Heisinger or no teacher at all for us this year." Mrs. Traub collected a parcel from the storekeeper and stopped at Luella's side on her way out. "Oh, and, Mrs. O'-Connell, do come up when you're finished here. I've some of that poison you've been wanting to rid yourself of the mangy cat under your house."

"No one's going to take him, Callie. He's not young and pretty." Bram and Callie were supposed to be collecting wooden crates from behind the commissary to break into kindling. Instead they were trying to find another home for Charles. "He'll just head for our cabin the minute he's let out."

"Ma'am cut a square of good beef from the middle of the roast before she put it in the pot and took it out the back door." Callie was sure it was poisoned. She'd searched but couldn't find it, had found Charles instead. "And she'd been to tea with Mrs. Traub."

They'd tried to convince the storekeeper that the commissary needed an experienced ratter in its storeroom but had been unsuccessful. Now they entered the cookhouse, found it abustle with men at their supper, the sounds of crunching, slurping, burping, rough talk, and the clang of tableware. Young boys rushed among long tables carrying bowls heaped with boiled potatoes and platters of beef. A waist-high hole in the wall gave access to the kitchen for empty platters and dirty plates and egress for the mounds of food handed out to the waiters. Charles stiffened, moaned warning, and batted at Bram's chin.

"When you coming back to work, schoolboy?"

"Why should he when he can look at that schoolmarm all day?"

"Hey, Miss Callie, I'm still waiting for you to grow up so's I can marry them dimples."

"What you bringing that dirty critter in here for?"

"That's no dirty critter. That's King Charles of Alta, ain't that right, Callie, honey? Helps me eat my dinner at the mill every day. Right regal about it he is too."

"Here! Take that animal from my cooking house." Mr. Mueller leaned out the kitchen hole and gestured so wildly with one thick arm he nearly sent a bowl of gravy flying out of a young waiter's hand. "What are you sinking?"

"But he'd catch the rats in your kitchen," Callie pleaded. "And he's wonderfully lovable." Charles hissed, spat, struggled to get out of Bram's arms.

"No catzes. Not one catz. For you, Callie, a piece of Heinrich Mueller's apples pie, two pieces for your tower of a brother even." Mr. Mueller's red face reddened with emphasis. "But no catzes. None!"

"Aye, and wot's a 'catzes,' Mueller?" Laughter and a chanting of "catzes" and then foot-stomping to the rhythm of the chant throughout the dining room sent Charles into a frenzy of scratching and biting and Heinrich Mueller into a frenzy of fist shaking. All but Charles came to a breathless halt as a hole sizzled into the wall beside Callie. Bram's jaw dropped and his arms loosened.

Callie caught Charles in mid-leap and turned to face the lady who'd left her book of drawings on the ground by the mill. The lady wore pants again and an odd puffy mackinaw that hung open in front. She had a man with her, a man taller than Bram with hair cut rounded and fluffy and so long it covered the tops of his ears. His skin was darkened by sun and his cheeks cut vertically by deep creases. They were both in the process of removing huge eyeglasses, smoky-colored, as if dipped in flame. They stood on a pile of fallen, grayed boards. They stood in bright sunlight, a deep green forest behind them.

"Callie, don't go to Telluride," the lady said as though terrified at the thought.

"Who are you?" Callie asked. "Where do you come from?"

"Aletha, Aletha Kingman. Promise me you won't go."

Callie heard the scraping of chairs and benches against the wooden flooring and in the general rush of boots she shoved a writhing Charles at Aletha. "Ma'am's going to poison him. Please find him a home."

"Are you Bram?" the dark man asked her brother. "If you are, don't go in the mine. There's going to be a cave-in if there hasn't been already." A squirrel perched on a tree limb above his head and scolded them all. And above the tree in an otherwise cloudless heaven a narrow band of cloud trailed all the way across in a perfectly straight line.

"If you wait here, I'll run and fetch your book," Callie offered.

"I thought you said Miss Heisinger had it."

"Miss Heisinger? Why would she have your book?"

"Callie, never mind that now. Just remember to never go to Telluride and, honey, I can't take your kitty." Charles climbed stiff-legged up the lady's chest in agreement. The man caught him as he was about to jump off her shoulder.

"Please, Aletha, you're the only one who can help. His name is Charles." The fuzzy edges of the hole moved together and squeezed out the sunny green world, the strange couple, and the dirty white cat.

Mr. Mueller came from the kitchen doorway, cautiously felt the wall with the palms of both hands. "I see it, yes. I believe it, no. Who is that woman with the trousers on, Callie? Where did she go?"

"She's Aletha." The privy smell came through the loose-fitting boards of the wall. Next to the lady and her companion had been a seat still standing with the outhouse fallen from around it. She'd

just sent Charles to a land where this building would be a tumble-
down ruin. Either that or it was a fairy-tale land. Or maybe heaven.
Whichever it was, poor Charles would be better off than he was
here.

"Do you think Jesus lives with them?" Callie asked, but Bram
pulled her out of the dining room, through the gathered miners,
and around to the privy side of the building.

Mr. Mueller followed. "Go and eat your suppers, you brave mens.
The children and I have encountered with the danger."

The privy stood whole and smelled even stronger than inside. The
wall next to it was solid. "We forgot to ask her how she makes the
hole without leaving a mark, Bram."

Irregular rows of tree stumps marched to the curve in the road
and continued on the other side in dots of gray up the mountainside.
No green pine branches to harbor that chattering squirrel. And the
couple in the oval had stood in the bright sunlight of morning, where
here the light was dusty with the approach of evening. "I wonder
how she knew Miss Heisinger," Callie whispered.

But Bram just stared straight and still. "Where is Charles, Callie?"

"He's with Aletha now. You know we couldn't keep him."

"Maybe he's dead. Maybe they were angels."

"Und so? What you do? That angel he said for you to not go into
the mine. He said there is coming a cave-in."

A silence overcame the small band of miners who'd straggled
along behind them. It was followed by a low buzzing of male vocal
cords and fear. It finally thinned out to one whispered word that
passed around the building and even crossed the road to the boardinghouse—"cave-in."

11

"HEY now, what if a lady with half a bedspread over
her head peeks in here?"

"I just want you to hold me," Aletha said. They both trembled
with cold and reaction, lying on one sleeping bag and covered by

the other, inside the tent, and still wearing their down parkas. The sudden and short-lived Alta winter had extinguished the fire. "And they were shawls, not bedspreads. Callie was small and young again. And it was winter there. Things . . . or time, is getting mixed up."

"So am I. You'd better let me go build a fire. Make us some coffee."

"But can't you help explain what's happening?"

"Yeah. You're seeing things that either did or did not happen a long time ago. And you're making me see them too."

"Maybe it's not me. Maybe Callie is the catalyst you and Tracy say I am. And who's this Bram Callie talked of?"

"Somebody close to her. Poor kid was sick about him being in the cave-in." He reached over her to unzip a fly window on the tent door and peered into the night. "How'd they manage a mine and a mill in all that snow? Still can't feel my feet. Rest of me is warming, though." He moved back over her. "Coffee, cocoa, or me?"

"I'm not . . . I don't want to lose my freedom again. Relations lead to relationships and freedom goes right out the door."

"So do I. I'll build us another fire. We can take off our shoes, warm up our toes."

"Wait. Don't go. Yet." She couldn't see much more than his shape in the dark but his impatience was a palpable thing in their tiny enclosure. "What if those old-fashioned people come back?"

His lips found her throat. His hair tickled her nose. "They're liable to get the old-fashioned shock of their lives."

Aletha knew she'd stalled past the point of being able to call the shots. "What is Cree short for?"

"McCree."

"McCree Mackelwain?" She tried to laugh but he was too heavy and it came out more as a cough. Why was it men never wanted to talk at a time like this? "I think the world was a better place in Callie's day when there wasn't all this promiscuity, don't you?"

"And dirty old men like me could visit the cribs on the line and leave nice young things like you alone? You have the nicest, roundest little buns I ever squeezed." And that was the last he would say.

Removing clothing in their cramped space without socking each other was nearly impossible and the awkwardness might have ruined the mood for Aletha. But the thought of Alta's dead people standing around outside the tent shivering in their shawls, up to their crotches in snow, their gasps of surprise shooting steam puffs into the night, mittened hands pointing to a galloping blue-and-yellow tent that must appear filled with a convention of whirling dervishes—the thought began as a humorous one and then slipped into a fantasy so erotic she scared herself. And when movement quieted down in the tent a few of the bolder, moral leaders among Alta's women bent to peek in the open fly of the doorway, shielded now only by mosquito netting. Of course, they wouldn't have been able to see anything, but in Aletha's fantasy they saw plenty. And to be caught in forbidden fornication by a bunch of Victorians . . .

"Uh . . . history's a real turn-on for you, isn't it?" Cree said finally.

Aletha took her rehydrated scrambled eggs and her new sketchbook onto the roof of the Datsun. She sketched what she saw and tried to add what she could remember from the night before—the porch on the boardinghouse, the snowshed, and the top level of the mill. But she kept seeing Callie's stricken look in the harsh lights reflecting off night snow.

"For an old-fashioned girl, you look pretty this morning." Cree handed her a cup of coffee. The softening of the usual edge in his voice had startled a squiggle from her pencil. "See, you can even blush."

"I'd hardly call my behavior last night old-fashioned." She drank in a gulp instead of a sip and burned her mouth. "Or pretty." "Pretty" was an old-fashioned word too. She loved it.

"It's not last night." He glanced from her sketch to the boardinghouse and gave her a slow smile. "More your reaction to it now that's old-fashioned." He drained his own coffee, set his cup on the Datsun's hood, and wandered down to the mouth of the mine, peering into the air around him as if he too were trying to reconstruct the snowshed that had connected it to the mill. For a time he stood with his hands sunk deep in his pants pockets and rocked back and forth on his heels. Aletha thought she could detect his lips moving and wondered if he was talking to himself. She tried to sketch him into her drawing, but she wasn't very good with bodies. The proportions were always wrong. Aletha hadn't taken up drawing until prison, part of a rehabilitation program. It had helped save her sanity then and had become an entrenched hobby since. But now she struggled with a form she'd drawn too large for the picture, his legs too long for his body and top half too bulky in his waist-length jacket.

Aletha threw the sketchbook onto the car seat and walked down past the boardinghouse to join him. The hole in the hillside gaped mammoth and black. An ominous turquoise drool of water bubbled out of the darkness to one side, flowed over rocks and humps to a crest that had once supported the mill. A few yards inside the opening stretched an iron wall set with a door locked in rust and padlocks. The chill felt deep and permanent here. "How could they get people to work in places like this?"

"It was dangerous, exciting work. Paid well, involved gold and silver, took he-man strength, and offered a chance for a tiny few to strike it rich. And everyone thought he'd be numbered among the tiny few. Life was one big lottery." On the side of the iron wall where the water escaped, the earth that abutted it had crumbled away in places, possibly helped along by tourists. Cree slid sideways through the opening.

"What's in there?" Aletha stood at the edge of the vertical crevice and tried to peek in without blocking his light. The black looked like a solid thing. The odor of damp dirt and mold blew out at her on cold air.

"Narrow-gauge tracks. Couple of ore cars. And one Mountain Dew pop can. I've been in here before." His voice came hollow, as if he spoke from a vast cavern. Then he was back sliding through the opening. "Feel sorry for that Bram, whoever he is . . . was."

"I can't even stand to think about it." Aletha stepped quickly out into the sun.

"Well, you've had your night in Alta," Cree said.

"Maybe if I stay awhile longer, I'll have another experience." He dropped an arm around her as they walked up to their camping area and she added, "I mean with Callie."

"I don't think I want another experience." He pried tent stakes out of the ground. "Ten minutes after they happen I begin to doubt they happened. It's disorienting as hell."

"I suppose you do have to get on with your mission." She unzipped her parka as the sun began to penetrate. "Is it something to do with the dead friend you and Renata Winslow have in common?"

He sat back on his heels and studied her. When he spoke the

edge had returned to his voice. "I see no need for you to know."

"Look, if you think all this secrecy makes you sexy, forget it," Aletha snapped. "You couldn't have any secrets worse than mine." She stood next to a building, the back portion of which was still upright. In the center of a room mostly roofed over was a large iron-and-porcelain stove with a pipe that vented straight up through the roof. A waist-high shelf lined the room for work space, with rows of open shelving above and below for cupboards. Two great metal sinks proclaimed this a kitchen geared to feed a fair number. "Cree, come see this."

He already had the tent packed into its little bag with the draw strings and was beginning to batter a down sleeping bag into a stuff sack. "I really have to get back sometime today." But he came to stand beside her. "So what's to see?"

She pointed to a wooden seat with three holes in it. "What's left of an outhouse. But it's almost attached to this building which was probably a restaurant by the size of that stove. Can you imagine the smells and the flies in summer? I always thought an outhouse was out and away from the house-house. Think of the germs. No wonder people used to be sick so much."

Cree stepped around the shelf seat to stand on a heap of boards. "Probably the dining hall for the boardinghouse. With a door right here so the miner full of a hot dinner didn't have to wade through cold snowdrifts to relieve himself. Germs are fairly recent anyway. Before germs, people got sick due to bad air, bad blood, bad luck, and the good Lord."

"When you get going you're a philosopher, historian . . . what are you really?"

"Bad news." He pulled her close for a kiss and their sunglasses clicked. His face felt warm and scratchy against her nose and men's voices chanted far away. Chanted something that sounded like "cots is" accompanied by a rhythmic rumble of stomping feet. Ghostly sounds to be hearing in a ghost town, like the special effects in a scary movie. It drew closer, louder. As she turned around, Aletha wished she'd listened to Cree and they'd not stayed in Alta for any more of this. The sun dimmed. She pulled off her sunglasses to a darker world.

A spreading hole in the air with edges that sizzled parted the view and opened onto the interior of a room in which Callie held up her arms toward a white cat leaping across midair, its claws extended, ears back, and tail bushed out. A tall boy stood beside her in high-water pants and a collarless shirt with a slit in the front so he could slip it over his head. His arms cradled awkwardly as if he still held the cat. The room behind them had open beams with bare, clear light bulbs. It had tables cluttered with dishes and glasses and men in high boots, little mustaches, and suspenders. The chanting choked off in groups as they noticed Aletha and Cree. Smiles straightened. Raised forks or hunks of bread lowered carefully to plates.

A youth in knee pants set a metal pitcher down on a table and backed toward a door across the room. Aletha could see the Lizard Head and corner of the commissary roof through a paned window. Chairs scraped. Throats cleared mightily. The men began to follow the youth's example.

"Callie, don't go to Telluride," Aletha said quickly, remembering how short-lived these glimpses into Callie's world were. "Promise me you won't."

A heavy man leaning out of the service window from the kitchen finally lowered his arm on the sweat-stained triangle in his shirt. After asking Aletha's name and without warning, Callie shoved the cat and all its claws through the hole. Aletha reached for it automatically, touching the back of one of Callie's hands. The cat smelled of sulfur.

"Ma'am's going to poison him. Please find him a home."

The cat stood against Aletha's chest, legs stiff, body trembling. She held him under his armpits, afraid to move. The cat had murder in his eye.

"Are you Bram?" Cree said behind her, and the tall boy looked up, closed his mouth to swallow. "If you are, don't go in the mine. There's going to be a cave-in if there hasn't been already."

Callie offered to find Aletha's book. The cat hissed like a snake and waved one set of claws at her face while the rest dug through her T-shirt and several layers of skin. "I thought you said Miss Heisinger had it."

"Miss Heisinger? Why would she have your book?"

"Callie, never mind that now. Just remember to never go to Telluride and, honey, I can't take your kitty." She pulled the cat loose to pass him back. He slipped like grease through her hands, mounted her front, and jumped off her shoulder.

"Please, Aletha, you're the only one who can help. His name is Charles," Callie said as the oval began to close. The last thing Aletha saw in Callie's world was the window across the room filled with mustachioed faces and rounded eyes. Then the dining room was gone and they had a clear line of sight to a roofless commissary and the Lizard Head in the distance. Cree held Charles now and Charles sniffed at his chin on a wary inspection.

"Looks more like a 'Charlie' than a 'Charles' to me." A certain gruffness beneath the casual tone suggested just how shaken Cree was.

"Waaaaa," Charles said, sounding like a baby with laryngitis instead of a cat. He twisted and sprang away, landing on the three-holed seat and then in the weeds. He vanished around the kitchen, to reappear as a white flash racing past the commissary.

"This is the Charles Callie asked about when I saw her at the Senate. He's living proof that what we've been seeing is real, Cree. I don't think you can deny it now, no matter how you try to fool yourself."

Cree had a long scratch on the back of one hand. Blood bubbled out in droplets between black hairs. "Well, he's living anyway."

"Living now. And all those people he was with a moment ago have probably been dead for years. Other people will have to believe us." She skirted the dining room's rubble and started after Charles. "We can't lose him. That's a real Victorian cat."

"What are you going to tell these other people? A bony white cat born around the turn of the century is alive today because a little girl pushed him through a hole in the scenery? You're going to end up in a kind of place that reminds you a lot of prison."

Charles sniffed around the foundation of a vanished mill but ran across the road and under Callie's house when he saw them. They called him "kitty, kitty, kitty." They called him "Charles" and "Charlie." Cree even called him a few un-Victorian names. But Charles remained cold and aloof and always out of reach. His dull-hued eyes reminded Aletha of the ancient Mildred Heisinger's.

12

MANAGEMENT was most unhappy at the latest shut-
down of the mine at Alta. First the unfortunate Haskell Gibson had
been caught in the works at the mill; then a lightning storm had
shut down operations in the same summer. Now in the first week
of September men refused to enter the mine for four days in the
belief that angels had appeared to them to warn of an impending
cave-in.

"You expect me to believe an angel would appear in the cookhouse?" A rising blood pressure showed up as blotches beneath the
skin on Timothy Traub's face. The mine manager fairly danced
around his office in the building behind the cookhouse. "I've heard
the language and the stories bandied about in that place. No angel
would go near it!"

"Where would you expect an angel to show hisself here, in the
privy?" one of his men asked. "Ain't no church, you know."

"And they tommyknockers has been cutting up something fear-
some," another offered. " 'Tis a double-edged warning and sure as
a gun it is too."

Traub beat a fist on the same metal safe Aletha had seen on its
side in the weeds, rusted and doorless. "You try to explain tommyknockers and angels to the owners."

While the manager fumed, Luella had to take Callie and Bram
out of school because loitering miners pestered them to explain the
manifestation of trousered angels who'd spoken to them personally
and even accepted Callie's offering of a stray cat. John O'Connell
finally took Bram off prospecting. Uncle Henry traveled down to
Telluride to see Aunt Lilly. Fighting broke out sporadically in the
boardinghouse, where young men spent too much time, energy, and
money over a pack of cards. Poor Miss Heisinger grew bilious because of the difficulty in sneaking in and out of privies with both
shifts from the mine and three from the mill hanging about to watch

her every move. Callie became sluggish and lonesome for Bram and Charles, missed the stimulation of school.

But while the company watched the "angel strike" eat into its profits, the single miners and mill hands accrued no pay and still owed a dollar a day for room and board at the cookhouse. Those with family could afford the layoff even less. And so they drifted back to work. But they moved warily through the levels and drifts, the crosscuts and stopes. They started each time a tommyknocker tapped over their heads or a drop of water splashed too loudly. And when a miner spit a fuse he hurried away from it a little faster than before.

Luella put up wildberry jams and jellies, ordered up sacks of cornmeal and flour, potatoes and dried pinto beans, coffee beans and sugar. At night mice chewed holes in the corners of the sacks. She set out traps for the first time since they'd moved to Alta. The kitchen was so crowded only a path remained between the table, stove, and back door. Sacks of provisions huddled along the wall under the stairs and beneath the beds in the loft.

Alta's children ranged far and wide to cut down aspen trees with yellow-gold leaves for firewood. Men with chains and horses hauled whole tree trunks to Alta, sold sawed-off sections to people squirreling away for winter. Heaps of firewood grew massive on the back porch.

Callie began knitting a neck scarf in the evenings while her mother knitted woolly mittens. The O'Connells nailed heavy blue denim over the floor and walls of the sitting room. At night under their naked electric bulb the room took on a somber winter hue and the skin on their hands and faces looked blue-tinged and eerie.

Late one afternoon as Callie and Bram dragged silver aspen up Boomerang Road, they met Miss Heisinger out for a walk. Callie and the teacher chatted while Bram walked on stolidly, saying nothing. Miss Heisinger wore a hat of black straw with a wide brim that shielded her face from the sun and from his view.

"It must be tiresome for you to not be able to go anywhere except Bertha's house and the schoolhouse," Callie said.

"To be unable to go anywhere except," Mildred corrected. "I don't know how I'll manage this winter when I can't sneak off on these little walks." She tilted her head to peer prettily up at Bram from under her hat. "I've worn a path between the tree stumps behind Mr. Traub's coal shed and through here." She gestured up an incline that led to the backyards of the nice houses on the hill. "This way I can avoid the camp altogether and take the air without causing some old grand commotion. Don't you tell anyone. It's just a secret I'm sharing with the two of you."

Bram didn't figure anything she did could be much of a secret for long, and soon there'd be men lining her path. He wished they hadn't met up with her. Callie always slowed down when she talked and the teacher couldn't walk very fast in all her long skirts and pointed shoes. That gnawing need to eat, which rarely left him, practically made his head swim now and he knew a dinner of chicken and dumplings was readying at home.

Miss Heisinger stopped them with a hand on his arm and one on Callie's shoulder. "Before I turn back to my private path, I must speak with you. Your birthday is next week, Bram, and so is Jennie Tyler's. I thought we might plan a little celebration. Perhaps carry our lunches to Alta Lakes and—"

Bram took a firmer grip on the aspen trunks and pulled them away from her skirts, trailing leaves the size and color of gold coins. They gave off a smoky, mossy smell. Why this woman took such pleasure in tormenting him he did not know. But if the wrath she raised in him ever got out, he was doomed and that he did know. "Birthday celebrations are for children."

He walked off and left Callie calling after him. Bram wanted to hurt Miss Heisinger physically and he wanted to hold her, caress around on her body. He was shamed by both thoughts.

"Bram, wait. Stop." She was running up the road after him. "I merely thought—" She cut off with a gasp and he didn't hear her heels clicking on pebbles behind him any longer.

"Are you hurt? Bram, help—" Callie had dropped her branches and run to the teacher's side. "She turned her ankle." Bram fitted his teeth together hard, laid down his load, and walked back to them. Miss Heisinger, with a hand on Callie's shoulder, tried to take a step and groaned, lost her balance, and sat in the dust in a billow of skirts. Her hat went cockeyed. "Oh, this is so silly. I'm sorry."

It was just then that the devil spoke to Brambaugh O'Connell.

"I'll stay with her," Callie said. "You run for someone to help." The evening cold that he hardly felt had turned her little nose red already.

Bram handed Callie his hatchet. He stooped to gather up the

fallen teacher and tightened the muscles in his buttocks and lower back as John O'Connell had taught him to do when lifting a load. He noticed how high her little boots were buttoned, how white was the lace of her petticoats. He was surprised at how light she was and how quickly the devil had implanted the idea in his head. The pain in her big flecked eyes almost caused him to waver. But things had gone deep enough, he'd had all a man could stand.

"Oh, that's a much better idea." Callie skipped beside them. "Bram can carry you home."

Miss Heisinger fitted nicely in his arms and he drew in a breath of power. This was the first he'd seen her so dangerously discomposed and in possession of not one iota of authority. When her hat had gone askew it left her hair untidied and his carrying her that way put a shocking amount of ankle and petticoat on display. "Thank you, Bram." Her bones relaxed against him trustingly. "But we mustn't go this way. What will people think? If you could just help me back to my secret path."

"That's right, Bram, and it would be shorter too." Callie screwed up her forehead. "What *would* people think?"

But Bram kept on course, actually felt the smile as it spread across his face. He tightened his hold. Mrs. Fisherdicks, who lived next to Aunt Lilly and Uncle Henry, stopped shaking the loose flour out of her bread cloth and stared from her doorway. She didn't even answer Callie's bright "hello."

"Brambaugh O'Connell, did you hear what I said?" Miss Heisinger whispered between her teeth. Her face had gone red and her bones stiff again. "Turn around this instant!"

"Bram, don't you hear her? Oh, hello, Mr. Crowe. The teacher twisted her ankle and Bram's carrying her home." Cyrus Crowe, the mill foreman, tipped his cap and forgot to replace it, just stood with it half on and half off and watched them pass. Bram nodded manfully.

"Not past the boardinghouse. You must be mad." Miss Heisinger struggled and kicked and her hat came off, causing more of her hair to come down. She was beginning to look as if a horse had run away with her.

Callie picked up the hat and found the long hat pin that had pulled out of it. She ran ahead so she could study his face while walking backward. "Are you just being mean to her?"

Bram would have given his soul to have never had to see that disappointed look. But he couldn't stop now. Even with all the practice he'd had on Callie, it was difficult to tickle the teacher while carrying her. Finally one hand managed to find the spaces between her stays and he surprised a squeal and a giggle from her. Miners standing in line to get into the cookhouse turned to follow them instead. They picked up more from the boardinghouse porch.

"Need any help there, boy? Be glad to give you a hand."

"What'd she do? Meet up with a bear?"

Bram pretended not to see John O'Connell coming out of the changehouse as they turned at the commissary and he led the procession up the road toward the fancy houses on the hill.

"He did it to be mean. She told him to not go through the camp. When we took her into Bertha's house she even started crying."

"Can't go back to school now. It's all anybody's talking about. Some say they even heard her laughing," John O'Connell said cheerfully, and slapped Bram on the shoulder. "Looks like you outsmarted the teacher and Ma'am too."

"I can't believe you'd be so cruel as to purposely endanger the reputation of a schoolteacher just to go back to the mine. She might never find work again." Ma'am looked to be on the verge of tears herself. She set down her fork and left the table. Callie couldn't eat her dinner either. She refused to speak or even look at Bram. Finally he stomped out to sit on a cold stump and brood. But not before he'd finished up two plates of chicken and dumplings.

While she washed dishes, Luella peered out the window over the dishpan as if she could see him in the dark. "It's all my fault. If I hadn't insisted on his going to school—"

"He knew exactly what he was doing and he wanted to do it. I saw it in his eyes. I'll never forgive him."

"What can we do for that poor teacher?" She handed Callie a cup to dry. "I'm afraid Mrs. Traub is already set against her."

Bram turned fifteen and stopped brooding on his misdeeds. Luella and Callie soon forgave him because he was theirs. He went to work in the mine and seemed to lose his clean, sun-browned look overnight.

Mrs. Traub delighted in nursing her captive schoolmarm. Mildred

Heisinger was forced to be off a swollen ankle for two weeks and she limped for another two after she opened the school again.

The snows came early and heavy that year. Even before Christmas the roads were impassable and the only way in or out was the tram buckets. No lady would ride on the dirty concentrates down to the Loop. And riding the empty, swaying buckets back up was too dangerous for children. Only the men could get out of Alta.

Every day before and after work in the mine John and Bram shoveled out the path to the privy. In between shovelings, falling or drifting snow filled it up again. Callie walked in cold white tunnels with only a band of sky above. When the sky was clear it formed a blue ribbon overhead that contrasted sharply with her snow canyons and made her squint her eyes to slits. When the sky was overcast or snowing it sometimes seemed to blend with the walls of snow and put a gray ceiling on a gray prison. Where paths were not shoveled but packed hard by heavy traffic she had to walk a careful line on top of the drifts. One step off a packed trail and she'd flounder in a snow morass. Bram cut steps in the snowbank that separated them from the mill so Callie could climb up out of the house to go to school.

Miss Heisinger had grown distant. She seemed to have lost enthusiasm for her teaching. Callie felt miserable when she remembered how much more they'd all enjoyed school before Bram had humbled the teacher. It seemed to Callie that her own happy world had been changing for the worse since she'd given Charles away to the lady in pants.

One evening while she knitted on the neck scarf in the blue glow of the sitting room, the winter wind shrieked and howled around the house, causing the cloth lining of the room to puff in and out where it wasn't held down by furniture or nails, and made the stovepipe rattle against the wires that fastened it to the wall. A coal fire was banked for breakfast in the cook stove in the kitchen and the little heating stove in the sitting room burned crackling aspen. It gave off so much heat Callie's forehead felt scorched, yet shivers tingled up between her shoulder blades as winter seeped through the wall behind her. Bram and Pa lay out on the floor half-dozing. A wild pounding at the door startled them all and when Bram roused to answer it, Uncle Henry fell into his arms.

"You didn't ride the tram up in this storm," John said as Bram tried to hold the man and close the door on the gale at the same time.

Henry Ostrander was short and stocky with heavy brows and bright blue eyes. The dark brows were coated white now, and so was his mustache. His whole face looked frosted over. He stared speechlessly as John and Luella fussed about, helping to remove his snowy outer clothes. Finally Luella stepped back and said softly, "Henry? It's Lilly, isn't it?"

And Uncle Henry began to sob like a woman. Callie had never seen anything like it and it was the saddest sound she'd ever heard. She moved closer to Bram. When he could control his voice, Henry asked, "Would you please send the children upstairs?"

"Would you please send the children upstairs?" Bram mimicked. He was on his hands and knees trying to slap the snow off the coverlet on the big bed. "I'm not a child."

Ma'am had let them bring up a coal-oil lamp and they'd set it on the floor at the end of the beds. Callie shook the snow from her quilt and crawled under it. She could remember when she and Bram shared a bed, and nights like this they'd huddle together. Then one day Ma'am had decreed mysteriously, "Bram's too big." Ever since then winter nights had been cramped because Callie had to curl up so tight to keep warm. He lay out on her parents' bed now with his hands behind his head and his feet hanging over the end.

"Bram, Aunt Lilly's dead, isn't she?"

"Either that or terrible sick, Callie girl, to cause a grown man to break down that way."

"But why couldn't we hear about it?"

"Maybe he doesn't want us to see him embarrass himself any more or he wants to spare us the sadness of the details of it."

"Remember how she used to laugh and tease us before she grew all fat? And she was so pretty and always saying surprising things. I don't want her to be dead." They watched the shadows twitch around on the low ceiling as the drafts pried and dipped into the lamp's glass chimney. Grains of snow sifted down like fine white flour when the wind shook the house. The salty smell of frying bacon drifted up to them as Ma'am prepared Uncle Henry a supper. "Tell me what it's like down in the stopes again."

"Not tonight, Callie. I'm feeling too tired and sad for Aunt Lilly."

"Aren't you afraid of the cave-in the lady's husband warned you about?"

"If it was going to happen, it would have happened before now."

"You know what the Bible says, 'As ye sow so shall ye reap'?" Charles was gone and baby Henry and now Aunt Lilly. Bram must not leave her too. "Bram, you don't suppose you'll reap a cave-in because of what you did to Miss Heisinger?"

13

"I think that big kid was Bram, don't you? I mean, the way he looked at me when I said his name . . ." Cree lay spread out on the ground on his stomach, pitching rocks under Callie's house in an attempt to dislodge Charles.

"We're terrifying him. But he can't stay here. There's no town left. No one to feed him." Aletha had found a long stick to poke and prod with. Charles spat and hissed and backed himself into a corner where some of the flooring had caved in.

"He's an animal. He might make out all right."

"He's a domestic animal and he's Callie's cat. We're not leaving without him. Your mission can wait, McCree." Aletha slid on her belly over the rocky, disturbed earth beneath the shack and tried not to think of what kind of creatures might have been digging here, perhaps have homes under her. She had to pull her souvenir pendant out of her sweatshirt to keep it from cutting into her. Just as she reached for a handful of cat tail, Charles broke and scooted past her face, made a wrong turn, and Cree had him by a hind leg an instant before he would have been free.

"Poor kitty, he's out of time and out of place," Aletha said when she drove them down the mountain. Charles lay across Cree's lap, hiding his face in the darkness of the crook of Cree's elbow. When Aletha stopped before pulling out onto the highway, he raised his head and panted with terror as a dog would with the heat.

"He's caught in time. What if we'd been caught last night?" Cree stroked a dirty spot on Charles's white coat. "Last night when it happened, the old times were all around us. And when it stopped we sort of fell back into our own time. This morning we merely glimpsed Callie's world through a hole. And when it closed, old Charlie here stayed with us instead of falling back into his own time." It sounded like he was peeling a carrot when he scratched his unshaven chin. "It must be the place. Or you and the place."

"And Callie."

"Callie wasn't at that roadblock. We didn't hear her when we heard the tram and those voices. It's you. And if I hadn't met you I'd be worrying over my own life. Not wondering if that Bram kid went into the mine."

"What if we changed history by warning them? Maybe Callie didn't go to the Senate. You know, if her teacher's still alive, she could be too."

She held Charles while Cree went into Rose's Market in Telluride for cat food and kitty litter. They discovered their new Victorian friend was not housebroken shortly after they turned him loose to sniff around the condo. Cree put him in a bathroom with food, water, and the kitty box and closed the door. "Could be why Ma'am threatened to poison him."

"Shouldn't we talk to him, soothe him down? This is all so strange to him."

"I don't know what we're going to do with Charlie." He turned her away from the bathroom door. "But there is something we can do for you."

Cree walked Aletha out to Lone Tree Cemetery. The toe of her tennis shoe nudged the flat stone in the grass. "It might not be our Callie." Her voice was husky with tears that weren't in her eyes. "Could have been a very popular name years ago."

Cree wished he hadn't been so abrupt, had warned her on the walk out. He turned away feeling like an ass because he didn't know how to comfort her. Instead he poked around in the grass nearby for other buried markers and found one almost completely grown over. He pulled away grass and weeds, dug out dirt with bare fingers, wiped repeatedly at the inscription, hoped it wasn't somebody named "Bram." This marker was larger than Callie's and looked as if it could once have sat upright. Some of the inscription was indecipherable but he did make out the words "Beloved Husband and

Father" and "Haskell Gibson" and the birth and death years—1880 and 1900.

He brushed off his hands and quelled an urge to look for more stones. That boy, even with his funny haircut and big ears, had struck a chord in Cree. Perhaps it was just that the kid was the healthy type, that if a man ever wanted a son . . . well, this Bram was the kind you'd want to show off to other men. Cree snorted self-derision and found Aletha watching him.

"Do you know you talk to yourself? I think that's kind of nice."

He knew he talked to himself, but he never realized he'd been doing it until the conversation was over. It had embarrassed him more than once. "So what did I say?"

"I don't know. You just move your lips. Hey, there's nothing the matter with being human."

Cree kissed her to make her shut up and took her to the Floradora for lunch. A barn had been stripped of its weathered wood to line an old building on the main street. The Floradora boasted the requisite bar, stained glass, hanging plants, and prints of Telluride's mining days, but it also had a soup-and-salad bar worth the price.

Aletha's honey-colored hair usually hung smooth to her shoulders and turned under at the ends, but now it was mussed by wind and tucked behind an ear on one side. Her cheeks were flushed with the outdoor activity and with sadness over Callie. Cree could well imagine her in a Caribbean tan and a nifty bikini surrounded by palm fronds and sand. He could not imagine her in a federal prison. She was too trusting.

"Are you married?" she asked him suddenly.

"Eat your salad."

"Least you could do is talk some about yourself. Especially after taking advantage of me that way last night."

"Advantage? I was practically attacked!"

"Are you married?" She lifted amber-colored eyebrows that matched her eyes.

"Was. Didn't work out." That wasn't all that hadn't worked out.

" 'It didn't work out'—that's become a cliché for a sick society." She waved her fork as if directing the sixties music playing from the speakers in the corners and originating at the local radio station.

"You're not only old-fashioned, you're a prude."

Aletha laughed then whispered, "I wish I'd never gotten involved with Callie. All I can think about is her. I walk around jumpy-like, not knowing where or when a hole into another world will open up."

"And possibly swallow you like it did Charlie. You might get stuck in Callie's world sometime. Ever think of that?"

"I don't ask for these things to happen. What can I do?"

"Get out of Telluride, maybe even out of Colorado. I've got a Cessna at the Montrose airport. Take you anywhere you want to go."

"You're a pilot. I knew you must have done something before you were unemployed. You certainly don't seem to lack for funds." She contemplated a cucumber slice on the end of her fork and then pointed it at him instead of putting it in her mouth. "I've got to know what happened to Callie. And there's only one person who can tell me. Mildred Heisinger."

"What about Mildred Heisinger?" Renata Winslow slid in beside Cree. "And where have you been? You missed a shift at the San Juan Bordello but Barry wants you at the Senate by four." Cree chose to ignore the raised eyebrow and questioning glance she turned on Aletha and then on him.

They stayed to have coffee while Renata picked at a lunch and regaled them with stories of the incompetents she'd been known to hire, and then softened it all with a coating of wry sophistication that passed for charm. She was one very smooth lady but she didn't seem like Dutch Massey's type. Renata had moved to Aspen from the West Coast, she'd told Cree, looking for reality. She'd owned a boutique there for a few years and moved on to Telluride, he supposed because she hadn't found reality in Aspen. He couldn't believe she'd found it here either.

"Cree and I have been seeing people and things happening in the past," Aletha said. "They even gave us a cat this morning."

"Oh, are you into the occult?" Renata's pause was minuscule. "They're talking about having a workshop on that next year between the hang-gliding conference and the film festival. There're already a few loons in town trying to drum up business."

"She didn't turn a hair," Aletha complained when they walked back to the Pick and Gad. "I don't understand this world even when I'm not in prison."

Cree had been assured that locks were unnecessary in Telluride but he'd always locked up the condo. That's why he noticed his key locked the door instead of unlocked it. He drew Aletha back and entered carefully, pushing aside the contents of the coat closet to gain entrance. Everything in the place had been tipped over, pulled apart, or dumped on the floor. He headed for the bedroom. The dresser in the corner angled out into the room, the carpet pulled back to expose the pad and the tack strip and the absence of the folder. How had they found that one section of loose carpeting in the whole place? And why today in daylight when the condo had been empty all night?

"Charles is gone." The fear and suspicion in Aletha's voice had nothing to do with the cat. "I don't know if whoever did this took him or just let him out."

"Probably let him out. He had no value to anyone. Listen, I have to borrow your car."

"The car'll just scare him. Shouldn't we look for him on foot?"

"I have something more important to do than look for a cat." Cree held her gently, spoke slowly. He clamped down on a surging impatience that wanted him to shake the car keys out of her and the sense of what he had to do into her. "You may have the keys to the condominium for what good they seem to be. I think they found what they were after and won't be back. But I need your car, now. Please?"

She didn't look convinced but she did pull the keys from her pocket. "That car is one of the few things left in this world that belongs to me."

"I'll take good care of it. May not be back till tonight or even tomorrow. Do not, I repeat, do not report this to the marshal."

Aletha was late to work at the Senate because she'd roamed Telluride asking after a dirty white cat with the palest of green eyes. She had no luck. Tonight she had a room but no car and she'd lost Callie's cat.

"Well, if it isn't the Witch of the West," Tracy greeted her. "What have you been up to lately? On second thought, I don't want to know. No tricks or whatever it is you do tonight, okay?"

"What's this Tracy tells me about you being haunted?" Barry took her aside later in the evening. "Haven't been hittin' the 'shrooms,' have ya?"

"I've been having strange experiences since I came to Telluride, and without any hallucinogenic help. Don't worry, I won't say anything to the guests." Aletha had learned there were two kinds of people here—locals and guests. And since tourism was the only industry left, the locals—mostly refugees from either coast looking for a mythical small-town way of life—could not survive in their mountain paradise without a continual stream of guests to bring in money.

"Oh, I don't know. Might help the trade." He stared through her a moment, jutted out his chin to scratch at the neck under it, and grinned. "Don't think even Aspen's got ghosts."

The Senate sided on an alley across which were the back ends of the businesses that fronted on Colorado Avenue, Telluride's main street. Many of brick, all built in the heyday of the mining boom, their behinds were an interesting hodgepodge of architecture. While some abutted directly on the alley, others were inset as much as half a lot space, the whole effect reminiscent of a mouth packed tightly with uneven teeth. Though there was a streetlight, the alley was, as alleys should be, heavy with shadow and mystery. It was also well populated by cats, Aletha learned when she stepped out the door of the Senate's kitchen with a plastic garbage bag.

She hadn't seen many this afternoon when searching for Charles, but now one jumped out of the dumpster as she pitched in the bag. Another sat on the edge of the dumpster across the alley, swiping its whiskers under the streetlight. And there was an all-out hissing fight taking place somewhere in the shadows. Aletha stood still, listening for the congested wail of her Victorian friend. She heard a "mew," several "meows," and some threatening moans that could have come from any cat.

"Charles?" she called tentatively, and that was a mistake, because all the cats shut up and listened back. The one on the edge of the dumpster eyed her as if she were an alien. Behind her, dishes clanked, the human dishwasher swore, the mechanical one sloshed and rattled. Someone on Colorado Avenue shouted. An engine that needed a muffler rumbled on a side street. A mountain night, chilly, dark— and somehow the human sounds did not seem a part of it. If Charles was in town, this would be the time to look for him.

The alley didn't feel friendly. Aletha opened the screen door. Heat and the stink of cooked cauliflower and chemical detergent hung like an invisible barrier at the doorsill. "Herm, do we have a flashlight?"

The tattooed dishwasher scratched grease from the splatter panels. "*We* do not have shit. *They* have a flashlight." He reached into a cupboard, handed her a slender cylinder but didn't release it as their fingers met. "You got a smoke? A joint? Forget it." He let her have the flashlight. "Just where is it at that you come from, dear? Do you even know?"

"Yeah. Prison." Aletha stepped back into the alley to the tune of his laughter.

"You are lost, lady," Herm called after her. "You am lo-ost."

14

UNCLE Henry gave up his cabin and moved into the boardinghouse. If there was a funeral in Telluride for Aunt Lilly, no one spoke of it to Callie and Bram. They couldn't have gotten down for it anyway. Luella was so strained and white that no one spoke of her sister to save her the pain. Her tonic ran out and she caught a lingering cold.

Callie's cheerful home had grown gloomy, and to add to it, the school session ended. One afternoon she climbed to the top of the drift in front of her house and felt like she was standing on a mountain on top of a mountain. She could even see the Lizard Head in the distance over the sloping mill roof. The sky snapped blue and the snow snapped tiny brilliants back at it. The cold and dry pricked the inside of her nose as if it wanted her to sneeze. Moisture from her breath caused the knitted strands of the scarf tied around the lower half of her face to freeze scratchy in front of her mouth. Her toes hurt already in last year's fleece-lined arctic boots. Callie had planned to visit Bertha Traub on the hill but a crowd had gathered around the tram house below the mill and she changed directions.

The tram house was a small wooden building on a tower with a long ladder instead of stairs. Empty buckets coming uphill entered a doorway to one side of the wooden ladder, rounded a horizontal wheel inside and were filled with concentrates from a chute leading down from the mill. The filled buckets emerged from a door on the other side of the ladder and the concentrates began their ride down to Ophir Loop and the railroad which carried them to the smelter in Durango.

Callie was startled to see a large clothing trunk strapped on top of a bucket emerge from the tram house. A flash of emerald green beneath a black coat caught her eye as Mr. McCall tried to help Miss Heisinger up the steep ladder. But he had to back down or find himself peering up her skirts and she meanwhile kept stepping on those skirts each time her foot attempted another rung. It was awkward and embarrassing. Callie turned away. Some of the men shouted encouragement. A few of the ladies snickered. Johann Peterson, the school troublemaker, hooted.

When Callie turned back, another trunk exited the tower and several buckets later her teacher swung out sitting atop the dirty concentrates, clumsy arctics jutting from beneath her skirts, lovely head all but covered by scarves, one arm wrapped around the cold center pole. Even the bucketmen leaned from the tower to watch the spectacle. Her head and back straight as a pick handle, Mildred Heisinger disappeared down the hill.

"You ever seen such a ridiculous sight?" Mrs. Fisherdicks asked Mrs. Traub.

Callie had lost her desire for an afternoon of play. She made her way back to a cramped and stuffy cabin.

Bram was deep in the stopes working a muck stick and so did not see his tormentor leave the camp. But he heard about it when his shift gathered around the potbellied stove in the commissary after tally. Luella was touchy and tired at supper and so no one brought it up. Callie ate in silence with only recriminating glances for him.

"Teacher's work was done here," he whispered to her in the fleeting moment after she'd left the kitchen and Ma'am still worked. "If she hadn't gone down on the tram she'd be here the winter." One of the things Bram enjoyed about working rather than being a student was the unspoken understanding that he had no household duties other than carrying in water, coal, or firewood.

But what he enjoyed the most about working, he decided the next morning, was the mornings. Not the rousing from a deep warm slumber, but meeting the other men at the changehouse, his belly full of breakfast, lining up outside, and parrying insults with his friends. It was dark when he went into the changehouse these winter mornings and dark when he came out. Bram would not see daylight until he worked the night shift. Tiers of pegs along the walls, a row of benches beneath. Bram lifted down a pair of overalls frozen so solid he had to beat them against the planks of the floor to limber them up enough to step into. He exchanged his clean jacket for the mud-crusted one he'd worn the day before and pulled on boots that came to his knees. Beneath this outer layer he wore a full layer of wool clothing.

And all around him the man sounds—grunts, snorts, coughing. And unending clearing of throats, the rumble of belching, the sharp blats of men farting. Bram loved it and the splendid feeling of belonging.

The back door of the changehouse opened directly into the long snowshed where he followed John O'Connell along a narrow lane between stacks of baled hay for the mules and piles of heavy timbers for bracing. Once inside the adit, the air dampened but warmed. In the depths the temperature varied little from its approximate forty degrees winter or summer. They stopped to collect their ration of candles and Pa his powder, then moved on along rusting tracks. Boots crunched on rock and grit between the rails. Pa snorted and spit into the inky drainage ditch at the side of the track, his stiffened slicker crackling as his pick swung rhythmically on one side, his dinner pail on the other. The clearing of rheumy throats sounded hollow in here. There was little talk now. The workday had begun.

Bram fitted a candle into the black-iron candlestick in his cap and waited his turn at the hoist that lowered the men into the sublevels. John O'Connell went down with his own crew and a "Tap 'er light, lad," for Bram. Bram crowded into the cage with his foreman, a taciturn Finn named Knut Talse, and a big Swede. They were careful to keep elbows and heads away from the jagged rock walls rushing by.

Electricity lighted the major tunnels, but followed behind the drilling, mucking, and timbering. The new carbide lamps were expensive and used mainly by the supervisors and surveyors. Each station had open wooden lockers for storing dinner pails, extra gear, and candles. After stopping at the lockers, Knut placed his crew along a drift face and motioned Bram on down a side tunnel.

Their boots sloshed in water now and the candlelight made the shadows of their legs move like elongated scissors on the walls. Water drops plinked. Picks clinked and hammers rang. A mule brayed objections that ricocheted through the network of stone passageways. Rocks thudded where men barred down the loose stuff from the last firing with crowbars. Machine drills spat "rat-tat-tats" interspersed with whines. A blue tinge hung on air heavy with the gassy smell of dead powder and the reek of water-soaked timber and human excrement.

Knut set Bram to mucking a round, which meant shoveling up the gob and rock brought down by a round of blasts. Nippers ran dulled steel drills up to the machine shops for sharpening. Powder monkeys took orders for and delivered dynamite. These jobs were handled by boys. Muckers needed more brute strength and were often older than Bram but still unskilled labor. It was Bram's ambition to work up to be a quartz man. Pa and some of the other men were already showing him the intricacies of rock drilling, loading, tamping, and spitting fuses.

But for now he took the miner's candlestick from his cap and jabbed it into a timber by its sharp iron prong. He took the muck stick or shovel and dug it into the mud-goo and rock, then shoveled it into a wheelbarrow, or "Irish buggy." When it was full he pushed it back through the tunnels to the end of the tracks and dumped its contents into a wooden chute that emptied into one-ton ore cars. When a car was full a trammer, with the help of a mule, would tram it to the cage, where the hoistman would lift it to the surface level. There another trammer would tram it out through the snowshed to the mill, where it would be crunched and sifted and jiggled and chemically tortured until only a coarse gray sand remained—the concentrates high in precious metals.

Mucking was exhausting work but Bram felt the exhilaration of prolonged exercise and pride in his growing strength. He was mucking out a stope—a room-sized cavity blasted into the rock where the vein ran deep. His shadow bent, scooped, rose, bent again. Mica crystals winked in the edges of his wavering light. A dislodged pebble clattered down a wall and made a "ploomp" when it hit the water on the floor. Glistening water drops from the roof worked their way beneath his collar and Bram was soon soaked to the skin. He paused to catch a breath and wipe a mucky coat sleeve across his forehead, heard his heart beating strong and true and a wee tapping noise overhead that caused a shiver to skip along the bones in the back of his neck.

The tommyknockers had come over the sea with the Cornish miners, although the Irish claimed them too. Tiny elfin spirits whose sole purpose, as far as Bram could determine, was to either warn or to bedevil the men who worked inside the earth. And there was never any telling which it was they were doing. Their quiet tappings came eerie in the stopes and drifts and sounded like nothing else at all. Tommyknockers warned a miner that either something was about to happen or that something wasn't. The miner then cleared out of the area and saved his life if catastrophe befell or he cleared out of the area and was roundly cursed by his foreman when nothing happened. Or he gambled with fate and stayed where he was.

Ma'am declared tommyknockers to be only superstition. Ma'am had never worked the stopes.

Bram stood back and watched the play of candlelight on the walls and roof that made them undulate with shadow. But they appeared in reality to be standing firm. The earth did not seem to work. He could see no small circles tamped with mud in the rock face that would signal a missed hole, a charge not yet fired that could go off unexpectedly. He had a swift memory of Callie's angel with the fluffy hair warning him not to come down here. But Bram decided to gamble and he went back to his muck stick and his Irish buggy.

Bram won that particular gamble and Alta drifted into spring, a highly illusory season at that altitude. The nights were still bitter although an occasional warm afternoon set the drifts to melting and seeping into the mine tunnels, and the blizzards hurled larger, wetter flakes. Before Bram went on night shift he had a long day—a thirty-six-hour break during the changeover. He ate and rested, made a snowman with Callie, and squinted like a mole in the snow-reflected sunlight.

Since John O'Connell still worked day shift, having Bram on nights upset the routine of the household. There seemed always to be someone sleeping and needing tiptoeing around. And food had to be organized for a dinner pail twice a day. Luella and Callie rose earlier to prepare a huge breakfast which was really supper for Bram and then reheated it when John came down from the loft.

One evening when Callie had dressed in her flannel nightgown in front of the stove and Luella had brought out the rags and dipped a comb in a cup of water to wet a strip of Callie's hair, the siren's shriek startled her so she tipped over the cup on the table. John came up from his doze on the floor, the blood already leaving his face. The three O'Connells looked at each other wordlessly.

"Bram," Callie echoed all their thoughts and broke the spell. There was a scramble for coats and shawls and arctics.

"Whole shift working the mine and mill. Could be it's nothing to do with Bram now," John tried to reassure them as they slipped and slid on ice-covered snow up the hill, but Ma'am was already making crying sounds in her throat. Callie gasped at the shock of cold air in her lungs and hurried on ahead, only to stop at the edge of the crowd, afraid of what she might hear. She heard it anyway. It seemed to ripple toward her from different directions in cries and whispers and choked-back panic.

"She's caved!"

"Level four."

"Talse's crew."

Pa rushed into the snowshed where men shouted and passed around shovels and picks. Mrs. McCall hugged Luella. Luella turned to sob on her neighbor's shoulder. Callie couldn't breathe. She doubled over. When she managed to straighten she saw Aletha and her husband standing next to the commissary. They wore the same puffy coats they had last summer.

"Callie," the lady called.

"It's Bram. Bram! He's in there." Aletha's husband had tried to warn Bram. Would he help them now? She reached out to him with a desperate hope. "What can I do?"

"Don't go to Telluride," the lady insisted as she had last summer. "Callie, do you hear?" This time the edges of a hole didn't close up over them. This time they just began to fade. "Callie!" the lady screamed, and disappeared.

15

ALETHA had called "kitty, kitty, kitty," once. She now had a string of meowing friends following her down the alley like the victims of the Pied Piper. Some tried to rub against her ankles and trip her up. Not one of them was Charles. Most weren't strays either. They were fat and trusting.

A dog barked and the felines scattered to the shadows and the streetlight at this end of the alley went out. Aletha looked over her shoulder to find the one at the other end still lit and turned back to a bowlegged bulldog baring his teeth in the small pool of light her flashlight made. He was standing in mud. She wasn't—it hadn't rained for days. He had the snub-snout and jutting lower jaw she'd seen only in pictures, the type of dog favored in her mother's old advertising posters. His growl came low from a massive chest.

"Humphrey?" a woman called from somewhere. "Here, Humphrey."

The dog didn't move and neither did Aletha. A horse snorted as it cantered by on the street, riderless but saddled, stirrups swinging casually, hooves slinging mud. The piles of new lumber on the lot next to her had become a shedlike building. A man stood in front of it and held up a museum-issue lantern. "Well, Fanny, you're late. Been nipping at the trail sides, have ya?"

"Humphrey—sorry, miss, he don't mind the Lord, let alone me." A small figure in a long silky dress and a hat choked with feathers stepped into the light pool, grabbed the dog by the loose folds of skin at his neck, and took a horrified look at Aletha. "You ain't dressed for the night. Even here. In need of help?"

"No. I'm . . . uh . . . looking for Charles."

"Like as not he'll find you first." She had a nasal voice and smelled strongly of funeral roses. "His money, ain't it?" The woman walked Humphrey off into the dark.

Dread and curiosity mixed like bubbles in Aletha's blood. "What if you get lost in time and can't go back?" Cree Mackelwain would be saying. The comforting streetlight still shone at the other end of the alley. Her cat-following had disappeared into another decade.

Aletha held her breath and stepped off into the mud. It oozed cold through the open toes of her sandals, tried to suck the straps off her heels, insinuated through the mesh of her hose. When she'd passed the false-fronted livery stable she could see tiny lights twinkling high in the mountains at the head of the canyon and shadows of familiar peaks against dim moonlight. The sweetness of recent rain didn't mask the stench of garbage and yeasty beer. Over the slamming of her pulse in her ears she heard voices raised behind closed doors and the splash of the San Miguel River down at the end of the street. The thudding sound of distant mills provided multiple heartbeats for this mountain night.

A woman carefully silhouetted in a window scratched her head. Row upon row of cribs, interspersed with larger frame houses. This part of Telluride was built up solid as far as Aletha could see in the night light. A few moments ago there'd been empty lots, raw condos in-the-building, and only remnants of the old left behind.

Buildings replaced the trees and cut off the view of the Pick and Gad from Mildred Heisinger's cupola. The Big Swede, the Monte Carlo, the Idle Hour—all names in scrolly print on lighted windows. A straining violin tried to accompany an out-of-tune piano and something made the sound of two pieces of wood slapping together repeatedly. Two men leaned against the Monte Carlo's lighted front, each with a heel up against the building, a knee bent, each with hands deep in his pockets. Horses dozed at hitching rails.

The brick Pick and Gad had a light over its front door too and it wasn't red. Except for the lurid brocade at the windows it looked disconcertingly the same. There was another such house next to it, noisier, not as fancy. And then the railroad tracks shiny with use on a raised bed of cinders, and dark shapes of wooden boxcars. Aletha turned around and almost lost a sandal. If only she could be invisible and wander these streets safely.

The two men holding up the Monte Carlo had their heads turned her way. They looked more like cowboys than miners, but their pants were baggy and worn inside round-toed boots. They wore hats with rounded crowns that resembled state-patrolman hats rather than Stetsons. They did have holstered guns hanging from their middles, though. She'd lose her shoes for sure if she tried to run in this mud.

"Hardly no clothes," one of the cowboys said overloud so she would hear. "Think she's tetched, Jesse?"

"Lookin' for business, more like."

"Why'd she chop her hair off then?"

Aletha pretended not to hear, glanced nonchalantly down Pacific Avenue to see Miss Heisinger's house lit even to the cupola and funny round window in the attic room. Shivers came over her in spasms, from the damp chill, from the excitement. It was all laced with a hearty dose of misgiving.

"I'm paranoid," she said aloud to keep the freaky night at bay.

"I'm Jesse," a voice answered right behind her. "This here's Carl."

Aletha left her shoes in the mud and ran. The light from her flashlight bounced and blinked off buildings and street with a strobe effect. Both her feet slipped and she nearly ended up doing a split. The man from the livery stable leaned against the door frame and watched her. She could hear Jesse and Carl not far behind, laughing, cursing the mud.

There appeared to be a great deal of light, people, and noise on Colorado Avenue up ahead, but Aletha had lost her curiosity. She turned and slid into the alley leading to the Senate. Why hadn't she listened to Cree? The comforting light at the other end of the alley was gone now like the cats. The mud didn't end where it had begun before. The shadows had deepened, taken over. She was afraid to go on, and afraid not to.

"Forgot your wooden shoes, lady." One of the cowboys dangled them in front of her by their muddy straps. He smelled as if he hadn't bathed or changed his clothes for a year—and that in an alleyway redolent of rotting food, outhouses, and the horsey stable.

"Iddy-bit scrawny, ain't she?" The other man appeared and doubled the stench. Aletha brought her hand up to breathe through and the flashlight up to shine in his face. "Ever see'd such a little light bulb? Where's the cord at?"

Aletha decided to scream, long and loud, because she didn't know what else to do and she thought it might put them off for a while. But somebody beat her to it. It came jarring, wrenching, bone-tingling that scream—drawn out and then strangled off at the end as though murder had surely completed it. The man from the livery stable ran around the corner and stopped when he saw Aletha, as if he'd expected to see her lying in a pool of blood. Lights came on in small buildings on one side of the alley and some of the apartments above the stores on the other.

A shadow figure walked through a shadow and into the light, turned first one way and then the other. Tracy Ledbetter.

"Now, that's more to my liking," one said.

Aletha sidestepped her antique companions. "Tracy, was that you?"

"I walked out the back door looking for you, and everything was . . . different." Tracy stared around at the people staring at her. "This is your doing."

"Careful," Aletha whispered, and turned to Jesse and Carl. "Sorry, we're . . . uh, booked. Booked for the night." She took Tracy's elbow and started them toward the Senate. "Just walk and shut up."

"Those two guys are following us," Tracy said between chattering teeth. "They have guns." They paused at the back door of the Senate. It would be senseless to walk into a kitchen full of strangers, so they continued, arm in arm, to the street. A sign read *Pabst Milwaukee Bottling Works* on the building across the alley from the Senate, where there had been only a dumpster and some cats. A boy in knickers and sagging knee socks raced down the board sidewalk, pausing to hand them each a sheet of paper from a stack under his arm.

Aletha swerved Tracy around the corner and made her run past the Senate's front door to the empty lot on the other side and into the shadows. "Maybe those cowboys'll think we went inside." She stubbed her toe on a board and had to hop. "Maybe if we go around to the kitchen it'll be our time now."

"Will you just quit maybe-ing and do something?"

There was a regular maze of little outbuildings behind the Senate and they tried to tug each other different ways in order to thread them. Aletha kept stepping on rocks and other sharp, unknown dangers in the mud. No smelly cowboys awaited them when they reached the alley again, just the rich smell of beef frying in the kitchen. She turned off the failing light. They held on to each other in a dark recess between the restaurant and a shed behind it, unsure of what to do next, hoping only to be present when a hole opened onto a more familiar world.

"What if we can't get back?" Tracy echoed the fear Cree had expressed in Alta.

Cree Mackelwain sighted in on the Lizard Head, then turned the Cessna's nose in the direction of Alta. The world always looked cleaner from above. At home the terrain below would have been the sear of brown rolling to mauve, gashes of crimson in the crevasses, tan string roads laid across empty miles, all blending sensibly. Here jarring contrast offered a different beauty—pockets of yellowing aspen, pieces of red ground cover, slashes of harsh shadow through sun-bright foliage. Green forest abutted beige rock and swept to the base of gray crags. The crag tops were frosted with snow that glittered against the endless depth of sky.

Cree had known he wanted to fly about the time he discovered birds. He opted to earn an engineering degree and then try to get into commercial flight school after, especially since his inheritance from his maternal grandfather, Douglas McCree, had been earmarked for a university education only. But he'd figured without Elaine. They had married when she became pregnant in his senior year at UCLA. Her brother was a roughneck on an oil rig in Wyoming and making "fabulous" money. Elaine's folks had plastic deer and pink plastic flamingos stuck into their front yard on metal rods. They talked Cree into roughnecking a year or two. Elaine and he could live with them. Babies didn't come cheap these days, they explained to Cree.

"Hell, I wanted to do right by the kid." There were no cars in Alta. Cree'd flown over this area before. And with the information in the now missing folder he'd found nothing. The hints in his partner's papers had convinced Cree that the stash was either in the mine in Alta or in one of the many in the mountains nearby. Why hadn't they assumed the same? Perhaps they'd already found it and left.

Elaine had miscarried during Cree's second week in a camp next to a rig out in the boonies. The camp consisted of five house trailers connected together. Cree worked two weeks for each week he had with Elaine. She grew used to living with her folks again. Cree grew used to making lots of money, came to prefer the rough camaraderie in the camp to Elaine's parents and their everlasting TV set.

The Cessna followed the road to the Alta Lakes. A couple of tents. A figure in waders fishing. A pickup truck. How had Cree thought he could do anything from the sky? Or did he just fear some dangerous involvement on the ground?

"After what happened to Dutch I've got damned good reason." Dutch Massey ran a small air-freight service out of Casper. He had only three planes when Cree met him but did a good business flying roughnecks, supplies, and light equipment out to remote rigs and the men back to town on their free days. Cree'd had a pilot's license since the day he was of age and he began to do a little flying for Dutch on his week off just to get in the air and away from Elaine. She'd taken a perverse pleasure in showing him off at cowboy bars. Every guy who pounded nails or sacked groceries during the day traveled at night in a Stetson and a pickup with a rifle slung across the back window. There were a lot more paunches in those cowboy bars than there were bowed legs. And the kind of macho-bluff he was used to out at the rig tended to turn nasty when mixed with liquor and women in town.

"Shit, she even tried to pick fights for me." But Elaine got to liking those places so much she took a job at one after her second miscarriage. By the time of the divorce, Elaine was pregnant again, and not by him. And Cree had enough money saved to buy into Dutch Massey's little air-freight business. Before his partner's murder, Massey-Mackelwain was flying a total of twenty-one aircraft out of Casper, Cody, as well as Butte, Montana, and had forty-two on the payroll.

Now Cree turned the one remaining plane back toward the pitched roof of the boardinghouse in Alta for a last flyover before returning to the Montrose airport and at an altitude his experience told him was lower than it was wise. Still no cars parked where he could see them. If it hadn't been for the all-pervasive engine noise he might have heard something before he noticed the small holes ripping in the Cessna's wings.

Someone was shooting at him.

16

"KEEP that up, boy"—Knut Talse took a pinch of snouse, the miners' snuff, fingered it into a ball, and tucked it under his lip—"and you'll be walkin' down the hill talking to yourself."

Bram leaned on his muck stick, listened to the new timbers creak in the stull at his back. "Ground's working, Mr. Talse."

"Thank you very much for that engineering report, Mr. O'Connell. I'll pass it on to the shift boss, huh?" Talse was a little man with massive chest and arms, whose mood could be read by the positioning of his eyebrows. Now they moved up under his cap. "Speakin' of which," and he kicked the shovel out from under Bram in emphasis, "he should be here any minute."

But Bram couldn't shake off his unease, continued to stand there trying to talk himself out of it. There were always dangers in the drifts, but as Pa had told him so often, a greater percentage of women died in their beds giving birth than men working underground.

"Is yoost the snow melt seeping down," Gus Lundberg, the big Swede, assured him. Bram had yet to meet a little Swede. Gus was known as one of the best machine-men in the San Juans. "It makes the dirt to svell there, shift here."

"That a fact now?" Sully, an Irishman whose real name was Thomas Sullivan, rolled his eyes at the roof so that a good portion of the whites shone out of a dirt-blackened face. As if on order, the little hollow, ghostly, shivery tappings began all around them. Bram's candle went out. "And what'll be making *them* noises, do ya think?" Sully whispered. "Snow melt?"

Even the bohunks framing timber for drift sets further down stopped their foreign chatter to listen to the tommyknockers.

"Don't hear me no hammers," Talse yelled down a manway from the stope where he and Shorty Miller were hand-drilling. Rock sloughed down a wall between lagging timbers behind Sully. The tommyknockers grew silent.

Bram was almost afraid to breathe but he relit his candle, bent obediently to the muck stick. Sully went back to his single-jack, a heavy hammer he used to drive a star-steel drill ever deeper into the rock face to make a hole to fill with powder to blow up the face so Bram could muck it out and the mill could pulverize it. Gus inserted new steel into his machine drill to do the same, adjusted the air hose, and let rip.

The Irishman's hammer clanged. The Swede's drill spat and whined. Bram's shoveling made a slicing-sucking noise. But he could still hear the water streaming into the levels instead of seeping. He could still hear wrenching timbers creak in agony all the way back down the drift. Had those sounds ever seemed so ominous? A shout came along on sluggish air from where the rest of Talse's crew was driving a crosscut. "Fire in the hole!"

The warning wafted down to them just before the round fired and blue smoke trailed along behind. Bram, Sully, and Gus had moved as one away from the creaky stull as the blast reverberated down the drift. It shoved a puff of air before it that set the candle flames lying over on their sides. Bram's eyes watered in the stench of burned powder. But the stull and lagging around them creaked no more than usual and they drew a relieved breath. They'd just turned back to their work when more shouts cracked through the smoke like shots from a repeating rifle.

Then came the awful, dreaded sound of breaking timbers and grinding rock. A far more violent rush of air exploded on them this time with a pressure that "whumped" in their ears. It was filled with dust so thick it quenched the smoke.

The candles snuffed out completely. A depressing silence weighed down on the blackness. And there is no blackness like that hundreds of feet deep in the earth where sunlight, starlight, or even shadow was never meant to reach. It pressed on Bram's eyelids and against his eardrums. He straightened from the cringing expectation of having the roof crash heavy on his body. He coughed out dust and grit, and the sound wakened others to scuffle their boots and clear their throats.

"Whore's shit." Sully's voice came out of the dust-clogged dark with an almost tender slowness. He managed to add a mixture of anger and resignation to the exhalation that came with it. One of the bohunks began a whispered chant in what might have been Latin, surely was Catholic, and sounded a lot like prayer. Then Knut Talse's growl as he climbed down the manway, the hissing of his carbide lamp, the metallic grating as he tried to spark the flint wheel, and the "pop" when it ignited. The pointed yellow flame seemed small and weak now, moved silently up the drift, raising to study the quality of the fear on each man's face as it passed.

Shorty Miller limped along behind Knut. "Told you, after them angels in the cookhouse give warning, it's dangerous crewing with that big bastard."

The word "bastard" came just as Talse had lifted the lamp to Bram's expression, and the foreman pursed his lips at the reaction he witnessed. "Shut up your head, Shorty, or I'll have the kid knock out what's left of your teeth."

"She's caved," Bram said stupidly. What difference did it make if someone called him a bastard when he was as good as dead anyway?

"Another engineering report, Mr. O'Connell? We'd best go have us a look then, hadn't we?"

The stull they'd all been so suspicious of had held fine. They tramped on past the station, all crowding as close as they could to

Talse's light. The dust hung unmoving now. Bram put his hand-kerchief to his nose to breathe through. Piles of earth had sloughed to the floor, narrowing their passage and forcing them to spread out more than they wanted. They came to the new end of the drift before they came to the crosscut where the others had worked. Rubble heaped tight to the roof. Knut played the light from top to bottom, side to side. Water covered the tracks, but the air pipe stuck out broken off and clear of the water.

"Think the rest made it?" Shorty asked. No one answered; no one knew. He knelt to the pipe and sniffed, put a hand over the jagged break and tapped his signal with a crowbar. The silence and the crew waited for an answer that didn't come.

"Too soon." Knut Talse coughed and the light jumped around on the wall of debris. "They have to organize a rescue. Meantime we'd best plan."

"Want me to start mucking this?" Bram needed something to do. He kept picturing how cowardly he'd look dying, and Ma'am's stricken whiteness when she heard of it.

"Where would you muck it to? There is more there than just a little plug, boy. Could go as far as the hoist even, if George and the boys brought it down driving the crosscut. Take days to reach us. You save your strength for living long enough to greet 'em when they get here." Knut led them back to the station and collected the remaining candles and snuffs from each man. He sorted and stacked all the food in one locker. Then, back a ways where the ground was good and the drift widened, he set them to building two platforms from the timbers the bohunks had been using for drift sets. They nailed a cap box to an upright timber between the platforms to hold a communal light and an empty powder case at one end of each platform for a thunder mug. The spent carbide from lamps that had been dumped near the lockers would serve for deodorizing these crude privies.

When their homes were finished there was room for each man to stretch out and stay up away from the water. Knut portioned each man a bite of sandwich and sent Shorty up the drift with the lamp to signal on the pipe again. "Tell 'em we are fourteen left here."

Bram had been numb and unthinking while they worked and planned for their survival, but now as he sat with his back against the wet wall in the smothering black waiting for Shorty and the light, and full weight of dread was upon him. He'd always known things such as this happened in the mines. But he'd never really believed it could happen to him.

Shorty came slopping down the drift. "They're comin' for us, Talse, but they're clear back at the hoist like you thought." No signals from the rest of their crew. It could take weeks to reach here if they had to spile as they went in unsure ground. "John O'Connell's at the other end." He handed Bram the lamp. "Better go let him know you're alive."

"And don't steal none of the food," Knut warned.

But for once Bram wasn't hungry. The light danced in his trembling fingers as he made his way to the compressed-air line. He bent to tap it lightly but there was no response. He tapped his signal again, two taps—a pause—and three taps. He put his ear right down to the pipe and John O'Connell's signal came to him faintly. And then Uncle Henry's. And some of the others he should have recognized but was too distraught to remember. Kneeling in water, holding the lamp carefully, Bram leaned his forehead against the new wall formed by the caved-in roof and sobbed like Uncle Henry had when he brought news of Aunt Lilly.

Pa and the others would work night and day to reach them. When the word was passed of miners trapped, hard-rock stiffs from all over the San Juans would be riding the tram buckets to Alta to lend a hand. There'd be hand drilling and machine drilling going on side by side and around the clock, and more men in the tunnels than could be put to good use. But they'd have to timber some as they went and the level above would have to be shored so as not to come down on this one anymore, and who could say what had happened above that in this rabbit warren of a mountain? And who was to say this cave-in was to be the last? Bram had heard stories of more rescuers than rescuees perishing when she caved again.

The food and candles would last awhile, but not nearly long enough. Water they had in excess and a man could live a long time on water alone. But first he needed air and Bram knew their greatest danger was the buildup of mine gases in this closed-off part of the drift. And then there was still water miraculously working its way through the plug in the passage, as well as dripping through cracks everywhere. How long before it filled up the workings below and stopped draining off, began to fill up their "home" until it drowned them all?

Bram expected a cruel razzing when he rejoined the others. Everyone must have heard his cowardice. But Gus patted Bram's knee when he sprawled on the platform and old Sully gave him a wink and a nod. Knut put the lamp in the cap box nailed to the upright beam to hold back the black for all of them. A bohunk walked over and offered Bram a chew off his plug. They were all treating him like the baby he was and Bram was bigger than most of them. The tobacco tasted bitter and hot and made him a little sick.

"Bohunk" was a general term for a wave of immigrants from Central Europe. Their poverty and foreign ways kept them somewhat segregated. Bram had thought they all looked alike, like Chinamen did, but he studied them now and realized this was not so. None as dark as the Italians nor as light as the Swedes, they ran the gamut in between. They were generally on the short and stocky side but within a few days he would learn their distinct and separate identities well.

Knut's carbide gave out and they started on the snuffs, little candle ends that were left of their work candles, while they had more strength to be up and changing them often, saving the long candles till last. The minute one began to flicker, Shorty or Gus would stand ready with another and light it off the last just as it was about to die so they'd have the full use of it. Knut and Sully would take a shift to spell them and Bram would help keep watch. Once they all slept and a candle went out. They carried wooden matches for lighting work candles but with their soaked clothing and the pervasive wet on the air, none would light. Knut felt his way out to the lockers in the station, where he'd seen some matches at the bottom of a metal dinner pail when he'd gathered up the food. He found one that would light, the rest useless.

Now they had to watch the light closely and it added more tension to the waiting. Sleep would have passed some of the time with less pain, but it was hard to do when worrying that the man assigned the candle would fall asleep. Every few hours Knut sent someone up the drift to tap on the air pipe, so the stiffs would know there was still someone alive to rescue.

Bram lay watching the mica crystals glitter in the candlelight and pretended they were winking stars. The red iron stains in the wall made him think of blood and the green and blue and purple flashes of the copper ores brought to mind Mildred Heisinger. Time dragged slower every hour. The bohunks sang songs and mimed bawdy stories that were funny for a while. Gus told a long story that Bram lost track of but he took comfort in the Swede's beautiful singsong. The tommyknockers were perfectly still now and Sully said it was because the wee people had given up hope for them. The food began to look funny but didn't smell yet. Knut ordered them to eat it all so it wouldn't have to be thrown out. Within half an hour they were every one retching violently.

Bram felt it was his insides having the cave-in this time and that his rib cage must be creaking and wrenching like the timbers in the stull had. The sickness lasted long past the time any of them had anything to heave but his guts. The stench added yet another unwelcome odor to the still, putrefying air.

"Any woman even had known better than to save the food past its spoil time," Knut blamed himself disgustedly, and leaned out over the platform to gag. "I never knowed nothing about food." When they all lay helpless and sweating and Gus had managed to hold himself up long enough to light the next-to-last candle off the previous one, a heavy shot from the rescue teams caused a concussion that jolted the platforms and put out the light. There was no way to light another now. "They're shootin' that heavy, must be hitting big blocks of solid rock," Shorty bemoaned the obvious. "Don't look good for us, no sir."

Brambaugh O'Connell turned into the eternal darkness to choke on sour juices ripped up from his stomach. Inside himself, he cried out for Ma'am.

17

NEXT to the alley across the street stood a false-fronted saloon lit to the rafters. It took Aletha a moment to recognize it as the building that was still there but boarded up and moved way back on the lot. A sign announced it as the Belmond, and through its storefront windows she could see a great many black-coated men with little round hats. In fact, it looked like every guy in there had bought his clothes off the same rack. There was a lot of noise coming from the place—shouting, jeering, the rumble of men's voices, the light ring of women laughing.

A couple stepped out of the Belmond. She wore gray from head to toe, but the way she let the man snuggle her neck and the way she tried to hurry him along made Aletha think she must work in the district. The couple had just crossed the alley when they disappeared, the Belmond went dark and moved back on its lot, the dumpster stood where the Pabst-Milwaukee Bottling Works had been, and the ankle-deep mud turned into the flat baked-hard alley again.

"How'd you do that?" Herm said from behind the screen door. "Just appear out of nowhere like that?"

Aletha and Tracy nearly knocked the dishwasher over in their haste to get inside, and Aletha welcomed the familiar odors of cooked cauliflower and detergent. She handed him the rolled-up paper a boy in knickers had shoved at her instead of the flashlight. Herm held it to the light. " 'Dr. Miles's number one hundred and fifty specific mixture. Guaranteed a sure cure for gonorrhea and gleet. This preparation is prepared according to the formula and will be found a positive cure. It is perfectly safe and harmless as it contains no poisonous ingredients. Prepared by Bartholomew Holder, Apothecary.' " Herm looked up. "What's gleet?"

"I went out to find you," Tracy said to Aletha, "to see if I could spend the night in your car too, but being around you is more excitement than the frail Ledbetter heart can stand."

"What about your boyfriend? Your apartment?"

"We couldn't come up with the rent and got kicked out. He skipped, left me owing." She shrugged matter-of-factly but she was still trembling from their time excursion and looked anything but casual. "He never wanted me, just liked being waited on and getting his rocks off whenever he felt like it."

"Cree's got my car," Aletha said, "but we have the keys to his condo."

"I think your Cree could use a housekeeper," Tracy remarked when they entered the condominium at the Pick and Gad.

"Help me put enough of it back together so it's livable for tonight at least." The place had obviously been ransacked but Aletha refused to answer Tracy's questions about it. After they'd restored some order and showered, Aletha made tuna-salad sandwiches and coffee.

"Two girls I know rent one of the old cribs in behind the Senate and Silver Bell. They're leaving town and I've got my name in for that crib."

"Can you afford it?" Aletha sat on the tiled edge of the empty Jacuzzi and cupped her hands around her hot coffee mug. "Without a roommate?"

"No and I had considered you as a roommate, but if I lived with you in a crib I'd probably have a steady stream of long-dead miners at the door, money in hand and their flies open."

"I'd pay my share and I even have wheels to take us places." Aletha hurried to refill Tracy's coffee cup. "Please?"

"Look, I like you. It's just you scare the hell out of me." Tracy took a small packet from her purse. "There's some high-rollers in town this week. Got this as a tip. Want a toot?"

"Do you know what they cut that stuff with?" And while Tracy snorted a line through a plastic straw, Aletha told how she'd landed in a federal prison.

"You shouldn't go around talking about that kind of past." Tracy sounded as if she'd developed a sinus condition and cleared it, all in the space of a sentence. "Nobody would suspect it of you, and what people don't know about you makes them feel better. About you, I mean."

Aletha felt uncomfortable and began to babble on about Callie's cat and how she lost him. And about meeting Jesse and Carl.

Tracy pointed the straw at her. "Life before this time mess started happening must seem pretty dull, even considering prison, huh? I think you get high on the danger of it. I think you're getting addicted to that high. It's becoming your toot." She leaned back, her pupils dilating. "What bothers me is, what are we going to tell Barry? We have to warn him. He could step out the back door of the Senate some night and meet face to face with Wild Bill Hickok or something."

Cree and the Datsun had not returned by morning. Aletha worried even though he'd told her he might not be back. Whoever searched the condo was not a nice sort of person and Cree'd had blood in his eye when he left. She should have checked in with Renata, but she talked Tracy into helping her search for Charles instead.

"You're looking in the wrong places," Tracy said. "You got to put yourself in his place. I can remember how I felt in his time last night. Shit scared. He's probably hiding in some building, not roaming the alleys. Not out getting high on danger like you would be. Now, there's some old buildings," she said when they stood outside the Pick and Gad, and pointed across the empty lots where the Big Swede and the Monte Carlo had stood last night, to the rotting outbuildings behind Mildred Heisinger's house.

"But he's an Alta cat. I'm sure he's never been to Telluride before. And those buildings weren't old in his time. What would a cat know anyway?"

"You got a better idea?" They walked around to the back of the lot with Tracy staying five steps behind Aletha. "If I see you disappearing into yesteryear, I'm going to run. Leave you to your own, toots."

The rear building looked like it might once have been a carriage house. Instead of pigeons, crows peered down at them through holes in the roof. The second building was a shed and a third a barn with leaning stall partitions. Ancient coal dust blackened one stall. A huge weathervane tilted against a corner, a prancing horse atop the crossed direction indicators. Two dilapidated steamer trunks stood open and empty on a dirt floor.

At first Mildred Heisinger was just a shadow silhouetted by sunlight which in turn was bordered by a dark door frame. She stood pointing a cane at them. Her dress hung formless to where her knees bowed painfully outward. But her spine was still straight and her head and neck unbowed. Her shoes were sturdy and laced, with thick-cushioned soles. They looked massive on the end of her tiny frame. Above her rolled anklets the red and blue highways of her blood were mapped across the unnatural white of her skin. "What you doing now, snoop? Going to clean the barn?"

"What year is this?" Tracy asked suspiciously.

"We came here looking for my cat, Miss Heisinger," Aletha shouted, remembering the old lady's hearing problem. "I live across the road and my cat ran away."

"White cat? Big tom?"

"Have you seen him?"

Mildred worked her mouth around the false teeth, up and down, as if trying to shrink them to fit more comfortably in a shrunken face. Finally she poked the cane down into the dirt and used it to help her turn. Her straight shoulders drooped now. "He likes chopped liver and mice. I got plenty of both."

It seemed to take Mildred forever to cross the short distance to the house. Charles rose from a wicker basket beside the kitchen stove. He arched and stretched and yawned, then rubbed the side of his neck against Mildred's stick-thin leg. His throaty purr throttled up and down with his breathing.

"This one yours?" Miss Heisinger sat in a chair and Charles jumped on her lap. "Seems to like me better." They looked up at Aletha with similarly blank expressions and the same color eyes.

"Did you buy him a basket already?"

"Had that a long time. Always a cat or two around here. Always died before I did. Didn't get another one after the last time because I was sure it'd outlive me and somebody'd shoot it or gas it or whatever they do nowadays. This one just walked in when I opened the door like he owned the place. Not too well housebroken but he likes to watch the television with me."

Tracy was giving Aletha pleading looks over the old lady's head.

"He does seem to like it here," Aletha said. "If you're fond of him—"

"No, you take him back, snoop." She pushed Charles into Aletha's arms much as Callie had. "I'll probably die tomorrow. You'll outlive him."

"You could borrow him for a while to keep you company."

"Then I'd hurt when you came to take him away. Young people don't stay in one place anymore." A lonely look crumpled her features and she glanced away from Charles. "People my age ought to keep to themselves anyway. Things don't hurt 'em then."

"I promise I won't take him until you want me to. He likes you better than he ever did me."

But Mildred Heisinger went into her parlor, turned on her television, and told them to go away and take their cat with them.

"Kitty, you'd found the perfect home," Aletha said as they filed through the gate in the wrought-iron fence. Charles wailed and struggled when a car went by. "A Victorian cat and a Victorian lady. It's a match made in heaven, and I had to blow it."

"I feel so sorry for her. Hope I never live that long." Tracy stared back at the house and almost tripped. When they turned him loose at the Pick and Gad, Charles prowled and yowled and refused the fresh can of cat food Aletha put before him. "All you have to do is open that door and he'll head straight back for her house and they'll both be happy."

"She's so deaf," Aletha said. "What if she doesn't hear him at the door? And she's so stubborn. What if she doesn't take him back now that she's refused him?"

Cree Mackelwain had parked Aletha's Datsun behind an abandoned building down at the Loop and hiked the old tram route up to Alta, telling himself the whole way that he was stupid, inept, unarmed, and a coward anyway. All he had going for him was anger, and anger tends to poop out pretty fast when you're climbing a couple of miles at a steep incline at that elevation. Whoever had shot at him could be a coward too, but he had a weapon. And he probably had food and a coat and company. Cree had a light jacket that was too hot on the way up and not hot enough when night fell on the ghost town. The Cessna had reached the Montrose airport with no problem and now sat complete with bullet holes for someone to report to the police so they could come and ask him more questions.

When Dutch Massey was slaughtered and the investigation had turned up evidence of the drug trade, Cree had come under suspicion. He still was. He wasn't interested in talking to the police again—he didn't know anything then and he didn't know anything now. Well, he'd known Dutch to supply a few bindles now and then out at the rigs when Cree had been roughnecking. But Cree hadn't questioned, until it was all over, how their business could have grown so fast, how his partner always had so much cash on hand (and as it turned out, he didn't know the half of that), or how and why Dutch took so many vacations. Dutch had handled the paperwork, Cree some of the flying and much of the personnel management.

"Maybe things just seemed so good at the time I didn't want to question much." Right now he couldn't say. All he could say was he'd just spent one of the coldest, hungriest, and most stupid nights of his life. There were three of them and they were still working over the town when he'd arrived. Eventually they took lanterns and went into the mine. They had a four-wheeled Bronco that looked brand new parked off in the trees. Cree thought about the big sack of groceries in it all night long, but if they found anything missing they'd start hunting him. And the memory of Dutch's body plastered around the office, some of him sticking by his own blood to the walls, kept Cree and his hunger in line. They'd used an automatic weapon and enough ammunition to stop a regiment.

All of Dutch's property and most of Cree's had been confiscated by either the courts or the IRS because it was held in joint ownership. Cree got away with one plane and his car. It was in his car he found the folder. He came across it one morning while looking for a whisk broom under the front seat. Dutch had hidden it there when he knew there was trouble, which proved Dutch Massey was no professional and no genius either. "Just dumb luck I found it instead of the narcs."

"Well, old buddy," Dutch had written, "if you're reading this it probably means the worst happened and I didn't get a chance to remove it. Which also means I'm probably in jail or had to leave the country. Anyway, I just want you to know I haven't left my partner high and dry." Dutch went on to inform Cree where he'd buried some "cash deposits" and that the key taped to the folder was to a condominium in Telluride, Colorado, that Dutch had bought in his mother's name and had been using for several years. His mother had died the day the Japanese bombed Pearl Harbor.

And then Dutch had explained to Cree about the cache in the ghost town of Alta.

18

Several days passed before Bram could keep any water down. Even though he could hear the stiffs working their way toward him, most of his hope had gone out with the candle. In the darkness sound intensified, perhaps because his eyes could no longer focus his attention elsewhere. The dripping water, the snoring sounds of sleep, the groan as a man turned over, and the clump of his boots on the platform kept Bram awake and abraded his nerves. One moment he felt weak and listless and wanted only to die, and the next he felt angry and sure he could not withstand one more irritation. That it would send him screaming in madness up the drift to bash at the wall until he bled to death.

They were all weakening sooner than they should because of the sickness the food had brought on. He knew they couldn't last until help arrived. No songs now, no jokes or stories. Just the dripping, snoring, coughing—none of it in unison but all in a senseless off-rhythm that made his body want to twitch and jerk in accompanying spasms.

"Water's risin'," Shorty announced after a trip to the end of the workings.

So that was how it was to end. Drowning. One of the things Bram had enjoyed about the cold, damp, exhausting work in the stopes was the anticipation of the warm, dry comfort of home after tally and the pleasure of having earned it. Now he longed for the comfort and loved ones there and could not imagine how he'd ever chosen to leave it for work in the dank earth. His tears were silent and private in the dark, but scalding hot on his skin.

Knut gave up trying to find encouraging things to say and only spoke when he decided it was time to send someone to tap a signal to the stiffs. Gus, the stalwart Swede, took over the morale boosting and would periodically swear that he heard the shots coming closer. The water was dripping less. The air was freshening up a bit. "Soon tings ben hunky-dory, you vill see."

When next it came Bram's turn to signal on the pipe he had to crawl on his hands and knees up the drift. The rescue efforts sounded fainter than they had the day before. He had to sit and rest a long time to clear his head enough to start back. It seemed the harder he breathed the less satisfaction he drew from the air. When he reached the platform, again on hands and knees, the water was up over his wrists.

His waterlogged clothing chafed against his skin and seemed to soften the flesh beneath. It felt to Bram as if there was no longer any connecting tissue between his skin and his flesh, nor between his flesh and his bones. The different layers would slide about independently when he rolled over. He came to picture his insides as a glass of Ma'am's slippery, clear, red-berry jelly. Tossing about became agony, lying still impossible.

The cold drips from the roof kept his topside frozen while whatever part of him contacted the platform warmed up. He was always half hot and half cold and his teeth took to chattering uncontrollably. He would hold on to his lower jaw for a while to keep it still and give it a rest. And when he did he heard teeth chattering all around him with that echolike emptiness sound makes in the drifts.

The water stopped its rising for a time as it filled up a stope lower in the workings. Bram realized that Knut wasn't sending anyone to signal anymore. He was going to mention it but lost track of his thoughts and forgot. It was Gus Lundberg, the strongest, most fearless, most hopeful of them all who broke first. He started an endless angry moaning and crawled over Bram's legs, making him cry out in pain. The moan grew to an unearthly intensity Bram would not have had the strength to produce. It sounded as if the Swede was bashing himself back and forth against either wall as he stumbled up the drift.

Bram called after him listlessly but his throat seemed clogged with itself. The ringing in his ears finally drowned out the Swede. Gus didn't return. Bram could tell when the water rose again because the bohunks came over to crowd onto his platform, theirs being lower. There was no room to turn over now, and breathing had become a gasping.

Sometime after that, it could have been hours or days as jumbled as his mind had become, he realized the water was lifting him off the platform. Someone insisted he wade up the drift to higher ground. Bram saw the love in Ma'am's eyes as she walked beside him and the pride in Pa's as he offered him a hand. Even in delirium, Bram could not bear to think of his little Callie girl. That would have been the final agony.

Callie tried not to think of Bram, but the reminders were endless. His cot in the sitting room, his spare pants on the peg, his hunting rifle under Pa's on the wall, the piece of his old shirt she used as a dustrag. Callie and Luella threw themselves into cooking and baking for miners who'd come to help in the digging out. They carried loaves of bread and covered dishes and desserts up to the cookhouse to help Heinrich Mueller. There was always a crowd just come off the digging that had to be fed. They'd stop at the boardinghouse on the way back to pick up washing from the visiting rescuers, who were stacked like cordwood in the rooms and hallways. Anything to keep busy, exhaust themselves enough to sleep.

Alta began to hurt for supplies and the call went out on the camp's one telephone in the manager's office. Donations of food and blankets came up the tram from Ophir, Telluride, Rico, Placerville, Pandora, San Miguel, Ouray, and great hunks of beef and mutton from the ranches and farms around. A doctor from the hospital in Telluride stood ready to take the train and ride the tram up when word came that rescue was close.

Wicker body baskets were stacked in the snowshed entrance to bring up the dead and the basket cases—those alive but not enough to stand up in the hoist bucket. John O'Connell had to look away every time he passed them going to and from the digging out. He worked so desperately that sometimes he came home with his arms draped over the shoulders of other men, his feet dragging out behind. They'd sprawl him across Bram's cot and help Luella remove his boots. He wouldn't eat until he woke and didn't want to pause long for that, but Luella would force food on him. "No sense in losing you both," or, "Our Bram will have a better chance if you can hammer steel with fed muscles."

The outside world knew from the signals how many of the twenty-two men on Talse's crew had survived the cave-in and who they were. There were widow's weeds going about Alta already, even though no bodies had come up yet. A twelve-year-old powder monkey had perished. He'd been sent to Talse's crew with an order. When Callie'd heard Bram was one who signaled, she dared to hope. But as time passed a heavy pain grew in her chest and she knew the meaning of the term "heartsick."

A special railroad car with two nurses arrived to wait on a siding down at the Loop to take the worst of the basket cases into Denver, where hospitals had the latest in lifesaving equipment. The ground was working on level four and the stiffs had to spile as they went, using up precious time the men at the end of the drift could ill afford. And the contrary weather turned warm, causing snow to melt away from the beaten paths until they stood up like bridges from the surrounding snow. Melting snow poured down the mountain and into old surface openings and cracks where the ground had worked, leaving mud slick everywhere to further hamper rescuers.

"Fair number of union men up here," John O'Connell said one

night over the food his wife insisted he eat before he took another turn at the drilling. "They say this wouldn't happen if the stiffs was to be organized. If we was organized we could force the management to slow down the work so the timbering was done solid behind a man before he goes spittin' fuses hundreds of feet down."

"The earth caves in on union men too," Luella said. "And just today the management here, Mr. Traub, told me the company would help with expenses since Bram's not insured."

"Funeral or hospital?" John said with a bitter sound that could have been a laugh. Both Callie's parents were so white and drawn that the bones in their faces stuck out and their eyes and cheeks sank inward. Under the electric light bulb they looked a generation older than they had before the cave-in. "Callie darlin' "—Pa drew her onto his lap—"don't you be listening to us now. We're just tired, your Ma'am and me. He'll be all right, our Bram."

And then word came. The survivors had stopped signaling. Callie and Luella had been kneeling by Bram's cot, praying silently to Jesus to save Bram. Callie had pointed out to him that since he already had Aunt Lilly and baby Henry, he didn't need Bram too. But since Callie had only one brother, she did. Ma'am must have seen the stubbornness in her eyes because she said, "Little girls do not lay down the law to the Lord, Callie. I think you'd best start over."

When Pa and Uncle Henry came to tell them the bad news, Luella rose from her knees and leaned against a wall, hugging herself, staring dry-eyed at nothing. John took Callie on his lap again, hiding his face behind her back where she could feel wetness through her dress. She wished Bram had listened to the man who'd come with the lady to the hole in the cookhouse. She'd decided now she was not about to ask Jesus for anything again.

The next morning, Mr. McCall came by. "We've hit water, John. Having to pump. But we're about through to them. You want to be there? I'd understand if you didn't."

Pa put on his coat and left without a word. Luella set down her Bible with a sigh. "Come, Callie, we might just as well go on up and wait for the news."

The door to the snowshed stood open and men were carrying the baskets off toward the adit. It was warm and sunny and the slush leaked through Callie's arctic boots as she leaned against Ma'am.

It seemed as if all the starch had gone out of Callie's bones. A quiet crowd gathered with them. There was just the usual coughing and an occasional sniff. Every now and then someone would pat Callie on the head. The doctor from Telluride and Mr. Traub entered the snowshed all togged out in boots and slickers with carbide lamps on their hats.

Sometime later a mule began to bray in the adit as if he was being beaten with a hot poker. He made such a racket it was a while before Callie realized there was a great shouting going on as well. The people around her began shifting from one foot to the other in dread and expectation and a need for any kind of end to this ordeal. Uncle Henry came running out of the snowshed door and refused to speak until he'd found Luella and Callie. "He's alive. Just barely, but Bram's alive."

Luella swayed and nearly knocked Callie off her feet. Uncle Henry turned to talk to those crowded around them. "Nine are still alive. But they're in bad shape. Doc says he's sending all nine on the train to Denver and going with them. Talse, Sullivan, Shorty, Bram O'Connell, and five of the bohunks."

Callie wasn't allowed to see Bram when they brought him up. She just saw the edges of the body basket hanging over the tram bucket on its way to the hospital train down at the Loop. Luella rode standing in the next one.

In Telluride Mildred Heisinger had heard of Alta's tragedy. The newspaper listed the names of the survivors and Brambaugh O'Connell was the only one she recognized. She felt a certain ambivalence. Mildred had troubles of her own.

The first week after she left Alta she'd reveled in the warmth and privacy of a room on the sunny side of the New Sheridan Hotel, hot baths, and gourmet food. She'd read and visited the shops and tried to recover from her humiliation. The second week she placed an advertisement in the newspaper offering herself as governess or tutor, hoping to find a position in a comfortable home. There was much wealth in Telluride and many of the rich had young children. The advertisement garnered two interviews but her lack of references ended both sessions on a cool and final note. And the town was not so large that word didn't spread quickly. She was even told that there was no opening for one of such meager credentials at the public school.

There were few other positions open to women except housewife, prostitute, and dressmaker. Mildred had been gently raised, but in the poverty of a homestead in Nebraska. Her parents, born to culture and wealth, had moved west when fortunes declined, determined to renew those fortunes on the dream of a fading frontier.

Mildred's mother had lost her dream and her life in a sod hut while giving birth to a stillborn. Mildred's consumptive father moved her, the books, and the piano to Denver in hopes of regaining his health and wealth in the pure air of a gold-laden Colorado paradise. Instead he married a widow with some money and thereby managed to send his daughter to a normal school which trained teachers. Before he died, he did manage to instill in Mildred a hankering for the good life, something she knew of mostly by hearsay.

The widow had children of her own and little sympathy for her good-looking stepdaughter. Mildred studied magazines for fashion. She'd learned much of decorum and language from her parents, but she'd come to find her looks and tastes to be more of a curse than a blessing.

She sat now with her feet against the radiator in a third-floor room on the cold, shady side of the New Sheridan Hotel, its one window overlooking the alley. Her money was nearly gone. She couldn't believe how quickly it had melted away. She'd managed to sell some of her clothes, but could find no buyer for her books. Reduced to one meal a day and washing in cold water from a basin, she'd soon be carrying slops in a boardinghouse. Or worse.

Mildred stood to pace the tiny room to warm herself. What was it in her that called out such cruelties in others? She'd never harmed a soul. In neither of her posts had Mildred been openly accused of anything, so she'd been unable to defend herself against the charges, whatever they were. With her two trunks, mostly empty now, the room allowed her only a few paces in any direction and she grew dizzy moving with her thoughts. She stopped at the window to peer down into the alley. A stray cat, as gray as the weather and swaying from hunger or disease, lurched through mud and snow to a trash bin outside the kitchen. Mildred couldn't bear to watch, see if it found food or collapsed trying to get into the bin.

When Bram O'Connell had carried her through that horrid mining camp, no one had mentioned it to her afterward. But he had been taken out of school and that mysterious shutter other women wore behind their eyes had closed them away from her.

There was a rapping on the door and Mildred paused before opening it for so long the rapping came again. It was Mrs. Stollsteimer, the housekeeper, a large-boned frump of a woman who wore nothing but deepest black offset by startling white aprons and white lace dust caps. She too had that shutter of the sisterhood behind her eyes that excluded Mildred Heisinger. "A gentleman in the lobby to see you." She used the same tone she did to terrorize the poor children who worked for her. "He asks your company at luncheon in the dining room in half an hour."

"Certainly not. How dare you assume I—"

"It's Lawyer Barada, Miss Heisinger." Mrs. Stollsteimer's expression indicated that fact surprised her too.

"Oh . . . well . . . yes. Of course. Please inform Mr. Barada I shall be happy to meet him for luncheon." Lawyer Barada was a leading citizen of Telluride. He had represented the Smuggler-Union Mining Company against the labor unions, and the Tomboy Mining Company as well.

Mildred Heisinger smiled at her image in the mirror and ignored the hungry cramping in her stomach as she prepared a careful toilet. Lawyer Barada and his widowed daughter lived in one of the finest houses in town, and the daughter had two small children just the age to need a governess.

19

DURING his night vigil in Alta, Cree Mackelwain noticed a few differences from his previous visit. History stayed in its place this time. Alta's ghosts did not awaken. And there was no horny woman to soften the night chill.

When the three men emerged from the mine tunnel at dawn they didn't appear to be carrying anything extra. Cree had been inside it several times. The lower levels were flooded and the main tunnel blocked by rubble after a mile or so. It seemed a logical place for Dutch to have hidden the cache but Cree had found no trace of it. He watched them from behind a tree on the hill above the tunnel entrance and wondered again exactly who they might be. They weren't being particularly careful. Two were short and rather stocky, one was tall. All three looked to be something over forty. One was balding. There was little distinctive or memorable about them.

From what Cree had been able to translate during the confusion of the investigation into his partner's death and the subsequent trial by the newspapers, Dutch was one of several local lone entrepreneurs in a disorganized business that organized crime decided to organize. Others were eliminated by similarly nasty methods. There was to be no mistaking those deaths as accidental. Cree should have had an inkling of how deeply Dutch had become involved when he discovered apparently senseless break-ins both at the office and at Dutch's apartment that went unreported. Dutch simply explained nothing had been taken. But the investigation uncovered the fact that sharks as well as organized crime were working the area.

A shark was a type of thief who lived off small-time drug dealers. These dealers had to hide quantities of drugs and cash somewhere and for obvious reasons did not report thefts to the police. So Dutch had taken to hiding loot in increasingly remote and unlikely places. He had, according to the letter left in Cree's car, taken possession of some "merchandise" while in Telluride and had hidden it in Alta when he suspected sharks had discovered his condo. He wrote that the stash was very large, suggested Cree waste no time finding it because "the stuff don't keep forever," and there was a sizable amount of money with it. Cree couldn't know if the men now driving off in the Bronco were sharks, representatives of organized crime, or organized law enforcement. Any of the three spelled trouble for him.

When he could no longer hear the Bronco, he made his way down to the vast yaw in the mountainside. Dutch's instructions had been purposely unclear. He'd indulged in a sort of amateur riddle to throw off anyone who might steal the folder. In the process it had thrown Cree off too. Dutch had conveniently marked the spot with a white flag. "Some tourist probably took it home for a souvenir."

If his partner had included a map instead of a riddle, Cree would have found the treasure by now and been gone. Cree took a last look at the hole and wondered again if the boy, Bram, had heeded his warning or if his bones lay crushed and rotted beneath tons of rock deep in the earth. Hunger drove Cree down the mountainside to Aletha's car.

In Telluride he treated himself to a hearty breakfast at Sophio's over a copy of the Telluride *Times*. Tracy met him at the Pick and Gad. She was straightening the condo up in payment for a few nights' lodging. Renata Winslow had called Aletha to wait tables at the New Sheridan Hotel. Before Cree could crawl off to bed Tracy went into a drawn-out tale of how she and Aletha had spent part of last night on Telluride's line in the days when it was thriving. "We got to do something about her, you know?" Tracy fixed him with a glance of significance and nodded sagely, "What she does is dangerous—for her, for people around her, and probably for people who've been dead for decades. I mean, even on *Star Trek* they try not to mess up other people's time."

Cree agreed but fell into bed, too tired to know what to do about Aletha Kingman. He woke to find Tracy gone and Charles sleeping against his legs. He made it to the New Sheridan in time for a late lunch. For Telluride, it was a hot day and most of the tourists were in shorts. Between the hotel and the corner was a wide concrete patio with tables. He ordered and waited to catch Aletha's eye as she busied herself at other tables. She looked tired, some of the bounce gone. When she bent her head to add up a check her hair fell over it and she tucked it back behind her ear impatiently. Worry lines etched her forehead. When she was old they would be permanent.

"Your car's back home safe and undented," he said when she could get over to him. "Tracy tells me you two went gadding in time last night. Don't you think you're playing with fire?"

"Speaking of which, legal people report break-ins. Those who don't have something to hide from the law. And they tend to be very secretive about their personal lives."

"When do you get off work?"

"Three-thirty. But I'm going up to the museum. I hear it's supposed to close soon." The museum operated on a small grant and opened only in the summer months when it didn't have to be heated.

"That's the woman who was with Callie at the Senate," Aletha told Cree, and pointed to the nude in the painting on the second floor.

"According to a legend, that's Audrey." He reached out to touch the surface. "Wonder if this is the original or a copy." He stepped back to inspect Audrey's exposed curves. "I don't know if there's any truth in it but the story goes she was one of the girls on the line and she let this artist paint her because he couldn't get man's work with his lily-white uncallused hands. The painting hung behind the bar in various saloons and the artist and Audrey got married and lived happily ever after on the sunny side of town."

"The story may be legend but that woman was real in Callie's time."

"Let's let her stay there." He took her shoulders and turned her to face him. "This thing is getting out of hand. More and more people are being involved."

"I don't want her to come to Telluride and end up on the shady side of town. I'd bring her here if I could."

"How would she adjust, torn from her family? God, she's just a kid. You get her here and you say to this little girl—'You'll never have to worry about childhood diseases or epidemics again. If you get pneumonia a doctor can cure it and we'll even straighten your teeth. All you have to worry about is missiles with nuclear warheads, rapists, drunk drivers, herpes, the cancer rate, and the poison in your air, water, and food. Oh, and would you like to see your own grave out in Lone Tree Cemetery?"

Aletha had continually to revise her judgment of him. He could flip off the most rude statement one minute and be sensitive the next. "Okay, Herr Professor, I agree. Your logic is unassailable."

"Good, then let's go up to the museum and get our history where it belongs."

The museum sat on the edge of the sunny northern side of town and Aletha grew breathless trying to keep up with Cree's long strides on an uphill slant. Back off Colorado Avenue, Telluride looked like most any small town with a mixture of Victorian and modern, elegant and modest. But the colossal mountain backdrop crowding in on it, hovering above its steeply pitched roofs, set this small town apart. "I don't do anything to cause this time thing to happen. And I don't know how you expect me to stop it."

"You're sure nothing like this has ever happened to you before?"

"Nothing. And I don't understand why it should be me or Callie or even be happening here instead of San Diego. Unless this sort of thing happens more than we know and no one talks about it because no one would be believed. Or there's something about Callie and me that connects across time somehow, and once I came here where Callie had lived, the connection opened up. But I didn't see any sign of Callie last night when Tracy and I roamed the red-light district."

"That's all crazy . . . but well reasoned." He stopped to study her. "Why is it I keep thinking you're such a fluff brain?" The museum faced the end of a street—two-story, pink sandstone block, third-floor dormers and gray lightning-shaped streaks where mortar had been used to fill cracks. The entrance was through a concrete-block enclosure painted to match the building.

"In Callie's time this was a hospital," Cree said, his voice soft and faintly reverent. Aletha wondered how he could get almost drippy over dusty historical relics when he'd witnessed the real thing, live. But she wandered the artifact-filled rooms, listened to his mini-lectures, and had the growing urge to get snuggled.

Somebody had gone to a lot of trouble to arrange and display a wealth of donated objects, from hand tools used in the mines to utensils used in the kitchen. In a glass case sat a round cardboard token worth twelve and a half cents in trade at the Cosmopolitan Saloon, with a picture of a girl younger than Callie, but with the brown sausage curls, dimples, and plump-cheeked innocence.

It was in the old-clothing display that Aletha found the sandals she'd lost to the mud and two cowboys named Jesse and Carl the night before.

20

MILDRED Heisinger did her best to eat slowly and in a ladylike manner. But she was so hungry the oyster soup, pork tenderloin, canned vegetables, and hot rolls seemed to disappear in record time.

Lawyer Barada, a small formidable gentleman with a shock of white hair and liver spots, picked daintily at his meal. "Does me good to see such appetite in a young lady. All this fasting females do nowadays just so their waists can be cinched an inch smaller is certain to bring harm to future generations," he said over coffee and lemon torte. "But then, unquestionably, a lady of your tastes can appreciate the menu here. I've been all over the country and rarely found better. It's always been my theory that a certain select few are chosen by God himself to know and appreciate the finer things. Don't you find that to be true, Miss Heisinger?"

"Yes . . . yes I do." Mildred was not at all sure where this conversation was headed. The lawyer's daughter and grandchildren had not been mentioned. She hoped she'd not made a mistake in dining with him, but he'd hinted at nothing improper. Replete and warmed at last, she felt blessed and secure for the moment. Sun had emerged to shine golden rays through windows draped in rich material. Her thin shoes nestled in soft carpet.

Lawyer Barada rang for more coffee. "An obvious example of the opposite is some coarse miner striking gold in the hills, accruing all the manifestations of wealth but in actuality remaining the coarse miner he was to begin with." The lawyer raised his cup to her as if in a toast. "Breeding will tell in people as well as horses, my dear, and every time."

Something was amiss. Mildred couldn't put her finger on just what. Her delight in this temporary comfort began to dim. The upper half of one wall in the dining room consisted of sliding panels which opened now to reveal several of Mrs. Stollsteimer's little girls cleaning the musicians' loft. Panels on the other side of the loft opened onto the barroom and the third side onto the ballroom. In this manner it was possible for one orchestra to entertain any one or all three rooms at the same time, depending upon which partitions were thrust aside. Mildred studied the little girls, all dressed in black like their mistress, to give herself time to think of a response to the lawyer's inscrutable remarks.

"I would expect, then, one would be most careful in selecting a governess for one's grandchildren," she said, blatantly bringing him to the subject uppermost in her mind.

"Governess? Grandchildren? What . . . oh, I see. You thought I'd asked you here to . . . It's not that at all, my dear Miss Heisinger. A governess's lot is a sorry one indeed. I wouldn't think of asking someone such as yourself to stoop so low. Poor things are paid a pittance and dismissed as soon as the last child is ready for boarding school. Then she must look for a position in another family, and when that is over, another. Do you know my very own governess ended her days in poverty? The most wretched poverty. I didn't hear of it until years later, of course, or I would have done something for her. Poor old Miss Brewster."

Mildred felt as if the ceiling and its chandeliers were lowering on her. "I should like to be independent in my life, sir. There are not many ways for a lady to—"

"Independent? A governess is at the beck and call of spoiled brats and their rude mothers, the harassment of the men in the family. The least indiscretion or mere suspicion of one sends them packing without references to ensure another such miserable position. I can't imagine a lady like yourself considering such employment, Miss Heisinger."

Mildred could feel the blush on her face. "Then what, Mr. Barada, did you—"

"Oh, I've come to offer something much grander than governess. I'm sending my grandchildren to the public school here when the time comes in any case. They need an end to the mollycoddling of a permissive mother who—" He reached across the table but did not quite touch her as she made preparation to rise. "Please hear me out and excuse an old man's wandering. I can see what you are thinking, but at my age I had nothing of the sort of proposition you had supposed in mind. I've been too slow to come to the point—a lawyer's failing. Miss Heisinger, I've come prepared to offer you a strictly business proposition from the town of Telluride, or at least some of its leading merchants and citizens."

Mildred sat very straight on the edge of her chair, still prepared to leave in haste and indignation. "The town?"

"Where else were we to find such independence, breeding, and taste in one person? And with the energy of the young to boot? Most ladies are very dependent, you know, or married. Which adds the same. In fact, the town's woefully short of the female gender altogether. And that's why we've come to you. Young men arrive here by the trainloads but there's a dearth of the fairer sex. And the town is growing—much of it on the wrong side, if you get my meaning. We are in need of young feminine persons for clerking, office work, laundresses—oh, I can't tell you all the work going undone. And when a young man from the mines decides to take a wife, where must he go? To the sporting section and make some soiled dove respectable and his life's companion. Now, what kind of place are we, to offer no better than that? And what can we hope to become?"

Mildred settled into her chair more comfortably. "I don't understand what you want of me."

"We want you to travel to the cities of the mid-continent and the seacoasts to tell young, capable ladies of the opportunities in Telluride. You'd travel only in the best accommodations and need to dress accordingly if you are to represent us. I am commissioned to offer you a handsome salary and, of course, all expenses." Lawyer Barada handed her an envelope. "It takes more than men and sporting women to make a respectable community. Ladies are such a good influence on a rough camp like this. Their gentling natures are so needed here. And you could live again as you obviously are accustomed and deserving to do. You'd be doing the town and yourself a great service."

He rose abruptly, as if the audience was over. Mildred stood, still clutching the envelope, and saw the gray cat in the alley through the window next to her. It lay still and stiff, its eyes and mouth open. When she turned back to Lawyer Barada he was holding out his hand to her—whether to take her elbow and guide her through the empty ballroom to the lobby, to shake her hand on a business agreement, or to take back the envelope, she didn't know. But with the starved gray cat very much on her mind, Mildred Heisinger took the lawyer's hand in a handshake and drew the envelope to her breast. "I should be most happy to accept your . . . the town's offer of employment, sir."

With Luella gone to Denver with Bram, Callie and her father carried on as best they could in the cabin in Alta that spring. In some ways it was pleasant. School started again in May with a new teacher. Mrs. Traub had Callie up to the big house to play with Bertha, often sending Callie home with good things for their dinner, and Mrs. McCall next door helped when Callie's baking or the cook stove gave trouble. Mr. Mueller up at the cookhouse always had extra pie or strudel that his "little Callie" must take home so it wouldn't spoil.

John O'Connell, when he wasn't up at the commissary discussing the great labor strike at the Smuggler-Union, a huge mine up out of Telluride, would sit after dinner and tell her stories of his life while she did the dishes. He'd had grand adventures, her father. He'd run away from his home in Bantry when his father beat him once too often, and had sailed on great sailing ships to Africa, New Zealand, Australia, and eventually jumped ship in San Francisco. He'd worked building railroads, driving freight wagons, and mining. John was on his way to the East Coast just to see what it looked like when he ran out of money in Ohio and stopped to work a few months at Grandfather Midden's farm and met Luella and the baby, Bram. "And I decided right then and there to bring them back out here where a man with a family can make something on his own and not have to work for another man until he dies."

Callie dried the soap from her hands and crawled onto his lap. She'd heard the stories before but felt a comfort in the familiar voice telling them again. "I'm lonesome for them, Pa."

"And so am I, Callie darling, so am I. Won't be long now and they'll be home with us again. You'll see." But Callie heard the doubt in his every inflection. She knew that Mr. Talse had died on the train to Denver and some of the others since. The last word they'd had, Bram still lived.

And then one day Pa came home with a different story and different plans for them. "Callie, you've been a fine brave girl. Ahhh, when bad luck strikes an Irishman it don't settle for a half-measure." He sat heavily on Bram's cot and felt for the hair that no longer topped his head. "It's your mother now. She's taken sick and had to find a warmer room in Denver. There's only so much highgrading a man can get away with, and they don't pay near its worth in town. Callie, we're going to have to give up the house. I'll be moving into the boardinghouse and I've found a place for you."

"But we're waiting for them to come home. We have to wait here."

John gave her his big bear hug. "Bless you, it's only for a small time. We'll soon all be together again in a far more splendid house than this here."

"You can't leave me too," Callie said desperately. "Pa, please—"

"Now, hear me out, child. It'll not be so bad as you think. And you can do something for Bram. What do you think of that?"

"Can I go to Denver?"

"No, Callie. You're going to Telluride. It's a lovely place and you've never been. There's this big, fancy hotel there and a lady by the name of Mrs. Stollsteimer who needs help with the cleaning of it. She's a sister to Mrs. Fisherdicks and Mrs. Fisherdicks told her of our troubles. You'll be working with girls your own age, wearing a fine dress and a lace cap. And your bed and board comes with the job. All you earn will be sent straight to Denver, where it's needed bad."

"The lady who left her drawing book here told me never to go to Telluride."

"And will you listen to a stranger and not your own father, then?"

"Pa, when she came to the cookhouse and I gave Charles to her, her husband told Bram not to go in the mine. And Bram didn't listen. And look what's happened to Bram."

"Callie, if I listened myself to all the warnings I've had in my life, I'd not set foot outside the door. The tommyknockers are ever telling me not to be going up a raise or to hurry and run out of a stope. We'd all starved to death if I'd listened." He set to heating water so she could bathe. Tomorrow, he was taking her to Telluride.

Callie O'Connell had left many rented houses before, but never with the sadness and fear she did the one in Alta. Everything she owned fit easily into a small carpetbag and Callie slipped the lady's book of drawings in it too. "I know it'll be seeming hard, now," John said to her as she rode in a stagecoach for the first time. "But you'll be seeing it's for the best. And you'll find Alta was a dull place indeed after you've been to Telluride."

"Will I go to school there?" Callie had heard Telluride had a big stone schoolhouse with only one class to a whole room.

"No, you'll be working and earning for Bram, like I told you. You'll be learning more of what a girl needs to know than in a school, and they'll be paying you to learn even. And you'll not have to read no books either."

"But I like books, Pa. I don't like cleaning things."

"Now, don't you be sounding like your Aunt Lillian." The stage mired down in the mud three times before they arrived. While Alta sat up among the mountaintops, Telluride hunkered low in a dark valley at their bottoms. Mountains seemed bigger, more forbidding when looking up at them; they glared back down at Callie. Horses drawing carriages and wagons kicked up mud and made slopping, sucking sounds in the street. Harness clanked and jingled. Wagons creaked. Drivers yelled and "hawed." Many of the buildings were of brick and stone instead of wood, and Callie held on to her hat to stare up at the three-story hotel. It looked taller than the boardinghouse in Alta.

A man in an apron stepped out of one of the two great doors in the hotel. A heavy scent of cigar smoke came through the door with him. He lowered a striped awning by a handle that squeaked with every turn. John led her to the other door. Stairs so wide that three angels abreast could descend them without brushing wings reached straight up to the top of the building, and so steeply she had to hold on to her hat again. She felt a little shiver of excitement even in her terror, and her breath made noise.

"And what did I tell you?" Pa propelled her around the staircase to a metal cage with a spectacled man inside. "Here to see the housekeeper," he said importantly.

The man in the cage stuck a finger inside one end of his spectacles and rubbed an eye, his elbow pointing straight out. His other hand pointed around the corner. "Up the service stairs. Across the landing." They followed his finger to a door and behind it a smaller set of narrow stairs that rose in the opposite direction to the wide ones and reached a landing between them.

Mrs. Stollsteimer sat behind a desk in a cubicle hidden from the great staircase by a wall. Callie had never known a lady to have a desk unless she was a schoolteacher. Mrs. Stollsteimer was mountainous and the keys on her belt clanked like harness. Her cap looked like a doily with a bun in the middle.

"John O'Connell, ma'am. And this here's my Callie come to work for you, she has. Your sister Mrs. Fisherdicks up at Alta, she—"

Mrs. Stollsteimer waved him quiet with a hand as large as his. "I've been expecting her."

Something inside Callie hardened when John O'Connell left her with assurances that he'd be back to see her soon, that when her mother and Bram returned they'd all come to Telluride to get her. If John didn't make his lucky strike prospecting first, which would mean he and Callie could go to Denver and stay in style until Bram recovered. They'd visit him every day. His promises would have gone on for hours if Mrs. Stollsteimer hadn't insisted he leave. Mrs. Stollsteimer stood looking down at Callie. "How old are you, Callie O'Connell?"

"I turned eleven last week."

"You're young and you're small." She took hold of Callie's shoulders and switched her this way and that. "But you look sturdy enough."

Only yesterday Callie had played with Bertha Traub and her cat in Alta, blissfully unaware of the change her life would take today. The housekeeper rummaged through a cupboard beside her desk and drew out a black dress and white apron. Callie wondered if it was because of Mrs. Stollsteimer that the lady in pants warned her never to come to Telluride.

PART TWO
TELLURIDE

21

CALLIE thought the dress made her sturdy brown shoes look silly and made her look more grown-old than grown-up. The white apron and cap were smaller versions of the housekeeper's. "The girls should be gathering for their lunch now." Mrs. Stollsteimer had shown her into a small room on the third floor crowded with six narrow cots. "Come along."

She led Callie out to the staircase and to the second floor. Callie looked down at the golden pool of sunlight on the bottom stair and the lobby floor below. Dust motes glided through it. She had an urge to sit in that bright pool awhile and warm away her dread and the chill of that third-floor room. The hotel had service stairs at the rear of the second-floor hallway also, and these led directly to a busy kitchen. Pans clanged and people scurried. Callie's throat caught at all the staring strangers as she followed the housekeeper to a corner where five girls dressed just like Callie sat at a table.

"Callie O'Connell"—Mrs. Stollsteimer held her shoulders again to be sure she faced them—"I'd like you to meet Olina Svendt, Elsie Biggs, Opal Mae Skoog, Grace Artherholt, and Senja Kesti. Girls, this is our new helper." Each girl blinked as her name was said and Callie in her embarrassment forgot each name immediately. Her starched apron humped up as she sat and they giggled behind their hands when she tried to poke it down. The housekeeper brought her a bowl of soup with pieces of chicken, potatoes, and tiny green things floating in it and a glass of milk almost too cold to taste. The girls whispered among themselves, but addressed not a word to Callie. One handed her a plate of dark bread, another the butter, and they all watched her, as if to see if she knew what to do with them.

The soup was tasty and the bread rich with molasses and raisins. The other girls had hints of mischief and laughter lurking behind their eyes, but Callie didn't see them again until supper. Cora, a chambermaid, taught her how to tuck in the corners of bedsheets so they wouldn't pull out, how to clean carpets with a carpet sweeper and the carpet runner on the stairs with a whisk broom. Callie learned to scrub out indoor toilets and porcelain bathtubs. The rooms at the front even had their own. Chambermaids wore gray dresses with white aprons and dust caps. Cora told Callie that if she worked hard, she too could become a chambermaid.

The next day Callie was again on the grand staircase that cut up through the center of the building. This time she swiped with an oiled dust mop at the wooden ends of each step where the carpet runner didn't reach and she was again gazing longingly at the spot of sunlight in the lobby below when it disappeared. Not because of a cloud but because a wall closed over the staircase hiding the lobby. The edges of the wall sizzled like spattering meat in a fry pan.

Callie dropped the mop to clatter down to the second-floor landing where the staircase now ended. She hadn't expected anything like this to happen in Telluride. But now she expected to see the lady who wore pants, and perhaps her husband too. Callie saw a lady. But not the one she'd anticipated. This lady stood in a gilt frame and was, except for a wisp of floaty gauze, as naked as it was possible to be. Callie plunked down hard on a stair, almost too astonished to breathe. The white flesh fairly shimmered against a dark background ominous with storm. The lady's hair was down and flying about. And it was all bumpy, as if she'd braided it wet and let it dry before taking it down.

"Better not let Mrs. Stollsteimer see you sitting there," Opal Mae Skoog whispered from where she dusted the balustrade. Her head stuck out between two of the posts. Callie could only point at the new ending to the staircase. Opal Mae turned to gasp and stare and then tried to pull her head back without first straightening it, and was caught between the posts. She struggled in such panic Callie thought she'd choke herself, and ran down to help. When Opal Mae lay on the hall floor, crying, but with her head still attached, Callie looked back at the naked lady to find the stairs and the patch of sunlit lobby had returned instead.

Opal Mae's father had been killed in the Smuggler-Union Mine. She had three brothers and three sisters. Her mother took in boarders, and all the children who could, worked. Senja Kesti's parents came from Finland. That's why she had such an odd name. Olina Svendt was the biggest and the oldest. She instigated most of what little mischief they had time for and managed to avoid most of the blame. She had very pale skin and hair, and wide, even teeth. Callie noticed gentlemen noticing Olina on more than one occasion. Elsie Biggs had fair hair and blue eyes too, but there the similarity to Olina ended. Quiet, timid, sallow—she seemed younger than Callie but was over a year older. Elsie was not clever and usually received the blame Olina avoided. Grace Artherholt was an orphan put out to work by her aunt, who already had a houseful of children.

All of the girls resented the fact they were not allowed to keep any of their wages. Much of this Callie learned in the third-floor room where they giggled and whispered in the dark and Olina told scary stories. Sounds from the streets came up to them until they fell asleep, and sometimes woke Callie in the night. Shouting and piano music and bursts of laughter and horses whinnying in alarm. Sometimes even gunshots. The town seemcd never to sleep. Yet it was a quiet place compared to Alta, where the mill thundered. Here the mills were faraway pulses, only there if you listened for them.

The night after Callie and Opal Mae saw the painting on the staircase, Olina hung her blanket over the transom so they could switch on the light to look at the drawings in the book from Callie's carpetbag. The other four didn't believe the story about the naked lady on a wall that didn't exist and agreed that Olina's stories were better. But all were fascinated by the drawings.

"This is the hotel, but where's the office building next door?" Grace asked. "Why would your lady have drawn tables with umbrellas there instead?" They decided the Chevy Citation was an enclosed buggy lacking its wagon tongue.

"That's down there, I think." Olina pointed mysteriously south toward the river and the railroad tracks when they came to the picture of the Senate. "On *that* side of town. Across from the jail." Olina admitted to peeking down side streets when she was out on errands.

Callie wished she'd be sent on an errand. In her first two weeks at the New Sheridan she stepped foot out of the building only once and that was into the back alley. She kept expecting her father to visit as he'd promised, and still prayed to some vague hope she couldn't name for her brother to get well. Now that she was away from the solicitous ladies of Alta, Callie missed Luella most of all. She'd sometimes see a figure that looked like her mother from behind but who always turned a stranger's face to her.

When a letter finally came, Luella wrote that Bram improved slowly. That she'd feared they'd lost him several times. "Callie, you wouldn't know him, he's so thin." He slept better now, had fewer nightmares. Her mother had not been well herself. "I'm troubled that we are all apart. I was angry with your father when he wired that he'd sent you to Mrs. Stollsteimer, but I've written her and she's replied. She assures me you are well cared for and kept too busy to be lonely. I think of you every hour and we're grateful here for the money you're earning." And the rest was a plea for Callie to stay in or near the hotel and not wander about the town. That she be off the street before three o'clock in the afternoon.

At three o'clock that afternoon, Callie feather-dusted a second-floor front room and looked out to the street below, wondering what was so magical about that hour of the day. There were not as many people about as in the mornings, but still a good deal of activity. Mrs. Stollsteimer had even more warnings than Callie's mother. "Never be rude to the guests of the hotel." How could she be rude to people who didn't even see her? "Never enter a room when the gentleman is present." "Never leave the hotel unless sent on an errand, and always return before three o'clock." That night, Callie asked the girls about three o'clock in the afternoon and it seemed they'd never stop laughing. Finally Olina said, "Because the bank is robbed promptly every afternoon at three o'clock and the streets are full of madmen taking potshots at everyone in sight. Especially little girls with shaggy hair."

Callie had trouble tying her own hair up in rags and had been letting it go straight. "There wouldn't be any money left to rob."

"Because that's when *they* come out," Elsie said solemnly and with a suggestion of fear or awe. Elsie didn't often say anything.

"Shut up, dunce. Let's not tell her. Let's show her. I'll think of a plan." Olina was very good with plans. Several days later she found Callie with Opal Mae and Grace polishing silver. "If we're a little late, you're to say we're finishing up the sinks in the common toilet on second," she told the other two, and grabbing Callie's hand, hurried her to the kitchen door. "We're to pick up Mr. MacIntosh's boots." He was a guest with his own toilet, and everyone ran for him.

The mud in the alley had dried enough that they could walk along the edges without sticking. Crows fought over the garbage mess behind the buildings and eyed them skeptically. Callie knew two people wouldn't be sent for one pair of boots. "But what if Mrs. Stollsteimer goes up to the common—"

"Callie, you'll never learn anything if you don't take a chance." The sun was out and the birds sang; summer was so short in the mountains. Callie wanted to hang back so the outing would last. Every other building on Colorado Avenue seemed to be a saloon with its doors open in invitation. But there were also shops that had fanciful clothes in the windows. On the way back they stopped to look in several of these and Callie was embarrassed to see lacy, beribboned corset covers displayed openly just like in the mail-order catalogs. Suddenly Olina pulled her around a corner and into a side alley, put her finger to her lips, and pointed to the street. Some miners stood in the doorway of a saloon; a wagon piled with sacks of feed lumbered past. And then everything seemed to grow as still and breathless as Callie felt. The miners all looked down the street.

A light ringing of ladies' laughter, the high rattle of their chatter. Three ladies walked by the alley, arm in arm, dressed in the loveliest dresses Callie had ever seen. Prettier than Miss Heisinger's, brighter and silkier. The sun caught in the plumes on their hats. Their parasols were fringed and the slight sway in their walks set the fringe to dancing.

"*Them*," Olina whispered. Two more, then three. Callie finally breathed. Another group, still all marvelously clothed. One turned her face to them. A thin dark smudge showed under each eye; her lips and cheeks were bright.

"They're painted!" Callie said and Olina said, "Shush!"

More and then more. And not one of them had a husband with her. The miners called to them and they waved back and laughed. One lifted her skirts an inch or so and did a little skip. Right behind that group came two ladies alone and on Callie's side of the street. They were deep in conversation and took no notice of the miners across the way or the girls in the alley. They were as beautifully dressed as all the rest. One was rather fat, with red hair. The other was Callie's Aunt Lilly.

22

THE sandals in Telluride's museum had wedged wooden heels, webbed leather tops, and were toeless and heelless. Streaks of copper-brown remained but most of the color had aged to beige. Aletha even recognized the dart-shaped hole torn out of a sole edge by a department-store escalator. "There's no way these can be your shoes." Cree doubled over to stare at them. "They've been here for years. You just got to town."

A typewritten message Scotch-taped to the underside of the glass case's top announced that the contents, as well as the hanging clothes displayed on the wall behind, had been found in trunks and boxes stored in the historic bordello, the Pick and Gad, and had been worn by the soiled doves who worked there. A smaller note, self-propped like a place card, sat beside Aletha's shoes and pointed out how these resembled more modern designs, and ended with the cliché of there being nothing truly new under the sun. It didn't try to explain the obvious differences between Aletha's sandals and the other shoes in the case. The latter were either black or yellowed white with high button tops and pointed toes that had curled with age to suggest they'd belonged to overgrown pixies. They looked exactly like the shoes worn by the good women on the sunny side.

"I still don't believe it." Cree straightened. "The same pair of shoes could not have been on you and in here at the same time."

Aletha shrugged and walked out of the museum.

"Look, I've picked up some books and pamphlets on Telluride's past. I'll lend them to you," Cree said when he'd caught up with her. "This, for instance"—he waved at a two-story building that housed the laundromat in its basement—"used to be the Miners' Union Hospital. The unions didn't trust the money withheld from their pay to provide medical care and built their own hospital. Aletha, next time the tear opens, promise me you'll—"

"I'll read your fucking books, okay?" She stopped in mid-stride and turned on him. They collided. "But they won't tell me what happened to Callie. They'll be full of man stuff. And this world is so boring compared to Callie's. I'm not sure I can resist if temptation offers." They walked on in silence, Cree making disapproving noises under his breath.

"You sound just like a spoiled adolescent—" He threw her against the side of the post office and bent over her as if in an embrace. But his head turned to watch a shiny Bronco round the corner and move up the street. "Uh, friends of mine. And you think this world is dull." He released her so fast she lost her balance and fell against the wall again. "I have to know where they go. See you for dinner." He took off at a run.

Aletha picked up some steaks and a slab of raw calves' liver on her way back to the condo. The liver had the consistency of a drowned corpse when she cut it into tiny bits, but Charles relished it. He made snorting noises while he gobbled. Then he purred and rubbed against Aletha as if she were Mildred Heisinger. "Here I thought you wanted a Victorian home with a Victorian lady. Is it just the liver?"

She made a tossed salad and put it in the crisper, poured herself a glass of wine, and settled on the couch with some of the material on Telluride's history Cree had left on his night table. No mention of Callie, but Aletha tingled with the awareness that she read of Callie's world.

In prison the boredom had been so intense it numbed. Life was either monotonous or dangerous, each new cellmate a threat until Aletha could psych her out, each work or exercise period a potentially treacherous time even with guards in attendance. Kitchen duty was the worst because of the availability of weapons. But the periods of boredom stretched long between the moments of danger. And sometimes the only grist for her thoughts was rehearsing and planning for the scary times. Despite all her efforts to blot out those relatively few but momentous months in her life, Aletha had to admit it was possible she'd brought along an unsuspected abnormality with her into freedom—a dangerous need for excitement.

There were hazards in Callie's world, too, and not all in the mines or on the line. In the early years of the century Telluride had a war. The miners formed a union to protect themselves from the insensibilities of a management working for indifferent and unaccountable absentee owners in the money capitals of the East and Europe. The management formed an "Alliance" against the threat of ignorant and greedy labor to run things to suit itself, and against the very idea of organized labor—a threat not only to democracy but to the ability of the industry to make enough profit to warrant investment and provide jobs in the first place. Wringing golden glitter from the cold hard Rockies was as expensive as it was inefficient.

It all sounded a little like Republicans and Democrats, more like liberals and conservatives, and mostly like two distinct classes of people, each determined not to understand the problems of the other.

"Who was W. J. Barney?" Aletha asked Cree over steak and salad that evening, hoping to get him off guard.

"Barney . . . ahhh . . . some mine foreman who disappeared mysteriously at the time of the troubles. He turned up dead after a long while. The Alliance blamed it on the union. Put his skull in a store window to prove a point. The identification hung on his red hair, I think."

"And who were the guys in the Bronco you didn't want me to see, so you plastered me to the side of the post office?"

"I didn't want *them* to see *you*. My guess is they were the ones who strip-searched this apartment."

"Why not report them to the town marshal?"

"Because I can't prove it was them, and besides, nothing—"

"Besides, nothing was taken." The piece of juicy steak went dry as wool and she spit it out. "Cree, are you a dealer?"

"Christ, first you call me a narc and now I'm a dealer." But an unfamiliar flush stained his face.

"And I was even beginning to like you." She dropped her fork and stood. "It's like I never learn." She scooped Charles up off the couch. "Come on, kitty, we'll go spend the night in the car. You, McCree, ought to get along special with Tracy. She likes her toots."

Charles did his rigor-mortis routine. He had a real thing about being carried. He also had bad breath and made an effort to wail his protest right in her face before he tried to climb her head. Aletha pulled him down, clamped him to her chest, and marched toward the door. She marched headfirst into Cree Mackelwain.

"You belong on the stage."

Aletha swung at him and lost the cat. She knew better than to take on somebody his size without being sneaky, but it was too late to call her fist home. It bounced off the arm he held up in mock terror.

"You do have a real flair for the dramatic." He moved to block her path as she tried to step around him to the door. "If you'll just stand still, I will tell you my big secret. I may have involved you in something by being around you."

"Why," Aletha asked later when they sat over coffee, "do you suppose so many innocent lives get messed up because of cocaine? I mean . . . people who don't even use it or sell it? Pretty soon it'll be the whole world."

"Most people live totally unaffected by it. You and I just happen to have been unlucky in our associations. I do think you and Tracy better disassociate yourselves from me until this is over or they leave town."

"But the coincidence is a little much. Almost as if time had planned it all. Or once Callie and I met, this whole thing started coming together. We sort of set time's plan in motion."

"You're being a flake again. Time is not somebody who plans things. Time is an 'it' to or in which things happen. Life is full of coincidence."

But the next morning when Aletha cleaned rooms at the New Sheridan Hotel, she mulled over all the instances in which her life had touched with Callie's, trying to discover a pattern. These thoughts helped her through several vicious chemical attacks on bathrooms and endless push-pulling with the vacuum.

She'd stepped out onto the balcony hallway on second to deposit some dirty linens when an older couple passed her on their way to the staircase. Aletha could have been a potted plant for all the notice they took of her. The woman dripped ashes from her cigarette waving in the air as she upbraided her companion for dressing too formally for the day's excursion, for walking too slowly, and for drinking too much the night before. He winced and dug his cane into the carpet with each step, his expression one of weary endurance.

Aletha had just turned back into the room to retrieve the vacuum when the woman's scratchy diatribe ended in a gasp. Aletha wondered if she'd sucked the cigarette down her throat or if he'd summoned the energy to hit her over the head with his cane. When she looked out, the couple stood on the landing, stiff, motionless. She leaned forward. He took her elbow.

"Oh, that's only Audrey, she—" Aletha reached them in time to see the problem was not Audrey. In fact Audrey was gone and the staircase descended to the lobby, ended in a splash of dusty sunlight worthy of a religious experience. The carpet became a narrowed runner of a different color where it met the absence of the wall. It wasn't the same lobby. It had a double door with glass windows. And when the door opened a man in floppy trousers stood looking up at them.

"Good Lord, madam, your skirt," he said to the woman with the cigarette, and doused his cigar in a white vaselike thing filled with sand. The sweet-sour smell of barnyard wafted up from the open door below, and creaking sounds. It was fascinating how these history people all looked so normal, even with their funny clothes, crooked and sometimes yellowed teeth. Aletha could see this one's stiff collar working as he tried to force a swallow with his head tilted back to stare up at them. His necktie was a short wide thing tied more like a lady's scarf with the two ends spread side by side instead of one overlapping the other.

The hole closed as the man below blinked and fled out the door. The nude Audrey traipsed dramatically across the forbidding backdrop of her painting. "That was a supernatural experience." The woman flipped her cigarette into a pot of phony ferns and turned on her heel. "I'm going back to the room. I think it gave me the shits."

"I suspect whatever we thought we just saw is best forgotten," the man with the cane said, eyeing Audrey and the wall and avoiding Aletha's eyes. "Enough trouble in this life the way it is."

Cree helped Aletha pack her suitcase. Tracy Ledbetter was moving her belongings into the vacated crib and Cree had talked her into taking in Aletha and Charles until he was convinced those around him would be in no danger. "I think I'm going to miss you," he said to Charles, but then smiled at Aletha. They carried everything down to the Datsun and came back for Charles.

"It seems like there's more and more happening, like it's speeding up." Aletha opened the door and entered first. Charles stood in the middle of the room, his tail puffed to twice its normal size. Part of the tiled Jacuzzi had faded into dim light. Next to it a deep bathtub sat up on molded ankles and slender human feet instead of the usual antique animal paws. Steam twirled up from it. A woman stood wrapped in a towel, a load of hair pinned up on top of her head, one strand escaping to curl down over an ear, promising to get wet. She was slender, straight, pale. What showed around the towel was flawless. Aletha could hear the change in Cree's breathing.

Shadows moved across the small mirror beside the bather's head. Wrought-iron curlicues painted white formed its frame and provided fastening to the wall. Aletha had seen its like in an entry hall filled with such mirrors. She'd seen the tub before, too. And the pale green eyes that stared at her now in startled outrage.

"Mildred?" Aletha couldn't believe it. "Mildred Heisinger?"

23

ANOTHER little something hardened up in Callie after her forbidden excursion on the street. Everyone had allowed her to believe her Aunt Lilly was dead, yet the world expected strict honesty and openness from Callie O'Connell. That excursion after three o'clock was never discovered and she was sent on a legal one early the next morning. This time with Elsie Biggs. They were to carry a valise up to the hospital and not dawdle along the way. Mr. MacIntosh, whose boots Callie had collected with Olina, had succumbed to a mysterious stomach ailment during the night after a sumptuous dinner party he'd thrown for friends in the hotel dining room.

"If it was such a grand dinner, why didn't we have to stay up and work?" Callie asked as they trudged along Fir Street.

"There weren't any ladies present." You had to lean into Elsie to even hear her soft speech. One of the ways she wasn't like Olina was her teeth. Not wide and even, they were bad and often pained her. But Elsie Biggs rarely smiled. Her family put her out to work because they wanted her to learn responsibility and not grow into foolish ways. They lived in Pandora at the head of the canyon. Her father worked in the Smuggler-Union stamp mill there. Her mother came to see her once a week. But Pandora was only a mile or two from Telluride. John O'Connell had sent word through Mr. McCall, when Mr. McCall came from Alta on his long day, that he'd be down to see Callie over the July Fourth holiday.

The hospital blocked the end of Fir Street. A wide covered porch spread on two sides with wooden steps at one end, and giant brick chimneys reared up on two ends of the building. Great snow patches on the mountain looming behind and above the hospital put a cold wet smell on the breeze.

"I wonder if Mr. MacIntosh is dead yet," Elsie breathed. "My pa says people only come to the hospital to die."

Callie thought of her brother and had the urge to kick Elsie, but she read the sign that warned them to be quiet. They turned the valise over to a lady dressed in starched white. Callie had expected to hear screams of pain and agony but all was as quiet as the sign suggested it should be. Back outside, Callie slowed her steps gradually, dazzled by the brilliant colors of sky, young grass, and exuberant dandelions. An enclosed school wagon pulled by two white and two brown horses bumped along the rock-pitted street. It was bigger than a stagecoach and the driver sat on the very top. Children's elbows and heads and hats hung out the side windows. Taunts, squeals, whines, hoots, and laughter replaced the birdsong. Someone yelled, "Elsie Biggs! Hey ho."

Elsie waved and blushed. Callie was surprised at how pretty she looked just then. "They're from Pandora."

"Where's the school? I want to see it."

"We'll be late back . . . but well . . . only if you hurry." They picked up their skirts and ran. Beautiful, monstrous houses—some with fences and their own sidewalks. And then the school, bigger than the hospital. It was made all of stone and sat in the center of a large piece of land. Callie counted ten arched windows across the front of the top story, and the building was longer yet going back. Wide concrete stairs led to the arched double doorway.

"Aren't you sad to not be going there every day?" Callie asked. "They must have many books in so important a school as that." But Elsie just hurried her back to the hotel. Callie tried to imagine the inside of that school for weeks afterward, fantasized that she and Bram attended it. She even peopled every room with a beautiful Miss Heisinger.

But Callie had to watch the summer disappearing through windowpanes. "I'm here to see you earn your way," Mrs. Stollsteimer told her when she found the girl dreaming about the school and watching the languid dust motes in the sun at the bottom of the staircase. "Someday you'll thank me. Now, run down and help the girls in the ballroom."

There was to be a special dance and late buffet dinner. The girls had to rush about to clean themselves and change into fresh uniforms after cleaning up the ballroom. They helped set up the buffet tables in the dining room and then carried platters of bite-sized meats and cheeses and cakes, and tiny sandwiches without crusts, to the people standing and sitting out in a ring around the dance floor.

". . . eight-hour day. Just give the lazy rascals more time to gamble, drink, and fritter away what means their labor has earned them."

"Unions only keep the honest man who's willing to work from selling his muscle as he sees fit."

Threading her way through the canyons of adults reminded Callie of the snow tunnels to the privy Pa and Bram had shoveled in Alta. But the canyon sides here were dark and gave off heat, were starched and corseted, mustachioed and tuxedoed. Voices echoed over her head, usless little hand fans flapped like bird wings. Hands accepted her delicate offerings, offered on tiptoe and with outstretched arms. Eyes looked right into her eyes and out through the back of her head. Callie thought she could have made rude faces at them and they'd never have noticed.

"Timber as you go. Ignorant rednecks have no idea the cost of such a thing. Don't have the timber or the time anyway. Damn few cave-ins for all the mining operations around here, if you ask me."

On the dance floor the ladies looked like princesses in the ruffled skirts and high-piled hair. And the gentlemen looked like sissies, pointing their toes, bowing and scraping. Then the orchestra in the loft speeded up, the violins fiddled instead of squeaked, the older people left the dance floor, and the younger ones paired off to jump around, lady and gentleman together. The chandeliers shook and jingled. Cheering, stomping, and rough voices accompanied the music from the barroom through the slid-back panels in that wall. Cigar smoke wafted gray-blue from the barroom, over the heads of the musicians, and into the ballroom. And when the orchestra stopped to rest, the clicking of the gambling wheels from the same source formed a constant background.

There was no smoking in the ballroom, but a great many unsuccessful attempts to spit at the brass cuspidors. A steady stream of gentlemen made their way through a door to the side of the orchestra loft and into the barroom and came back smelling of something stronger than punch. There weren't enough ladies for the dancing anyway, and only the very old and crippled were allowed to sit out.

"Aren't having trouble hiring nonunion men up at the Smuggler, are you, Collins?"

"Running full shifts. Out-of-work men coming in on the train every day."

Olina Svendt wore her pale hair in one neat braid that she could sit on if she wanted. It trailed down her back and over the bow of her apron strings. She was approaching Callie with a tray of cut-glass punch cups when a gentleman reached over to give the braid a quick, forceful tug. Then he looked back to the man speaking to him; except for the good-natured sparkle in his eyes, the man went on as if nothing had happened.

Callie caught the smart of tears the gesture had brought to Olina's eyes and determined she'd not aspire to become a maid no matter how fine the hotel. Perhaps she'd be a teacher like Ma'am and Miss Heisinger. She'd never known anyone but her brother to take such advantage of a teacher.

"WFM, Western Federation of Miners, they call themselves. Wastrels, Foreigners, and Misfits is more like it."

"Insurrectionists is what they are. Country's going to the dogs when these scalawags get in power. Owners ought to band together and get the Pinkertons in here. Infiltrate and investigate these socialist buffoons before we have another Coeur d'Alene on our hands."

An elderly lady sitting bolt upright, her old-fashioned bustle holding her at least six inches from the chair back, motioned to Callie with little eyeglasses on a gold rod. She took two wafers from Callie's platter, never taking her eyes from the dance floor, and Callie moved down the wall to offer the platter to Mr. MacIntosh, who had recovered from his hospital stay despite Elsie's misgivings. He was also elderly and he didn't look at her either, but took a wafer with one hand and began kneading Callie's bottom through her skirts with the other. Mr. MacIntosh made her skin creep up her bones.

For a moment she worried she'd throw up her supper all over the gruesome-smelling, sludge-colored liver mixture smeared across the wafers on her platter.

"Building their own hospital to avoid health deductions. Wait till they see the cost of that and they'll change their song."

"What about that Barney chap that's missing? Nonunion man, wasn't he, and a shift boss to boot?"

"Probably just the heel-itch. You know these miners—always moving about. If he's the one I think he is, he's got carrot-red hair."

"Shift bosses don't move around so much. Union's done away with him."

Callie, sick and angry, reported Mr. MacIntosh to Mrs. Stollsteimer. She expected the formidably moral housekeeper to march out and confront him, but found herself hushed instead.

"Don't say such nasty things about poor old Mr. MacIntosh," Mrs. Stollsteimer whispered, and took Callie off to a corner of the dining room. That was the first Callie knew the woman could whisper. The words "discreet" and "ladylike" hurried from the housekeeper's lips, and the admonition for Callie never to place her backside within reach of a gentleman. Callie came away with the feeling that she was the nasty one.

When the girls lay exhausted in their darkened room, Callie asked Olina about the right and wrong of the matter. Gentlemen and men in general, Olina explained none too patiently, had certain urges in their natures that caused them to do things a lady did not discuss and did not entice a gentleman to do in the first place. Men could only control these urges if a lady behaved herself. Olina then promptly fell asleep, leaving Callie wondering if the ladies flopping themselves around on the dance floor enticed trouble for their backsides. And what about *them*, those gorgeous creatures who paraded with her Aunt Lilly after three o'clock in the afternoon?

The ball had set off the three-day July Fourth holiday. But Mrs. Stollsteimer's girls and the rest of the staff at the hotel did not have a holiday. The work load doubled on Colorado Avenue when the merrymakers streamed into town. Callie worried her father wouldn't be able to find her as she gulped gluey oatmeal under the housekeeper's impatient eye. And she'd saved up so much to talk to him about. First she'd confront him with the presence of a live Aunt Lilly in Telluride, then tell him about the wonderful big schoolhouse here and ask if she could go there as soon as Bram left the hospital and didn't need her wages. Callie still did not like cleaning things. And she wanted to write to her mother and brother, but had no money for paper and postage. And her shoes were too small, causing her toenails to turn back into her flesh to fester and bleed.

When John O'Connell did find her, Callie was on her hands and knees scrubbing around the battered cuspidors in the ballroom. She stiffened in his embrace, remembering Mr. MacIntosh's hands, and knew she'd never be able to tell him about it. But Pa was just as eager to be away as he had been to hold her. "The stiffs are marching," he said mysteriously. "And it needs doing. I love ya, Callie darling, and here's a letter from your Bram that came inside one to me."

Callie couldn't understand why the miners would be marching today since the parade wasn't until tomorrow. She bent listlessly to the gruesome floor, Bram's letter unopened in her pocket. She'd save it as something to look forward to, to help her get through the terrible tedium of her day.

"Eight-hour day," Mrs. Stollsteimer remarked at supper, "even my girls work longer than that."

There'd been a clamor in the street—yelling, with gunshots for emphasis, and occasional powder blasts that shook the hotel. Callie had assumed it all part of the festivities until there were wild scurryings among the more genteel in the hotel.

"The bastards have shut down the Smuggler-Union!" a gentleman cried to another, and almost tripped over Callie, again on her hands and knees. Apparently some union men who'd struck in May had surrounded the Smuggler-Union and forced the scabs hired to replace them to stop work. The first report was that a hundred lay dying, but the figure kept coming down all day. By supper the hotel staff learned that union men forced the scabs to march over thirteen-thousand-foot Imogene Pass to Ouray without shoes and told them never to come to Telluride. Callie hoped these union men weren't the stiffs her pa was marching with and that he hadn't joined the union with Ma'am too far away to stop him. She didn't see why he should; they already had an eight-hour day at Alta.

The next morning Mrs. Stollsteimer surprised the girls by letting them watch the July Fourth parade from a third-story window. There was a subdued expectancy instead of the boisterousness this holiday usually generated. The governor of the state of Colorado was sending the lieutenant governor to try to talk the union and the management of the Smuggler-Union into a peaceful settlement of their dispute. It was rumored that Arthur Collins, manager of the Smuggler-Union, had asked the governor to send troops. The latest tally of the results of the disturbance of the day before was three dead and three hurt.

Even up above it all now Callie could feel the tension in the air. For one thing the fashionable ladies and gentlemen stood on the hotel side of the street. Miners, some with families, crowded the other side. She looked among them for Pa but didn't see him.

Boys darted about setting off firecrackers, horses whinnied in terror, dogs barked and ran around in confusion while men cursed them. Babies cried and giant powder exploded at unexpected intervals on the mountainsides. But the red-white-and-blue flags stuck in the storefronts and the small ones held in hands fluttered halfheartedly. Someone had even shoveled up the street, and only a hint of blotchy stains from the horse traffic showed on its dirt surface.

A brass band marched by in straight lines, tooting mightily with only a few squawks, and for a while tension eased. A fire wagon pulled by huge horses followed, and then a team of barefoot men in their long underwear pulled the hose cart. Wagons rolled beneath her, festooned with pine boughs and young ladies in lovely white dresses. They looked like floral bouquets sprinkled amidst the green of pine needles and made Callie hate her old-lady black dress even more. Men sat ramrod straight on prancing, shying horses. Others walked in uneven rows and some wore strange robes and hats or gaudy costumes or uniforms. All were faceless under their hats from her vantage point above.

"Knights of Pythias, Order of Redmen, the Masons," Opal Mae identified each group in a tone of wonder Callie couldn't fathom. Half were tripping on their skirts or couldn't keep their swords hanging straight.

The sound and panoply moved away down Colorado Avenue and the flags went limp and the smell of fresh horse droppings rose in the mountain sunlight to Callie's window. And the people shuffled and stared at each other across the street once more.

24

MILDRED Heisinger absently pressed and pushed at wrinkles in her white gloves, licked a finger to brush at a smudge on one of them. Two engines pulled the train straining around a mountain curve so convoluted she could see the engines across a ravine out the window of her car. The lead engine billowed gray-black smoke that obliterated all sight of the mountainside on which it traveled. The second engine did the same with white steam, and the two vapors mixed to twine through pine and aspen and looked like a grounded thundercloud. The trip back had been long and tedious for Mildred. She looked forward to the suite at the New Sheridan for which she'd wired ahead. And a deep hot bath to cleanse away the grit of the train cloud blowing through open windows. The air had cooled as they'd gained elevation, but the scented pads shielding her travel suit from her armpits gave off unpleasant reminders of the tax one paid to travel.

The young ladies with her were agog, fluttering among empty seats to catch the vistas on either side, gasping and chattering at what they saw when looking down, holding on to their hats and leaning far forward to look up. They were seven in all. A discreet advertisement in a Kansas City newspaper had netted twelve applicants from which she'd selected nine, and at the last minute two had grown faint of heart at the thought of leaving home. Still a goodly number considering the commission she was to receive from the town for each, in addition to her salary and expenses. And they were all young, of good moral character, and every one had at least a year of work experience. Her prize, Audrey Cranston, settled across from Mildred now, excitement sparking in her eyes like the sparks from the engine stacks. Audrey had worked three years as a bookkeeper for a foundry and came highly recommended.

Although these young ladies were from modest backgrounds, they had a flair for independence and self-support with which Mildred could identify. They'd heard so much of the "wild west," the "Rocky Mountain Majesty," and the lore of the mining camps that her job had practically been done for her. They couldn't believe that an entire town wanted them. And that someday when they did decide to give up their independence to marry (which all young ladies except Mildred planned to do eventually), Telluride overflowed with strong young men from which to choose.

"Will we see Indians in Telluride?" Audrey asked her now.

"It's possible. Races are held along the railroad track on the July Fourth holiday and many Indians and Mexicans come to race their horses. There may still be some lounging around the depot." Mildred was confident she'd found the perfect employment as she gazed with fond good humor at her enthusiastic charges. She'd warned them of the vicious storms of winter, the rudimentary services and shopping available in a mining camp. But they were on a pioneering adventure and Mildred felt a glow at having helped others find their dreams. And all she need do was to stay in fine hotels, dine out, visit museums and department stores, dress in the latest fashions, and read. On this trip she'd limited her interviews to three hours in the afternoons and had the rest of the day to do as she pleased. Mildred wondered at other women's desire to marry and had noted long ago how quickly all but the rich wearied and faded once they began the inevitable childbearing.

Charlene Rassmussen sat beside Mildred and gave her an impetuous hug. "Thank you, thank you, thank you. It's all so beautiful and I'm so happy."

"You haven't even seen Telluride yet." Mildred noticed these women did not shutter her out with their eyes but regarded her with respect and something akin to awe. Charlene had worked on a telephone switchboard for a year and had confided to Mildred that her parents insisted she marry a neighbor man with bad teeth, bad skin, bad breath, and thinning hair. Rather than do so, Charlene had left home to come to Telluride.

Mildred and her companions had attracted a good deal of attention on their trip and particularly the farther west they traveled. One gentleman pointed out an eagle to them now. Charlene smiled at him. He did not have bad teeth or skin or thin hair but was rather handsome in a ruddy sort of way. His speech was educated but his clothes those of a rough workman and his mustache needed trimming. His eyes seemed busy catching every detail both inside and outside.

Mildred forgot about him as the train crossed a high mountain valley with vast herds of cattle, stopping at each little settlement along the way, and her new friends exclaimed at the number of young cowboys hanging about the depots. But she noticed the ruddy man again as they all stretched their legs on the station platform at Ridgway before boarding the narrow-gauge train that would take them into the even loftier San Juans.

"Do ya live in these parts, miss?" He appeared beside her and now his speech matched his clothing.

"I live in Telluride . . . for the moment." The fact was she had no permanent address and the idea that she might like to invest some of her earnings in a house came to her just then. It was suspect for a woman not to have a home. But then, almost everything but marriage was. "And you?"

"Oh, I've come to work the mines." He watched her like he seemed to everyone and everything. "Hear a man can make his fortune in the San Juans."

When they reached Telluride he tipped his hat to them and swung off down the tracks with a bedroll over his shoulder. No Indians were there to meet them but Audrey seemed not to notice, just swirled her skirts in an effort to take in all the peaks at once, and a piece of her unruly hair loosened from her coiled braid. "I know I'm going to like it here."

An agent from Lawyer Barada introduced himself and guided them to a livery surrey. But Mildred feared the hanging dust from the streets and mule droppings from a loading packtrain along the way might dispel the good intentions of the town's greeting. The agent deposited her at the New Sheridan, explaining that central lodgings had been provided for her charges at the Victoria Hotel until they were settled in employment. Lawyer Barada was not in his office at the Sheridan Office Building next to the hotel, so she left the list of the young ladies' qualifications with his clerk. Though weary, Mildred felt good about her trip as she shook out and hung the new clothes she'd bought in Kansas City. The next trip would be to Chicago, with Lawyer Barada's approval.

Callie witnessed her ex-teacher's grand entrance but Miss Heisinger looked right at and through her like the other guests of the hotel. The lieutenant governor of the state of Colorado had arranged a truce between the management of the Smuggler-Union Mine and

Miner's Union No. 63, Western Federation of Miners. Now the stiffs at the Smuggler received a straight three dollars for an eight hour day like those who worked the other mines around, and the town returned to a wary peace. The mine owners were less than happy with the arrangement. Callie heard much mention of "damned red-necks" and the injustices of a pro-labor government in Denver as gentlemen passed her in the halls or lobby.

And it was in the lobby she loved to be, especially when the sun shone in to warm her. The day after Miss Heisinger arrived, Callie was sent to dust the moldings, tables, Mr. Root's cage front, and the top strip of wood on the wainscoting. Callie was hoping to chance upon a daydream to help her through the day when the housekeeper swept in from the hall to the ballroom and caught her gazing out the window, feather duster stilled in midair.

"What am I to do with her, Mr. Root? She's not worth the money to feed."

Mr. Root just shook his head and polished his spectacles with a handkerchief. When the spectacles were off, one of his eyes wandered off by itself.

"Callie, Opal Mae is sick with a bad tooth and can barely raise her head. You'll have to hurry and finish here and help Cora on second."

Callie climbed to her room before going to help Cora and reread Bram's letter. Her brother had wanted to die but Ma'am wouldn't let him. Now he wanted to leave the hospital and Denver. "I'm lonesome for you, Callie girl, and still so weak. Please write. Ma'am wonders why you don't write also."

Callie took off her shoes and rubbed the sores on her toes. She had highgraded some writing materials from the hotel but she was afraid to highgrade coins for postage. Callie buttoned on the torturesome shoes again, slipped into the hall and down the staircase to Miss Heisinger's suite. Just as she put her knuckles to the door, her teacher opened it.

Miss Heisinger was dressed for dinner, a summer dress of lace and bows. The ruffles were wrinkled some but her hair and skin shone. Her long gloves and reticule matched perfectly. She smelled of soap and powder and she walked directly into Callie. The girl fell backward onto the carpet runner.

"I'm sorry. I didn't see . . . Callie? Callie O'Connell?" A gloved hand reached down to help Callie to her feet. "What are you doing here?"

"I'm sent out to work." Callie looked away in embarrassment at the memory of her brother carrying a kicking, disheveled teacher through the heart of the camp. How could she ask her for money to send a letter to that very brother?

"Why are you sent out to work so young? You are such a fine student."

"My family has troubles just now, ma'am. My brother—"

"Oh yes, your brother." Miss Heisinger's voice lowered and Callie winced. "I heard of the accident. I'm sorry."

"Callie, there you are." Cora peeked out the door next to Miss Heisinger's. "Hurry, we must finish this suite before the evening train arrives. A very important guest is coming."

Callie turned back to Miss Heisinger, only to find her gliding away down the hall.

Where was she to get the postage money? Callie swiped at dresser tops and windowsills as Cora fussed about with a carpet sweeper. It wasn't as if she needed a great fortune. As the train whistle signaled the imminent arrival of their important guest, Callie paused to look out the window. The buildings across Colorado Avenue were lower than the hotel and she could see over them to the dark side of town. Daylight seemed always to linger longer here. There buildings were well lit and through the glass she could hear already the low murmur that hummed on those streets at night.

Her Aunt Lilly lived. And she lived over there. And she loved Bram as much as anyone. If Callie could find her, Aunt Lilly would surely see Bram's letter sent off to Denver.

25

CHARLES lay on his back on Tracy's bed, his hind feet in the air, his tail up over his lower stomach concealing his nether regions in a modesty suitable to a Victorian cat. The pink lining of his ears, the pink slant of his closed eyelids, the pink outline of his nose and mouth were the only color on him. The rest was snowy fluff. The soft life was making Charles fat. And clean.

Two daybeds, two dressers, and a TV set shoved up against the outside door about filled the crib's front room. The back room was a kitchen except for a small section walled off for a bathroom. The place was even smaller than Callie's cabin in Alta.

Tracy lay on her daybed next to Charles and watched television. She'd hung her *Dr. Miles's Number One Hundred and Fifty Gonorrhea and Gleet* poster over a bad patch on the wall and a sketch that Aletha had drawn over another.

Aletha stretched out on her own daybed and attempted to read one of the books on Telluride Cree had lent her. *The names of the fabulous gold and silver mines of the region will live forever in the annals of man's wealth and greed, fortitude and destructiveness. The great Sheridan Mine, the Tomboy, the Smuggler-Union, the Blackbear, the Nellie, and the Gold King—to name a few of the larger employers—hired hundreds of miners, millmen, engineers, and office workers. Their combined payrolls supported most of the business in town. So when strife emerged between management and union—*

"So when it comes to dishwashing detergent there's no substitute for Subdue. Mrs. Callus's spotless glassware demonstrates why."

—of the Smuggler-Union, an Englishman, Arthur Collins, was hired as manager. Familiar with the methods used in the copper mines of Cornwall and aware of the need for greater output and profit, Collins instituted the fathom system whereby a miner was paid by the fathoms of earth broken rather than by the regular eight-hour shift at the standard rate of three dollars. Men found themselves working longer hours for less pay. The union struck and Collins hired scab labor to continue operations and hired it at the regular three dollars for an eight-hour shift for which the union had struck to begin with. On July 3, two hundred and fifty striking miners attacked as the night shift of scabs came off work. Four men died in the battle and the offending scabs were forced to march over a rocky divide without shoes and told never to return. Peace was restored for a time through the efforts of the state government but—

"Aletha, I got to tell you something."

—and the tragic fire at the Smuggler-Union Mine the next November when twenty-eight men lost their lives. A series of avalanches at the Liberty Bell—

"And now, Mrs. Hannah, can you tell me for four *hundred* dollars what is the name of—"

—*the dashing Bulkeley Wells, Harvard graduate, son-in-law of Colonel Thomas Livermore of Boston. Livermore owned the New England Exploration Company which in turn owned the Smuggler-Union. Wells oversaw his father-in-law's mining interests as well as the vast Whitney holdings from his offices in Denver and fully supported Arthur Collins's antiunion stand.*

"Aletha, I lied to you about why Larry left."

—*when Arthur Collins advertised that he would rehire the scab labor on a published list of—*

"Will you listen to me? This is important."

"Why did Larry leave you?"

"Because I gave him herpes."

—*the bloodshed. Arthur Collins was murdered in his home in Pandora, a settlement with giant stamp mills in the valley below the Smuggler-Union tunnels, by a gunshot blast through the window as he—* "You gave him what?"

"You heard me. That was the only breakout I've had since I came to Telluride and I haven't had one since. Honest."

Charles rolled over onto his stomach. He watched Tracy cry. His slant eyes held no trace of sympathy.

They worked the Senate that night and were invited to go to a party at Renata's afterward. Renata lived several miles out of Telluride on a narrow mountain road with nothing but mailboxes and driveways to suggest there might be houses hidden off in the trees. Aletha found it only because Tracy had been there.

Renata greeted them at the door of a multilevel wood-and-glass thing that climbed a hillside. Where did she find the time and the sun to maintain that tan? She wore a creamy-colored backless pants outfit. Why didn't she have goosebumps? She drew Aletha into the room, leaving Tracy to fend for herself. "And where's Cree, do you know? I haven't been able to get hold of him."

"I think he wants to be alone for a while."

"Please tell me he is not writing a book. Writers ask a lot of questions and then want to be left alone for a while. And take it from me, they are the most insipid people you'll ever meet."

The first floor had a sunken living room and greenhouse with a frothy hot tub. A ledge and steps separated the two. The kitchen monopolized a mezzanine and the two levels above were given over to bedrooms. The front walls were all glass. Most of the people here were in their thirties, a fair number of them pregnant. Blue jeans and designer thighs were much in evidence, especially as one got out of the other to slip into the hot tub.

Aletha watched a woman cut piles of cocaine with a razor blade into lines on a glass tray in one of the bedrooms, watched the excitement of those around her with rolled bills already in hand. The coke reminded her of Cree, of the people who had cut down his partner and might now be after him.

Renata's wall art was art—paintings, sketches, watercolors, prints, and rather surprisingly all Western. Aletha would have expected Renata to go for something more "in." And on the wall along the staircase leading to the kitchen was an original signed by Jared Kingman. Aletha almost spilled her wine down her front. She'd had a running fantasy in prison that her father broke in and rescued her, took her to a hideout somewhere on the desert. And she lived happily ever after keeping house for him while he painted and she never saw another living soul as long as she lived.

Aletha's first ten years of life had been hand-to-mouth (the Phoenix Kingmans would have said squalid) but she was generally content with the long warm afternoons of the Southwest that offered hours of outdoor playtime after school, the freedom of having a working mother unable to organize them for her, and a father largely absent. She did object to the constant moving, often just ahead of the creditors. Life was a succession of rented rooms with a blanket concealing her parents' bed from hers, meals bought from carry-out joints or snatched at restaurants and taking up most of the money not spent on rent. But it was the change in schools and friends that was hard. Aletha never overcame her terror of entering a classroom of strange faces waiting for her to do something embarrassing.

Aletha was born in Taos, a scant two months after Jared married her mother. Helen had wandered in from Missouri. She had no close family ties. Jared had been born to a family in Phoenix who rejected him because he chose the bohemian life instead of the professional career intended for him. Two drifters had drifted together. Aletha adored her father, probably because he'd done little parenting. She'd heard him referred to as a "beatnik" and a "deadbeat." Sometimes their lodgings had television, usually a shared one in a central lobby, and Aletha had noticed that Jared wasn't anything like the father on *Leave It to Beaver*. He deserted them in Tucson. It was shortly after that that Bertie Hollister began visiting Helen and life took on some changes. There was suddenly money for a real kitchen, gymnastics classes, a bicycle, an orthodontist.

Bertie was a contractor with a wife and three children. When he divorced them, he married Helen and moved her and Aletha to San Diego. He did well there. Helen changed into a matron-type like on TV and Aletha was sent to a private school where she was miserable. The polish took in some places but was superficial in others and tended to rub holes in the social fabric. She began to feel like two people. Bertie was good to her but California never felt like home and when it came time for college she opted to go back to New Mexico. But Albuquerque didn't feel right either and Aletha realized she had no home and this unsettled her even more.

The known list of her father's paintings was small and many had ended up with the Kingmans in Phoenix. Aletha had not seen this one, but it was typical. A picture of a peaceful pueblo, Indians going about the business of life, carrying water jugs up ladders, eating on a rooftop, children playing with dogs—all unfashionably realistic, the colors so perfect you could smell the smoke from the cooking fires. Too perfect. Except that all the human figures and even the dogs had grotesquely shortened legs. Down in the left corner a rusting automobile sat on blocks.

There was always something jarring in the idyllic scenes her father created. Maybe he'd been two people too. Helen contended he just never grew up. Helen had several of Jared's paintings. One was a landscape with interesting shadows, cactuses, textures in the sandy earth, deserted fenceposts dragging their wires on the ground, and in the background two saguaros copulating.

Renata Winslow appeared at her side. "I hear there's naughty stuff going on upstairs. Would that help you get in the party mood?"

"There is. It wouldn't."

"There's always the hot tub. Your glass is empty. Let me get you . . . white wine?"

"Red."

"You do buck the conventions, don't you?" Renata led her to a wet bar tucked under the redwood stairs. "Hey, loosen up. We'll just ignore what's going on upstairs and hope there're no undercover task forces around. What can I do? Drugs happen." A table had appeared on the ledge between the greenhouse and living room. Pâté, raw veggies, deviled eggs, spicy things in unknown wrappings, fruit, cheese, pastries.

"Catered," Renata answered the question Aletha hadn't asked. Aletha had been thinking of Callie just then, wondering what was happening in her world at this moment. She had the feeling that the past was happening right now just on the other side of the wall. And she wanted to erase Jared Kingman again.

"There are two things I insist we discuss." Renata helped her fill a plate and moved her away from the lines forming at the table. "First, what's this Cree tells me about you pulling magical tricks? Are you holding out on me? Are you connected with the film festival?"

Around gobbles of egg, sips of wine, crunches of cauliflower and broccoli dipped in herbed-yogurt goo, Aletha whispered to her employer about Callie, holes in walls, even Charles and the two filthy cowboys. Suddenly it felt good to talk about it.

Renata folded her arms and the sheen of her hair and outfit blurred in Aletha's eyes before Renata stared her down. "I don't believe a word of it."

"Of course not. What was the second thing you wanted to discuss?"

"Well, this you'd *better* believe. The sheriff says that Cree has an airplane at Montrose airport."

"So? I knew that."

"Did you know it's full of bullet holes? Did you know that some sort of investigator from Wyoming is in town asking questions about Cree? I don't want to get involved, Aletha, but I think Cree should be warned. If he's not dead already."

26

"MY dear Miss Heisinger, your concern for qualifications is most laudable," Lawyer Barada said as he led Mildred into the hotel dining room, where females were admitted in the evening only if accompanied by a gentleman. When she dined alone it was either in her suite or in a small room set aside for ladies. "But unfortunately the need is such that the town cannot afford to be quite so selective. Commercial interests here are willing to train the young and inexperienced and, in fact, prefer ladies at this stage if the ultimate goal is to enlarge the pool of marriage partners for our robust miners." He seated her in a private booth but did not bother to draw the curtains. They were early for dinner and there were few in the dining room. He pressed a button in the wainscoting to indicate their readiness for service and a bell tinkled faintly by the entrance to the kitchen. Then he leaned back and studied her under raised white brows. "I must say employment and travel do suit you."

Mildred lowered her eyes in modest embarrassment, rejoicing at how well she knew she looked. "I feel worn after such an extended journey and fear it shows to my disadvantage."

"Poppycock, you look fresh as a flower in May, Miss Heisinger." He rubbed his hands together in the gesture of a much younger man. "And I hope you'll say you're ready to travel again soon. The damsels you brought us yesterday have only whetted our appetites."

"I tried calling on them this morning at the Victoria and found them gone."

"I too thought it distressing they'd not had time to settle in and have a look at the camp before being snatched up by their employers, but they were the first batch and the need was great. I daresay you'll see them about the shops as they've trained for their new duties." He ordered for them both—vichyssoise, baked ptarmigan in sauce, vegetables in pastry, fruits fresh from the counties around, imported cheeses.

Mildred was not as impressed by the cuisine as the last time she'd dined here with Lawyer Barada. In fact, a plain stew would have sounded more appetizing. She'd eaten in so many elegant hotels since, that her hunger for rich sauces was more than sated. In the cities the dining rooms were larger than this but the somber thick carpets, the brown wainscoting that reached seven feet up the wall, and the wallpaper not much lighter above that—all were reminiscent of the dark masculine luxury that pertained to hotel dining rooms in general. When the main course arrived she said, "I rather thought I'd like to stay for a bit and perhaps look for a small house."

"Excellent idea. I was intending to counsel that you invest some of your earnings toward a more secure future. And what better way than in the very town that provides your wages." He set down his fork with the food still on it and raised his wineglass to her. "Really, Miss Heisinger, you surprise me. You've a head on your shoulders worthy of a man—although far prettier." He chuckled a dry coughing sound and drank to her. "But let us not bother that pretty head over such matters as houses when my agent can scout about for one while you are scouting for more young females for Telluride."

"But it would take very little time, as the town is not large and is overcrowded. There cannot be so many choices, after all. And I don't wish to presume upon your good offices any more than I have done already."

"Nonsense, my dear. No presumption on your part. I insist. Besides, I have contacts that you do not and can hunt out the best possible properties."

"I don't have the money to purchase a home at present. I thought merely to look around and determine prices, establish an account at the bank to save toward—"

"After another successful trip for the town your credit will be good in Telluride, Miss Heisinger. Which reminds me . . ." He slipped another bulging envelope across the table to her and raised his glass once more. "To the continuation of a fruitful partnership and to a safe and profitable journey for you. Your ticket on tomorrow's train is included as well."

"Tomorrow. But I've not had time to—"

"And time is of the essence, I'm sure you understand." He turned as two gentlemen entered the room. "Buck? Buck Wells, you young rake, is that you?"

One of the gentlemen was more handsome than any drawing Mildred had ever seen. Tall, slim, and aristocrat-straight. From the polish on his shoes to the glossy sheen of his black hair, the perfectly matching arch of heavy brows over enormous dark eyes to the flawless bone structure and clean-shaven chin—this was a vision Mildred could not have fantasized whole even in a girlish daydream had she not first seen him as a model. "Dashing" was downright paltry for description.

"Homer, you old shyster, good to see you." He towered above the lawyer, who'd risen to greet him, cuffed him on the shoulder and pumped his hand. His voice was a mellow, studied rumble, his consonants clipped in the Eastern fashion. "I've come to confer with Collins here on the redneck problem."

"Not surprised. Terrible injustice being done in this region. But what of the Colonel? And how are Grace and the children?"

"All well and hearty. And you, sir?" And the vision turned to Mildred. "You seem always to be in good form . . . and company."

Mildred glimpsed a world beyond her own pretensions and for a moment even realized them as such. She felt like a servant girl masquerading in this place, in these fine clothes, in this presence.

"Let me introduce you. Miss Mildred Heisinger, formerly a schoolmistress, presently a true friend of the camp. Mr. Bulkeley Wells, formerly of Boston, presently of Denver. Mr. Arthur Collins, formerly of England, presently manager of the fabulous Smuggler-Union."

Mr. Collins, a sallow creature next to his companion, nodded curtly. Mr. Wells actually bowed and smiled. The misalignment of his front teeth did nothing to dispel the dazzle. But both men's eyes followed her hand as it slipped the fat envelope off the linen tablecloth onto her lap.

"Delighted," said Mr. Bulkeley Wells, and Mildred felt the relief of air returning to her lungs as his remarkable eyes turned back to the lawyer. "We could use your counsel this night, you old war horse."

"Well, I have dined but I might sip a brandy while you are at your dinner. I'm sure Mildred will excuse us. My dear, do not miss your train."

Mildred couldn't leave the dining room fast enough, couldn't sleep that night for the vision of hypnotic eyes and gleaming hair, for the discomfort of feeling so out of place in a world in which she thought she'd finally found a place. As she left her suite for the train the next day she met him again, coming out of the door next to hers.

"Ah, the beguiling Miss Heisinger." Once more he bowed, this time deeper, and reached for a hand she hadn't offered, brushed his lips across her glove. Was he trying to make more of a fool of her with his old-fashioned ways, or did people of his class still carry on in this manner? "I'm saddened to see that you're leaving so soon upon my arrival. Perhaps another time?"

Mildred had never swooned and had no intention of beginning the silly practice, but she did feel dizzy looking up at him and decided she must be too tightly laced. He steadied her by the hand he still held and looked over her head.

"Are you Doud?" he asked someone Mildred hadn't realized had come up behind her.

"I am, sir."

"You'll excuse us?" Mr. Bulkeley Wells bowed again and Mildred hurried away again, but not before she'd seen the man, Doud. He was the ruddy gentleman determined to be a miner who'd traveled on the train to Telluride with her and her charges. She heard them talking out of sight above her as she descended the stairs.

"I've seen that lady before and she's seen me. What if she talks out of turn about us meeting?"

"I shouldn't worry, Mr. Doud. She's leaving town for some while and women of that stripe are rarely listened to seriously."

Mildred paused on the stairs and brought her gloved hands to hot cheeks. *Women of that stripe?* What could he mean by that? Surely not what came first to her own mind.

Callie O'Connell fingered the crisp paper of her letter to Bram in her apron pocket for reassurance and slipped out the front door of the New Sheridan Hotel right behind Mildred Heisinger. Miss Heisinger stepped into the livery carriage, carefully keeping her skirts from the mud. Callie set off smartly down the sidewalk as if she'd been sent on an errand. It was possible that if she hurried she could be back before she was missed, but it wasn't likely.

It was a good while before three o'clock in the afternoon, though, and her presence on Colorado Avenue caused no startled glances. She expected something terrible to happen when she turned off into the forbidden south side of town. But all was unnaturally quiet. There seemed to be no one about but a couple of stray burros rummaging in an offal heap in the alley. Many tiny houses like the ones in Aletha's drawing book crowded together, but there was no life about them. She could hear the train chugging at the depot and the river splashing across the tracks. Finally she found a man sweeping out the livery stable. She had to step over piles of horse dung dumped in the gutter. Flies made an awful din in the quiet here.

"Please, sir, I'm looking for my Aunt Lillian. Can you tell me where she lives? She's fair and pretty and—"

"Lil? I think there's a Lil at the Pick and Gad." He pointed down the street toward the river. "But I don't think you should be going there, lass." He eyed her uniform. "You one of Mrs. Stollsteimer's girls?"

"Thank you, sir." Callie hurried on in the direction he'd pointed. Her heart pounded in expectation of some catastrophic retribution that would fall from the sky. Guilt made her hands sweat and her mouth dry up. But she couldn't *see* what was forbidden about this place. It simply looked run-down and crowded.

The air was heavy with beer and refuse and she welcomed the cool, sweet breeze that came down off the mountainside. Most of the big buildings had names written on their windows and appeared to be saloons. The Pick and Gad had a small sign over the open door. Curtains hung out of two windows upstairs like white lacy flags. Callie knocked on the door molding and waited, finally entered a dark passageway and continued along it to the back of the house and the light at its end, surprising a woman mopping a kitchen floor. "What are you doing here, child?" She was short and round and untidy. "Are you one of Mrs. Stollsteimer's girls?"

"I'm looking for my Aunt Lil. I was told she lives here."

"Lil? An aunt?" She scratched her face. It wasn't painted. "Oh, I don't think so . . . well . . . wait here." She slapped the mop back into the bucket and went to a door at the side of the kitchen. "Leona, there's a little girl here. Says Lil's her aunt."

All Callie heard of the answer was a throaty chuckle. A lady sat at a dining table when the scrubwoman motioned Callie into the room. She wore a robe over her nightdress and had droopy streaks of color on her face. She was eating from an egg cup. A ledger book lay in front of her on the table.

"I don't know what you're about, my girl, but Lil has no kin." Sunlight from the window behind Leona glistened on the flyaways of her hair, made them look like broken spiderwebs. She was apparently one of *them*, and *they* certainly were unlike any ladies Callie knew.

"I'm looking for my Aunt Lilly Midden Ostrander."

Leona smiled so big all her teeth and gums showed, and one tooth had a darkness to it. But when she turned her head to the scrubwoman it caught the light like a jewel. "Do you think she means Floradora? She was a Lillian, wasn't she?"

"My aunt's not Floradora, she's—"

"Names change here, and fast. But I think it's Floradora you want. Too independent to work for me, that one. You remember, Sarah, that's the one thought she'd make it alone in a crib like the scragglies, keep all her money, and get rich. She'll be back. But by then I may not want her." She rose and closed her robe around her with a hand that had rings that glittered like her tooth, then led Callie out a back door and between two of those tiny houses to a street. Callie had never known a grown woman to step outside in her nightdress if her house wasn't on fire. "That's the Silver Bell on the corner there. You want the crib but one behind it. Best knock on the back door. Who'd have thought to see one of Mrs. Stollsteimer's girls on Pacific Avenue?" She laughed, patted Callie on the top of the head. "Tell your aunt you was sent by Diamond Tooth Leona. And then get the hell out of this part of town."

Callie ran. The likelihood of her absence at the hotel going undiscovered grew ever thinner, but she still had hopes. By the time her Aunt Lilly answered her knock on the back door of the tiny house, Callie was near tears. But Aunt Lilly let hers fall, as she hugged and kissed her. "Callie darling, oh . . . you shouldn't be here. How's Bram? I've been so worried. How'd you get to Telluride?" Aunt Lilly smelled strange.

That night up in Alta, John O'Connell poked in the dirt beneath the house where once he'd lived with his family intact. He was grateful for the pounding of the mill and hoped the night would hide his legs sticking out for all to see as he lay flat on his stomach and tried to explore the ground by feel. He could hear footsteps on the boards above him as the new mistress prepared her kitchen for the morrow.

He'd left a hunk of highgrade here, thinking it to be the safest place because it had always been, and where had he to hide it at the boardinghouse? John was back for it now because he'd received word from Luella that she and Bram would soon start home. That Bram would live but his health had broken. The doctors cautioned he'd be best suited for the life of a sedentary scholar. The thought of that strong young body wasted brought a pain to John's throat that wouldn't swallow. He'd settle them in Telluride, where there was a high school. It seemed that Ma'am was to get her way after all. John would hire out to one of the big mines close to town so he could see them often.

He'd planted the highgrade four hands from a support post and thought sure he could find it even in the dark. And he'd not buried it deep. Perhaps he remembered the wrong post? He crawled farther in, cursing the rocks and stones that jabbed through his clothing. Luella had long ago torn the weather protection off the base of the house so no cat would ever be tempted to live there again, and moonlight appeared suddenly on the ground outside. It glowed on broken crockery in the refuse dump. But something else glowed closer to hand, under the house with him. A piece of white cloth partially buried. As he pulled it free he dislodged earth and felt something smooth beneath it. It wasn't highgrade but it wasn't anything that belonged there, either.

After much digging in the disturbed earth with his hands, John uncovered a round bowl-shaped thing about as large as a dishpan and covered tightly by a lid. It had a smoothness to it he couldn't describe, almost the feel of a rain slicker or glass that had been softened somehow. Beneath that was a package wrapped in a paper-thin oilskinlike material.

He pulled both objects out into the open and slipped over to the mill to inspect his find under one of the outdoor light bulbs on the side of the building. The package contained stacks of paper money, the bills too small to be real and too intensely colored. The bowl was a milky white and had "T-u-p-p-e-r-w-a-r-e" embossed on the lid. At first he thought it was filled with sugar that had a strange opalescent sparkle in the artificial light, but it had a bitter taste and began to numb his tongue as he slipped the fake currency back under the house and kept the bowl in exchange for his highgrade. It wouldn't bring as much, but if it was what he thought it was, perhaps he could convince an apothecary to pay something for it at least.

27

CHARLES prowled Mildred Heisinger's kitchen looking for either chopped liver or mice, Aletha supposed. The ancient lady had called her "snoop" again but let her in. Aletha had stopped at the Chocolate Moose for calorie-laden pastry first and Mildred condescended to put in her teeth and make some of her weak coffee. Mildred offered Charles a bite of éclair. He sniffed it and walked off with one of his more disdainful wails. "Had so many cats in my time, can't remember all their names."

"Can you remember Callie?"

"Didn't have one named that."

"Can't you remember anything about what became of Callie and her brother?"

"I remember the Depression. Hard times they were." Her head trembled constantly as if she was always shaking it to answer "no."

"You must remember something before that." Mildred would have been middle-aged by the time of the Depression, Aletha realized, already middle-aged when Aletha's mother was born. "Were you here when the miners went on strike and Bulkeley Wells—"

"He shot himself in the head out in California. I been to California and I don't blame him." Mildred sat quiet with her thoughts for a few minutes and then sighed. "Pictures in the paper when he died showed him going bald. He was a patrician," she said with a smirk and a bitterness that surprised Aletha, who'd decided the old gal didn't really care about anything anymore. "Been dead longer than you been alive. Had eyes on him so big he could hypnotize whole crowds. They'd do whatever he wanted. Even persuaded the governor to send in the militia. Bunch of boys with rifles—didn't know one end from the other. Threw those union men and anybody else Captain Bulkeley Wells didn't like onto the train and hauled 'em away like cattle. Ruling classes had it all their own way then too."

"Why did Callie O'Connell come to Telluride?"

"Pinkerton detectives in town, pretending to be miners, spying for the Owners' Association and the Alliance."

"Did Callie ever work at the Senate or the Pick and Gad or any place like that?"

"Bob Meldrum, he wasn't afraid of old Buck Wells. He wasn't afraid of anyone. He'd shoot men and kill 'em after he'd picked a fight, just to get a reputation. But he worked for the owners too. Deafer than I am now he was."

"I mean if you lived in this house then you must have known something about what went on in this side of town. Did Callie become a prostitute?"

"Had myself a grand big house on the sunny side of town till the Depression. Used to go out horseback riding with Mrs. Bulkeley Wells and her rich friends from Denver."

"Then why did I see you in the Pick and Gad about to take a bath in a body younger than mine is now?" But she couldn't bring herself to say that loud enough for Mildred to hear. "Do you ever have the feeling that the past is still happening?"

"What did you say your name was, snoop?"

"Aletha. Aletha Kingman."

"There's a book of drawings upstairs with a name like that on it." The fragile skin on her forehead rumpled as if she was trying to remember something. "Haven't looked at it in years."

"Did Callie give it to you?"

"I took it from her. Little sneak."

Aletha must have spent two hours searching through stacks of books and antique magazines before she found it. It was old and dirty and crumbly in places and someone had written *Aleetha* on the front of it. How could Aletha have come to Telluride less than a month ago and sketched those pictures while they'd already been moldering in this attic for decades? Like her sandals up in the museum. How could objects not yet manufactured, let alone conceived of, be deteriorating with age at the same time? They couldn't unless the two times were happening at once. Even then they couldn't.

Mildred Heisinger slept in front of her flashing television when Aletha came downstairs, so she took the sketchbook and Charles and headed back to the crib.

Tracy just rolled her eyes and shook her head when Aletha claimed the sketches were ones she'd done upon first coming to Telluride. "Your stories are so confusing I can't understand them, and I even lived one of them." She was painting her nails a sick purple. "Listen, Renata called. She's got you a job at the Floradora over the dinner hour, and here, Cree left a note for you."

"Oh, good, Renata's got me scared to death for him and he told me not to try to contact him."

"He just stuck it in the screen door. Don't know why he didn't come in. I've been here all morning."

"Says, 'Aletha, please meet me in Alta by the old boardinghouse. I'm desperate, Cree.' "

"Sounds fishy. Is it his handwriting?"

"I don't remember ever seeing his handwriting."

"It stinks." Tracy flailed purple-tipped hands about in the air. "I wouldn't go if I were you. You said he was involved with some dangerous creeps. And I didn't actually see who left the note."

"What would you do, leave him up there alone? Desperate? He doesn't even have a car."

"Then how'd he get up there? I mean he was just here putting the note in the door, right? Why go all the way to Alta to talk to you?"

"Maybe he thinks no one will see us meeting up there, where here they would . . . You're right, it stinks. Go with me? You don't have to be to work till four."

"Oh, so we can both get in trouble if there's some to get into? Nice the way you include a social leper such as myself in your dangerous plans."

"Oh, shut up."

But Tracy went along—on the condition that they stop the car down the road and walk up through the trees to see if this was trouble or not. Once they were away from the road, all the trees looked alike. Aletha just kept them headed uphill until they came to a wooden tower black with age, its top falling over, thick rusting cable hanging from one side and a pine tree trying to grow up its middle. "This must be a tram tower, so if we follow the cable we should get there."

The cable disappeared but a swath of stumps and newer, shorter growth pointed the way. They stayed in the trees to the side, puffing thin air on the up slope. The way Tracy broke twigs climbing over deadfalls and swore when her thin shoes caught between branches, Aletha wondered how much of a sneak operation this would turn out to be. "Hey, I appreciate your coming along. I mean, it's not your problem."

Tracy gave her a crooked grin. "You really got it for this Cree?"

"I'm attracted but leery. Of the two men I trusted most in my life—my dad deserted and a boss got me put in prison." Another falling tower and the view opened onto Alta. A black-and-silver Bronco was parked near the commissary. A man sat inside reading a newspaper. Another man, a long one in blue jeans, lay stretched out facedown on the slope between the mine entrance and the board-inghouse.

"Oh, Aletha, he doesn't look desperate," Tracy whispered. "He looks dead."

Aletha handed her the car keys. "You go back the way we came. Bring help."

"You're not going out there? That's just what they want. Cree's a decoy."

"I think the lady had a real good idea," a low voice said behind them. "In fact, I think it's so good you both ought to go on out there. Now." He sounded like he should have been seven feet tall, bearded, and carrying a submachine gun. But he was a short man with a rifle, clean chin, and nasty eyes. Tracy's eyes were full of accusation again. "Heard your car coming for miles, quiet day like this," he chided, and poked the rifle barrel into Aletha's spine. She'd toked up on adrenaline when she'd seen Cree on the ground. Now, walking out into the open with a gun in her back, Aletha had so much extra nerve juice it made her ears ring. A marmot sat in a boardinghouse window hole. Another whistled up on the mountainside. "Hey, Duffer. She got here. Brought a friend."

The man in the Bronco stepped out, folded his paper, and laid it on the car seat. He stuck a thumb and forefinger in his mouth and whistled twice. An answering two whistles came from down the road. Aletha knelt beside Cree and pulled him over on his back.

"Careful," the man with the rifle said. "I think he might have some broken things."

Cree had swollen lips and blood stringing down from his hairline. But he had a pulse.

"There was some information he refused to share with us," Duffer explained.

"He doesn't know where it is and neither do I."

"I expect he'll be slightly more helpful if he sees that you will be hurt far worse than he is now if he doesn't help. Perhaps we could persuade you to persuade him even."

"Why?" Aletha's stomach cramped. "You'd just kill us all if you found it. You'd have to."

"I'd certainly have to if I didn't," Duffer said pleasantly. Tracy made a noise in her throat. A third man walked up the road from the direction of Callie's house. He had a handgun, out and ready, and an expression of detached disinterest. Duffer didn't look up from his examination of Cree Mackelwain's bruised face. "Wake him. His girlfriend's here."

The new man found an empty beer bottle in the weeds and held it down in the stream that flowed out of the mine's entrance to let it fill with the milky-turquoise water. He poured it slowly on Cree's upturned face, and clotting blood thinned to pinkish rivulets. Aletha reached up to push the bottle away and the man kicked her in the face with his boot before she had time to move or even think. Now Aletha lay on the ground, her mouth so alive with pain it made her nose run. When she wiped it away, blood mixed with mucus on her hand.

"Amazing how easy it is to make a pretty girl ugly, isn't it?" Duffer said, and when Cree moaned he ordered the other two to get him on his feet. "He can see better what we do to the girlfriend."

It was the total lack of emotion that deadened all hope around these men. They didn't even seem to enjoy brutality that much. It was as casual as eating a sandwich. And killing would be too. Aletha could tell from Tracy's expression that this had occurred to her as well. The two gunmen held Cree swaying between them each with an arm through his, leaving them a spare hand for their weapons. He kept coughing and gasping with the pain it brought. He wasn't aware of much else yet. Aletha felt terrible for him but mostly worried she was soon to die while incongruously feeling for loosened teeth with her tongue.

"He thought it must be in the mine, but couldn't find it there," she heard herself saying as if a part of her imagined there was some use to even talking to these machines. And then she listened. Everyone but Cree listened. A car engine? Airplane?

"Into the tunnel." Duffer grabbed the handgun and his friends dragged Cree away while the gun motioned Aletha to her feet.

"We told the sheriff we were coming up here," Tracy offered as she squeezed through the opening between the metal door and the wall of the mine.

"Stuff it, dyke," Duffer told her, and followed Aletha through the opening. The only light in the place came from that crevice they'd entered by, and it didn't come very far. Aletha wanted to bolt for that light, but it would make her such an easy target. Cree moaned and coughed out of the dark.

"Put him down and those two with him. I'm going for the lantern."

Someone grabbed Aletha's hair, yanked her backward until she fell, stuck cold metal behind her ear. "Not one sound. You don't want I should get startled."

The pulled hair smarted and her nose ran again. The light blurred and wavered as her eyes watered, but shadowy objects appeared slowly. She blinked tears and a squarish thing sat in front of her on little wheels. The rock in her necklace lay warm and scratchy between her breasts and then grew almost prickly hot but she was afraid to reach for it with the gun at her head. Duffer returned with a light that hurt her eyes. "Just a pickup passing through to the lakes. Now, where were we?" The light came back to Aletha. "We were going to entertain the girlfriend. He conscious?"

"What the shit?" the man behind Aletha said as more lights appeared above them. Cruel fingers released her hair.

A string of lights appeared on the ceiling. And sounds—the background rumble of the mill in a mining town alive, a clanging of metal striking metal, men's distant voices, the sneezy smells of raw timber and dusty hay. The iron door to the outside had dissolved and the gray-metal skeleton of the snowshed extended toward the mill. In the other direction the overhead lights stretched into the distance and disappeared. The cavernous tunnel had no end now. Duffer switched off his battery lantern and turned a complete circle, staring at the change in the scenery. The man with the rifle walked a short distance down the track.

"Aletha?" Cree was sitting up holding his head and squinting at her. "Run. Get out of here!"

The growls of clearing throats, snorts, hacking coughs, laughter, boots crunching gravel—a group of men, perhaps twenty or more—moved along the tunnel toward them. They carried small round pails with lids and long hammers and other tools Aletha didn't know. They wore droopy water-stained hats, a few with unlit candles in metal holders still in the brims. The man with the rifle raised it. His face had lost its mechanical look.

"Aletha," Tracy said in a breathy voice, as if she'd been running, "I think for once you did something right."

"You did this?" Duffer turned to Aletha and then quickly back to the advancing men. Their faces were so dirty they looked as if they'd tried to disguise themselves with blackface. The ones in front slowed and stopped, and were jostled from behind. They spread out. The laughter and coughing quieted. Eyes rested on the guns aimed at them.

"Hit's the angel wot warned of the cave-in."

"Angels don't bleed."

"Them women are wearing pants."

"What do we do, Duffer?"

"We get out of here. Cover our exit." Duffer was already backing down the tracks into the snowshed. He dropped the lantern. He turned and ran between stacks of lumber and baled hay to a side door. The other two followed, not bothering to keep their weapons trained on the miners, who were beginning to growl again, but not from phlegm this time.

Cree lay back down, coughing and groaning. As Aletha started for him, he and the light closed up in the cat-eye oval and disappeared. Tracy stood in the niche between the iron door and the earthen wall.

"Help me with Cree," Aletha told her. "He's right over here."

But the muddied miners and the sounds and the smells and the injured Cree Mackelwain were gone.

28

Mrs. Stollsteimer met Callie O'Connell at the kitchen door off the alley as the girl tried to sneak back into the hotel after her visit to the shaded side of Telluride. The housekeeper gave Callie the nastiest duties available and promised to end her employment the minute she could contact one of her parents. But John O'Connell arrived in the next week to talk her into reconsidering. He promised Callie would never do such a thing again. "She's but a child, ma'am, here to learn under your fine teaching." He explained that his ailing wife and invalid son would soon be returning from Denver and he'd been able to find only a room to house them. They needed Callie's earnings as never before. He'd found himself a place at the Smuggler and a bed at its boardinghouse. He took Callie aside and gave her a wink. "It'll not be long and we'll all be together, darling. You'll do it for your Ma'am and your brother?"

"Why did you tell me Aunt Lilly was dead?"

"Did I ever say she was? Or that she wasn't? Your Ma'am will explain such things as a man can't. Are you not just filled with longing to see them, Callie?"

Her father hadn't noticed that Callie was limping, but Aunt Lilly had and she'd measured Callie's feet. One day a new pair of soft black boots arrived by way of a gentleman staying at the hotel. "I see that father of yours finally bought you some new shoes," Mrs. Stollsteimer said when she noticed the boots. "They appear costly for someone in such a precarious financial state as he claims."

Callie allowed the housekeeper to think what she would and reveled in her new comfort. But her general unhappiness grew at the thought of having to live apart from her mother and Bram when they moved to Telluride. Word came at last that they were settled in a rooming house in Finntown and Mrs. Stollsteimer gave Callie permission to leave the hotel to visit them. Finntown was a section around the depot inhabited largely by working-class Finns. It lay on the south side of town but was separated from the bawdy section by an invisible curtain of respectability and in some places by a buffer of warehouses.

Her mother was waiting for her on the landing of a staircase attached to the side of a house with pretty wood banisters around its front porch and a gleaming picket fence. Callie hid her face in Luella's clothing. Her mother had never carried much extra flesh but now it seemed all that lay beneath the dress was bones. Finally Luella held Callie away and knelt in front of her. "Has it been so very bad for you?" There was a blackness to the skin around her eyes. "You've grown so since last I saw you."

The room held two cots with a blanket hung between on a wire. It had a wardrobe, Ma'am's trunk, a small table with two straight-backed chairs, an oval braided rug, and obviously no room for Callie. Bram's liquid eyes looked huge in his skull-face and were about all that reminded her of him. A knitted cap covered his head. His hands hung massive at the end of stick arms. He was still very tall but seemed to have shrunk because of a rounded stoop. He lowered his eyes and turned away from her, folded himself onto a chair with odd jerky movements. Callie put her arms all the way around his shoulders, a thing she never could have done before, and clung to him without speaking as she had to her mother. When she didn't release him he finally relaxed, laid his head against the side of hers.

Luella didn't notice the new boots until Callie's second visit. Callie was sitting on the edge of Bram's cot while he rested, telling him about the funny people who stayed at the New Sheridan Hotel and Miss Heisinger's grand clothes, when Luella returned from helping Mrs. Pakka in the kitchen. A portion of their room and board was deducted for this service and Luella garnered extra scraps for Bram. But most often he refused them. "Callie, those are lovely new shoes but why would your father buy such dear ones when we're in these straits?"

"Aunt Lilly gave them to me. And money to send Bram's letter too."

"But she's dead, Callie." Bram's voice had deepened, seemed too powerful for his new body.

"She's not, Bram. She's just Floradora now and she lives right here in Tell—"

"She is dead." Ma'am stood over them, arms folded and face ashy-colored.

"But I talked to her and she—"

"She is dead to us. And as good as dead to herself. You are never to speak to her again or to mention her name. And, Callie, you are never to go near that side of town again. Do you understand?"

Callie did not understand and on her next visit when she'd coaxed her brother out for a walk in the sun, he wasn't much help. "She's done something evil," he said sadly. "I'm not to speak of her to you." He scratched at the knit cap. Bram had caught a fever during his illness and wore the cap because he'd lost his hair. "Don't go that way. People will see me."

Her brother shuffled his feet now like old Mr. MacIntosh. Ma'am had brought books home from the wonderful stone schoolhouse for him but soon he would have to join the other students in the classrooms and face the cruel stares his appearance elicited. When Pa had first seen him he'd gone out into the hallway and wept. Aspen flamed yellow and orange on the ridges that were too high or too far to have been cut away and the air was crisp and afloat with spicy, drying smells. But Bram just watched his boots crunch cinders along the railroad tracks.

"At least you don't have to clean things," Callie said, searching for something to cheer him. "And you have so many books." She tried to keep the envy out of her voice. "Aunt Lilly, I mean Floradora, lives over there." He still didn't look up. "She paints her face now." Callie tried a few skips and left him behind. It was like having a whole new brother to get used to. She slowed and let his misery overwhelm her.

Mildred Heisinger was not as pleased with the second group of young ladies she escorted to Telluride. She'd lost the sense of pride that accompanied her return the first time. Lawyer Barada was so insistent on numbers, Mildred had accepted all who had applied. There were thirteen, of every shape and size, and not one of them could be termed brilliant. Mildred stood on the station platform now waiting for the lawyer, who, his agent said when he came to collect her new charges, had found a house for her and wished to show it to her himself. He would be along shortly.

"You!" a hate-filled voice said behind her, and Mildred whirled to find Charlene Rassmussen in mild disarray. Charlene was one of her finds on the Kansas City trip. Her hair straggled down beneath her hat as if she'd lost her combs. Her travel suit needed sponging and her enthusiasm had turned to outrage.

"Charlene . . . are you not enjoying your new employment here?"

Charlene became white at the lips, widened her eyes in a maniacal manner. "I am more fortunate than the others, you bitch. I have a benefactor. Mr. Whipple has wired me fare home and offers marriage in spite of you."

"Mr. Whipple . . . but isn't he the neighbor with the bad skin, teeth, and breath and little hair? The one you fled here to escape? What has happened that would cause you to return to someone whom you loathed so?"

Charlene Rassmussen spit directly into Mildred's face. "Audrey's vowed to kill you. And I hope she does."

Mildred wiped her cheek, unable to believe this carefully chosen young woman capable of such repulsive behavior. "Is Audrey unhappy with her employment also?"

Charlene gave out a choking sound and turned on her heel, leaving

Mildred with that familiar snaky coldness in her middle. Deep inside, where she couldn't inspect it carefully, there had been a suspicion that something was not quite right about all this. It was too easy, too perfect, paid far too well. She'd tried to convince herself that common shopkeepers could afford her extravagant salary and expenses to obtain clerks and bookkeepers. That they were sufficiently selfless to be concerned about the supply of marriageable females in the camp. She greeted Lawyer Barada coolly when he drove up in a smart little buggy with a black horse.

"You were right, my dear, it was extremely simple," he said with enthusiasm as though he didn't notice her stiffness. "There was but one house for sale in all the town." The feeling in her middle compressed to a sick hardness as he turned the buggy the wrong way on Pacific Avenue. "I took the liberty of investing your current salary and commissions as a beginning payment. The demand for this property would have made it unavailable by the time of your return." He pulled the buggy over and stopped the horse on a corner. "Well, what do you think of it?"

The house was newly painted, had lovely ornate trim at the eaves, and a charming little cupola. It had a carriage house and stables behind it, all sparkling white, and a black wrought-iron fence. It was not large or imposing but roomy enough. From the outside it would have been a home she might easily have chosen herself. Had it been in another section of town. Had it not been overshadowed by the two-story perversion of human greed next to it called the Big Swede. A saloon downstairs, and she dared not think what it was upstairs. Men lounging in the doorway were already staring at her.

"You must be joking," she said finally to the lawyer beside her.

"On the contrary, Miss Heisinger, it's a fine property and fills all your requirements. It even comes with a few of the essential furnishings left behind by the previous owner, and I've taken the liberty of hiring a girl for you."

"You take far too many liberties, sir."

"But someone must look after it while you travel about, and see to your comforts when you return home weary. She comes for practically nothing and I have it on good authority she's an excellent cook."

"I insist you drive me to the New Sheridan Hotel at once."

He raised snowy brows and shrugged. "As you wish." He had

the nerve to maintain a light one-sided banter as they drove up the street, as if everything were normal. "You have much to learn of the world of work, my dear Miss Heisinger, but then, you are young," he said kindly as she stepped from the buggy unaided. "Your little home awaits you should you change your mind. Your most recent earnings including the commissions are already invested in it, remember."

Mildred needed time to collect herself, to decide what to do. Now she was hungry and tired and there were no beds available at the New Sheridan Hotel. Nor at the Victoria. Nor at the New Colombia. And the looks she received at each of these places raised her suspicions. There were no vacancies in the few boardinghouses on the north side of town that accepted ladies. She even went out to the Italian Catholic section to the east. Late afternoon was turning into chilly evening as she raised her chin and hurried back up the street. She stopped a woman with wrapped parcels. "There's boardinghouses down in Finntown that take in ladies, I believe."

"Mrs. Pakka and Mrs. Riconola rent rooms," a man on the street in Finntown told her, and pointed out both houses. No sidewalks here, and Mildred's skirts gathered dust as she stepped around animal droppings. Mrs. Riconola's rooms were filled. A lanky scarecrow of a man sat on the steps of Mrs. Pakka's house.

"In the kitchen, straight through to the back," he said, and dipped his face into the collar of his coat. Mildred was halfway down the hall when she recognized the hollowed eyes. Brambaugh O'Connell. She had to stop and clutch a door molding to let that face sink beneath her own worries. And in the kitchen she confronted his mother. Mrs. O'Connell had always looked worn for her age but now she looked nearly as eroded as her son. "Miss Heisinger?" She wiped her hands, large and reddish, on her apron. "I've worried for your welfare since the unfortunate turn of affairs at Alta. It's good to see you looking so well."

"Heisinger?" Mrs. Pakka brought a bowl of steaming soup to a sideboard. The kitchen smelled of yeast and boiled meat and other good things. The warmth was heavenly. "There's no room here for your kind, woman." Her eyes had that shutter behind them Mildred had hoped never to see again.

"But, Mrs. Pakka," Mrs. O'Connell said, "she's a—"

"She's the lowest among the crawling things on God's green earth.

Luring innocents to their destruction." The landlady picked up a wooden chair, her expression every bit as outraged as Charlene Rassmussen's. "She's a procuress, Mrs. O'Connell."

"Oh, surely not. You must be mistaken."

But Mildred watched the shutter close over Mrs. O'Connell's open and concerned expression, mere doubt shuttering Mildred out for all eternity. She backed away as the chair legs poked at her, prodding her through the back door as if she were a dangerous animal let into the house by mistake.

29

CREE Mackelwain hurt. Two stubby miners tried to help him out of the snowshed and ended up dragging him. They smelled of sulfur and brimstone and dirt mucked up from the devil's playground. "Where are the women who were with me?"

"Got closed up in a hole in the air some ways. Those three men are running scared down Boomerang Road. Bunch of stiffs hard on their tails."

It would have been a relief to be deposited in the chair in the miniature office if the bending of his body hadn't felt so dangerous. There was a miniature desk and a metal safe on wheels with golden curlicues painted on it. Cree tried to stretch out his legs but the mustachioed men gathered around him made it impossible.

"Timothy Traub," a man with clean skin said. He wore a suit coat, vest, and a bow tie that had tails on it. "Manager here. Don't suppose you could tell me what it is you was doing in the adit?" Cree watched Timothy Traub separate into two identical men.

"Cuts his hair like a foreigner, Mr. Traub."

"You an American? Were you born in this country? Union men do this to you? You insured?"

Cree blacked out. He surfaced to hear someone say, "Careful now. Easy. Long son of a bitch, ain't he?" He could feel himself handled, the movement of air past his face. He sank back into the black that eased his pain. The next time he was aware of himself, he was lying on something brick-hard. He moved his hands outward and decided it was not very wide.

"Here we are, awake at last. What say we open those eyes and have a look at the world, hah?" A tight wrapping around his chest kept him from filling his lungs deeply.

"Aw, leave him be, Nurse Swengel, poor man must be paining after such a beating as was give to him," said a voice farther away with a soft roll.

"Time he was awake and eating if he intends to heal, Mr. Pangrazia. And the sheriff would like to know his name."

"McCree Ronald Mackelwain," Cree said, and opened his eyes against his better judgment. "What year is this?"

"Well, now, you haven't slept *that* long." Nurse Swengel was small and wide and her clothes rustled. "It's still nineteen-aught-one." She put a hand on his forehead and against his cheek, tilted her head back to look at him through the little squares of her eyeglasses. Then she tilted it forward so she could study him over the tops of them. Her bodice and sleeves puffed with starch. When she lifted him to drink from a thick glass, his middle refused to bend at the waist and chills, sweats, and nausea attacked him all at once. She lowered him carefully.

"You're one strong lady for your size," he told her through gritted teeth.

"That I am, Mr. Mackelwain." She reddened, smiled. Her teeth were a mess. "Just you remember that when it comes time to take your medicine." She arranged a series of hard little pillows under his back so he could be raised without bending above the hips and introduced his ward-mates. Three lay ominously still and flat. One lay on his side snoring softly. One moaned and gurgled and wheezed. Mr. Pangrazia sat on the edge of his bed. He was minus a leg. Every bed in the ward was filled. Nurse Swengel disappeared to find Cree some soup.

"This isn't Alta, is it?" he asked Mr. Pangrazia.

"This is Telluride. You sure got bumps on the head. You don't know where you are or even what year you are in." Mr. Pangrazia shook his own head sadly. The place reeked of urine and carbolic acid, held a deepening chill. Wind rattled at the windows. Snow blew in sandblasts, swirled in gray-white shapes that hid the rest of the world, piled powdered-sugar-fine in the corners of the windowsills. "Gonna be a terrible winter," Mr. Pangrazia said, following Cree's gaze. "My son, he tells me every burro and squirrel has fur three inches thick already."

"Great." Cree tried to sigh but his sore ribs objected. Aletha's little time switch had saved them from a nasty fate at the hands of Duffer and the boys, but the very thing he'd feared would happen to her had happened to him.

At the Floradora, Aletha carried plates of the special of the day, Smuggler-Union Lasagna and Miners' Salad, ignoring the looks her swollen lips attracted.

"Just don't eat anything solid till your teeth feel firm again," Tracy had said. "You won't know if any are dead till they start turning gray."

Aletha had a dental appointment in the morning. Bertie would turn gray if he knew all the money he'd sunk in orthodontics for her smile was in extreme jeopardy. She and Tracy had left Alta without Cree and with the black-and-silver Bronco sitting alone by the commissary. She wondered what Callie's world would do with Cree and how it would handle those three goons. As Tracy said, they had to eat and pay the rent, so they'd come back in time to go to work.

Aletha, however, had decided to search for some old-fashioned clothes, at least a long coat, to cover her modernness, and the next time that time decided to do its thing, she'd walk off into history and try to find Cree. She just hoped somebody was tending to his injuries. Since the odd occurrences seemed to happen around her, maybe she could be with him when the hole opened again and bring him home. This was not exactly the kind of problem she could take to the county sheriff.

Aletha had had a small brownish patch where the pendant lay against her skin when they came down from Alta that she'd thought might be a burn but found was just a stain that washed off with a little scrubbing. She wore the pendant outside her blouse now and wondered if, because it seemed to heat up at times when history opened up, it had some magical property that caused the phenomenon. Which was silly, but she continued to wear the pendant just in case it was her only way of making contact with Cree.

The Floradora had a less expensive menu than the Senate and

attracted more of the working locals. Backpacks instead of purses, big mongrels tied up outside, sad-eyed and patient. "What'd your friend Mackelwain do, bust you in the mouth?" A man swung around on a bar stool in time to catch her arm as she headed back to the kitchen for some Tomboy Chili and Prospector Bread. He had blond hair down to his collar, the requisite flannel shirt and work boots, and very professional eyes. He was trying to look like just one of the guys but had a few more years on him than most everybody at the bar. "Know where I can find him?" he asked. "He could be in some bad trouble."

"The last I saw him he was up in Alta. Maybe you should start there."

The county sheriff stopped by and introduced himself as Tom Rickard. He had big shields sewn to the sleeves of his shirt that said "SAN MIGUEL COUNTY" and a white star patch in the center that said "SHERIFF'S DEPT." He had crinkles around his eyes and fluffy hair cut a little short for Telluride. Aletha told him the whole story. Except about Tracy, no sense getting her involved. And except about the hole in time. Which left some fairly large holes in her story.

"Get any names?" The crinkles stayed around the edges of his eyes but the expression on the inside flattened out to weary boredom.

"The other two called the chief honcho 'Duffer.' "

"And they walked Mackelwain into the mine and never came out."

"Right. And their Bronco was still sitting up there when I left."

"And it never occurred to you to seek help for Mr. Mackelwain."

"No. I mean yes. But I didn't know who to go to. I didn't think you could do anything."

"You'd be surprised what I can do. For instance, I understand you spent some time in the Federal Correctional Institute in Fort Worth. Didn't seem to teach you enough to stay away from drug dealers, did it?"

Aletha felt a protective numbing. When life went downhill, it accelerated like it was on wheels. "That conviction was reversed."

"But not erased," Sheriff Tom Rickard said. "Don't leave town."

The next day when she stepped out of the dentist's office a sheriff's deputy was waiting to drive her up to Alta. The dentist's prognosis had been the same as Tracy's.

The black-and-silver Bronco still sat by the commissary. All its doors stood open. Other officers and a number of nonuniformed men poked about the ghost town. One held out a jacket for a hyper dog to sniff. They disappeared into the mine and the dog's incessant barking sounded suddenly remote.

"Thought you might be able to remember a little more if you came up here." The sheriff had shields sewn on his jacket too. It was cold and cloudy and trying to rain. A dispatcher sputtered over a patrol-car radio nearby. The sheriff's sunglasses kept studying her. An officer with a flashlight came out of the mine where the dog still barked far away. "Gets to one spot and stops. Keeps going back to it."

"Get a shovel."

"Area's hard as rock, hasn't been disturbed in years. It's like they got to that one spot and vanished into . . . someplace else."

"Wonderful." A great drop of rain slid down one lens of his sunglasses. Sheriff Rickard turned to another officer coming up the hill. "Watcha got?"

"Newly disturbed earth. Under a falling-down shack."

Aletha followed them to Callie's cabin. She knew it wasn't Cree in that disturbed earth. All she wanted was to go back to Telluride and find that coat.

"Too small for a human grave."

"Some animal digging maybe. Or drugs. Or drug money."

They'd dug less than a foot when they came across a rock the size of a small football wrapped in a rag. It was milky speckled quartz on one side and a dull gold color on the other.

The sheriff of San Miguel County in 1901 wore a three-piece suit and tie. Cree counted seven buttons on his vest alone. He wore a watch chain and a mustache and smelled of sweet cigar. A big man compared to the others around here.

"Those fellows beat me and when I woke up I was inside the mine." Cree tried to slow his words to match the relaxed style that prevailed here. "I don't know what they wanted."

"You ain't the best liar I ever heard, Mr. Mackelwain," Sheriff Cal Rutan said good-humoredly. "But I don't approve of what they did to you. Have all three of those boys in the jail and all they do is complain about the cold, the food, and the lice. And the drunks in there with them." He picked Duffer's battery lantern up off the floor. "Suppose you could tell me what this is?"

"No, sir. Seems to be made of funny stuff."

" 'Funny stuff,' yes . . . well, watch this." He pushed the switch and the light came on. Mr. Pangrazia sucked breath in between the gaps in his front teeth. "Maybe they were after this?"

"I've never seen anything like that before, sir."

"Well, I've never seen anything like these before, sir." The sheriff produced Cree's running shoes. "And you came in here wearing 'em. Where'd you say you was from again?"

"Wyoming. Cheyenne. I had those specially made for me there."

"And you have no money, no family, no previous occupation. Sounds to me like you got about as much trouble as those boys in the jailhouse. Winter's coming on hard. I'll get a wire off to Cheyenne. They didn't teach you to talk like you do in Wyoming, friend." Sheriff Rutan gathered the lantern and his overcoat and left Cree with, "You're not careful, you'll end up in Stringtown."

"Stringtown," Mr. Pangrazia explained, "is where the very poor live." He practiced with his wooden leg and crutches in the aisle between rows of beds. Cree's bed had the metal foot rail extended, with pillows to fill in between it and the mattress. The man with the gurgling lungs had been carried out dead. "Drunken men, Indians, prostitutes too old and ugly. My son, he tells me they eat stray dogs there. They live by a string, Mr. Mackelwain. Some don't make it through the winter. It's across the river on the east edge of the camp."

That's the town park, Cree thought. I'm in the museum, and skid row is in the town park. His injuries did not encourage laughter so he shook his head like Mr. Pangrazia. Snow still blasted the windows. Cree didn't think his feet would ever be warm again. "What month is this, February?"

"November," Mr. Sorenson answered. His bed was next to Cree's. He was rarely awake.

"November 1901 . . . oh, God, they had the fire yet? At the Smuggler?" Twenty-eight men perished. There would be a mass grave in Lone Tree Cemetery. "I think it was 1901. Maybe it was eighteen men. Maybe it was the twenty-eighth. I'm sure it was November."

"My son, he works at the Smuggler-Union. No fire there. November, she half-over already." Mr. Pangrazia hopped and hobbled and shook his head sadly. "Bumps on the head, poor man. Bumps on the head."

30

JOHN O'Connell was feeling his age. He swung an empty dinner bucket and watched the younger men jounce along as if they hadn't just put in a grueling shift. His wife but a poor bag of bones. The boy unfit to work probably ever. His prospect still not located. Little Callie forced to wipe up after swags. John could ill afford to wear down now. He did a man's work and was proud of it but he was thirty-six and his tired bones told him he couldn't keep this up indefinitely. He coughed as the smoke from the rounds firing below passed him on its way to the outside, and followed it to the cold mountain day already dimming toward night. The chill cut through his damp clothes and set his skin to bracing up with goosebumps. Spitting biting juices from the plug in his cheek, he waited as an overloaded hay wagon pulled up in front of him. When he stepped around it he could see more snow had fallen while he was down, feathering over the bare ground where the wind brushed it so, filling up rock crevices and drifting deep in the protection of buildings that clutched the mountainside. It spread over the stubble of stumps on the slope above like shaving soap.

Almost every inch of the flat shelf here that wasn't road was given over to buildings, along with every additional inch that could be gouged and flattened out of the rock-hard mountain. The Smuggler-Union had several adits but the main passage to the fabulous Bullion Tunnel opened onto this steeply pitched slope, forcing most of the support buildings—machine and blacksmith shops, boardinghouse, assay office, storage sheds, and tram station—to crowd around the opening. There was little space for a man to stretch his legs except on the road. An old story told of a miner who walked in his sleep off the boardinghouse porch and was never seen again. The outhouse required no digging. It sat on a platform that emptied out over space. It was said when winter got deep enough the cold drafts came up the chute under the privy and made a man's testicles try to crawl up his bunghole.

John chuckled and it eased his exhaustion. There were some good stories of this place and some of them might even be true. And the working stiffs here had shown the owners they wouldn't stand for unfair wages. Next they'd work for safety measures so a man needn't risk too much every day—proper timbering and ventilation, no shooting of rounds till dinner break or tally and the boys safely away.

He stood at the edge of the precipice and watched the camp robbers fly and screech around the kitchen slops dumped over the side, as the gulls had done when he'd been to sea. The Smuggler's mill was down in the valley at Pandora, but he could hear the muted thump of the vast mill over at the Tomboy across the abyss, the clickety-clack of the tram buckets, the braying of mules, the clink of the smithy's hammer.

He straightened sore shoulders and inhaled the clean brisk air. Well, it was a grand country and a man like John O'Connell could find his fortune yet. And he'd managed to pay some ahead for Luella and Bram at Mrs. Pakka's from the sale of that white powder he'd found up in Alta. Too bad the stuff wasn't worth more.

John was swapping stories with the boys in the dining hall halfway through a supper of boiled beef, cabbage, and potatoes and looking forward to the selection of pies even now being sliced on a nearby sideboard when the hay wagon he'd met coming out of the tunnel caught fire. Every man was called out to fight it. The wagon had been unhitched on the road and left right where he'd seen it. The night shift had just gone to work and wasn't available to help. John had no doubts they'd lose the wagon but still figured they'd have it out in time to eat some of that pie. They'd always been short of water at the Smuggler, there being no mill to demand it. Most of it was hauled in winter. A horseman was sent racing off to the Tomboy for aid and water. Men began shoveling snow at the burning hay and flapping at it with wet blankets.

A wind with whirly, thin snow swept up the valley just when the fire looked to be containable and by the time help from the Tomboy arrived there were burning patches on almost every building and the few barrels of water the visitors could spare were about enough to wet more blankets to fight sparks on roofs. The wind howled as if in glee at this. Then it bellowed the sparks into conflagrations that sent the firefighters and their blankets off the roofs fast and backing down the road. John wasn't the first to notice the smoke leaning toward the adit instead of spiraling upward. The foreman from the Tomboy ordered anybody who would listen to close the safety doors on the tunnel.

"Don't have any," John yelled over the snap and whoosh of the flames.

"Then we'll have to dynamite it, fast!"

"That'll ruin the tunnel," Mr. Collins, the manager, shouted. He and a horde of others had just stepped off the tram, having come up in the buckets from Pandora.

"There's a whole shift in there. They'll die from the smoke sucked into the workings."

Thor Torkelson, the shift boss, handed John a wet blanket. "Men dying vile they ben yapping. Got to tell those still alive to run to the other adits, not try this von."

It certainly wasn't that John O'Connell wanted to risk his life. But it didn't take a man long to die breathing smoke that thick. There wasn't time to reach other adits and then gain the workings. The boardinghouse came down on his pie as John wrapped the blanket about and over him, leaving only a slit to peek through. The heat outside scorched his skin; inside it was heavy as a locomotive and airless. Flame had been sucked surprisingly far in. A horse, screaming like a banshee, came out of the smoke and nearly trampled John in its panic. The man hanging on to its tail and racing along behind had his hair on fire.

John lost track of Torkelson. He came across another horse dead in its traces, the trammer hanging lifeless over the edge of the tram car. John's blanket had gone as dry as the linings of his nose and lungs. Each breath was choking, burning agony even filtered through the blanket, and about as satisfying as rocks to a starving man. He'd stumbled into walls and across huddled shapes of more dead before he heard the thunder and whump of the explosion. Someone had finally blown the adit.

Bram O'Connell was out walking the tracks that night. Ma'am kept warning him to stay in Mrs. Pakka's heated parlor with his studies, to conserve what little strength he had and not risk cold and pneumonia. But sharing that tiny divided room with her was suffocating him, and the parlor where the boarders gathered after supper was even worse. Yet neither compared with school. He'd been attending for about a week now and had already earned the nickname "scarecrow." He was not allowed to wear his cap in the classroom to hide his baldness. The girls giggled behind their hands, the boys yelled insults from around corners. And in his dreams he repeated the slow agonies of drowning.

In order to sleep, to work off a growing restlessness, to vent his rage at his helplessness, Bram had taken to walking the railroad tracks at night, where no one paid him much attention. He'd walk the track through the sporting section halfway to Pandora, turn around and walk it again. It took more walking each night to settle him.

This night Bram was on his second time back through the sporting section and ignoring occasional invitations from the hags who lived in the tiny shacks scattered along the tracks when he reached Spruce Street and heard a great commotion in front of the Senate. He followed the shadows until he reached the Silver Bell, where a crowd had filed out into the street.

"Fire at the Smuggler . . . smoke in the tunnels, down the shafts."

"Men dead by the tramloads."

"Old man Collins wouldn't blow the adit till it was too late."

"His lordship was afraid of losin' his precious money while men was losin' their lives." There was a low rumble of male anger as the streets continued to fill. Bram took his own anger back to the tracks and ran to the boardinghouse, having to lean against Mrs. Pakka's coal shed to recover from the exertion and to fight the terror. If only he could be a man again, he'd go up and fight through smoke and fire and worse to bring John O'Connell out if he was in that hellhole.

When Luella O'Connell heard of the disaster she went to her trunk for a packet of the powders she'd purchased from a peddler with a portion of her tiny funds. She'd come to prefer the straight powder to that diluted in tonic and found that when applied to the inside of the nose and mouth its healing of nervous disorders and exhaustion was much enhanced. The peddler had assured her that the powders were even better than food for nourishment and restoration of the energies of the body. And if John were one of the dead, she would need all the strength she could muster.

Callie didn't learn of the fire at the Smuggler-Union Mine until the next morning. She and Opal Mae had huddled together on the same cot all night, partly for warmth and partly for comfort. The cot next to Callie's was empty. Elsie Biggs had been dismissed that morning. She'd committed the cardinal sin for Mrs. Stollsteimer's girls. She'd entered a room while the gentleman was present. "If she hadn't been a ninny and screamed, no one would ever have known," Opal Mae insisted. "The gentleman wouldn't have told, would he?"

"Not on himself," Callie answered. "Elsie probably didn't even know he was in there."

"Let this be a lesson to the rest of you," Mrs. Stollsteimer had told them sternly. To be sure they behaved themselves, she decreed they would henceforth work in groups; the three youngest—Callie, Opal Mae, and Senja—would work together and Olina and Grace would do the same. "I don't ever want to see any of you parading about separately."

Callie, Opal Mae, and Senja were trying to scrub and scrape dried tobacco juice off the wainscoting in the dining room the next morning when they heard about the terrible fire at the Smuggler and the estimates of the dead.

"Bodies already being stacked like cordwood at the mortician's," a guest said to another as they waited at the door for the dining room to open.

"That's what those foreign buggers get for organizing unions, if you ask me. Good Lord just 'struck' back." And the man laughed.

31

ALETHA found the coat at the Old Claims Trading Post among a wide assortment of items—secondhand, just old, and valuable antique. It was heavy, made of gray scratchy wool, with black piping and buttons. It had darts pulling it in at the waist and reached the tops of her tennis shoes. It smelled musty and dusty but appeared sound enough.

Her mouth felt considerably better. Her front teeth had not turned gray yet but she still ate carefully. The film festival was due to start the next day and the conversations in restaurants, stores, and on the sidewalk had taken on the broad A's of those who had trained their speech habits or those who wanted one to believe they had. But the festival did mean work for her. Renata warned that after the festivals and before the skiing there would be an off season and work would be scarce. Aletha's problem was keeping the coat and her black dress boots with her in case the hole opened up. She decided to wear them to work.

"What a cool coat," one of her fellow laborers remarked at Sophio's the next day. "It even stinks old." No one else noticed it. You had to get pretty far off-the-wall to be noticed in Telluride. But she couldn't wear it while actually waiting tables so she hid it behind the antique sideboard on the restaurant's balcony where her tables were assigned and then was nervous whenever she had to go downstairs for burritos and margaritas. She needn't have worried because nothing happened that day. It happened the next.

She was in the bathroom at the crib, washing out the towel with a circle cut in its center that she used on the toilet seat just in case Tracy's disease of the decade could be spread in that manner, when Tracy started yelling and racing between the front door and the back. "I'm not getting caught this time. Which is it? Front or back? I don't want to be wherever whatever it is, is."

Aletha dropped the towel, slid into her boots and coat, opened the back door. Charles bumped off her in his haste to get in. It was a sunny afternoon, just as it had been a moment ago, and a pickup sat in the alley. "Tracy, nothing happened. It's still now."

"Yeah? Take a look out front."

The front room was chilly compared to the kitchen. Charles hid under a bed, only his puffed-up tail showing. Aletha peered through a window onto Pacific Avenue. All she could see was fog, a dark fog, as if it were night in front of the crib while afternoon in back. She tried to swallow down the rush of excitement. She was doing this only for Cree, not as a fling. This time she wasn't wearing the quartz pendant either. So much for that idea. But she grabbed it off the top of the TV in a sort of superstitious hope it would bring her luck in finding Cree in Callie's world. She pulled the TV away from the front door, calling over her shoulder to Tracy, "Wish me luck."

"Don't go out there!"

But Aletha was out there. On a board sidewalk in the cold. The fog had an empty feel to it. She could see a smear of light across the street and a watery streetlight that hung on invisible wires over the intersection of Spruce Street and Pacific Avenue. No tinkling pianos, rough laughter, or clicking gambling wheels. Just the whisper of the fog and the distant heartbeat of the mills. It wasn't right and it was spooky and Aletha decided to look for Cree another time, but the door to the crib was locked.

"Go away," some women who didn't sound like Tracy answered her knock through the door, and the light went out inside. There was no answer at all to her second knock. Aletha buttoned up the coat partway down the front. Stealthy footsteps approached from the direction of Spruce Street and she slid around the side of the crib.

"Tap 'er light," a voice whispered out of the fog, and one set of footsteps crossed the street while the other continued up it.

Aletha stood chewing on her knuckle, hoping for an idea as to what to do next, a shiver tickling her spine at the ghostly sound of that whisper. Her boots crunched on snow when she stepped into the side alley a couple of cribs down. But the fog was even darker here, so she followed the sidewalk to the corner, trying not to let her boots clunk where it was hollow. Her breath made its own little fog and she stuck her hands deep in the coat's pockets. Her ears felt frozen and numb. She didn't like the feeling of going directly from afternoon to night in a few steps. It felt like accelerated jet lag. If the Big Swede or the Monte Carlo, the Idle Hour or the Pick and Gad were operating tonight, business was slow. She could distinguish few lights and no sounds from that direction. From the other, horses stamped and snorted in the livery stable. Aletha turned that way, imagining all sorts of threats in the fog.

How had she imagined she'd get to Alta from here? Fly? Was Cree still there? The fog, filled with the smell of wood smoke, thinned and thickened without warning, came to her in chunks. It couldn't be the absolute dead of night when everybody slept, because there were lights in the apartments above the stores. She reached Colorado Avenue and again a watery streetlight hung dead center over the intersection. Nothing doing here either. What was this? Horse's hooves thudded on dirt in a slow walk.

"Who goes there?" someone called from up the street.

"Sentry . . ." and words Aletha could not hear, male voices. The horse hooves began again and the horse with a white streak on his nose cut through a chunk of fog into a thin patch. The fog clustered in little beads on the hairs in his ears and on the mane that straggled over his forehead. He snorted steam in her face. The rider was dressed like a cross between a Canadian Mountie and a Boy Scout. "And who goes here?"

Aletha backed up against a building and the horse followed her onto the sidewalk. "Where is everybody?"

"In their homes as they should be." The Mountie-Scout dismounted and the saddle creaked like a dead tree limb in the wind. "By order of Governor Peabody of the state of Colorado. The town's under martial law and there's a curfew, miss. I'll escort you home."

"Uh, I just got here and I don't have a place to go."

"You must have come from somewhere and in a hurry. You've come out without your hat." Leading the horse with one hand, he took her arm with the other and showed clearly what he thought of her by walking them back into the red-light district. "Surely you have friends who'll take you in? The penalty for breaking curfew is arrest, and the jail and Redmen's Opera House are filled with ruffians. They are no place for a woman of any sort."

"I don't know anybody—except Callie O'Connell. She works at the Sheridan Hotel, or did . . . or will." The horse whinnied back to his friends locked up in the stable as they passed. "Oh, and I know Mildred Heisinger. But I don't know if she lives here yet." She knew she was chattering insanely. "What I really need is to get to Alta."

Another sentry commanded them to halt and stepped out of the fog with rifle lowered. "Ah, Captain Webbley, sir. All's quiet that we can see, but I think they're out and about. In this fog we can't fire on 'em for fear of hittin' one of our own."

"Yes, well, I have a culprit here. Says she has no home but knows a Mildred Heisinger somewhere who might take her in."

"She'd be the house with the iron fence and cupola right over there, sir. It's the lighted window you're seeing through the fog."

Captain Webbley jerked Aletha forward. "I don't think Mildred's expecting me," she said.

He tied the horse to the fence and guided her through the gate. There was a stained-glass panel in the door now. A black woman let them into the entry hall. It had a small table with a lamp and a coat rack instead of the many mirrors it would have. The worn linoleum had given way to polished wood and an oval throw rug. The black woman moved like the fog, with hardly more than a whisper. A short man stepped out from between the curtains that hung across the parlor door.

"Mr. Meldrum." The men shook hands and the captain explained Aletha's presence in a loud voice. Mr. Meldrum's frosty blue eyes watched Captain Webbley's face and not until the captain had finished speaking did they turn to Aletha. There was the same emotional blankness in them that had troubled her about Duffer and his goons.

"What's she done, bobbed her hair?" He worked the inside of his lips around on his teeth, pursed them a couple of times. Mr. Meldrum spit at a corner of the floor. It was brown and Aletha half-expected it to steam. He wiped his mouth with the back of his hand. "Millie? Come on out here and see if you got any use for this."

Aletha was aware of the smell of her old coat in the small entry hall. The young Mildred Heisinger made her feel like a frump in comparison, like Renata Winslow always did. Mildred emerged from the parlor in an ivory-colored gown puffed at the upper arms and bosom, slimming to waist and wrist and flaring gradually to the floor. The bodice was all lacy and the dress looked much like those Aletha had seen at the museum, but not yellowed, dusty, limp, or worn with age. And neither was Mildred. Pale hair, skin, dress, and eyes— she looked almost like a marble statue and held herself like one. A thin feathery curl hung down in front of each ear, the rest of her hair swept up in an impossible scheme.

Captain Webbley drew in his breath and stared. Then he explained Aletha again. Mildred didn't watch him speak but watched Aletha instead. Aletha could only stare back and wonder at the change the years would bring. "She has obviously fashioned a story for your benefit, Captain. I have never seen her." Even her voice was lovely.

"But I do agree she can't be put out on the street with all the unpleasantness. Perhaps Leona would have room for her."

Aletha was struck by the complete lack of sympathy in Mildred's tone. No empathy for another female here. Her eyes held more of a studied disinterest than the cold of Meldrum's. "I'll take her off your hands," he told the captain now and reached around the curtained parlor door for a gun belt with two filled holsters. "Going that way myself." He took his coat from the coat rack. It had a star pinned on it. He and Mildred exchanged looks and then he hustled Aletha out the door. "Come on, girlie."

"Who's Leona?" And when he didn't answer her—"I really have to get to Alta. Is there any way you could help me? It's very important." He just strode through the fog pulling her along with him. Even when a sentry ordered him to halt Meldrum didn't stop until he saw the rifle pointed at his chest. "Oh, sorry, Mr. Meldrum. I didn't know it was you."

Meldrum stared the sentry down and continued on his way with Aletha in tow, not by the arm as the captain had, but by a handful of the coat's shoulder pad. He was headed for the Pick and Gad. "Uh, listen, I'm no angel but I'm not ready for that place. Will you stop and listen to me?"

It was then she remembered her last conversation with the old Mildred Heisinger. This was the Bob Meldrum who murdered men by picking fights and outshooting them. And he didn't listen to her because he couldn't hear. "Deafer than I am now," Mildred had said. Aletha would have thought somebody would sneak up from behind and shoot him if he couldn't hear well.

The scream of a horse. Dogs barking. Men shouting off in the fog. Popping sounds. Aletha would have liked to think they were firecrackers but she feared they were gunshots. This old town was obviously a town at war and Aletha had picked a lousy time to visit.

32

CREE Mackelwain found himself evicted from the hospital. Not because his body had fully healed but because he was a pauper and because those injured in the Smuggler-Union fire filled the town's small hospitals. Nurse Swengel rewrapped his rib cage and gave him a last breakfast of oatmeal and coffee.

"We don't treat vagrants kindly in Telluride," Sheriff Rutan told him. "Now, we could send you out on the next train. But then, you owe money around here. Hospitals don't come free." He stretched his upper lip down over his front teeth and scratched absently at his mustache. "Then again, you could find yourself a place in String-town. 'Course, with winter that could be uncomfortable. You don't have much in the way of a coat and your feet'll freeze in them fancy cloth shoes." He waved his cigar around and the smoke drifted toward the little stove in the corner of his office in the courthouse on Colorado Avenue. Cree kept edging closer to that stove, longing to put cold wet feet up against it and get them away from the drafts on the floor.

"And Eugenio Pangrazia tells me this wild story about you fore-telling the fire at the Smuggler. Now, I don't believe in foretelling, so that leaves me with the possibility you might know somebody who was planning on flicking a match into that hay wagon."

"Mr. Pangrazia must be mistaken, sir. And I would like to stay in Telluride if you could suggest a way I could keep from starving and freezing."

"You're one mighty polite fellow, you know that? And a mighty suspicious one too." The sheriff stood by the stove with his back to it, lifted his coattails to warm his ass. "First, the union's blaming management for that fire—should have had safety doors, say they. Should have blown the tunnel mouth right away, say they. Then management says the unions probably started it to cause trouble, which is what they do best. Now me, I don't know. But I don't like unions. And if I find out you're working for St. John, Haywood, and that outfit you'll think freezing and starving heavenly compared to what I'll see done to you." Sheriff Rutan watched the smoke from his cigar for a while, turned his front to the warmth, and spoke over his shoulder. He seemed the antithesis of the harried lawman of Cree's day with nothing else to do and crowds swelling the street.

"Personally, I think you're a spy for one side or the other, got caught up in some troubles you won't talk about. For all I know, you're working for Mr. Bulkeley Wells himself. Because, friend, you ain't from this part of the United States of America." He moved to a table under the window and picked up a bundle that unfolded into a coat. "But seeing as you're such a polite bastard . . . this belonged to a big German by the name of Brandt. Went out and forgot it one day last week and walked right in front of a passing bullet. Too bad they buried him in his boots. They might have fit you too."

The coat smelled sour, was heavy and black and a little short— but it was warm. "Thanks. What about the starving part?"

"Ain't no excuse for a man to starve in this country, friend, unless he's afraid to work. And last I heard, Willy down at the Cosmopolitan was looking for someone to muck out the barroom. His nigger got in a fight in Stringtown and died on him. One free meal comes with the job, and wages. Just in case your other employers don't pay up soon." Cree thanked him for the tip and was almost out the door when Sheriff Rutan called him back. "Just one more thing, Mr. McCree Mackelwain. Since you didn't die and we needed the room, we had to let your three friends out of the jailhouse. You might want to keep a watch out for them."

Cree hadn't felt this helpless since he was a kid. He'd been unemployed once, but in a world he understood a little and there'd been unemployment checks to ease the strain. Now he didn't have shelter, he didn't have a cent, and at least until he talked to Willy he didn't have a job. He could see his way out of this bondage to history only if he could make contact with Aletha. If she ever visited Telluride in 1901 again.

Colorado Avenue was black with men in dark suits and derby hats. The quietest mob Cree had ever seen. The men formed orderly lines and waited to move forward. Grim faces turned toward him and Cree scrunched into Brandt's coat collar and hurried across the side street where a brick building sat on the corner in place of the New Sheridan's patio. Church bells clanged hollowly in the narrow valley. People stood on the sidewalk watching the silent parade. It was the funeral procession for the men killed in the Smuggler fire. He'd read where thousands of miners from all over the region had come to march in this procession. Under other circumstances this would have seemed a miraculous opportunity to indulge his penchant for history. But if he was to spend the rest of his life in it, history seemed more frightening and lonely than intriguing.

He asked a woman where he could find the Cosmopolitan and she directed him two blocks down, where a handwritten sign on the glass door read, *Closed until after the funeral.*

Where much of the Colorado Avenue Cree had known consisted of vacant lots, this Colorado Avenue was crowded on both sides with commercial buildings, many of brick, two-story, with people hanging out of apartment windows above. Cree was the only person on the street without a hat. Even the kids wore hats here. A woman at an open window next to an elaborate sign of *The Knights of Pythias* pointed him out to the man next to her. Cree felt like the bum they probably thought he was and walked on quickly with an unreasonable sense of shame and embarrassment. Of course it didn't help that he still had swellings, cuts, and bruises on his face. And he still limped to protect a tenderness in his groin where one of Duffer's little helpers had kicked him repeatedly.

At six-foot-five and surrounded by generally short stocky miners, Cree could see above the crowd. Not that there weren't a few other tall men. He noticed one in particular as he overtook the head of the slow procession. A huge blunt-featured guy, wearing a black Stetson instead of the small-brimmed, rounded hats of most of the men. When his glance settled on Cree over the heads around them, one eye didn't move but stared straight down the road. Big Bill Haywood, a labor legend whom Cree had seen in pictures, would someday become so discouraged he would end up dying alone and disillusioned in the Soviet Union.

Haywood wore a black armband and a sprig from an evergreen branch in his lapel. as did all the marchers behind him. In front walked the families—the women with their grief hidden by veils, trying to keep their backs fashionably straight under a load of despair. Five wooden wagons with flat beds extending a couple of feet out over the metal-rimmed wheels and draped in black cloth lumbered ahead of them. Horses jangled their harness, impatient with the morbid pace. People sniffed and coughed. Shoes shuffled on frozen ruts worn thin of snow. Cree realized why all these sounds seemed so loud. The eternal mills stood silent. Suddenly three men broke ranks, ran to the fourth wagon, and pulled the driver off the seat. One took his place, while the others pounded him to the ground.

"He weren't union," someone shouted in explanation, and coffins—narrow, wooden, plain, black—jiggled and shifted as the new driver hurried the team to catch up. By the time the first wagon turned into Lone Tree Cemetery the marchers filled the road clear to town. One giant pine stood almost in the cemetery's center. It would be long dead in Cree's time, like those who lay beneath it. Four or five private graves had been excavated, as well as the big trench, and piles of earth and rock sat beside them, their snow covers melting into mud. Crows, dozens of them, scampered black against the snow, cawed their irritable laughter at this human intrusion.

Cree wanted to stamp his freezing feet but feared attracting attention during the graveside services held for all in front of the mass grave. It didn't look more than three or four feet deep and seemed shallow even for this rocky soil, considering the dead and most of the mourners had made their livings as hard-rock miners. Both a priest and a Protestant clergyman officiated and caskets were lowered into the trench while others were carried off to family plots.

Big Bill Haywood took the sprig of evergreen from his lapel, tossed it into the open pit, and stared after it solemnly. "Tap 'er light," he said softly, and turned away. One by one men filed by and each tossed in his sprig. As Cree turned to go he noticed Callie O'Connell standing in a group of mourners near a family plot, staring at him wide-eyed. The last time he'd been to Lone Tree Cemetery he'd taken Aletha to see Callie's gravestone.

The gaunt woman at Callie's side fidgeted with Callie's hat. Her movements were jerky and nervous. The man on the other side of Callie held his derby in his hand. His balding head was bowed and an angry red puckered the skin of one cheek and ear. He didn't even look up when Cree approached and said to Callie, "If you see Aletha would you tell her I'm looking for her?"

Cree had joined the miners filing out the gate, passing men still wearing their sprigs and filing in, before he recognized the tall figure standing behind Callie. The boy named Bram. The once-magnificent kid looked as if he'd been attacked by cancer. Cree wondered if he'd warned him from a cave-in only to have him fall victim to disease. The ravaged face and shell-shocked expression would haunt Cree for a long while.

Gone was the giant mound of mill tailings extending out from the head of the canyon. Exploratory drilling and dredging marred the valley instead. Across the river there was a grouping of low shanties, some no more than wooden packing crates. Stringtown. "Nice coat." Duffer fell into step beside Cree. "You want to tell me what's happened?"

"Mine disaster. Funeral." Cree stepped up his pace.

"I know that. Listen, Mackelwain, you help us get back and all else is forgotten. You can keep the stuff and the money and we won't touch a hair on you, okay?" He hunched into his rumpled tan jacket, his ears red with the cold. "What do we do?"

"If I knew that I wouldn't be here, would I?" Cree looked over his shoulder to find the other two right behind them. "Who are you, anyway?"

"Man I work for decided your partner had something belonged to him. Sent us after you when he couldn't find it on Massey. Sort of wanted to make an example to others, you know? Hey, you help us out and you won't end up like Dutch Massey. The chick who showed up in Alta with your girlfriend said Kingman caused this. Where's Kingman?"

"She didn't follow us into the past, Duffer. You're on your own." Cree turned into the Cosmopolitan Saloon. Right now all Cree wanted was to survive. Just in case Aletha happened to turn up at the right place at the right year. Because merely surviving was all he had left.

33

ALETHA stood in the kitchen of the Pick and Gad. Bob Meldrum had taken her around to the back door. "Got to get her off the street for tonight, Leona," he said now, and stripped off Aletha's new-old coat so fast half the buttons came with it. She stood exposed in jeans and grungy sweatshirt. "This a woman or a boy?"

"It's a woman," Leona yelled, and circled Aletha. She had a darkened front tooth. "What's your name, honey?"

"Aletha Kingman."

"Well, Aletha Kingman, you can stay the night. Looks like someone's hit you in the mouth already."

Aletha would have expected the occupants of this place to be running around in nightgowns or underclothes like in the movies, but they were dressed from neck to floor. Perhaps because of the chilly drafts that seemed to flow from all directions in this house. A plump woman stood in a doorway, playing cards fanned out in her hand. Another peered over her shoulder.

The kitchen had one brick wall and a cook stove. The rest was wooden and oiled and polished, and layered with the smells of stale cooking in spite of the drafts. The proportions seemed wrong— ceiling too high—room, furniture, doorways too small. Even the handle of a broom leaning against the brick wall seemed shorter than normal. Heavy boots sounded on the floor above them, voices raised in hilarity. The clank of spurs descending a staircase. Leona and her women exchanged glances and watched Meldrum. Three men entered the kitchen. They spread out and stopped.

"Deputy Meldrum," said the one in the middle, and continued to pull on gloves with gauntlets. He was so handsome he didn't look real. And he knew it. He wore a uniform, a gun at his belt, and jodhpurs tucked into polished boots that reached to his knees. He wasn't as tall as Cree but he was a lot taller than Meldrum. "Just looking over the premises to be sure everything is locked up for the curfew," he said with a good-humored smirk.

"As you say, Captain Wells."

"And who is this Diana in tight pants?" Captain Wells peered down his nose at Aletha, huge eyes more amused than curious. "The latest act at the dance hall?" He started past her then backed up for another look, squinted as if he recognized her and was trying to remember where he'd seen her.

"Got caught breaking curfew. Could hardly take her to jail or Redmen's," Meldrum said.

Could this be the Bulkeley Wells old Mildred Heisinger said would grow bald and shoot himself in California? Hard to visualize him as anything but perfection in jodhpurs. But then, look what would happen to Mildred. If anything would cure Aletha of an addiction to dangerous historical entertainments, it was this out-of-place feeling, that she was an impostor among real people because this was their world, not hers.

"Interesting gamine, Leona. You could do worse. And now I'm going to skulk out the back door." But Captain Wells left straight and proud and laughing.

"You know full well, Bob Meldrum, I couldn't turn him and his friends away," Leona answered his glacial stare.

He stood unblinking as if forming a judgment or making a decision. "Where's Audrey?"

"She ain't here," Leona said. Meldrum grabbed her elbow and twisted. Some place in her arm popped and she gasped. "Upstairs, you son of a bitch."

"Don't swear, Leona," Bob Meldrum warned, and crossed to the hallway through which Captain Wells and company had entered.

"Get me Sarah," Leona said in a half-choked voice as the two women led her from the room. Aletha stood listening to Meldrum's measured tread on the stairs and what sounded like a door being kicked in. She decided this was no place for her and grabbed her coat off the floor. She was free to run out into the cold fog and get shot by the militia. A woman screamed upstairs and Aletha went for the door.

"Damn, he's a mean one," one of Leona's girls said behind her, and reached around to close the door. "Don't go out there, honey. Sarah'll fix you something to eat after she sees to Leona. You can sleep here by the stove."

Sarah didn't appear pleased at the prospect. She had been prepared for bed, but she puttered around the stove in her heavy housecoat, her hair all pushed up into a net cap. She fed Aletha some tasty but greasy soup, milk, and bread at the kitchen table while several of the girls gathered around to watch. Aletha was a little too worried to be hungry but ate most of what she was given under Sarah's grouchy stare. Sarah had pits and bumps all over her face. No one but Aletha even raised her eyes when Bob Meldrum came down the stairs and strode through the kitchen and out the back door.

Sarah gave her a couple of rough blankets and a pillow and told her to sleep on the floor. It wasn't bedtime by Aletha's internal clock and when all was quiet in the house she slipped down the hall, past a staircase illuminated by a light left on in the upstairs hall. She felt around on the wall inside an open door to her left looking for a light switch. What she found was a round knob that turned clockwise, but a chandelier sprang to light on a crowded room with a small bar, silvery heating stove, piano, couches and chairs and tables in conversation groups, fringy lampshades.

There was another sitting room across the hall that had no bar or piano, but this one was cozier and the walls were crowded with paintings of nude women in various poses. The one of Audrey held center stage between two long windows dressed in velvet. It looked like the one hanging in the New Sheridan but the dark background colors were richer, Audrey's skin lighter. The contrast in the dim light made the woman seem about to fly out into the room.

Aletha didn't think she'd slept until she became aware of people standing over her, some fully dressed, others in warm robes. One of them was Audrey. She wore a long braid over her shoulder and a bruised look, not of the skin but of the expression. "It's her. I seen her at the Senate, back by the kitchen. She and another one carrying trays of dishes, their skirts way up to their knees. I thought they was ghosts, but here's this one in the flesh." Audrey hunkered down and pinched Aletha's cheek, bringing with her the scent of stale underarms.

"Must be foreign, the way she's dressed, and her hair," another said. "You a heathen, miss?"

"I'm a person. And I'm sick of being treated like a stray animal." Aletha pushed herself off the floor and the young relics backed up. "And I come from the 1980's."

"Oh well, that explains everything. She's a loon."

"My father says the world will come to an end by 1925."

"Your father's a loon too."

"So Miss Not-so-fancy Pants, what are you doing here in 1904?"

"I'm looking for a man named Cree Mackelwain."

"Never heard of him."

"Ain't that the very tall gent was here a couple years ago? Had dents in his cheeks. Sort of a bummer but he had the whitest teeth."

Aletha backed toward the door, feeling really afloat now if there wasn't even to be a familiar Cree in this world. "What happened to him?"

"Moved on, I guess."

"Thanks for the food and the floor." Aletha slipped out the kitchen door to sunlight on snow. Cree had made it from Alta to Telluride, but Aletha was here in the wrong year. If the time tear wasn't going to find her, perhaps she could find it. She didn't want to end up as one of Leona's girls. She headed back toward the crib because that's where time had caught her up. But the streets were lined with cribs and she had to count back from the Silver Bell to be sure she had the right one.

"Who are you really?" Audrey had thrown a shawl over her robe and followed. "Where do you come from? Callie said she knew you." Audrey stared beyond Aletha, covering her mouth with her hand, and Aletha turned at the sound of applause and cheering. All the cribs but three were gone and Pacific Avenue was closed off at the north edge with crowds behind the ropes and the sheriff's and the marshal's cars flashing lights on either end.

"Stunning visuals," a man said, and stepped over the rope to pump Aletha's hand. She turned back to find Audrey gone.

"You want to take a bow?" the sheriff of San Miguel County asked Aletha, "and then tell me what the shit is going on?"

"Aletha, did you find him?" Tracy dived under the rope and practically dived into Aletha's arms. "What happened to the fog?" Minutes later in the sheriff's office she confided, "I told them the whole business about your time trips. They don't believe it. Well, would you?"

"But why the crowd and cops on Pacific?"

"The film-festival types came down from Colorado Avenue when they saw the fog. Thought it was some promotion stunt, I guess. And the cops thought the fog was some kind of public menace. Then it seemed like it dissolved the minute you stepped out of the air."

"Okay, I want to know what you know about that fog and what you know of the whereabouts of Cree Mackelwain," the sheriff said. "And I want to know right now, lady."

"I walked into the fog to find him but the girls at the Pick and Gad said I was a couple of years late." And Aletha recited faithfully just what had happened, knowing it was useless because it was unbelievable.

"I think you need analysis," Sheriff Rickard said when she'd finished.

And Tracy said, "Aletha, you couldn't have spent the night on the floor of the Pick and Gad in 1904. You weren't gone more than an hour and a half."

34

CALLIE had thought she was mistaken when she first saw Aletha's husband at Lone Tree Cemetery. But then she noticed his bright blue shoes and his height. She'd felt so good at being with the family again and so guilty at feeling good on such a sad occasion. Pa and Mr. Torkelson were heroes for going into the fiery portal to save others first. Pa had come out with burns and Mr. Torkelson had died. The O'Connells sat up front in the little church with Mrs. Torkelson, while many had to stand outside. No one but Callie and Bram even seemed to notice Aletha's husband. Callie wished he hadn't been there. He'd become a harbinger of bad things. And Aletha too.

On the way back to town Bram slouched along. He hated to be out where people would look at him, and never had Callie seen so many people in one place. "People always looked at you, even before the cave-in," she told him as they walked behind their parents. "And you're still you. Still Brambaugh O'Connell inside."

"But you aren't the same inside, Callie girl. You've changed since you've come to Telluride. You used to love everyone and everything."

"I still love you. I just hate cleaning things and I hate to not have us all live together in the same house."

"You hate not having us all live together in the same house," he corrected, and looked down at her from such a great height she wondered if he could still be growing for all his sickness. "You didn't used to hate."

"I don't hate you, Bram." And she took his hand that used to be warm and dry and strong. Now it was cold and damp and flaccid. She couldn't tell him that she'd turned sly and secretive.

The thing Cree Mackelwain found the most unusual about the Cosmpolitan Saloon and Gambling Club was the total absence of females. Not that they were forgotten. They sat astride horses, perched on stools, lounged in sunlight, and generally displayed their naked selves from paintings and photographs all over the walls. But there was not so much as a barmaid or scrubwoman in the saloon area. This was a man's world and a man didn't have to remove his hat or guard his tongue or hit the spittoon if he didn't want to. Although there were a good number of cowboys in and out, this was certainly different from the cowboy bars his ex-wife had dragged him to in Wyoming. Instead of across the back windows of pickups, men wore their guns around their waists hidden by suit jackets. Cree had subscribed to the scholarly theory that the wearing of six-guns was largely a Hollywood myth. But not so in Telluride at the beginning of the century.

Willy Selby was the proprietor. He left the dining room to the chef and the headwaiter and spent his time behind the bar in the saloon. Raucous behavior ended and hats came off at the door to the dining room. Cree's one free meal came at midday, when he was sent back to the kitchen to eat on a stool. The first day, a cook asked him if he wanted his beefsteak whole or ground. He ordered it whole and could see why the option had been offered. It had the flavor and texture of rawhide. Fried steak and fried potatoes and water was it for twenty-four hours. But the portions were generous and he swiped a piece of brown wrapping paper from a wastebin to wrap the last of the meat in and slipped it into his coat pocket. Willy expected him to work from eight in the morning until ten at night, and for this he would pay a dollar a day, but not until the end of the week. "More than I paid the nigger. He only got seventy-five cents."

Cree was responsible solely for the saloon and the bathroom leading off it, and with the long hours given over to it, the work was not that difficult. It was more the demeaning nature of the job that depressed him. Once he knelt down to polish the brass footrail on the bar or to pry up the scuddy gunk around the spittoons, these short men talked about him as if he was a kid or a moron.

"Where'd ya suppose he got shoes like thayet?"

"One more bend-over and he's gonna bust them britches clean open."

"Them big hands of his never done a man's work, I can tell ya."

Cree learned not to bristle when they called him "boy." They called each other boy a lot too. But "Steeplehead" began to grate. In the long leisurely hours of polishing and sweeping and waiting for some yo-yo to step away from his crushed cigar butt long enough for Cree to pick it up, he'd daydream that Aletha would come for him and just before stepping back through the tear with her he'd turn around and flip off Willy and the boys at the gambling tables.

He'd never realized how beguiling the thought of stealing could become. He had nothing but scraps saved from his lone meal and a dead man's coat, while stacks of gold and silver coins worth ten and twenty dollars apiece sat on the tables along the walls.

One of his duties was to keep the round stove in the corner stoked with coal, and at least he was warm during the days. But nights were long and cold. Cree stayed away from Stringtown, where all the other bums lodged, and found a boxcar with some loose hay down at the tracks instead. The hay and the heavy coat probably kept him from freezing the first night but they didn't help his disposition much, nor his skin, already itching from the bandages around his middle. He saved the scraps from his meal to eat in the night when hunger attacked the little sleep he managed. He fantasized about the Jacuzzi and the queen-size bed in the modern Pick and Gad. Things looked up the second night when Willy presented him with a knitted wool cap and scarf. "Told the wife about you. Said you was a proud man and might not take 'em. Belonged to her brother."

Cree took them. That night he removed his wet shoes and socks and wrapped the scarf around his feet. The wool was as scratchy as the hay and his bandages. He put the cap and scarf in his pocket when he went to work. He could easily carry all his possessions. "Don't even have a toothbrush."

"What'd you say, Steeplehead?" Willy leaned over the bar to peer at Cree on his hands and knees by a spittoon.

"I said I don't even have a toothbrush."

"What do you want a brush for your teeth for?"

"Think I'll moon all of you instead."

"Talks to hisself," Willy explained to a customer, and Cree tried to decide whether he'd hug Aletha if he ever saw her again or throttle her.

He was just getting used to being dirty when payday came around and he bought himself a bath at a bathhouse in the rear of a saloon, a tall narrow building on Colorado Avenue that would still be around in his day. He'd thought it leaned from age but it was fairly new now and seemed to have been built that way. It had round wooden tubs like hot tubs but with much less water and heat. It was after ten and most of the business was in the saloon, so Cree had a tub to himself. He unwrapped dirty bandages from around his rib cage and finally took a decent breath. A heavy set man replaced him at ten every evening at the Cosmopolitan. By the mess that greeted Cree in the mornings, he guessed the guy served more as bouncer than scrubman.

After his bath, Cree went to a barbershop, where he had a shave and his hair cut too short. This all totaled seventy-five cents and would have been worth that in dollars if he'd had them. Next he visited Van Atta's, "The Up-to-Date Outfitter," to look for a pair of boots. Rows upon racks of almost identical suits for men and shelves of derby hats like he'd seen in the funeral procession were offered for rent. Someday this place would sell skis, but now a miner could come down off the mountain dirty, clean up at the bathhouse, rent a full suit of dress clothes at Van Atta's, and be respectable for a night on the town. In the morning—having drunk, gambled, and whored away a month's pay—he could return the suit and collect the deposit to buy breakfast or rent a blanket and thin mattress in an unheated room and sleep off his excesses or rent a horse to get him to work.

Van Atta's sold clothing as well as rented, and must have stayed open most of the night, as did the rest of the town. Cree bought a pair of something called "Lumberman's Pacs" for $2.10 and two pairs of socks for fifteen cents. The pacs, as the salesman proudly repeated over and over had ". . . ten-inch legs of oil-grain leather with oil-pac leather uppers and double soles scwn and inserted with round cone-headed Hungarian nails." But Cree bought them because they were big enough to fit over two pairs of heavy socks. Since he'd worked a short week his grooming and shopping spree left him with $1.85 for the next week.

Although he smelled better he still was uneasy about stopping in at the Senate to delay his frigid night in the boxcar, but a bartender served him a five-cent mug of warm beer and told him to help himself to the free sandwiches and hard-boiled eggs on the bar. "Only what you can eat here," he warned, sizing Cree up accurately. "You're not to fill your pockets."

Thick slices of bread with hunks of chewy beef or sausages, dripping with butter and ketchup, sat on the bar. He took one of each and a couple of eggs to an out-of-the-way corner and felt like a rich man. The Senate, unlike the Cosmopolitan, had a piano player and women. Tobacco smoke swirled among the limbs of the naked statuette swimming above the tables. The pervasive odor here and in this whole sector of town was that of malt liquor. It had soaked into walls and floors and clothes and hair and wood and brick. It distilled into the air and oozed out onto the street, where it hung above the planked sidewalks like a sign and choked the alleyways behind. It was the best advertising a bar could have.

Cree sat back full and content, wiggled his toes in his new dry boots, and watched a fight brewing at a gaming table toward the center of the room. It was a big table with many men sitting around it, and two of them were insisting that unions weren't just for foreigners and that the fire at the Smuggler proved the working classes had to organize to protect their very lives. Others claimed otherwise and the shouting grew over the scraping back of chairs on the wooden floor.

Cree started when a man walking by him almost fell over his outstretched legs. "You union or are you not?"

"I'm just a poor man down on his luck, came in to get a beer so he could eat a free sandwich."

"Awww"—the man shook his head like Mr. Pangrazia at the hospital—"tha's not right in this plenteous country." He handed Cree a coin. "Go have yourself a woman." Then he turned into the room and socked the first guy to come at him.

Cree pulled in his legs and tried to look small. No chairs were hurled at the mirror and bottles behind the bar. There were some crunches and one man fell against a table, knocking over stacks of coins; then the bartender and two bouncers helped several gentlemen out the door and it was over. The two men who started the fight were still at their table when the room settled down. Those standing at the bar merely held their drinks up out of the way. Neither the piano player nor the gamblers around the edges had even paused. Hard to believe the horrors that would befall this town over that very argument. He'd seen better fights over a football score in Wyoming bars. Not one gun had been lifted from a gunbelt.

In the back rooms the suits didn't look rented, and complete dinners were being served. The gambling was quieter, the stacks of coins higher, and the women more relaxed. Cree felt shabby here and returned to the front room. He read his new coin. It was worth twenty dollars. He put it away quickly. Nobody would believe he hadn't snagged that off a gambling table. Before heading for his freezing boxcar, Cree climbed snowdrifts off the alley in back of the Senate to stare at the crib Aletha and Tracy would live in someday, in the dim hope of making contact with Aletha. This was the third night he'd done this, and tonight a town marshal approached him carrying a sawed-off pool cue for a nightstick and kept whacking it into his glove. "You want to give Floradora some business, boy, that's between you and her. You want to make her scared every night like she's been complaining of, and it's gonna be between you and me."

Cree slunk off. Even worse, Sheriff Rutan stopped in to the Cosmopolitan the next day to throw back a shot of rye and check up on him.

"He don't make trouble. Don't get drunk," Willy praised him. "Gets to work on time and don't lean on his broom too much. Real dependable fella."

"Glad to hear that, Willy, glad to hear it." The sheriff bent over Cree, who was on his knees shaking down the ashes in the stove. "Looks like your other employer hasn't paid up yet. Or is this a good place for spying?" When Cree didn't answer, he said, "You seen your three friends lately? I hear they could be stealing food and who knows what-all. See to it I don't hear that about you, Mr. McCree Ronald Mackelwain."

35

CLYDE Duffer spread cold hands to the tiny fire. He sat in a crate. They'd arranged three tipped-over crates in a triangle, leaving a space in the middle open to the sky for fires. It was not the Hilton. And it was snowing again. He hadn't seen so much snow since a television special on the Yukon. It crunched like broken glass as Maynard slid the other two crates apart enough to crawl into the triangle. Maynard had a package wrapped in butcher paper.

"What'd you do, roll a baglady?" Duffer asked him.

"Slipped into a few places and snatched the freebies off the bars. Got more beer joints in this damn place than houses. Garbage in the alleys is frozen so stiff you can't tell what it is. Have to fight the dogs for it." Maynard blew on his hands and presented Duffer with a pickle the size of an erection. "Got some sausages too. Figure if we held them over the flames—"

"Lenny getting the gun?"

"Grabbing firewood off wood piles. Hey, Lenny and me go out

and practically get wasted for blankets, clothes, and stuff—how come you don't go out?''

"I'm the planner and you're the gofers. How come no gun?"

"Everybody and his brother's carrying a gun out there, Duffer. It's like war, not the real world. Liable to get shot trying to nab one. What would you plan if we had one? A holdup? Hey, they got money falling off poker tables instead of chips in those joints, but it's all change. And every guy in the place watching you grab it is wearing a gun. Odds are grueling, man."

"Maybe I'm planning on visiting a joint and seeing for myself." Duffer's pickle was frozen already, crunched worse than the snow. "Secret-like."

"You'd stand out a mile. Not dressed for staying more than long enough to steal some food and run. I mean, they wear three-piece suits in them places, and hats yet. Besides, Duffer, I don't think they go in for long court trials and stuff here. Liable to get hung if they even suspect you."

"You put away a few souls in your day, never bothered you. Never had anything pinned on you either. What makes this place so different?"

"That's just it. In my day odds are I don't have trouble. Odds are different here. And I don't even know what they are yet." Maynard stuck a sausage on a sharpened stick and held it over the fire. He had a scarf tied over his head like an old woman's babushka and a floppy hat over that. With the seedy coat he'd yanked off a fallen drunk, Maynard looked the perfect picture of a hobo.

How had they come to this? Duffer had the gnawing urge to kill slowly and lovingly whoever was responsible for their predicament. But if you got right down to it, how could Mackelwain's girlfriend have pulled off something like this? Duffer's frustration was such that he'd eradicate somebody pretty soon anyway. He had to look like he was doing something. Maynard and Lenny just stuck to him now out of habit, fear of the unknown, and the dumb hope he could do something. The only reason Duffer hadn't killed Mackelwain out of spite before this was that he couldn't be positive the jerk wasn't their only ticket home.

Cree was more concerned about how to break his twenty-dollar gold piece without coming under suspicion of having stolen it than he was about Duffer and his boys. And he worried about freezing to death as every night the mountain town grew more frigid. Most of the saloons on Colorado Avenue encouraged their customers to visit the attached dining rooms when hungry, but down in the tenderloin every bar had free treats for the price of a beer. He made the rounds so as not to make himself too unwelcome at any one place and thereby managed another meal every day.

It was at the Silver Bell one night that he saw Bulkeley Wells, Arthur Collins, and two other dandies out slumming in this working-class bar. Bulkeley Wells Cree knew by his picture in the history books and Arthur Collins by the talk of the men standing next to him. Wells seemed truly above any of the mutterings either of discontent or of admiration that whisked around the place at his entrance, but Collins was clearly uncomfortable. Cree looked with interest at Collins, the man history had slated for assassination in a little less than a year. He held himself aloof while Wells joked with hard-rock miners, thumping them on the back. Just once, briefly, his eyes chanced to meet Cree's over the heads of others and Cree could feel the impact. Whatever the man turned his hand to, the power of his charm would turn others with him. Cree was again reminded of how much he wanted Aletha to come for him before this town tore itself apart.

The next time he saw Bulkeley Wells was in the Cosmopolitan. Wells sat at a table in the dining room with Collins, Sheriff Cal Rutan, and a stooped white-haired man. Cree was on his way back to the saloon from his meal of creamed chicken over mashed potatoes. They were dining on roast duck.

"Mr. McCree Mackelwain"—the sheriff gestured with a half-gnawed bone—"come over here." Rutan asked Wells, "This your man?"

"No man of mine. Any of your doing, Homer?"

"Never saw him before," the elderly gentleman answered. "You a union man, boy?"

"No sir, I'm unaligned."

"Talks funny," the sheriff explained. "Thinks he's educated. Says he's from Cheyenne. I wired up there and they never heard of him." People were discussing Cree as if he weren't present again.

"McCree . . . odd Christian name. His mother's maiden name, I'll wager." Wells looked at Cree more closely. "I see intelligence behind those eyes, Cal, and the smolder of violence."

"Meek as a kitten for as big as he is." The sheriff dismissed Cree with a wave of his hand. "It's why, I want to know."

"There's only one way to be sure of him, Cal," Wells said with a softness Cree could just hear as he reached the door to the saloon.

That night Cree started for his boxcar early and hungry because he'd run out of nickels for beer until payday. It was one of those clear nights when a full moon blue-tinted the snow heaped everywhere and sound snapped on rarefied air. A frozen burro lay on its side at the end of Spruce Street like a tipped-over statue. It had been there last night too and Cree wondered when someone would think to cart it off. Three or four men stood on the tracks stomping their feet and talking steam balloons between Cree and his boxcar, so he walked on down the tracks past piled lumber and the R. Wunderlich and Rella Bottling Works and Beer Storage. He turned off to the ice pond, a dammed-up offshoot of the river. The brick icehouse would someday be a restaurant but was now used to store squares of ice cut from the pond to distribute to Telluride's iceboxes.

They stood at the edge of the pond near a roped-off area and at first Cree thought they might be ice skaters. She had her hands demurely ensconced in a muff and pleaded with voice tone and movements of her head instead of gestures. He hunched into his coat, bent slightly toward her. They kept about a foot apart. Cree turned away, feeling as lonely as he had that day at Dutch Massey's funeral.

Then he heard her running toward him, light footsteps, and what he first thought were hiccups but realized soon were choked cries. She passed him in awkward hopping steps, hampered by her skirts, her arms held out for balance on the icy path between snowbanks. She slipped, skidded, and fell. The muff came flying back toward Cree. She was on her feet almost at once and racing over the tracks to the street on the other side. Cree braced his body to block the man if he was intent on chasing her and found himself facing Callie's brother.

"Aunt Lilly?" Bram called softly after the fleeing figure. He looked more like himself filled out by his heavy clothing, but he sounded stricken.

Cree walked the plowed tracks with Bram O'Connell. "I couldn't take her money," Bram explained, stroking his aunt's muff. "Not that we couldn't use some. Ma'am needs her medicine. Pa can't work till they rebuild up at the Smuggler."

"Why can't you accept help from your own aunt?"

"She's Floradora now. One of them. She's dead to us." For a boy who was so emaciated, he had a long, strong stride.

Cree worked to keep up. Bram formed an odd and tenuous link with his own world. "Tell me more about the cave-in."

"Who are you? You knew about it months before it happened," Bram said. "How do you close up holes without leaving any mending marks?"

Cree had no answer that would make sense, so he just said, "Charles is getting fat and lazy. Aletha spoils him."

"You warned me not to go back in the drifts up at Alta, and one caved in. Your lady warned Callie not to come to Telluride and she did. I'm afraid to ask what you plan for her."

"Bram, we didn't plan the cave-in. We feared it would happen. Aletha is worried that your sister might become like . . . like your Aunt Lilly, one of them." Cree was saved by Aunt Lilly's muff as the boy swung at him with the hand that still held it. He grabbed Bram in a bear hug and was almost thrown off the tracks. There was power in this kid still. "Listen to me, will ya? I'm not insulting your sister. It's just that Aletha worries for her. She loves your sister too."

"Then she'd never even think such a thing of my Callie girl."

"It's not thinking it that makes it happen. Weren't you a little surprised when your aunt became Floradora?"

Bram pushed Cree away and broke an ice chunk off the edge of a warehouse platform and hurled it into the night, his whole body behind it, a cut-off groan escaping his throat. He stared at Cree, his eyes shadowed by a bony face and the tilt of his head under a yard light. He wore a knitted cap like Cree's.

For a moment Bram's head reminded Cree of a skull. In Cree's reality, Bram O'Connell would have been dead for years, probably decades. All the background sounds of this mining camp seemed suddenly as remote and hollow as the wind. Cree shuddered, shook his head clear of ghosts. They tramped past the dead burro and around the curve in the tracks where the dregs of the prostitutes held court in sagging cribs. Bram stopped suddenly. "Are you my real father?" When Cree was too stunned to answer, the kid slouched farther into his shoulders and walked on. "You're so tall like I am and . . . you seem to search me out."

"But your pa—"

"I'm a foundling. But I always wondered what he'd be like. If he ever wondered too. Men don't, I guess." Bram stopped again. "I belong to John O'Connell and I'd gladly die for him, so don't think—"

"Bram, hey, I'm not your father. I'd like to be your friend." I'm a good half-century younger than you, kid. "But if I ever have a son, I'd be proud if he were like you." Cree wasn't sure how much he was talking aloud to himself, how much he meant to say.

"Nobody wants a scarecrow for a son, mister, a scholar who can't even swing a double jack."

"Where I come from, scholars do very well. Brains outweigh muscle every time."

"Where do you come from? You talk in a strange way."

"Wyoming."

"Do they have many scholars in Wyoming?" Bram scratched at his scalp through his cap. "Where I come from a man tests his mettle with a hammer and steel."

The next time Cree saw Bram, the boy told him he'd found work after school, loading and unloading boxcars at the R. Wunderlich and Rella Bottling Works and didn't feel the need to walk so much at night.

And the next time Willy Selby at the Cosmopolitan Saloon paid him, Cree bought himself a bath, rented a three-piece suit and a derby at Van Atta's, and took his twenty-dollar gold piece to the Pick and Gad.

36

CREE was sweeping out the Cosmopolitan Saloon the next morning when he saw Aletha Kingman. He always stirred up the fire in the coal stove first, then cleaned the toilet behind it where the flush tanks sat high on the wall. He'd clean himself at the sink placed just outside the door in the saloon proper. It had two faucets;

one ran cold, the other icy cold. He'd change the blackened four-foot towel for a clean one each day. Cree would spread buckets of sawdust on the floor to soak up any mud or tobacco juice that hadn't dried to concrete. With snow everywhere and mud streets thawing now and then at midday, the floor was always filthy. He'd sweep sawdust and everything that came up with it out onto the sidewalk and then shovel it and any new-fallen snow out onto the street. Last, he mopped the floor with soap and water.

This morning, Cree was still at the sweeping-it-out-onto-the-side-walk stage when Bulkeley Wells himself rode up on a sleek and nervous horse. He stopped and watched Cree over the snowbank. "I think, Mr. McCree Mackelwain, that this sort of thing does not suit you." His horse shied and pranced but he sat it as if he didn't even notice. "I think perhaps we can find something more to your liking. If you're interested, I should be in my hotel suite at the New Sheridan around two o'clock this afternoon."

Cree was interested in anything that would pay enough for him to rent a room and buy three solid meals a day. He was about to tell Mr. Bulkeley just that when he noticed Aletha standing across Colorado Avenue. He dropped the broom and the horse reared. "Aletha, I'm here. Over here!"

"What the devil?" Wells said, more discomfited by the sight across the street than by the dangerous antics of his steed. Across the street there wasn't any snow. The sun shone on Aletha's honey hair and the bare sidewalk was concrete instead of wood. Across the street Aletha looked comfortable in a light jacket. She started toward him.

"For God's sake don't come to me. I'll come over there." Cree recognized the building she'd been about to enter as the one where Renata Winslow had her office, and he recognized the woman who came to lean out of a second-story window as Renata Winslow. Bulkeley Wells's terrified horse practically ran him down as Cree raced across to Aletha, and he heard the snap of authority in the other man's voice as he tried to control the animal.

The herbal dusty scents of autumn instead of horseshit. And Aletha Kingman smelled blessedly of soap and hair rinse and toothpaste.

Aletha sat naked in the Jacuzzi in the condominium at the Pick and Gad. She sipped champagne mixed with orange juice and faced Cree through steam. The side of one leg gently brushed his as the bubbles frothed and lifted her while he told his story. "I'd just gotten my twenty-dollar gold piece broken so I'd have some money, and there you were. I couldn't believe it."

Aletha couldn't believe it either. She'd been on her way to find out if Renata had any work for her when she'd felt a cold wind on her back. Cree had rushed her here before Renata or anyone could question him. He'd showered, shaved, and brushed his teeth—to hear him tell it—forty-two times. When she returned with the fixings, he prepared fluffy cheese-and-mushroom omelets and a half-pound of bacon. They took the phone off the hook. The world would come down on them soon enough. "Love your new hairdo. Makes your ears stick out."

"And you have something the matter with your smile."

"One of your goon friends kicked me in the teeth. I'm lucky I'm only going to have to have one of them capped. What gets me is how you could have healed up so fast. There's only a few marks left on you from that beating."

"Well, it was over a month ago. Even old men like me heal eventually."

"Cree, you've only been gone six days."

"Six days . . ." He sat staring into the steam between them and then laughed. "When I left here it was September, when I got there it was November. And they were talking about Christmas when I left. I've been gone six days and lived a month."

"I went back for an overnight, but it was the wrong year." Aletha described the day of the fog. "A couple of the gals here at the cathouse did remember you though, Cree. Your stay couldn't have been all that much work and no play if they remembered you after two years. I mean, there was probably a lot of traffic in and out of this place." His gaze was steady, unrevealing. He didn't bother to comment. It was his business if he wanted to visit a whorehouse. It had probably been a very long month in those six days. It irked her anyway. "What if the time switch happens again? Right now, like we are? Here we'd be in the past with nothing but two champagne glasses, surrounded by a bunch of sweaty, gawking prostitutes."

"That experience was no joke. Promise me you won't mess with this again."

"I wish I'd taken your advice and left town when I could. But now the sheriff has told me not to leave. He's looked up my prison record, which was reversed but not erased. And I really feel responsible for what happened to you, but I can't stop it from happening again. I probably shouldn't go to work and expose others to God-knows-what, but I have to eat and pay rent. And the delicious, sexy mood the champagne and I were conjuring up is evaporating like the bubbles in—"

"Shush, please? Shut up." He pulled her toward him by her knees. "Don't get all simpy and weepy on me." He was just drawing her onto his lap when someone literally pounded on the door.

"I know you're in there, Mackelwain. This is the sheriff. Open up."

Aletha huddled in clothes still wet that she'd hurried into without drying herself off. Cree sat in a terrycloth robe at the other end of the couch. The sheriff, a deputy, and the town marshal swaggered around them talking tough. "Those three guys are mob, Mackelwain. You expect me to believe you took care of them?" the sheriff asked. "If so there's a lot in your background that is not known by the computer."

"I didn't do anything to them. Aletha did, and I told you how." But Cree explained again. "And when the tear opened up, they weren't around to come back. Guess they're stuck."

"Bunch of screaming nuts, all of them," the sheriff told the marshal. "And the reason you show little sign of the beating those guys gave you, according to Miss Kingman here and Miss Ledbetter, is because in the last six days you've been gone you lived a month in the year 1901 and had time to heal."

Cree winced, then shrugged. "Right."

"The mob goes after your partner, Massey, and he's dead. Now the mob is after you. What do you suppose they want? This?" And the sheriff took the hunk of rock his men had found in Alta from a bag. "Know what it is?"

"A rock?"

"Don't get smart. Most of this 'rock' is highgrade gold, the likes of which have not been seen in this county since the old days when they tore up the San Juans for it. Now it's worth bucks, but nothing like what your partner was into. Maybe Miss Kingman whisked this out of 1901 for us with her special powers?"

"They found that under Callie's cabin, Cree," Aletha said. "But the only time I've been under there was when we were trying to flush Charles. Remember?"

"Charles who?" The sheriff put a foot up on the coffee table and struck a pose.

"Callie's cat . . . my cat now. Callie's a little girl from the past. She—"

"Cat." Sheriff Rickard nodded patiently. "I'm not interested in cats. I'm interested in cocaine." He kept right on nodding. "Which happens to be relevant to your past and to Mr. Mackelwain's and what the employers of the missing Clyde Duffer, Maynard Bellamy, and Lennard Pheeney are interested in. I see a connection somewhere."

"You've had no reports of a sudden winter on Colorado Avenue this morning?" Cree asked. "What about the fog on Pacific a couple of days ago?"

The marshal looked interested and about to speak, but the sheriff cut him off. "The only snow I want to know about comes in kilos, grams, and ounces. You are both under investigation and I want you to stay where I can find you. You so much as take a walk in the woods, you check in with the marshal first."

"I'm going to enjoy the luxury of this place while I can," Cree said when they'd left. "It's only a matter of time before they discover it belonged to Dutch and grab it too. Or that sheriff will have me in jail for something I don't know about yet. Or the local narcs or the feds will have my balls for—"

"And you're glad to get back?"

"Sure beats hell out of a cold boxcar, lady." Cree reached for her again. And someone knocked on the door again. A more polite if insistent rapping this time. "Shit!"

"Cree Mackelwain," Renata Winslow said when he'd opened the door, "where have you been?"

"Right here. In 1901." Cree slammed around the kitchen, filling the teakettle and dumping beans in the electric coffee grinder.

"And you I had work for," Renata told Aletha. "But could I reach you?" She slipped the phone back on its cradle and turned to Cree. "And I thought you'd gotten killed like Dutch. There are all sorts of nefarious nerds ranging our tiny community and asking questions about you. And who was the gorgeous hunk on the horse in the snowstorm with you this morning?"

"Mr. Bulkeley Wells." Aletha leafed through a book on Telluride until she came across Wells's picture.

"He did sort of look like him, but Wells died out in California sometime in the thirties I think. The guy on the horse was young. And how did you manage that little snowstorm? Or the fog the other day?"

"Renata, I told you about my problem at your party."

"And I still don't buy it. But I know a few people who were at the film festival who would give their eyeteeth to know how you do this stuff. I can contact them if you're interested."

Aletha curled up in her damp clothes in a close approximation of a fetal position. "Why do all these things happen to me?"

"You didn't spend a month sleeping in a boxcar." Cree poured coffee into three mugs. "I just want to hide in here and never go out."

"Probably the first place the narcs will look for you," Renata said. "You work that snowstorm on the ski slopes in October and the town will hire you for life."

"I told Bram that Charlie is fat and sassy. Did you know Floradora was his aunt? He about killed me when I suggested Callie might go the same way. Floradora lived in the crib you and Tracy are renting."

"I know you two want to be alone," Renata said. "You can talk gibberish over my head all day. But I'm staying until I get some answers."

"What I didn't tell him about was the snowslide." Cree picked up the book and started turning pages. "At the Liberty Bell. Let's see, it was . . . oh, God, next spring. Figures. You should have seen the snow they have already. You have to climb over snowbanks to get down to the doorways."

"You warned him about the cave-in. What good did that do?" Aletha said. Cree and the champagne were giving her a headache.

"But he's going to school and working at a warehouse. Which he shouldn't be. Looks brittle enough to break. But there's no reason for him to go near the Liberty Bell." Shortly after noon, Cree picked up the phone and called MoNika's, Telluride's version of a carry-out, and ordered roast duck à l'orange, crab-stuffed artichokes, spiced fruit, French bread, and more champagne. "You should have met the sheriff then. Makes the present one look like a preacher. And the gamblers, the professionals that worked in those places. They could be steely-eyed and drunk at the same time."

Renata gave in halfway through the afternoon to go back to her business. "Watch out for the narcs, you two. They invariably arrive at the halfway point in a good climax."

37

THE winter of 1901–1902 was one of the worst ever known in the San Juans, which are fabled for their winters. Bram worried about the tall man, Cree, who slept in a boxcar, and he stopped to check for him often after work at night. But the car was always empty and eventually it was moved away. Bram lived in a sort of haze that winter. He'd grown so good at ignoring the taunts of his classmates they'd begun to ignore him. He concentrated on his studies in order to limit his homework so that after supper he could hurry off to the Wunderlich Bottling Works, where he marked order forms and stacked crates of bottles, readying for distribution by wagon in the morning. When the seven-o'clock train came in he unloaded barrels and crates into the warehouse. At first the work exhausted him, but eventually it made him pleasantly tired. Mrs. Pakka began leaving milk, cheese and bread, pieces of leftover meat pie, and cookies out for him at night.

John O'Connell returned to work after Christmas up at the Smuggler but Bram refused to quit his job. Instead he insisted they use the money to move Luella into a small room just off the parlor so she could keep warmer, and he moved into the attic, where as many as seven men could sleep on cots. In the beginning he had trouble sleeping for the cold, but soon the heavy work and food before bed kept his blood flowing hard enough to warm the blankets. The second week in January, Mrs. Pakka took in three new boarders and the dorm room was filled. The three were freshly shaven and smelled of the bathhouse, but their clothes were shabby and ill-assorted. They paid two months' rent ahead in good coin, though, and were quiet and orderly at table. They spent much of the day around the stove in the parlor like old women.

"His marks are good, Mrs. O'Connell, and his appetite is healthy even though he's very . . . lanky," Bram overheard Mrs. Pakka tell

Ma'am one evening. "He's a loyal son to you and seems to me he thrives on all the work he does."

"But the doctors in Denver warned of his fragility, Mrs. Pakka. They—"

"It's you I worry over, Mrs. O'Connell. And, pardon my forthrightness, but if there's another worry coming to you, it's your little girl, not your boy." Bram's heart turned cold.

It turned cold again the next day on his way home from school. Another blizzard raged and the students were warned to travel in groups. Bram, as usual, had no group and ducked his head into the sleety onslaught alone. Nothing moved but the snow. Buildings were shadow-blurs sometimes seen, sometimes imagined, definite only when he walked into one. He came across a man trying to tug a stalled horse and lost them instantly.

Bram tried to turn away from the wind to catch his breath, but whichever way he faced, snow gorged the air and he felt the return of the old terror of suffocation, the nightmare brought on by a caved-in drift flooding to its roof. The more he panicked and fought, the more the snow swirled into his mouth and reached for his lungs, filled his eyes to blinding and coated his lashes together. He found himself making a constant circle where he stood to fight for breath, terrified at his helpless isolation.

It finally occurred to Bram to pull his arms out of his coat sleeves and hold the coat up over his head to give himself some breathing space. He'd long since lost his schoolbooks and was stunned at how easily he could come to losing his life as well in the middle of a town. He'd walked into the train depot before he regained his bearings. It was closed up tight with no train expected in this storm. Bram remembered the abandoned feeling he'd had looking at the drawings of Callie's lady, Aletha, pictures of familiar places gone all strange and empty. He took off again at the angle that should lead to Mrs. Pakka's, not far from the depot. Just as he reached an outbuilding, he tripped over a sprawled body. He dragged it to the kitchen door by its ankles. It was Mr. Pheeney, one of the new boarders. He was half-frozen and he'd been shot.

In the parlor, Duffer and Maynard played gin rummy at a small table by the stove, unaware of what had happened to Pheeney. Now that they were warm and fed, boredom goaded them to bad temper.

They shared the parlor with the scrawny O'Connell woman and a drug salesman stranded there by the storm. He cleared his throat a lot and just sat. She had a perennial runny nose and her polite sniffing made them all the more irritable. She was reading the Bible again. She had to be the salesman's best client.

"I'd give my balls for TV right now and a case of beer," Maynard whispered.

"Shut up." Duffer jerked his head in the direction of the others in warning. But he agreed. How these people could be content to work their butts off one minute and be totally inactive the next mystified him.

Maynard lost the game because he was too busy watching the O'Connell woman. She'd picked up a packet of medicine she'd purchased from the salesman. "Hey, Duffer, she snortin' the stuff?"

Mrs. O'Connell had poured some powder into the palm of her hand and held it to her nose. Maynard startled her by leaving his chair suddenly and standing over her. Some of the powder fell onto her Bible and he dipped an index finger into it, tasted it, rubbed some on his upper gum. "This ain't street stuff, Duffer. It's pure. And this guys's selling it for almost nothin'."

Mildred Heisinger had a headache but no powders to take. She sat in a drafty railroad car stranded atop the Dallas Divide. Her latest batch of human freight hovered around the coal stove at one end of the car, cutting off the heat to the other passengers. They were from California and did nothing but complain, and they numbered only six, which meant that Mildred was going deeper into debt to Lawyer Barada and his unseen business associates. She no longer traveled in the style she had. Scrimping on expenses helped her to save something toward her debt, and there was no need to impress her charges. Her advertisements now left little doubt as to what was expected, although the careful wording didn't actually specify anything. Every trip garnered an innocent or two, desperate to get away from home or a violent husband, but Mildred's sympathy for respectable women had diminished. Her cozy house in the unfortunate part of town had become a haven to hurry back to. Lawyer Barada assured her that if she chose to run from her debts the guardians of law and order as well as the Pinkertons would hunt her down no matter where she fled. She believed him.

"You didn't happen to mention freezing to death, your ladyship," a floozy from Los Angeles whined. "Plenty of money and pretty clothes, says you. And beauteous surroundings." She looked around at the windows packed with snow. The couple with the croupy baby sitting behind Mildred moved farther away.

The baby ignored its anxious mother and began a congested wailing. Mildred retreated inside herself and away from the miserable company. Her inner eye watched herself sit at the end of her dining table nearest the stove while Letty served hot soup and baked chicken with peas. She didn't mind being alone at the long table, she felt safe and blessed. And since it was her house, she could even read while she ate. Mildred stood naked, dipping one foot in the steamy bathtub brought out to the cook stove in the kitchen, while Letty held her robe up behind to keep the drafts from her back, when cold drafts swept into the railroad car. The conductor and Mr. Bulkeley Wells swept in after them. The conductor looked red and pinched. Mr. Wells looked exuberant.

"I've ventured up to the front. The rotary train will be all night plowing its way up here," he said happily. "Here, you hens, allow that mother and infant to the fire." He had the floozies scattered and the lady and baby to the stove in seconds. Mildred's charges had the grace to look awed. "Why, my dear Miss Heisinger, is that you?" He bore down on Mildred. "How uncomfortable you look." And before she could protest, he'd drawn her from her seat and pulled her toward the front of the car. "We must do something for you."

"Did you see that? Her ladyship can blush."

Mildred was out of the car, across the connecting platform, darkened by snow walls, and being propelled down the aisle of the next car, still trying to shake free of Letty and the hot bath. "Mr. Wells, please!"

"The service on this railroad is abominable." He hurried her across another set of connecting platforms and into the unbelievable warmth of a private car. "But I'm always exhilarated by a good battle with the elements, aren't you?" He slipped her coat from her shoulders even as she resisted, and unpinned her hat from behind, lifting it off before she had the wits to grab it.

Wallpaper, couches, hanging lamps. Almost stuffy with rugs and cushions. Snow at the windows dimmed the light. He lit an oil lamp and tinkered with the heating stove. Mildred felt like a rabbit in a trap listening to the approach of the hunter. "Mr. Wells, you must realize how unseemly it is for me to be here," she said, and reached for her coat hanging on antlers fastened to the wall, but he blocked her by bringing a covered pot to the stove top.

"Unseemly?" He raised both eyebrows and the enormous eyes appeared to grow. "How can you even think of propriety at a time like this?" He blocked her way again, as if he didn't notice her attempts to reach her coat, and drew plates and dinnerware, a linen cloth and napkins, from a side cupboard. "Do you realize that at this very moment men are risking their lives atop these cars merely to keep the stovepipes from blocking with snow? Do you realize we may all freeze to death before rescue arrives? This is truly a time of crisis." He lifted bread and cheese and a bottle of wine from a hamper. Mildred refused to look at them. She knew the danger for her lay inside this car, not without. She also knew it had been long cold hours since she'd eaten. He lifted the lid of the pot on the coal stove, stirred the smell of cooked lamb and onions into the air. "Please do sit down and be comfortable, Miss Heisinger," he said as if he'd just noticed her rigidity. "The stew will take a moment longer to heat through. May I call you Mildred?"

When she neither answered nor seated herself, he paused in the process of removing the cork from the wine bottle and studied her. He still managed to block her escape and he did so in a manner she could not be certain was intentional. The coach was crowded with furniture, boxes, and luggage. They stood not so very far apart. Other than the draft in the stovepipe and the hiss of the lamp, the stillness was uncanny. The howl of wind and storm outside either had abated or was stifled by a blanket of snow. Mildred couldn't seem to look away from him. She was strongly aware of the ruin this man must leave in his wake as he dashed about his rich, eventful life. She had no wish to be numbered among the ruined, but she didn't know how to fight him. Like Lawyer Barada, he could assume the privileges of his class while working on her penchant for good manners to outsmart her. Mildred sensed that if he but touched her she was lost.

"I believe that you are afraid of me," he said softly, trying to sound surprised, but his eyes gave away his amusement. "Now, how can that be? You're a sophisticated, well-traveled lady and I merely offer you dinner to help pass the storm." He pulled out a chair at the table. "Beginning with my very own jellied consommé, followed by the tempting ambrosia heating on the stove and the other poor provisions you see before you. And I promise to deliver you safely afterward to your cold and crowded coach completely uncompromised."

"You promise? And what is it you expect in return?"

"The promise of a gentleman. And your lovely presence at my lonely table is more than enough compensation on such a bleak evening."

Mildred sat. But still she didn't trust Mr. Bulkeley Wells. The consommé was better than any she'd tasted on her travels. She took her first sip of alcohol, although she'd vowed not to touch the wine. The fragrant stew was warming but a trifle salty and he offered no water. She had also vowed not to relax, but she did. They discussed the novels of Mr. Dickens, Mr. Macaulay's histories, the poetry of Mrs. Browning. Mr. Wells told of his journeys abroad. It was difficult not to enjoy the evening.

"And so," he said finally and catching her completely off guard, "how's business? I understand you're helping to solve the problem of the shortage of working girls in Telluride."

Mildred felt an alarming tingling under her hair and along the backs of her hands. She didn't know if it was because of what he'd just said or because she'd drunk more of the wine than she'd intended during their stimulating conversation. He'd actually opened another bottle, she realized now. She started to rise, felt a tad dizzy, and sat again. "Really, Mr. Wells, your rudeness is scarcely gentlemanly."

"Mildred, Mildred, why this pretense of modesty and outrage? You are a businesswoman and I am a businessman. I'm in Telluride often enough, God knows, to be fully appraised of the nature of your business. Barada has seen to it that everyone in damn near the whole valley knows. Why this act of innocent primness?"

Mildred made it to her feet this time but held to the edge of the table.

"You parade around with the starch of a grand lady, demand lavish respect and careful manners from everyone, and yet you go about the country enticing innocent girls to—"

"No!" Mildred was dabbing her eyes with a linen napkin before she realized she was crying. "Don't you—"

"Let us be truthful for once." He rose and blocked her exit again.

"You are, quite simply, a procuress and everyone knows it." He held her wrists when she tried to push him out of her way.

"You promised"—her sobbing was uncontrolled and shameless now—"as a gentleman."

"And I'll honor that promise if you still wish it in a moment. But first . . ." Mr. Bulkeley Wells kissed a tear off Mildred Heisinger's cheek. "There, there, now, there's nothing so terribly wrong with what you do if it's looked at in a certain light." He kissed the other cheek. Mildred felt a frightening heat envelop her body. "I should think there must be a need or you wouldn't have been hired."

Even with all she'd been through, the stoic Mildred had wept like this only twice before in her life. Once when her mother died and once after Brambaugh O'Connell had carried her through the mining camp of Alta. Bulkeley Wells raised her head by holding to her chin and forced her to look into his eyes.

"No . . . you promised."

Then he pulled her toward him and kissed her mouth and Mildred was lost.

PART THREE

WAR

38

T HE rotary train rescued Mildred from the Dallas Divide but the winter did not improve. Bulkeley Wells admitted to feeling like a "cad" when he discovered the pristine procuress was a virgin. He would always wonder if she hadn't tricked him somehow. Mildred retreated to her haven on Pacific Avenue, thankful that the snow would keep her from traveling for a while. Wells had a long-haired kitten delivered to her door in apology. Mildred named it Cad. He was the first in a long line of cats to share her haven.

"He wasn't even armed," Duffer complained when Sheriff Rutan came to investigate Lenny's murder.

"The more fool he. Now, I wonder what's become of your other friend, McCree Mackelwain. He wasn't armed either. We find his body when the snow melts, and you're the first man I'm coming after."

Bram O'Connell was growing a new head of hair. Itchy, soft, silky, lighter, with just a touch of its former sandiness, as if his terrible illness had leached it of its color. The doctors in Denver had predicted he'd go through life bald or with a sparse fuzz at best.

February went out like a lion with a four-day snowstorm, wind-driven and so heavy the San Juans seemed shrouded in a deep twilight even at noon. On March 1, the slide next to the Liberty Bell Mine, above and to the east of town, overran its trough and scattered boardinghouse and tram cars and men down the slope like matchsticks. Rescuers from town raced to dig out the buried, and the slide ran again, taking some of the rescue party and the injured. As stunned survivors straggled back to town, another slide swept part of them off the trail. The dead totaled nineteen and the hospitals filled again.

A dazed Telluride gathered itself to bury en masse for the second time in a little over four months. The slides continued to run. Almost daily, tons of loosened snow thundered to the valley floor, carrying rocks and trees and death, rattling windows, knocking dishes from their shelves, making miners fear the trails and huddle in the saloons. Their talk was now that the management at the Liberty Bell had caused the trees to be cut from the hillside for timbering in the mine, thus widening the trough. And the buildings were built too close to the trough. And Eastern money didn't mind how many died as long as their investments prospered.

"First they complain the tunnels are not well enough timbered," Arthur Collins wrote to Bulkeley Wells in Denver. "Then they complain of the cutting. Whatever the disaster, management and owners are to blame. Meantime I'm hard pressed to keep the blighters at work and appeased. I preferred the scabs."

Stringtown flooded as usual with the spring melt, but more bodies were discovered this time, due largely to Lennard Pheeney's attempts to support himself, Duffer and Maynard. Duffer and Maynard had managed to live through the horrible winter without a weapon by rolling bummers, as the easy prey were called here. Duffer still felt uncomfortable without a gun but agreed they were under enough suspicion already.

It was well into summer before the last of the snow was gone, and the mud that followed seemed almost as deep. But the mountain flowers overwhelmed the denuded hillsides in bright apology and the sunshine cleared the air of discord and the miasma of death. The union sponsored picnics and baseball competitions. The wealthier ladies rode horseback through the town and down the valley or up the mountain roads. Peace and sanity reigned, on the surface.

Callie O'Connell was twelve now and able to enjoy some of that summer because she was allowed to visit her family and because she grew ever more stealthy in arranging to sneak out a bit. She'd even discovered that the rear door to a boot shop fronting on Colorado Avenue backed onto the alley that ran past the Senate and the outbuildings of the cribs behind it. If she was careful she could cross the alley and scamper between those buildings to her Aunt Lilly's back door with no one to see her. Aunt Lilly, or Floradora, made some arrangement with the bootmaker and he never seemed to notice Callie wandering toward the rear of his shop where she had no business to be.

The fall was warm and dry and promised to continue summer's

goodwill, but on Labor Day the union invited Big Hill Haywood from Denver to speak at the picnic. He told those assembled that the "gold barons" did not find the gold, prospectors did that. They did not mine the gold, miners did that. Nor did they mill it. Millworkers did that. Yet these gold barons ended up owning all the gold.

In October the Businessmen's Association asked William Jennings Bryan, the perennial presidential candidate, to speak on "The Evils of Socialism." He spoke from a raised platform on the sidewalk in front of the New Sheridan Hotel. Bunting draped the platform and the civic leaders sat on folding chairs to either side of Mr. Bryan. Nonunion miners and citizens opposed to unionism on principle mingled to cheer his warnings and drown out the prounion hecklers. The crowd was far larger than that which had gathered to hear Mr. Haywood. Callie, setting up tables in the dining room for the celebration to follow, heard the cheering but none of the speech. She wouldn't have understood it anyway, or that others were again deciding her fate.

The peace lasted through the pleasant fall and in November Arthur Collins, manager of the Smuggler-Union, deemed it safe to rehire some of the scabs the union had forced out of his mine. They were mostly American-born, of Northern European stock, hard workers, and they shared his philosophical leanings concerning capitalism. He advertised his intentions and listed their names in the area newspapers, hoping to attract them back.

When Clyde Duffer and Maynard Bellamy visited the Silver Bell the day the Telluride *Examiner* published Mr. Collins's advertisement, they were down to beer money and barely enough to cover another week at Mrs. Pakka's boardinghouse. They sorely missed the devious talents of Lenny Pheeney. The Silver Bell was packed with men and grumbling.

"Who's this Collins?" Duffer asked when they found a spot at the bar.

"He ought to be shot."

"He's a slaver, wot he is. I seen you around, you should know who he is."

"Uh, I been sick a lot, not out hearing things," Duffer said. He really didn't care about the much-reviled Collins but the mood of this place made him uneasy. The plate for snacks on the bar was empty. Duffer was beginning to give up hope he'd ever get home. If he did he'd be in deep shit trying to explain his absence to his employers. And then old Maynard, who'd never had an idea in his life, drained his beer, wiped off his mouth, and leaned across Duffer to the man on the other side.

"Hey, how much to take out this Collins dude?" Maynard's offer took some translating but a few drunks at the bar swiped some money off the gambling tables, which weren't busy because of the big debate, and Duffer and Maynard walked out of the Silver Bell jingling.

"We don't have a gun, you fuzz brain," Duffer said. "What you going to do, smile this Collins dead?" Maynard just smiled broader. Things were getting so bad old Maynard got high off one beer. "And the fact that we were seen at that dump the night the money turned up missing?" He listened to the jingle in his pockets as they walked back to the boardinghouse. "Wait, I get it. We got the money. Why worry about Collins?" He looked at Maynard with new respect.

Maynard scratched at his dirty neck and unshaven chin. "Sheriff keeps telling us to get a job, right? We got a job. We do it good and we might get us a career. This place is humming with hate, man."

"Thought you was scared of getting in trouble around here."

"I been reevaluatin' the odds, Duffer. There's another winter coming. You know we been here a year? What other skills we got?"

Aunt Lilly's front room was a bedroom instead of a parlor. A shelf ledge ran around the room three-fourths of the way up the wall. On it gaily painted plates stood on end between half-burned candles in silver candlesticks and beer steins with pewter lids. Rosy-pink wallpaper stretched from the baseboards to the shelf, pretty ribbon-bows at its border. Bright Indian rugs covered the floor. An iron bedstead with brass knobs filled one corner and had a saggy, stretched cover-spread and six fringed pillows. All three shelves of the bedside table were stuffed with neatly folded towels and wash-cloths.

Callie stood in the center of the little room and looked her fill. She normally wasn't allowed in here but she'd found a chance to visit this morning and discovered her aunt was not at home. Callie felt sly and secretive again. A rocking chair was pushed sideways against a window. Curtains hung from an oblong rod that circled out into the room and hid a rack upon which Aunt Lilly hung her wealth of clothes. Her trunk sat at the foot of the bed and it was full too. A commode and tiny coal stove completed the crowded room.

This was certainly an odd bedroom, and odd to be opening directly off the front porch, but what intrigued Callie most were the pictures on the walls, all photographs of Aunt Lilly. In one she sat on a chair in nothing but her petticoats and corset and her hair all down. In another she had her hair properly up but wore only a towel to cover her bosom and private parts.

A sudden knocking at the back door sent Callie scurrying from the forbidden room to answer it. An old Chinaman looked surprised to see her but handed her a package. "This for Miss Floradora. You give please?"

Callie closed the door wishing now she hadn't answered it. She'd been so guilty and flustered she hadn't thought. She wasn't to be seen here. She visited only in the mornings and often awakened her sleepy aunt. Callie put the package on the table and slid the twine off one end to peek under the wrapping paper. More towels, smelling of the laundry. Callie lifted the other end of the wrapping and found washcloths. She drank from the dipper in the water pail beside the dishpan and tried to understand the things she'd seen.

"You're a swell girl, Floradora, I'll give you that. Swell girl," a man's voice said in the other room, and the front door slammed.

"Let me get some water, John, and I'll be with you in a moment," her aunt answered, and giggled in a silly manner. Callie dashed out the back door and hid behind the coal shed. She checked the parts of the alley she could see and started for the rear of the boot shop . . . and stopped. John?

Callie slid back in behind the coal shed, then around it, zigzagged to the outhouse and then to the wall beside the kitchen window. Aunt Lilly ladled water from the pail into a porcelain basin. Her hat sat on the package on the table. She added something from a bottle, stirred it, and carried it into the front room. Callie slipped into the kitchen and waited. When nothing happened, she tiptoed across to the inside door. It was off the latch. A tiny shove opened it a crack.

All Callie could see was the man. He wasn't John O'Connell. He

wore a shirt, rumpled vest, and garters holding up black socks. Aunt
Lilly's hand washed his private member with a washcloth. Callie
had seen Bram's private member several times when he'd had to
relieve himself in the trees and told her to look away, but it had
been small and aimed downward. This man's member was fat and
long and it thrust toward the ceiling.

Callie left the crack in the door and hightailed it to the boot shop.

"This world sucks," Clyde Duffer proclaimed when he met Maynard Bellamy halfway to Pandora. Maynard pulled him behind a
rock outcropping. "Have to walk everywhere. It's cold and crummy
and . . . Sure you can find it again?"

Maynard had swiped a shotgun propped in a corner of the livery
stable and some shells from a packing case on a warehouse dock.
He'd hidden the gun out here so he wouldn't have to carry it back
and forth through town, but it was night now and there were patches
of snow, patches of shadow. The place looked different and he wasn't
sure he could find it either. Then he recognized the shape of the
bush in which he'd stuck it. There weren't any leaves, but the center
stalk was thick enough that you had to look twice to see the addition
of a shotgun even in daylight. He pulled it out, cracked it open,
inserted the shells. He didn't know when the thing had been cleaned
last, whether it would blow up in his face.

Still, it was good to be working again even if the odds for screw-
up were pretty high. There'd been no time for planning. Or even
being certain Collins would be home. They had to rely on some
jerk-off's description of Pandora at the dinner table at the boardinghouse, trying not to appear interested. And they couldn't sneak
up to it by a circuitous route because every yo-yo in the valley had
a big dog he let run loose. So they just walked down the road with
the shotgun tucked close to Maynard's side in hopes it wouldn't be
noticed in the dark. If they got away with this hit, they knew of an
all-but-bottomless exploratory hole in the hillside just above Stringtown where they could ditch the weapon. They planned to be back
in a bar in Telluride by the time news of the hit, hit town. What
the plan needed was careful timing and a better knowledge of the
terrain. They were both just too antsy to wait.

At least they knew what Collins looked like. Just that afternoon
Duffer had been standing on Colorado Avenue to disassociate him-

self from Maynard, who was stealing the shotgun. He heard catcalls and threats shouted at Collins as he drove a buggy into town and stopped at a storefront where gold-painted letters announced "The Smuggler-Union Mining Co. Employment Office."

As they approached Pandora now, the pounding of the mills drowned out the dogs' warnings. It masked their footsteps as well, and although they saw people moving behind lighted windows, they met no one face-to-face. Arthur Collins's house was easy to find because it was all lit up, with horses tethered outside that snorted and stomped discomfort at their approach. But again the sounds went unheeded because of the terrible clamor of the mills. A kitchen and a large dining/living-room area were lit up on the first floor. In the dining area people sat at a long table. It looked much like a movie set to Maynard—the costumes, the furniture framed by a square of windowpane.

"That's got to be him right here," Duffer said directly into Maynard's ear. The table stretched away from the window and all the unsuspecting diners were visible except the guy at the head of the table. They could see the back of his head and one arm as it gestured toward the chick on his right.

Maynard looked at Duffer. Duffer looked around behind them and to each side and shrugged. Maynard brought up the shotgun and emptied both barrels through window glass and the back of the man's chair.

39

"It was weird," Cree said, "the talk in the Cosmopolitan. Like the assassination of President McKinley. It happened just a month or two before I got there. Sounded so much like Kennedy. And the cowboys talked about—"

"I know, cows." Aletha ducked her head against the wind as they walked down Colorado Avenue. The wind was full of grit from the mountain of mill tailings east of town. The mammoth sprinkler system tried to dampen it but the water drops just blew away with the tailing dust.

"No, about grass and sheep and cattle. Cowboys don't talk 'cows.' You know one of the things I missed back then? Buns. Women wore so many clothes you couldn't tell if they had buns or not."

"Except at the Pick and Gad when you were changing your twenty. What if you'd picked up a . . . social disease there?"

"That's not all that hard to do here." He didn't want to talk about that visit to the Pick and Gad. "I think 'tap her light' means take it easy. Miners said it a lot. It may have had to do with sticking dynamite in a hole and carefully pounding it in. I suppose you'd better tap it light or die."

Aletha looked over her shoulder. They expected to be watched, but she didn't see anyone following. They were on their way out to Lone Tree Cemetery. Cree insisted upon looking up old friends. "Aren't you worried about going back all of a sudden? You know what happens around me."

He gestured toward the tailings pile, where dust devils played havoc with the town. "That whole thing wasn't there. Ended way back up at Pandora. And all this was mills and shacks and houses, and over there, the park was a slum area. Duffer and his crew had to live there."

"And if we suddenly went back? Duffer's still there."

"Probably hung him. Criminals didn't get far with the old law-and-order boys."

Cree had been gone less than a week and she didn't know him any longer. Her obsession had become his. It was depressing. "You once offered to fly me out of here, anywhere I wanted to go. Let's do it."

"Too late. Neither one of us can afford to get in any deeper with the law-and-order boys of today. With their computerized network they'd probably have every airport in the country waiting for my bullet-pocked Cessna. They've got our numbers down good now."

Aletha looked over her shoulder again. He was still talking and living the old days when they reached the cemetery. He started out around Callie's grave and began digging turf with his fingernails. Aletha just watched and worried. "Hey, whatever happened already has. What's the use?"

Cree wiped dirt across his forehead, sat back on his heels. "I'm going crazy, huh? Like you."

He brushed his hands on the grass and stood, staring down at the mess he'd made of the sod, then shook his head. His lips moved in conversation with himself. Finally he took Aletha's hand and they started toward the road, pausing at a long rectangular strip of concrete with names gouged into it along the top and bottom. "Fire at the Smuggler. I attended the burial." They hadn't gone ten feet before he stopped again at a group of headstones displaying the name Pangrazia. "I was in the hospital with Eugenio. He lost a leg when a wagonload of ore ran over him. Looks like he lived a few more years. But the son he was so proud of died young, about the time of the troubles."

"Cree—"

"I can't help it."

"I know." You didn't need things going bump in the night to be haunted. To one side of the gate in a sort of aisle stretched single graves in a crowded jumble. The small, slightly raised headstones were identical, with metal plaques on their surfaces. It looked like the area might once have been a road inside the fence that someone decided to put to use. One of the stones slanted to catch her eye had *Lennard Pheeney—1902* written on its little plaque.

"Probably not the same Pheeney, but it would raise some interesting questions, wouldn't it?" Cree said, and then wandered among the haphazard assortment of stones. "Planted this close, they must have been digging into old graves while trying to bury the new." He slid his hands in his pockets and hunched his shoulders. "Wonder what I'd do if I came across one that read *McCree Ronald Mackelwain.*"

Mildred Heisinger could not remember what had prompted her to climb the stairs to the cupola. She hadn't climbed stairs unaided for years. But here she was trembling and dizzy and alone at the top, clinging to the newel post, wondering how she was ever to get down. That was the trouble with getting old, you'd set out to do something and then forget what it was before you got to it. Like when she'd planned to have the house painted. She was sure she'd made arrangements to have it done, or had she just thought so? That was during the time all those ragged hippies were in town and

Mildred thought she might hire one or two to do the job cheap. Now, according to Doris Lowell, those hippies had grown up and were running the town. And the last time Mildred had ventured outside, the house still needed painting.

That snoop hadn't washed the window up here. Mildred's sight was fuzzy even with the heavy eyeglasses, but with the smudgy window glass as well, she almost thought she saw an apparition of the Big Swede. "Can't be. I burned it to the ground with my own hand."

Mildred had just climbed the stairs all warm from her bath, tired from her journey, looking forward to the hot bricks Letty had wrapped and placed at the foot of the bed, when she heard shouting and hooting and her name being called from outside. She hurriedly switched off the light bulb, and when her eyes adjusted she saw the lights on the second floor of the Big Swede and people standing on the outside landing and stairs. There were both men and women making shockingly lewd gestures at her house. One, whom Mildred recognized as having been garnered on a trip to California, turned her back, raised her skirts, and bent over, wiggling her bloomered fanny in Mildred's direction, causing raucous laughter from the others. Mildred kept the curtains drawn after that. But on occasion she would part them enough to peek at the doings on the second floor of the infamous Big Swede. Sometimes, when the evenings were warm, women would entertain gentlemen there without pulling shades, and Mildred would see things that troubled her sleep.

That was in the days when she slept up here in the room off the cupola and the bedroom she now used was a formal dining room. Now Mildred was old, confused, and clinging to the newel post. The Big Swede was no more. She could see right through it to the trees grown up to border the street, and the hazy outlines of the Pick and Gad through them.

"Mildred, __ __ are."

Mildred jumped. How long had she stood here?

"_ called __ __ __ phone. __ ___ answer." Doris Lowell led her back down the stairs. "Meal _____ __ nice. Mustn't _____ _____ stairs." Doris helped her into her chair and the woman who brought her hot meal put the tray across her lap. Doris turned on the television too low for Mildred to hear it, but the vegetables looked soft enough for once. One of them handed Mildred her teeth. "Now, __ _ __ a good girl."

That wasn't what they used to call her and Mildred hadn't been a "girl" since most people around here were born. How long could she go on like this? Her age was unseemly. Mildred didn't know how to stop being, and feared the alternative. She suspected she was eating some kind of fish, a square of something warm and salty. The buttered mashed potatoes and chocolate pudding were best. She felt so much better. Had she forgotten breakfast?

"__ __ think? All right __ __ stairs. _ __ __ worried."

"I'm just fine, Doris. Don't fuss." Mildred removed the painful teeth. She must wash them more often. That ridiculous child on the television was going to have another baby. Illegitimate of course. Doris was still watching her. Doris thought herself old for a few gray hairs, but she could walk, bend, carry without pain. Mildred could remember when Doris moved to town. "You go back to your family." That's right, Doris's family was dead or moved away. "I'll be just fine."

"__ __ coffee." Doris handed her a hot cup. Something was wrong. Mildred usually fixed her own coffee. Heat felt so good in her bones now that she was old. Letty carried pails and pails of water to heat for her baths. Something was still wrong. Doris was still here and the coffee was gone.

Tracy watched the same soap as was on Mildred's TV while Aletha sketched Charles, who sat on the windowsill watching the lack of acitivity on Pacific Avenue. After their cemetery excursion she'd left Cree gorging at the Floradora and come home to Charles, depressed and fearful of setting things off by her mere presence, losing Cree to history again. She felt cursed.

"So you come back to lose *me* in the past," Tracy said. "Thanks."

The process of sketching was soothing, the sweep and jerk of the pencil, the shape of the cat taking form. "Kitty, hold your tail still."

But the tip of Charles's tail twitched like a worm caught by a shovel edge. His purring increased and softened during dramatic lulls in the soap opera and five-inch whiskers trembled slightly in the light. His front toes tightened and stretched, the claws sounding a thin scritching on the old wooden sill. He made the shabby crib cozy just by being content, being Charles sitting in the window.

Superimposed on the tranquil scene, Aletha kept seeing Cree sitting back on his heels, a dirt smudge on his forehead, looking up at her from the cemetery sod. She was becoming dangerously dependent on him for something to think about.

Charles stiffened. His tail began to swell. He moaned warning in his throat and stared into the room unblinking, owl-eyed. A haziness formed over his head. Aletha thought she saw a shelf with a candle burning in a candlestick, a beer stein on one side of it and a decorated plate standing on edge on the other. She blinked it away and screamed. Tracy came off her bed and Charles soared into the room like a flying squirrel. "Run out the back way, fast!"

Aletha snatched Charles by the hind feet as he fought to scoot under her bed. She carried him twisting and clawing into the kitchen. "Callie girl," a voice behind her cried, a male voice, young, heartsick. "Callieeee . . ."

Aletha joined Tracy outside and righted the cat. He was so stiff he could have spent the night in a deep freeze. She looked around the corner of the crib. Pacific Avenue appeared to be the one she knew every day. She ran along the side to the street until she could see the Datsun parked where she'd left it. She fought cat claws to free a hand to open the door and hurled Charles in. He landed on Tracy, who was slipping in on the other side. Then it was a struggle to extricate the keys from her tight jeans pocket, and her heart felt like it was trying to pound its way up her throat. The Datsun tore up Pacific Avenue and headed for Colorado Avenue and out of town. Tracy heaved Charles into the backseat and braced herself against the dash like Cree did. "It was happening again, right?" Tracy shouted as if they were being pursued by the clamor of a hundred bombers. "I left the TV on. Where are we going?"

"If it happens because of me, maybe it won't when I'm gone, maybe we can outrun it." Aletha felt the quartz pendant hanging outside her shirt. It was definitely warm. Her hand came away with a faint rusty stain. "But I can't go anyplace old. It's old places, buildings—"

"Aletha, everything's old in Telluride, except new houses, condos. Aren't you supposed to report to the marshal before leaving town?"

"But the land they're on is old. We have to get away from Telluride. Someplace . . . I know, Renata's. That area is all new, isn't it?"

"The land is old everywhere. Who knows what was on it? It's Renata's day off."

"Good. Then she'll be home. We'll call the marshal's office from there."Renata didn't answer their knock, but she hadn't locked the door. "Renata? You home? It's Aletha." The refrigerator hummed on the kitchen mezzanine above. The heating system clicked and crackled softly. Sun bathed the greenhouse area, and the place had a slight muggy-jungle smell. Aletha released Charles, who plomped up the central stairs with a parting grainy "Waaaaa."

"Hey, Aletha, come see." Tracy stood between two cascading house plants at the front wall of windows and pointed to the deck outside that held a round picnic table and several lounges. An aluminum contraption that fanned out toward the angle of the sun contained a naked woman stretched down the middle.

"So that's how she keeps her tan." Aletha pulled the pendant up over her head and slipped it into her pants pocket, feeling a little silly, but maybe . . . She found a door to the side of all that glass and stepped out. "Renata, I hate to bother you on your day off, but I've got trouble."

Renata, with a white towel wrapped around her head and a white bathrobe, looked like a blue-eyed Indian as she handed them Perrier with ice and lemon. "You saw a shelf with a candlestick and beer stein on the wall and decided you must escape Telluride," she summed up what Aletha had told her with a studied blankness. "Aletha, there's a woman in town, a sort of counselor. I wonder if you'd consider telling her your story."

"It's not just her, Renata. Cree and I can vouch for this stuff," Tracy said as Renata led them down the staircase from the kitchen.

"That's my father's," Aletha said when she came abreast of Jared Kingman's pueblo scene. "I mean, he painted that."

"You're that Kingman family? Any idea where I can get more of those? They're worth a fortune now."

"How can you afford this setup on Renata's Helpers?" Tracy asked bluntly.

"Business"—Renata settled on a couch, drew her legs up under her robe, and stared Tracy down—"is good. And with two marriage

settlements, the sale of a business in Aspen, and some wise investments I assure you I can afford my life-style. I do not deal drugs,
if that's what you were thinking. And, Aletha, please tell me why
you honored me when you decided to escape Telluride."

"I thought if I came someplace where there wasn't any history it
couldn't catch me. There's no history here, is there?"

"As I remember, there used to be a sawmill on or very near this
site, and for all I know, Indians camped here while hunting before
that."

"You see a buzz saw coming out of a wall," Tracy warned, "don't
stand around and try to figure it out."

Renata called the marshal for them and then she called Cree to
persuade him to prepare dinner for them all. "He's one of the best
chefs in town."

She drove in to pick him up and buy some groceries and he made
them a creamy lobster-and-vegetable casserole. He and Tracy went
over their experiences in old Telluride while Renata came up with
sarcastic remarks. They were finishing their coffee when Doris Lowell called.

"Mildred Heisinger is poorly. Mrs. Lowell's worried." Renata
held her hand over the mouthpiece. "The old lady keeps asking for
'Snoop.' Doris thinks she means you, Aletha."

"Tell Mrs. Lowell I'll come in tomorrow. I'm afraid to go back
to Telluride tonight. It's like things are starting to happen again,
and—"

"At Mildred's age, Aletha, there may be no tomorrow."

40

THE O'Connells finally decided that after Christmas,
when the new school term began, Callie could give up her work and
go to school. Both Pa and Bram were earning now, and most of
their debts had been paid. Mrs. Pakka had agreed to allow Callie
to share her mother's tiny room off the parlor. Callie danced from
cot to cot in the hotel's third-floor room when she surprised the rest

of Mrs. Stollsteimer's girls with her wonderful news. She vowed secretly to end her visits to Aunt Lilly's.

Arthur Collins left a wife and two young children. The vicious murder sickened union and nonunion men alike. Vincent St. John, president of the local chapter of the Western Federation of Miners, offered a five-thousand-dollar reward for information that would lead to the capture of the murderer. This worried Duffer and Maynard, who hid their blood money under a floorboard in Mrs. Pakka's attic and took jobs carrying crates at the Telluride Transfer Station across the street from Mildred Heisinger's haven. A grand jury convened to charge Vincent St. John with the murder of Arthur Collins. A district judge threw out the murder charge for lack of evidence. However, in the minds of the majority in Telluride, the "Western Federation of Murderers" had been tried and found guilty. Mr. Bulkeley Wells, a man Callie had merely glimpsed during his stays at the hotel, arrived in his personal railroad car with his family and valet. He moved them into Collins's house and took over management of the Smuggler-Union. He closed operations down for a month in mourning for the slain manager, and John O'Connell had no work. Callie's reprieve was postponed for another school term.

"You'd be so far behind now, they'd just put you in with the little kids," Opal Mae Skoog said, thinking to comfort her friend.

"Don't know what you'd want to waste your time with books and figures for anyway." Olina Svendt stroked Callie's head in a motherly way. She'd begun to notice Callie's brother. The sun had mysterious ways of highlighting the bones in his face under the colorless, unruly hair when he met his sister in the alley behind the kitchens. Callie always found unused food, bread or meaty bones or cake, to take to him, and Olina had learned to hunt such things herself, to step out and offer him extra. His eyes said more than a schoolboy's should and his hunger intrigued her. Olina wore her long braid coiled on top of her head now.

Callie became a woman that winter, going through the messy menstrual rites with the aid of the other girls, who taught her the proper shame of it. This winter was not as harsh as the previous one and melted away sooner. When it did, the body of W. J. Barney was found in a ravine, nearly destroyed by predators and weather. Barney had been a Smuggler-Union shift boss missing since the 1901 strike during Callie's first summer in Telluride. She and the girls took turns sneaking out to see the horrible skull with a matting of red hair displayed in the window of a store. The sign next to it announced that this was the work of the union murderers.

Sometimes, when Callie had leave to visit her mother, she'd take roundabout routes between the boardinghouse and the hotel. This served to lengthen her time away from both. Luella had become difficult to talk to. Often Callie would go by way of the railroad station and clear up to the magnificent schoolhouse, then back down to the hotel. One of these times she noticed Miss Heisinger on the front of a livery buckboard, her huge trunks in the wagon bed behind. She'd not stayed at the hotel in a very long time. Curious, Callie followed and stood in the shadows of the stone Transfer Station as the liveryman handed Miss Heisinger down at the gate to a pretty white house.

Callie remembered Bertha Traub saying that the teacher had many fine books in her trunks in Alta. Perhaps that's why the liveryman struggled with them so now. Perhaps Callie wouldn't be as far behind in school if she could do some reading.

"Callie, why should she give you books?" Olina said when Callie discussed this with her friends that night. "And if she's a teacher, she might need them."

"Don't you think she might lend me just one?"

"Well . . . you might have to give her something of yours to keep so she'd know you'd bring it back and not damage it. Like the men leave a deposit at Van Atta's when they rent a suit."

"I don't have any money for a deposit." Callie reached under her cot for her carpetbag and looked through it. "What about Aletha's drawing book?"

"I can't think what she'd want with that."

But Callie took the sketchbook with her on her next trip out and marched right up to the pretty white house. A Negro woman answered the door and stared at her as if no one had ever visited here before.

"What is it, Letty?" Miss Heisinger called from the interior of the house.

"It's me, Miss Heisinger. I mean it's I, Callie O'Connell," she shouted past the black woman, who was clearly not going to invite her in.

Miss Heisinger appeared and nodded Letty away. She had a flush in her cheeks and no welcome in her voice. "What would you want here, Callie O'Connell?"

"Please, ma'am," and Callie told her ex-school mistress about her desire for books and her offer of a fine book of drawings as a deposit. Mildred stood poised and still as Callie rushed her sales pitch. She barely blinked all the while Callie talked. "If I'm to ever begin catching up with—"

"Ever begin to catch up." Miss Heisinger took the drawing book. Her face looked cold as marble as she leafed through it, and did not change when she finally looked over it to Callie. "Do you treasure these drawings for some reason, Callie O'Connell?"

"Oh yes, they're very grand. Everyone says so."

Miss Heisinger smiled a tight little smile and closed the door in Callie's face. She still had the drawing book and Callie had nothing.

In August the state government, now headed by a newly elected pro-business governor, sent one thousand National Guardsmen into Cripple Creek to crush a miners' strike, and less than a month later, just when Callie hoped to quit work and resume her schooling for the new term, the millworkers around Telluride decided they wanted an eight-hour day like the miners had won earlier instead of the twelve-hour shifts they worked. The union called a strike against the Smuggler, the Tomboy, and the Liberty Bell mills. One hundred millworkers walked out and the giant crushers ceased their din. The mines had to shut down and John O'Connell was thrown out of work. The family needed Callie's wages once more.

Callie decided to visit Aunt Lilly again. Aunt Lilly had given her small gifts of money or candy often, but this time she gave Callie a book. "It was left here by a friend, ever so long ago. I don't think he'll return for it, and since you fancy words so much, you can have it."

Indian Horrors; Or, Massacres by the Red Men. The colored engravings horrified, titillated, and astonished Mrs. Stollsteimer's girls for endless hours. None of them would ever look at the few ragged red men on Telluride's streets in the same way again. And while Callie read and reread the savage horrors aloud to the others at night with a blanket over the transom, the town roared outside. It was full of out-of-work men down from the mines. They slept on barroom floors and wherever they could, spending whatever they had on Pacific Avenue in a burst of holiday gaiety, sure that the owners must give in soon.

In a back room of the upper story of the Pick and Gad, Audrey Cranston posed nude against a black velvet draping. She felt cold and highly ridiculous under the sexless scrutiny of the artist. Diamond Tooth Leona had this amazing idea of having the girls painted in oil and hung in the waiting parlor. Leona had in mind not only encouraging business in this manner but speeding it up as well. And at the Pick and Gad, as in most businesses, time was money. Not only could a gentleman get his interest up and have it ready by gazing upon the available lovelies in the paintings, but he could make his choice among them more promptly by observing them all at once.

The artist was some bummer Leona had snatched off the streets when she'd seen the sketches he was trying to sell to buy food. Audrey noticed his brow furrow and his eyes squint as his concentration shifted from the form he painted to the human inside it. And she knew he was about to ask the forbidden but abiding question. "What would it be that could draw someone like yourself to this profession?" He colored slightly. "Or did you come upon some misfortune?"

"I certainly did, mister. Or rather she came upon me." It set her thinking of Mildred Heisinger again. Death was too good for that woman.

"Nobody's forcing you to stay," Leona snapped at her once. "All you had to do was earn enough for a ticket out of here, and you did that long ago." Which was true, but a ticket to where? Not back to Kansas City, where family and friends would question her about her time out West and surely read the guilt on her face. As a book-keeper she'd made enough money to live in a spare room with two other women who worked at the same foundry and to dress frugally but respectably, perhaps indulge in some frivolity once a month. She'd worked twelve to fourteen hours a day. Here a Chinese laundryman and Sarah saw to her vastly expanded wardrobe, lodging and food were provided, and there was a party every night. No cleaning, washing, ironing, cooking, baking . . . Audrey didn't like the life exactly, but she didn't quite know how to give it up either.

Just one more week, or one more month, she'd promise herself,

until she had some money put by so that life wouldn't be as grim
as it had been in Kansas City. But if Mildred Heisinger had not
lured her here, Audrey wouldn't have thought Kansas City so grim
and tedious. And the money seemed to disappear before she could
get it together to count. There were always dressmakers' bills and
a backlog from the shops on Colorado Avenue. Audrey could never
get ahead enough to feel good about leaving. The disillusioned
expression of the hungry artist made her decide to try again. "And
what brings a man of such talents as you to a place like this?"

"I came to the San Juans to make my fortune and found instead
that my slight frame and uncallused hands made me unfit to those
who hire at the mines."

"You'd rather be a miner than a painter?"

"I'd rather be a man of wealth than almost anything else." He
stepped out from behind his canvas and turned his head from side
to side studying her. "Try putting your left arm up and your hand
to your brow like this." He demonstrated a ladylike gesture of
distress that made her grin.

He was puny but interesting. And his disappointment in her needled
Audrey. The next day, as she returned from mailing a letter full of
lies to her parents, she saw Mildred Heisinger. Mildred rode sidesaddle, and for once not gracefully, toward the livery stable. Audrey
walked with Leona and a few others from the house, and Leona
grabbed her arm. "Mind your manners, now."

They'd all heard Audrey's threats against the hated procuress,
and the rest laughed as they passed, but Leona stayed behind with
her. "Think of the lovely clothes you have and the fun and the time
to yourself. Don't make a fuss."

The Heisinger bitch looked over their heads and guided the horse
into the big doorway. "I think I shall take up riding," they heard
her say to the stableman. "In fact, I may purchase an animal of my
own."

"She could have horses and even a carriage," Leona said thought-
fully. "Hire a bummer from Stringtown to feed them. All those
outbuildings behind her house and all."

The San Juan District Owners' Association organized by Bulkeley
Wells asked the governor of Colorado to send troops to Telluride
because the lawless strikers threatened anarchy to the town, not to

mention the free-enterprise system. Not only did they refuse to work, but they kept the honest workingman from his toil as well, causing hardship to him and his family.

"What they want is troops so they can reopen the mills with scabs," John O'Connell assured Simon Doud over a beer at the Senate, "and to be breaking the back of the union."

"But what can we do against trained soldiers?" Simon Doud was the ruddy-faced man Mildred Heisinger had seen on the train when she'd begun her travels, and again at the New Sheridan Hotel.

"Keep the buggers out of town." John stared glumly at his beer. No more rye-bright eyes for him. In fact he'd just finished a free supper at the soup kitchen set up by the union at the new Miners' Union Hospital.

"You mean . . . do something to the tracks?" Simon Doud looked astonished. He'd worked alongside John O'Connell at the Smuggler Union, mostly mucking, but John had been teaching him the ways of the hammer and drill.

"Well, now, there's an idea." John marveled at his new friend's ability to see solutions so quickly. Even drink didn't seem to fog the man. "Spit a few fuses under a trestle between here and the Dallas Divide and troop trains would not come a-crawling into this camp. I might just be bringing it up at the meeting tonight."

"But what's to preven . . . stop the foot soldiers and cavalry from unloading and walking into town?"

"Slow them down a mite. Cause hell with the supplying of them. A thousand militia was sent into Cripple Creek. Must take a heap of provisioning." John finished his beer and rose from the table. He'd put off a trip to Mrs. Pakka's to visit the wife long enough. They had to talk in the parlor in front of others. She seemed interested only in her medicine and her Bible. Too long since he'd had a woman. Not that he'd want to bother poor Ma'am with that now. If he hurried he'd have time to stop off at the bottling works and see the boy too. He longed for the day his little family lived again under the same roof. He nodded farewell to Doud and turned toward the door.

John froze as two women stepped inside, Floradora she was now and one other. He'd seen her around but this was the first they'd met eye to eye. She was dressed to the teeth, and prettier than ever she'd been back in Ohio or up to Alta either. Lillian froze too. Her smile, set to welcome the whole room, caved in at the corners. Color rose to fire her cheeks. She looked down first, as well she might. He knew women turned to this life, had had business with a few, but this woman he couldn't fathom. She'd had a good man to see to her and there was nothing so desperate in her life that time could not have fixed.

They stepped around each other, carefully. But the scent of her perfume haunted him as it sickened him all the way to the boardinghouse.

41

MILDRED Heisinger didn't know that Aletha, Renata, Doris Lowell, and the young doctor ringed her bed in the room that was once a dining room. Or that Cree, Tracy, and Charles waited in the parlor.

"Is she dying?" Aletha searched the room for any sign of history overtaking her, listened for any unearthly sound. "Shouldn't you get her to Montrose to the hospital?"

"It doesn't make sense to move her." The doctor prodded with her stethoscope. She made house calls because the local clinic had replaced her with a male doctor and she'd refused to leave town. "I'll see if I can jack up the clinic for an IV unit."

Neither the doctor's prodding nor Aletha's anxiety disturbed Mildred. Bob Meldrum did. She was riding her new mare up Boomerang Road to practice in privacy when he rode toward her. Bulkeley Wells and the Owners' Association had hired rough gunmen to help keep order and protect the mines from strikers, and Sheriff Cal Rutan had them deputized. Bob Meldrum was one of them. When she tried to ride past him, he turned his horse around to accompany her. "Ladies shouldn't ride out alone in these troubled times," he said. Mildred looked straight ahead, tried to hide her fear. "But then the other hens won't ride out with you, will they, Millie? No matter which side of Colorado Avenue they live on. Must be lonesome for you."

Everyone, even hired killers, knew of her. "My name is Miss Mildred Heisinger."

"You sit too stiff for the horse, Millie. You need to relax into her gait so's you don't jar your delicate little ass so bad."

On the shady side of town where Mildred lived, crude language and rude manners were common. She'd refused to acknowledge such behavior. Hired killer or no, Mildred hadn't the least intention of changing that stance now. With a hissing disapproval on the intake of her breath and a determined rise to her chin, Mildred jerked at the mare's reins to turn back toward town. The mare turned but then reared, almost dislodging her rider from the awkward sidesaddle. And when the horse came down on four feet, she refused to move. Instead she spread her hind legs and with a rumbling that began in mid-stomach she expelled blasts of foul wind and great plops of excrement onto the road.

Mildred was so embarrassed she forgot herself and looked up into the face of the dangerous man next to her. When he caught her expression he began to laugh in loud reverberating rounds. It was late November, with somber skies and little snow, chilly, bleak. A stand of aspen lined each side of the road, and the raw barren branches reared above his head like the antlers of a gigantic stag. After a siege of coughing he was able to control his mirth and it left his eyes almost instantly, the wintry emptiness of the killer returning. "Maybe I'll just have to teach you a few things about horseflesh, Millie. Teach you to ride like Mrs. Bulkeley Wells herself."

"Mrs. Bulkeley Wells herself," Mildred mumbled.

"Well, I'm going to go call the clinic about that IV. Surely they can't refuse the oldest living resident of Telluride." The doctor left the room.

"Look, I don't think I should stay in town too long," Aletha said. "Maybe I should go back to your place, Renata. Have Mrs. Lowell call if she needs me. Something might happen."

"I can't wait for something to happen. And I want to be right here with you if it does."

"She's talking again, Aletha. She might be coming out of it." Doris Lowell tucked the covers under Mildred's chin. "She might ask for you again soon."

* * *

But Mildred was watching Mrs. Bulkeley Wells ride by the train window as she came into town from yet another trip. Grace Livermore Wells rode with such ease in her dashing riding costume. She and the horse flowed together at a terrifying speed that left the train and the other mounted ladies behind. A picture in motion Mildred would never forget. That was before Bob Meldrum taught Mildred to ride almost as well. Before she acquired her first mare. Leona, the madam at the Pick and Gad, had helped her buy that first horse.

Leona pushed her way past a protesting Letty right into the parlor. "We're going to have us a talk, Miss Nose-in-the-air. One businesswoman to another, and right now." Her hair was about the shade of the skin of an orange. "Overheard you telling the stableman at Anderson's the other day you wanted your own horse." The creature settled herself on Mildred's nicest settee. She didn't seem to notice the fact that Mildred remained standing, an obvious indication of lack of welcome to most people. "Now, you could do better for yourself, and I happen to know how far you're in to that old bastard Barada. What you need is some advice on the type of girl needed here. The kind that'll pay and that'll stay."

Mildred had had no recourse but to listen. The advice had been profitable.

Aletha stood alone at Mildred's bedside. Doris Lowell had stepped into the bathroom and Renata into the parlor to talk to Cree and Tracy. The doctor had driven to the clinic for the IV unit. Aletha still watched the corners nervously and didn't realize Mildred's eyes were open until she had the feeling of being watched.

"Hi, Miss Heisinger. It's me, snoop. How you feeling?"

"Callie O'Connell," Mildred said distinctly.

"Oh great, now you're going to tell me about Callie when I'm a lot more worried about Aletha Kingman."

"They put her on the train and sent her away. Herded the women and children into boxcars like cattle. Bulkeley Wells and the Alliance and the militia. Found skeletons in the mountains for years afterward when the snow melted."

"Oh, surely they didn't send women and children out in cattle cars in winter." Aletha looked to Doris Lowell standing in the bathroom doorway. "Sounds like *Dr. Zhivago*."

"I'm afraid it was Telluride. And much of it is still hidden. For years history decided that Bulkeley Wells and the militia were right. They did speak for the majority."

Mildred was still watching Aletha, and Aletha leaned closer, hoping Mildred could read her lips. "Isn't that Callie buried out in Lone Tree Cemetery?"

"All gone now. Leona and Bob Meldrum and Bulkeley Wells. Even Audrey."

Charles slid in through the door Renata had left ajar. He jumped up on the bed and stuck his nose in Mildred's neck. "Waaaaaa."

"Cad? That you?"

"Leave him be," Doris said when Aletha made a grab for him. "Until a few years ago there were always a couple of cats around here. And one of them was always named Cad."

"Snoop?" Mildred called but then lapsed into her own world. Mildred stood naked but for a towel beside a lovely porcelain bathtub she would someday come to own. It was filled with steamy water and sat in the bordello known as the Pick and Gad. Mildred's skin crawled with the drafts rising behind her. No patient Letty there to hold a towel or robe up to block them. Sounds of revelry ascended from the floor below and the street outside. It had dinned on since the lifting of the curfew.

"Millie, you gotta have more fun," Bob had told her. "More friends."

"I have you and Leona and Letty. And my books, my riding. Cad."

"You can't hide in this little house all the time you're in Telluride. Come out to the party tonight at the Pick and Gad. Leona promises none of the girls will bother you. I'll be there to see they don't."

Mildred would rather have gone to the ball on Colorado Avenue or to see the Shakespearean players performing *Othello*. But Mildred would not be welcome there. Bob Meldrum could be very crude and very sensitive. But since she'd come under his protection she could venture out on these streets with no harassment. She'd come to the party, against her better judgment, just to see what it was like. And just for a short time. Bob had promised to stay at her side. But she met some of the players here who reenacted lines from *Othello* after their performance on Colorado Avenue, and some of the gentlemen who'd returned their ladies home after the ball.

Somewhere in the evening she'd lost track of Mr. Meldrum. And she'd drunk too much champagne, had apparently consented to be the prize in some wager she could not remember now, had insisted upon a bath first, hoping to go home to Letty and go back on her promise, and had found herself in this room instead. She wondered what Mrs. Bulkeley Wells would do in such a situation—Mrs. Bulkeley Wells would never find herself in such a situation.

Bob Meldrum had never touched Mildred. Nothing beyond taking her arm to guide her across the street. He would visit her, have dinner, watch her play the piano, have her read poetry to him. Often he would just sit and look at her. Then he'd visit the Pick and Gad.

Leona said he was horrible to the girls here. But although no gentleman himself, he treated Mildred like a lady, which was more than she could say for Mr. Bulkeley Wells. Perhaps Bob had not really disappeared from the party. Perhaps tonight she was to see the other side of him. She could not remember if he had anything to do with the wager for which she was prize. He could be "calling in his debts" as he often claimed to do. Then again, he could have merely stepped outside to kill someone. Killers . . . prostitutes . . . and a big white cat sitting in a hole in the wall. As if the wall had burned through from the next room in that one spot only. But there was no smoke, no flame, no scorching, just small fizzes of light popping around the hole's edges like the bubbles in a glass of champagne.

The cat's eyes widened. Its back arched and the hairs on its tail spread apart to puff it out of proportion. Behind the cat was a table with an enormous lamp, and part of a square chair that had upholstery cloth hanging to the floor. In a corner two people stood in a doorway. A girl and a very tall man. The girl that a young militia captain had brought to her door during the curfew. She wore trousers, a baggy overshirt, and something that looked like a pink rock for a necklace.

"Mildred?" the girl said as if she couldn't believe her eyes. "Mildred Heisinger?"

"That's the snoop," Mildred announced to the faces ringing her bed, and tried to sit up, but found hands pressing her back to the pillow. "The snoop!"

42

C ALLIE saw the troop train come into Telluride. She'd walked to Mrs. Pakka's boardinghouse and rushed out onto the porch when the citizens marched past to the railroad station. Mr. Duffer and Mr. Bellamy had just returned from work and they followed the crowd. Callie slipped in behind them. "What do you suppose these crazies are up to now?" Mr. Bellamy said.

"Looks like they're marching off to war," Mr. Duffer answered.

Tents were set up all around the station. Bales of hay were stacked everywhere. Men in uniforms with musical instruments formed along the tracks and began playing parade music as the train approached, strangely silent, without blowing its whistle. The engine pushed a flatcar piled with more hay. Rifle barrels stuck out of the hay at all angles, making Callie think of a confused porcupine. A group of horsemen rode up, the leader carrying an American flag. The horses danced and shied at the band music and the chugging and steam from the train.

This was the most excitement that had happened around Callie since Elsie Biggs went alone into a room with a gentleman present. The engine shrieked and then whumped to a stop. A head appeared over the hay-porcupine car in front of it. The lead horseman handed his flag to the rider next to him and saluted. "Captain Bulkeley Wells at your service, sir."

The head in the hay swiveled this way and that. Another rose behind it and then another. The faces on the heads looked terrified and Callie laughed in spite of the grand parade atmosphere. The bodies under the heads began to stand up. A strange device rose with them. It appeared to be many overlong gun barrels fastened together in a circle with metal bands. It pointed right at Captain Bulkeley Wells but he just saluted each new head as it rose from the hay. Down the track another train pulled in behind this one. Doors screeched open on both and horses jumped out of boxcars, men rushed to mount them. Commanding voices shouted orders all down the line and soldiers leapt out to lower rifles at the cheering citizens and the Telluride Cornet Band.

Somebody set off black powder high on the hillside and the soldiers fell to one knee, balancing their rifles on the other. The cavalry horses broke ranks and ran down some of the tents. And the crowd cheered louder. Callie didn't know what all this was about but she cheered too. Jubilation filled the air. And a great smell of horse.

A new figure rose up in the porcupine car. This man had a cape on his coat and wore a sword at his waist. Even the cheering subsided in his presence, and during a lull in the horse noise he saluted Captain Bulkeley Wells back and asked quietly, "Where, Captain, are the strikers?"

"Oh, they're all over, sir." The captain gestured so widely he set his mount to backing. "But not here."

"The strikers are all over, but they are not here?"

"Not right here . . . at the moment . . . there might be a few. But this is largely a welcoming committee, sir. I don't think it will be necessary to shoot anyone."

And as if in support of this, Senja Kesti's littlest brother, Lowri, waddled out from somewhere and threaded his way through the welcoming committee's horses to wave hello to the men in the porcupine car. The Kestis lived practically next door to the depot and Callie would often drop by on her way back to the hotel from Mrs. Pakka's to see if Mrs. Kesti had anything she wanted taken to Senja.

Little Lowri was something over two years, bundled against the chill, and fairly rotund anyway. His waving caused him to tip over and sit hard in the snow, which in turn caused him great anger. His screams brought several women on the run with Callie in the lead, when Captain Bulkeley Wells sprang from his horse and swept the child up in his arms. This brought applause from the audience but did nothing for Lowri, whose outrage escalated. The captain's horse took off down the tracks and his eyes settled on Callie. "Here, and watch your little brother more carefully. He could well have been trampled."

The captain turned away before Callie could explain that Lowri was Senja's brother but not before she recognized the gleam of fever in his large eyes. Certain kinds of excitement did that to men. She'd seen it in Bram when he was told he could go back to the mine and quit school, and in Pa when he'd dropped in to the hotel after not seeing her for months but could stay only a few minutes because the stiffs were marching and it needed doing. Callie put little Lowri down, took his hand, and led him home.

Soldiers walked the sidewalks now. Cavalry detachments rode the streets day and night. The militia guarded the roads to the mines and mills and a man needed a signed pass to get by them. One afternoon Senja's mother came to the back door of the hotel demanding to see Callie instead of Senja. "It's your father, Callie. They're sending him off on the train and your mother's too weak to control Bram."

"Who's sending him?"

"The Alliance and the militia. To Montrose. Deporting, they're calling it. Hurry, your brother's lost his wits with it all."

Callie was still confused but she raced after Mrs. Kesti. There weren't as many tents around the depot as before but there were nearly as many people. Most of the troops had been billeted in the town and the large boardinghouses up at the mines. But that funny gun was still there and it sat on wheels like a cannon. It aimed at the train, which was all steamed up and ready to go. The crowd didn't cheer this time and some ladies wept.

A line of men chained together were being herded into a boxcar, the chains clanking and thunking as each sat down. Captain Bulkeley Wells stood to the side, with two soldiers behind him holding on to Bram. They held Bram's arms behind his back. It struck Callie how straight her brother stood now, how much wider his shoulders looked than those of the men holding him. His face was still strange and bony but the rest of him no longer seemed like a sickly scholar.

Callie walked right up to Captain Wells. "Please, sir, may I have my brother?"

He glanced down as if she were a summer fly to be swatted, and back to the chain line. Then he glanced down again. "How many brothers do you have, girl?"

"Just that one, sir." She pointed to Bram but didn't meet his eyes. He looked murderous. Callie had come away without her coat and she shivered. Captain Wells leaned over her.

"You're one of Mrs. Stollsteimer's girls, aren't you? And your father's on that train?" He removed his coat and put it around her shoulders. It hung to the ground and the lining held his warmth. As the last prisoners entered the boxcar, the many-barreled gun was tipped upward and an officer "harumphed" unintelligible orders.

"They're going to shoot Pa!" Bram struggled with his guards.

"No, son, they'll merely fire a warning," Captain Wells said, not unkindly, and patted Callie's shoulder. "To warn them not to come back."

One soldier turned a crank, two braced themselves each against a wheel, and a fourth held steady a rack of cartridges. The gun revolved, fire and smoke spit from all its barrels, sounding like the roar of a hundred rifles firing at once but not in unison. Dirt and snow exploded on the mountainside above the boxcar and across the river. Stumps splintered and blew apart. A few fledgling pine trees were cut in half. Every dog in Telluride went into a barking frenzy and horses at the hitching posts by the depot reared trying to pull away. The engine steamed out of the station. Captain Wells stared across at the damaged landscape on the mountain and trembled. "Magnificent."

Callie decided he was cold and returned his coat. "Thank you, sir. Now I'd like my brother if you please."

He laughed. "They certainly teach you girls pluck up at that hotel." He nodded for the soldiers to release Bram. "Go home, boy, and behave yourself. See you don't get in the same trouble as your father."

Soon a train arrived filled with scabs from Missouri and militiamen guarded their passage to the mines and mills. The stamps thundered once more, bringing back the normal heartbeat of the valley. A judge in Montrose released the deportees and termed their expulsion unlawful. Governor Peabody disagreed and the militia was ordered to check the incoming trains. The union men filtered back into town anyway, but Callie didn't see John O'Connell until he'd been locked up in the bull pen on Colorado Avenue.

The bull pen was constructed of heavy timbers connected with rope and had a thick metal door. It sat in front of the bank on the sidewalk, its announced purpose to detain vagrants. The mining companies refused to hire known union men so a great many were "vagged" and the small jail could not hold them all.

Callie was on an errand for the hotel and a quick visit to Aunt Lilly's via the boot shop when she saw the men in the bull pen.

She'd turned thirteen the previous summer and still hated cleaning things. She'd learned to twist her bottom out of the way of any gentleman's grope and how to walk like Olina and Floradora. Not yet "grown," she still wore her hair down but she brushed it shiny every night.

Callie had to step into the street to pass the protuberance of the bull pen. It looked something like an animal stockade. Pieces of men showed through the holes between wood and rope. All Callie could see over the top were hats. She'd started to cross the street at the intersection when she heard her father calling her name. It was embarrassing to see grown men caged that way, and doubly so her own father. "How's your poor Ma'am, Callie darling?"

"The same. Are the soldiers hurting you, Pa?"

"No, and don't you worry now. This is the United States of America and justice will be soon done. Rest of the county don't approve of what this camp has come to." He removed his hat, rubbed his scalp as if there were hair to brush back off his forehead. "And the union has power in the state. Best not be telling your brother I'm here. With his temper, there's no knowing what he'll do."

That night as the girls were preparing for bed, Mrs. Stollsteimer came to the doorway of the third-floor room and ordered Callie to pack her carpetbag. She was being dismissed. "I've sent for your brother to come fetch you. The streets of this town are no longer safe, thanks to men like your father."

43

"WE really do have to get out of here," Aletha told Dr. Barbara.

"She settles down so at the sight of you. She's probably terminal."

"I just don't want this whole room to get terminal."

"Believe me," Tracy added from the doorway, "Aletha's the one who can do it." She came in from the parlor with an anxious Cree behind her.

"Snoop? It was Brambaugh O'Connell in that room," the old lady said, as if Aletha should know what she was talking about.

"Please don't get upset, Miss Heisinger. I'm sure everything'll be fine." When Aletha tried to move away from the bed an ancient hand clasped her wrist and the IV bottle swung on its rack.

"You were there, and the cat," Mildred said.

"Talk about callous." Renata tried to keep Aletha from freeing her wrist. "Now, stop this paranoia and help comfort the old woman."

"After all that came later, I forgot, you see," Mildred explained.

"Don't leave." The doctor bent to Mildred's chest. "I may have to send someone out for oxygen."

"She's just trying to die," Tracy said. "Hell, she's earned it."

"True. And so will we all someday." The doctor looked into every pair of eyes but Mildred's. "And so we are all obligated to make her death as comfortable as possible. As we'd like someone to do for us someday."

Mildred didn't see the expressions of guilt mixing with the panic of those edgy to leave her house. The mysterious hole had closed over the cat and the couple behind it and Mildred was too shaken and confused to be interested in the bath. But the door to the hall had been locked against her. There was no window. She'd lost her clothes somewhere. The hole with the dancing edges had swept the champagne bubbles from her head. There was one other door and she backed toward it, keeping her eyes on the mysterious wall. Shudders of cold and fear rattled her teeth.

In her desire to quit the smaller room she slid so quickly into the adjoining one she forgot to worry about what she might find there until it was too late. Mildred had an impression of crowded warmth, bright colors, a crackling sound from the stove in the corner, a bed with an excess of pillows. And a tall man, his back to her, his fists raised against the door to the hall. "Let me out or I'll break everything in this room!"

The laughter of both male and female voices came from the other side of the door. "Promised your pa I'd see you to your first bedding. Now, mind your pa, boy."

The man swung around, arms lifted as if to clutch the first thing he touched and smash it against the door. He was not quite the boy in her schoolroom in Alta, not the skeletal figure on the steps of the boardinghouse a year later, but the transformation was not so great that she didn't recognize the eyes under the colorless hair. The body had regained its flesh, added muscle. The face had matured to smooth planes and shadowed angles. But the rage was the same, the violence unleashed, checked momentarily by his surprise at finding himself not alone. The dignity she had sensed in her classroom was still there, and outraged again. His voice broke now from astonishment instead of adolescence. "Miss Heisinger?"

"Bram, I don't live here. I've been made the brunt of this joke too."

"You're trying to haunt my life." He picked up a small table from beside the bed and hurled it to splinter against the door; a trail of towels and washcloths marked its passage across the room.

Mildred pulled the bath towel tighter around her, tried to regain some of her own dignity. "I was about to take a bath and the wall—"

"You were about to take a bath here. But you don't live here."

"Someone took my clothes. Perhaps there's clothing in here. Turn around. Don't look at me. I can explain this as soon as—"

"It's not that I don't know what to do." He looked about as if for something else to pick up. "I've had enough teasing and mocking tonight." He picked up Mildred.

The old lady seemed to be sleeping, if fitfully. Her body jerked and her hand let go of Aletha.

"Is she dead?" Renata stepped back from the bed.

"No, in fact she's breathing easier." Dr. Barbara picked a limp wrist off the covers, checked the pulse against her watch. "This particular crisis might be over."

"If we could just get Aletha away from town," Cree said, "everybody else should be safe."

"I cannot understand why Aletha is so dangerous." Doris Lowell slipped Mildred's arm back under the covers. "You'd think she had dynamite strapped to her chest and was about to spit the fuse."

"We'll explain when there's time, and I promise you won't believe it." Cree guided Aletha to the door. "We'll be at Renata's."

"I'm going too." Tracy practically pushed them through the parlor and into the entryway. "We came in Renata's jeep. The Datsun's still at her place."

"Never mind," Renata said behind them. "I'm right with you.

Mildred doesn't like me anyway and I don't want to miss any magic film effects." They all crowded outside the door and stopped. Renata walked around them and stepped onto the shoveled path between looming snowbanks. "It snowed all this while we were in there?"

Aletha hugged her jacket sleeves. "It's not night anymore."

Cree tried to open Mildred Heisinger's front door. It was locked. There was now a glass pane in it.

Renata walked back from the gate, looking dazed. "The jeep's gone. There're all kinds of people in the street."

"I could kick this door in or break the glass," Cree said.

"And explain it to your friend Sheriff Cal Rutan?" Aletha asked. "Or Mildred's friend Bob Meldrum?"

"We'll freeze out here." Renata pounded on the door. "Doris?"

"Doris Lowell isn't in there, Renata," Tracy said.

Piled snow hid the street from them, but there was shouting coming from that direction, then a gunshot. Renata pointed to the building towering over the snowbanks and Mildred's little house. "How did that get there?"

"It's the Big Swede," Cree said dejectedly, and opened his jacket to envelop Aletha against him. "I suppose we could all go and huddle in a boxcar."

Aletha could hear his heart and could almost hear his despair. Then she heard shouting close at hand and felt him stiffen. When she peeked out of his jacket the cold tried to freeze the tears to her cheeks and two men had entered the snow tunnel from the street. One stopped hitting the other over the head when he saw them. He stood with a board raised while his victim ducked beneath it and escaped, leaving blood drops on the path.

"Hey, Duffer, come here quick!" Maynard Bellamy shouted.

"You let the guy get away. We were supposed to—" Clyde Duffer appeared in the tunnel to gape at them, scratching the stubble on his chin. Together they looked like a couple of clown bums in their baggy clothes and slouchy hats. "Mackelwain and the girl. After all this time." They moved toward Mildred's house in step, blocking the path, with identical dreamlike expressions, carefully, eyelids blinking rapidly as if they expected the group by the door to dissolve any minute. "It's time you took us home," Duffer said to Aletha. "Do your stuff."

Aletha hid her face back against Cree's chest.

"You want to freeze standing here? We're the ones with the warm clothes this time, Mackelwain. Better get her in gear."

"Well, I'm going back in this house," Renata said decisively, and stuck her fist through the glass panel in Mildred's door.

Aletha was in jail again. But this one didn't smell of evaporating plastics, steam-table vegetables, or disinfectants; this one smelled of the smoky wood fire in the potbellied stove at the end of the alleyway between cells. It smelled of the dirt of the floor and of human feces. It smelled of woolen clothing in need of dry cleaning and reminded Aletha of the long coat she'd bought just for visiting this world. The coat now hung in the crib on Pacific Avenue a good eighty years away. In eighty years this jail building would sit across Spruce Street from the Senate and would be the San Miguel Public Library, the tiniest library Aletha had ever seen. One room with a concrete floor and decent heating, it would have shelves of books and plastered walls. Now it was still across from the Senate but the inner walls were the same mortared rock of the outside and made for cold, bumpy leaning.

They'd each been given a blanket which Aletha was sure must be crawling with lice. They sat wrapped up on a bench at the back of the jail as near to the stove as iron bars would allow. There were two cells, running the length of the building. The alleyway between had wooden flooring and led to the stout front door. Each cell had a small wooden seat with a hole in it in one corner and a high barred window that looked out onto the street.

They'd all been charged with vagrancy, Renata with vandalism, and the three women with indecency, probably because they happened to be wearing jeans. Duffer and Maynard had evaporated after pretending to have discovered them breaking into Mildred Heisinger's house while hunting vagrants. When the black woman came home to find them crowded into the entry hall she'd run screaming for the marshal. Most of the inmates were vagrants awaiting a hearing or union men the mine owners refused to rehire. They answered Cree's questions readily enough but huddled away from his end of the cell, obviously embarrassed that females would be "vagged" and placed in a jail along with men. The blankets hid some of the women's form of dress but there were many curious glances at their shoes and the hair hanging loose about their shoulders. Renata's careful makeup became more apparent as she grew more tired and frightened. Several men singled her out for special smiles.

The door hinges squawked and screeched when a man came in to rebuild the fire. He ignored the miners' questions about when he thought they could expect to be fed. Just after he left, the door opened again and the man who entered this time practically blocked the alley between the cells. All grumbling hushed.

"Sheriff Cal Rutan," Cree whispered to Aletha, and sighed long and hard.

The sheriff searched the faces behind the bars on either side of him and stopped when he came to Cree. "Mackelwain, isn't it? Let's see . . . McCree Ronald?" In the pause that followed, Aletha figured she could have heard a worm turn in the dirt floor. Nobody even spit. "Looks like you got yourself some more of them fancy shoes and some fancy women too. And here I been worrying you'd been killed by your rough friends. Those boys got themselves jobs, been helping round up vagrants, becoming upstanding citizens. Misjudged them and you too. Thought you was smarter than to come back to Telluride, having skipped out on your debts." Sheriff Rutan turned his backside to the stove and rocked on his feet. "That sure wasn't smart, Mr. McCree Mackelwain."

44

BULKELEY Wells had been a captain in the National Guard in Denver, and Major Hill, the commanding officer of the troops in Telluride, persuaded him to form a local company of militia from the general citizenry to be known as Troop A, First Squadron, Cavalry. Captain Wells in his blue tunic and jodhpurs took command of Troop A. The enthusiasm of the town was such that a detachment of cadets from the high school, organized back in the days of the Spanish-American War, marched and drilled as well. Those "foreigners" would think twice before returning to Telluride. Bram O'Connell, refusing to march against his father, quit school in his last term before graduating and went to work full time at the Wunderlich and Rella Company Bottling Works. Ma'am was too sick and preoccupied to stop him.

On February 21, Major Hill and his troops withdrew from Telluride, leaving Captain Bulkeley Wells supreme military commander of San Miguel County. Wells continued the curfew and closed down the saloons, gambling halls, and the bordellos to keep the troublemakers from congregating. He ordered a stone fort built on top of Imogene Pass to keep any strikers from returning by way of the closed end of the valley while members of Troop A searched all trains, wagons, and coaches coming in from the open end.

Callie had wanted to leave the Sheridan Hotel for so long she was surprised at her thoughts that first night out of it as she lay in the narrow bed and tried not to touch her sleeping mother. At the hotel she'd had her own bed. She already missed the indoor toilets and the running water. It would be wonderful to be out from under the tedious work but she'd miss talking to her friends at night in their third-floor room. Mrs. Stollsteimer's girls had become a family to her. Ma'am had declined so, Pa was never around, her brother had grown to such a man he was unlike the Bram she'd loved before the cave-in or after when he was sickly and ashamed. She felt uneasy around him now, yet she daydreamed of herself and Bram living alone in a cabin high in a mountain meadow. The cabin was small so she didn't spend much time cleaning it and, impossibly, it had an indoor toilet.

Just as she was falling asleep, Bram went off to work a little mine he owned and Callie went out to ride one of the wild horses who lived on the meadow (they would allow no one but Callie to ride them), when along came Olina Svendt to visit, on the pretext of needing to borrow some sugar. Of course she stayed until Bram came home and asked him when he intended to marry and he said, "No need to marry. I have my little Callie girl."

The next day Callie ate the noon meal alone with Ma'am, Mrs. Pakka, and Mrs. Pakka's two daughters because all the men were at work or in jail. Just as they'd finished there were loud knockings at both front and back doors and outcries from the neighboring house.

Mrs. Pakka answered one door, her oldest daughter the other, and both ushered in members of Troop A. Mrs. Pakka wore her hair braided on top of her head like Olina Svendt. But the landlady's braids were thin and gray, the scalp beneath pink with irritation at being pulled so tightly. The pink spread down over her face now and she tightened her lips against her teeth. "They're here to search the house for weapons. We're to stay in this room until they're done."

Luella put a hand to her chest and knotted it to a fist as if her heart hurt. "I need my medicine. Callie, could you—"

"No, she can't leave to get it now." Mrs. Pakka gave Callie a look that said she didn't expect Callie could ever do anything useful and poured tea into Luella's cup.

"I'll fetch it when they've gone." Callie took her mother's hand and pondered Mrs. Pakka's look.

"It's me they're after, isn't it?" Luella peered up at the corners of the ceiling as if she expected members of Troop A to be poised there ready to leap at her. "I'd best hide." Callie's mother crawled under the dining table, leaving Callie and the Pakkas staring at each other openmouthed.

"That medicine is affecting her head," Mrs. Pakka said, "just like spirits do when a man can't stop the drinking. I can't get her to eat. Blood's so thin it makes her nose bleed. You and Bram ought to make her see a doctor. See what he thinks of this medicine she can't be without."

"Ma'am, come out from under there now." The thought of children "making" a mother do anything seemed fanciful to Callie. But she softened her voice as she would for Lowri Kesti or a kitten. "They're not looking for you, they're looking for guns." Still her mother didn't move. "I wish Bram were here."

"Not with his temper, you don't." The landlady winced as the searchers tipped over something upstairs. "And speaking of whom, he's not come up with the week's board money and I've given him more time. Now you're an extra mouth to feed on the poor boy's wage. You can work some of it off around here, miss. Must have taught you something up at that hotel besides swishing your skirts."

And so Callie found herself cleaning things again and tied down to the boardinghouse, keeping an eye on the increasingly erratic behavior of her mother. There was no hope of starting school until the fall term anyway. But one afternoon she saw Luella to her room for her nap, put on her coat, and made her way up to Colorado Avenue. There were surprisingly few people on the street and she noticed the closed doors on the saloons. She stepped into the boot shop, waved at the bootmaker, and slipped into the alley in back. Callie hoped her Aunt Lilly wasn't entertaining a gentleman. They needed money for the boardinghouse. She'd tell Bram and Mrs. Pakka the money came from her back wages at the hotel, although Mrs. Stollsteimer had made it clear there'd be none. Sly. Secretive.

"Oh Callie, I'm glad you've come." Aunt Lilly had two lady friends at her table. "I have something for you." She shook out her hair and disappeared into her front room. The other ladies had their hair down too, and damp, as if they'd just washed it. Their faces were scrubbed of paint. "Here, honey, have some coffee," one of the ladies said, "and see what Floradora has for you."

Aunt Lilly brought out a lovely dress—red-black-and-green plaid with lace at the collar. "It's almost new. And I know how you hate that black hotel thing."

The dress was a tad large but Callie was glad to take off Mrs. Stollsteimer's uniform. "I'll tell everyone it's a hand-me-down from Olina's sister."

She sat to coffee with the relaxed ladies and related the new troubles of the O'Connell family and her dismissal from the hotel. Once Aunt Lilly assured her she would help, Callie enjoyed the afternoon. They talked clothes and hairstyles. Callie drank too much coffee. Her nerves hummed in her ears. One of the ladies brushed her hair and tied a ribbon bow in it. Callie felt pretty.

She sensed that the washing off of a private part was not all that Aunt Lilly and her friends did to entertain gentlemen. And what they did do caused these women to be shunned by all others. There were certain matters Callie's normal curiosity shied away from knowing. And although the atmosphere was friendly, there was a certain line that instinct told her not to cross. She'd never mentioned Uncle Henry here. These women spoke carefully around her too. But she saw no harm in bringing up the fact of closed saloons.

"Captain Bulkeley and our own Troop A have closed down all the business."

"The bootsmith was open," Callie said. This drew laughter and winking.

"Well, then, certain kinds of business." Aunt Lilly turned to her friends. "I hear the Senate and some other places are serving early suppers today for . . . uh . . . ladies of the neighborhood so the food they'd already bought don't spoil. Promises to be cheap, and a working girl just has to knock discreetly at the back door."

Callie left as the ladies decided to put up their hair and go out for supper. She left with a nice collection of coins in her pocket but she'd overstayed her time and found the back door to the boot shop locked. She started down the alley toward the livery stable and met a lady who smiled warmly as she passed. Callie walked on a few steps and stopped. She knew that face. In fact, she knew the whole body. Callie turned in time to see the lady enter the alley door of the Senate. What would it be like to go out for supper? Aunt Lilly was going to the Idle Hour. Did the lady Callie had just met suspect her picture sometimes hung on the second-floor landing of the New Sheridan Hotel?

When Callie knocked discreetly at the Senate's back door a sweating man in an apron ushered her through the kitchen into a room with tables set up like those at the hotel dining room. The lady of the painting was the only other patron so far, and she sat at a communal table. Callie sat beside her. "Might as well have some fun, with everything closed, huh?" the lady offered by way of conversation. "Awful young, aren't ya? No scruples in this town. My name's Audrey."

"I'm Callie O'Connell."

"That your real name? You use your real name, you don't want to use the whole thing. If I was you I'd stick to Callie. What brought you to the shady side of town? Not the Heisinger bitch, I hope."

"You know Miss Heisinger? She was my teacher."

"Your teacher!" Audrey put her hand over her mouth as if she thought she'd be sick or had said an evil word. "And you not even with your hair up."

The sweating man brought them each a bowl of soup and stomped back to the kitchen as if he wished they hadn't come.

"Do you stay often at the New Sheridan Hotel?"

Audrey laughed. "You're a funny kid, Callie. Wonder if anybody else is coming tonight." She blew on a spoonful of soup. "My God, what's that?"

Callie looked up from her own soup to see the hole with the frying edges opening in front of them. It'd been so long, practically two years now, Callie'd hoped she'd outgrown these ominous experiences, as one outgrew earaches and bad dreams. But there stood Aletha, and this time not in pants. She wore a skirt so short it almost revealed her knees, and what appeared to be a piece of rough quartz around her neck on a chain. She carried a tray of stacked dishes. Another lady stepped out from behind her, her skirt even shorter, and she too carried a loaded tray. Audrey dropped her spoon, and soup splattered everywhere.

"Aletha? Miss Heisinger took your book," Callie said all in a rush before Aletha could pronounce some terrible warning Callie didn't want to hear. "How is Charles? Do you still have him?"

The lady beside Aletha made a funny sound and dropped her tray. Dishes broke and clattered. "Callie," Aletha said, "what are you doing *here*?"

But the hole closed up over Aletha before Callie could answer. Audrey pressed back in her chair and held both hands to her bosom. "Where'd they go?"

"That was Aletha," Callie said, the enjoyment gone from her evening. "I hope I never see her again." But Callie saw Aletha and her clumsy friend the very next day at John O'Connell's hearing in the San Miguel County Courthouse on Colorado Avenue.

45

ALETHA sat with Cree, Renata, and Tracy at the back of the courtroom. The seats were long hard benches like church pews. The flag next to the judge's desk hung in folds, so Aletha couldn't count the stars. The jailer had fed them fried potatoes and tough beef last night but no breakfast this morning. No one had slept much. Gunshots sounded throughout the night and horses' hooves pounded by on Spruce Street. The women had been escorted to an outhouse behind the Senate before they'd all been marched up here.

Aletha stood automatically when the judge entered the room. That's when she noticed Callie O'Connell across the aisle. Callie was older again, wearing the same dress and hairstyle as when Aletha had seen her for the second time at the Senate and Tracy had dropped her tray. Callie leaned around a tall man to stare back. The tall man was watching Cree. He was the boy, Bram. His hair looked bleached.

Judge Wardlaw cautioned those present that this was a hearing preliminary to nothing and the court would make suitable decisions on all matters brought before it. A Mr. Murphy and a Mr. Richardson had come from Denver to represent the union men and a Mr. Barada spoke for the Citizens' Alliance. Men were interrogated as to their means of support, hours of gainful employment, and summarily judged vagrants. Barada was small and elderly but he spoke with the strength and diction of a Shakespearean actor and made the union lawyers seem graceless, dull, and dumb just by the way he combined words, intonations, gestures, and expressions.

One by one the vagrants were led out of the courtroom and the crowd thinned. The elderly Barada announced a special case, that of John O'Connell, and across the aisle Callie and Bram sat straighter and Aletha could see the profile of the woman on the other side of Callie. It was the woman with Callie in August in Alta when this all began. Then her hair had been the same rich chestnut as Callie's; now it bore swaths of gray. Her husband was forced to stand at the front of the room with his hands cuffed behind him. Bob Meldrum stood guard next to him.

"This man, John Clarence O'Connell, stands accused of planning the bombing of the troop trains on their way to this camp, your Honor."

"Mr. O'Connell"—Judge Wardlaw looked up from his hands spread palm-down on a desk clean of paper—"are you a member of the Telluride Miner's Union, Local Sixty-three, of the Western Federation of Miners?"

"Aye, sir, and proud to be." John O'Connell put his shoulders back.

"And did you conspire to bomb the trains bringing the National Guard troops into this district?"

"I did not, sir."

"Your Honor, we were not informed of these charges," Lawyer Murphy said. We demand—"

"If it please the court," Lawyer Barada interrupted, "we have a witness."

"Your demands will be heard in good time, sir," the judge told

Mr. Murphy, and then muttered to himself and the room in general, "These Irishmen." To Lawyer Barada he said, "Call your witness, Homer." The witness entered from the judge's chambers with Bulkeley Wells. Wells stood off to the side but in full view, and Aletha could feel the radiation clear at the back of the room. Beside her Renata breathed, "Magnificent."

"Simon P. Doud," the witness answered Lawyer Barada.

"Would you please describe the conversation you had with Mr. O'Connell concerning the bombing, Mr. Doud?"

"We were drinking beer at the Senate and Mr. O'Connell said that blowing up the tracks between here and the Dallas Divide would keep the militia out, sir."

"It was you who suggested it," John O'Connell broke in, "and it was just talk. Nothin' come of it." Bob Meldrum nudged John with his shoulder.

"And why was it you were drinking at the establishment known as the Senate with Mr. O'Connell? And what was it that brought you to Telluride, Mr. Doud?"

"I work for the Pinkerton Detective Agency out of Denver and was hired to infiltrate the group of miners affiliated with the Western Federation of Miners employed in this district. I worked alongside John O'Connell up at the Smuggler."

"And who arranged this contract with the Pinkerton Agency, Mr. Doud?"

"Captain Wells and the Owners' Association, sir."

Captain Wells smiled pleasantly as the courtroom went still. Outside, snow drifted from a smudged sky and left splashes on the windows. Lawyer Barada raised spotted hands toward the ceiling in a gesture befitting a preacher. "You were hired as a spy, Mr. Doud, before the militia was even called up to pacify this district? As if some farsighted soul knew of the horrors to come?"

Let us now pay homage to the great god Wells, Aletha thought with disgust. But he surprised her. "If it please the court, I'd like to speak," came the low mellow voice. "I should like to beg leniency for Mr. O'Connell and to remind the court of this man's heroism in saving the lives of others during the unfortunate fire at the Smuggler-Union. He still bears the scars of these noble deeds. I happen to know he has a family and feel deportation enough punishment for his mistaken loyalties, with the provision of course that he never return to Telluride."

"Done," decreed Judge Wardlaw. "And, Mr. O'Connell, I hope you can see the charitable intentions here and will in future avoid any taint of conspiracy. Past heroics can only take a man so far." Bob Meldrum led John O'Connell out, and Bram and Callie rose. Bram's face was flushed, his jaw tight.

"Bram," Cree said softly, "don't do anything foolish now. They win." Cree nodded toward Bulkeley Wells at the front of the room. "They win the whole shootin' match. Damn your principles, son, you have to survive."

Bram hurried to support his mother, who'd faltered in the aisle ahead of him.

"Still foretelling the future, are you, Mr. Mackelwain?" Sheriff Cal Rutan said when the O'Connells had left. "You sure learn slow, boy."

Aletha was startled by a glimpse of what smoldered just under the studied blankness in Cree's eyes. Unlike Bram, who appeared ready to detonate at the least provocation, Cree would walk ten miles out of his way to avoid a confrontation. But back him into a corner and keep goading him and there'd be violence. "Remember what you told Bram," Aletha warned him. "Good advice for you too."

"That is all of the union business, if you gentlemen care to go have something to eat," Judge Wardlaw told the lawyers from Denver. "We'll discuss your complaints and demands in my chambers at two o'clock."

Sheriff Rutan walked to the low railing that separated the spectator pews from the lawyers' tables and the judge while the courtroom emptied. "I was helping the marshals clean out the jail, Judge." He made a sweeping gesture toward the rear pew. "Ah, this is what we have left over." He motioned for Aletha and those with her to come forward. Bulkeley Wells took a seat in the jurors' box.

"Why're they all wearing blankets? Do they think they're Indians?"

"Their clothes are improper, Judge, and not very warm," the sheriff said. A clock tick-tocked above the judge's head instead of buzzing. Judge Wardlaw leaned his chair back against the wall. "I can understand the jail needing airing about now, Cal, but what do you propose we do with them?" He yawned, stretched. "Any suggestions, Buck?"

Wells stood and walked to the railing. He clasped his hands behind his back and paced before them as if reviewing troops. When he stopped in front of Renata, Aletha imagined she heard the snap of electricity denied the clock. But he moved on to Aletha. "I've seen this woman at the Pick and Gad a few weeks ago and before that a couple of years ago in a patch of sunlight that did not extend to my side of the street. She's given to dressing like a man and disobeying curfew." He moved on to Cree. "And this man worked at the Cosmopolitan." Wells was tall but he had to look up at Cree, which made it difficult to look down his nose as he could with the others. "McCree Mackelwain," he said softly. "Cal thought he might be a man of mine. I did think to enlist him in our services because . . I don't know. A certain perceived spark of . . something useful? That I would prefer to have in my camp rather than the enemy's? But he ran over to her and the sunlight"—Wells nodded toward Aletha—"and disappeared. Totally. This woman"—he paced back to Renata—"was leaning out a window above."

"Excuse me, Buck, but you're not making complete sense of this," the judge said.

"I'm only too well aware of that, James." Wells rubbed his lips. They sounded dry. "I think I'd like to question them further. And then perhaps send them out on the vagrant train. They're not . . . not quite expected."

"Maybe not, but they're yours," Judge Wardlaw decreed. "Join me for lunch at the Sheridan, Homer? If we make it last all afternoon, I won't be here to meet those boys from Denver."

"My pleasure, James." The old lawyer stood, gathering his papers. "Be careful, Buck. I too find these vagrants unusual . . . possibly dangerous."

"I told Meldrum to come back here," Sheriff Rutan assured him, and then added when the lawyer and judge had left, "The tarts could find work after you lift the embargo on the tenderloin."

"And you, Mr. Mackelwain," Bulkeley Wells said, "where have you been all this time?"

"Home, in the future. Aletha, can't you think of some way to get us back?"

"Yeah, try concentrating on it," Tracy said. "Or meditating."

"Do all of you come from the future?" Wells asked. The sheriff snorted and lit a cigar.

Aletha concentrated. Renata removed her blanket and sat on the first pew. She ran her fingers through her hair and shook it out. "Aletha, get me the hell back. You've proved your point."

"The lady has the sound of authority." Wells perched on the railing separating them and eyed Renata. "Are you the madam of the group?"

"Who are you to call names? Railroading people just because they belong to a union and don't agree with you."

"There is no union here, Miss . . . or do you go only by a first name?"

"Winslow. If there were no union there'd be no trouble here."

"We refuse to acknowledge a union in Telluride, Miss Winslow, so it does not exist. And you are right, if it doesn't exist there will be no trouble."

"Sounds like Ronald Reagan," Tracy muttered. "Aletha, concentrate."

"I'm disappointed, Mr. Mackelwain. You let your women do all the talking," Bulkeley Wells said. "I sensed more of a man in that exaggerated length of yours."

"Sheriff, I'm ready to take the prisoners to the depot," Bob Meldrum said from the back of the room. "Even got a couple of volunteers to help me."

Cree groaned. Aletha turned to see Duffer and his friend Maynard standing beside Bob Meldrum. All three were grinning.

46

"I have often dreamed of visiting the past. A more simple time, when law and order was not so difficult to achieve and a man was born expecting to earn his way." Bulkeley Wells sat on a corner of the judge's desk slapping gauntleted gloves against his leg. "I hope that should such a thing happen I would comport myself with considerably more aplomb than you and your ladies, Mr. Mackelwain. I don't for a moment believe you all have traveled from the future. I do applaud the originality of the idea. And I did see that . . . that patch of sunlight."

"I'm surprised you remember so much after so long."

"I rarely forget. Neither does our fine sheriff. Do you, Cal?"

Sheriff Rutan puffed billows of choking cigar smoke into the room and coughed. "Still think we ought to keep him here to work off his debts."

Meldrum sat at the back of the room, but Duffer and Maynard had sidled up as close to Aletha as they could and kept staring at her so she couldn't concentrate. She felt hungry, dirty, irritable, and afraid, so when Bulkeley Wells said, "Perhaps you'd like to tell us something of the future, Mr. Mackelwain," Aletha answered instead, "You're going to go bald and shoot yourself in the head in California."

"No one really wants to know his own future," Cree warned.

"I noticed you conversing with the O'Connell boy." Wells changed the subject as if he agreed with Cree. "I'm curious as to your relationship with that family. The father's transgressions are rather serious. The son left our public school in his final term. It is rare for a miner's child to complete the fifth grade. This boy was at the head of his class. Rather far ahead of the others, I'm told."

"Bram's a friend of mine. I told him to cool his temper. That you and the owners would win."

"Is that before or after I shoot myself in a hairless head?"

"Before. You may win here, but eventually you lose. Mildred Heisinger says you're going to put women and babies in cattle cars and ship them out of town." Aletha caught Cree's expression. "Well, she did."

"If you're not going to take us home," Cree said through his teeth, "at least don't make things any worse."

"How would the Heisinger woman be privy to any supposed plans of mine? Did she bring you here?"

"I've told you your future. Well, Mildred lives forever. She's—"

"She's hardly that robust." Wells was watching Renata again.

Renata met his eyes. "History says that you are a womanizer," she said in her best bedroom alto, "that it brings you grief. You lose your shirt, but I understand you have great fun along the way."

He rose and motioned to Meldrum. "My interest in you has been out of curiosity. I regret there is too much at stake here for me to indulge myself any longer. The very basis of freedom is endangered—"

"Whose freedom?" Renata asked.

"Any man's if he wishes to sell his labor as he sees fit. It's more than a freedom. It's a God-given right."

"What about women?" she said as they filed down the aisle toward the door.

"If they possess any intelligence at all they will find a man worthy of their support."

"Oh yeah?" Tracy said. "Well, we've come a long way, baby."

"We've come a long way, baby," Cree mimicked as they walked to the depot. "Tell me about it when you're freezing your buns in a boxcar or getting them fondled in a whorehouse. They're not going to liberate women for years. Men can't even join unions freely. Have you noticed it's winter here? We're in a whole lot of trouble, ladies."

Bulkeley Wells rode a horse behind them. Bob Meldrum walked ahead, and Duffer and Maynard to either side. The streets were a hardened corduroy of ice ruts in the shady patches and mud ruts where the sun had worn through.

"When are you going to do your stuff?" Duffer asked Aletha.

"What ever happened to Lennard Pheeney?" she countered.

"Somebody shot him. We owe you one, right? And for two years in this fuckin' place."

"But if you get us home, all debts are off," Maynard added hastily.

Bob Meldrum strode ahead, deaf and oblivious of the low voices behind him. Wells seemed not to hear them over the noise his horse made. Many hats were doffed in respect to Captain Wells, many greetings called to him by women and children. He seemed to know everyone by name. When he sent Aletha off on a train, would that end her connection to her own time? Did she have to be where Callie was to move back and forth between worlds?

She recognized several of the modest homes in Finntown that would withstand the years and the inroads of condominiums. Tracks ran past the depot now and boxcars lined up on sidings. The windows on the depot were not boarded over, and inside, a potbellied stove made some of the wooden building dangerously hot while corners still held the chill of outdoors.

"You must've lost your stinking coat," Bob Meldrum said to Aletha. "Audrey said you just disappeared into a fog. You should've stayed with Leona when I took you there. See all the trouble you're in now?"

Bulkeley Wells drew Renata apart from the others and stood talking to her for some minutes. When he took his leave, Renata joined them on a bench along the wall. "Did he offer you a job?" Cree asked. "Better stick with Aletha. If there's any way out of this, she's it."

"He's one chauvinist-pig hunk," was all she would say.

"I don't know when your train arrives, so relax." Meldrum leaned against a wall and chewed on his chaw. Duffer and Maynard perched close by. Cree's stomach gurgled, Aletha's burned. Tracy wiggled. Renata seemed preoccupied. Across the room a man in a visor watched them through an iron grate and then turned as a clacking noise started up behind him. Meldrum sauntered over to talk to him and when he returned he said to Duffer, "Leaving you in charge. I'm going to go eat. I'll be back to take a turn. Looks like it'll be a while." He handed Duffer one of his guns. "Don't look away from them."

"You don't have to take a turn here. We'll stick with these bummers all day."

"Yeah, we ain't hungry," Maynard said. When Meldrum had left, he looked at Aletha. "Okay, now we're alone. Get a move on." But the day wore on and no threats brought the hole with shimmering edges. Antique people in antique clothes came and went. Aletha felt buzzy with hunger and terror that leaving Telluride would be leaving behind her only link to home. It grew dark outside the unboarded windows but the man behind the grillwork came out to turn on weak lights.

"What if I start killing your friends off one by one?" Duffer whispered. "All we need is you, right? What if I start with Mackelwain?"

"If you kill my friends I won't ever be able to concentrate." The buzzing in Aletha's head grew in volume when Duffer turned the weapon on Cree.

"Evening train's passed the junction," the man with the visor called out, and then, as if he just noticed Aletha's group was all that remained, added, "Won't have another vagrant train together till morning."

When the doomed sound of the whistle on the evening train moaned closer and closer, Aletha began to imitate it, first in her head and then aloud. Ignoring the startled glances of her friends, she let it grow into a scream. She wasn't positive she could stop if she wanted to. She wasn't sure how much was hysteria and how much her desire to keep the stationmaster's attention on them to make it more difficult for Duffer to shoot Cree without having a respectable witness looking on. Maybe she had flipped altogether, maybe it just felt good to be doing something less passive than she had all day. Maybe it was just the hopelessness of it. Life in either world with Duffer and Maynard likely meant death for them all.

"Here, now, we can't have that," the stationmaster said when she'd stopped to take a breath.

"Shut up, dyke," Duffer yelled when she started in again, and he raised the butt of the gun above her face. She didn't stop even when he brought it down to strike her. She was shoved aside so suddenly the gun butt hit the wall instead. Aletha really couldn't stop now. This must be what crazy is, she thought, but oh the wonderful release of it. Renata slapped her. Tracy shook her.

Cree and Duffer rolled about on the floor while the stationmaster stood by helplessly. Maynard circled the struggle, looking for an opening to grab the gun in Duffer's hand. Cree had Duffer by the wrist to hold the weapon away while he pummeled him with the other hand. Cree's face was flushed almost blue-red, his lips pulled back in a snarl. He fought disgustingly dirty. Aletha stopped screaming and began a hoarse giggling. She was losing her voice.

Renata motioned to Tracy to help her pry up a loose board off a bench and then tried to sneak up on Maynard with it. But the gun went off and everyone backed away. A hanging light fixture swung wildly. There was a new hole in the reflector. The swinging light bouncing off walls and faces made the whole scene even funnier but Aletha's giggling changed to tears and the train whistle did the screaming now, very close.

The gun hit the floor and Cree was free to beat on Duffer with both hands. When Maynard made a dive for it Renata brought the board down on the back of his head so hard her feet came up off the floor. Maynard stayed where he was.

A sudden sharp burning on Aletha's leg made her think she'd been shot too, but the bulge in her pocket reminded her of having stuffed the souvenir pendant in it and she drew it out by the chain.

The pink-stained quartz was definitely hot to the touch. The light had slowed its arc but still swung above them. Given the scarcity and weakness of the bulbs in the large room, all the corners were dark but the moving light illuminated a boarded-up window in one corner and a patch of wainscoting with the paint worn and flaked to almost nothing. A ripped cobweb drooped with dust . . .

"Tracy!" Aletha threw the necklace under a bench and shoved Tracy at the corner. She grabbed one of Cree's ankles. He'd gone crazy with rage and was no help at all. Renata just looked bewildered as Aletha struggled to hold on to him. Duffer's nose was bleeding and making the floor slippery. The train had stopped. Steam and smoke fogged the depot windows. The door opened to admit two trainmen. "Renata, if you want to go home, grab a foot."

Renata came to and they fought together to pull Cree off Duffer and face down toward the corner. Aletha smelled the air change to musty and saw Duffer roll over, crawl toward them on his stomach. "Maynard, they're gettin' away!"

Maynard still lay on the gun, unmoving. The lighted area around him, the gaping stationmaster, Duffer straining toward Cree's outstretched hands, and the top half of Cree Mackelwain narrowed till they disappeared in darkness. Duffer had been about six inches from grabbing onto Cree. They gave a last mighty yank and Aletha ended up on her fanny with Cree's empty shoe in her hand.

"Shit, I almost had him. I was going to kill that bastard," he yelled from out of the pitch dark . . . and then, "Are we home? I can't see a thing."

"You didn't bring Duffer along, did you?" Aletha asked.

"The last I saw was the look on his face when he realized I was getting away. Probably better than killing him. Renata?" And when she answered, he called out for Tracy. "We didn't leave Tracy behind, did we?"

"I'm over here. But you stay over there." And the smell of warm urine cut through the mustiness.

"Where are we now," Renata asked, "in limbo?"

"Probably in an ancient, closed-up, abandoned train depot," Cree answered close to Aletha, and she shoved his shoe at him.

"How'd you do it, Aletha," Renata said dryly, sounding more like herself, "grab Toto and click your heels together three times?"

They wandered into cobwebs, tripped on debris, assured each

other their eyes would adjust soon and they'd find a way out before time switched them back to a murderous Duffer. Then Tracy found an open space between boards and Cree helped her pound out a window hole.

It was still dark outside and wood smoke still hung heavy on the air, but the lights of a much smaller Telluride winked around them. Cree and Tracy went to Mildred Heisinger's, she to gather Charles and go back to the crib and he to collect Renata's jeep and get Aletha out of town as fast as possible. When he returned he was breathless. "Mrs. Lowell was out at the gate talking to the doctor. They hadn't missed us. Seems it's still Thursday. They claim we all left the old lady's house not more than two hours ago."

47

UNABLE to solve the disappearance of the four disturbing vagrants and with John O'Connell and the others deported once more, Bulkeley Wells decided to lift the curfew. Even the residents down at Mrs. Pakka's boardinghouse could hear the rejoicing in the streets when the saloons and Pacific Avenue opened for business again. A ball was to be held at the Sheridan and a group of Shakespearean actors brought in to entertain the town. Bram emerged from the bottling works to find two men awaiting him on the dock—Thomas Sullivan and Shorty Miller. Bram hadn't seen them since their hospital days in Denver. They too had regained strength and flesh since then, but both had aged a good bit.

"Sure but you've come back fit, lad." Sully had to stretch up to embrace him. "Good to see you."

Bram couldn't forget Shorty's calling him a bastard at that awful time in their lives. But when Shorty stuck out his hand, Bram shook it. They slapped each other on the back. There is an undeniable bond forged between those who almost die together but don't.

"Got us a message from your pa," Sully said. "He's in Ouray. Said to tell you not to be losing your temper and acting the fool. Just take care of the family for him till he gets back. Things'll be right between the union and Telluride soon. Ain't that what he said now, Shorty?"

"That and one more thing, Sully." Shorty showed all the extra spaces between his teeth.

"Oh, that's right. You go on home, boy, and clean up, have your supper, and then meet us at Van Atta's by seven o'clock."

"Van Atta's? I don't need clothes, Sully."

"Now, don't argue, Bram. You just mind your pa."

Audrey couldn't believe it when Diamond Tooth Leona told her who Bob Meldrum might bring to the party that night at the Pick and Gad. "And I want your word you'll behave yourself. Anybody knows how mean that man can get, it ought to be you, Audrey. Say one wrong thing to her ladyship and he could kill you."

While Leona and the girls fussed about with frills, Sarah and a raggedy group hired from Stringtown for the occasion strung streamers, inflated balloons, and arranged platters of fancy candies and sandwiches. Wagons delivered cases of champagne to the back door and a small ensemble set up in a corner to practice playing together for the first time. Telluride's tenderloin had been raucous a good part of the day but when the Pick and Gad opened its doors for a preannounced party, one and all cordially invited, the mountain valley seemed to explode. There was standing room only in the champagne parlor, the waiting parlor, the dining room, and even the kitchen.

At Van Atta's Sully and Shorty rented Bram a suit of clothes and outfitted themselves as well. "Shorty and me just got paid at the Maggie Breen, up out of Ouray, and the evening's on us."

"Your pa said as how he figures your education's been suffering with him gone so much."

"Shorty and me ain't union so we thought to get work here."

"It's not like we're scabs . . . just that we don't happen to see eye to eye with John about certain things. Exceptin' your education."

Bram walked down the street between them feeling ridiculous in the suit and hat. He knew what they were up to and couldn't believe Pa would condone such an evening for him. But then again . . . His two companions were short men and walked with their hands in their pockets, their hats pushed back, and jaunty swaggers. Bram walked stiffly. His coat sleeves were too short. He felt like a bear someone had dressed up to make fun of. He wanted to claim his rights to manhood and leave the embarrassments of boyhood behind, but then again, the transition could be the most embarrassing of all. Bram dreaded embarrassment more than most proud people because of the torture he'd endured from his schoolmates when he was a scarecrow with no hair.

He stood to the bar at the Cosmopolitan Saloon and downed a beer with them. Beer didn't bother Bram much after sampling the product at the bottling works for several years, but the pictures of naked ladies on the walls around him did. Next they stopped at the Brunswick, then at the Senate. Bram began to relax a little. At the Silver Bell he even bought a round. But the next stop was the Gold Belt Saloon and Dance Hall, and what the ladies did there, alive and moving, was worse than anything hanging on a saloon wall. He sat on a wooden folding chair at the back of the room. Sully and Shorty craned forward to see better. Bram's vision was excellent and he cringed backward, but he watched.

Five not very pretty ladies pranced about in what he assumed was a dance, to the accompaniment of a fiddler and a piano player and a man shouting a story no one could hear over the hooting and stomping of the audience. The bright lights made the dancers' bodies look creamy and smooth and their faces clownish with the exaggeration of applied color.

"Plump and pretty," Shorty yelled into his ear, and spit tobacco juice at the floor. The middle of the five was more than plump and the cheeks of her backside flopped and jerked with every step. Her smile was fixed no matter what the insults directed at her from the audience, as if she had not escorted her body to the stage. All the ladies wore their hair down and all wore the same costume, a costume similar to those favored by schoolgirls at poetry recitations— wreaths of paper laurel leaves on their heads, draped Grecian gowns. But these gowns were transparent. It was horrible and impossible to look away, to ignore the swelling ache of himself in his rented trousers.

"They were ugly," Bram complained, but he stuck his hands in his pockets and tilted back his hat as they left the Gold Belt. Is this what Pa did on his off days in town? Why would those ladies want to make such undignified spectacles of themselves?

"Didn't notice you sittin' there with your hands over your eyes."

"Now, you're not to be making fun of the boy, Shorty. If he likes 'em pretty, I sure know where there's some pretty ones, don't you?"

Audrey watched Mildred Heisinger and Bob Meldrum in the champagne parlor. She sipped champagne and he drank from the bottle. As the evening progressed Mildred relaxed her stiffness and Meldrum got slowly but definitely drunk. He introduced her proudly and then gave anyone so much as brushing against her a chilling glance. The next time Audrey noticed them Mildred was being entertained by some actors from a traveling troupe that had performed on Colorado Avenue earlier. Meldrum played poker nearby and kept looking over at Mildred's rapture.

Audrey couldn't understand the attraction between them. Mildred's throat and shoulders were bared daringly in a ball gown that drew much attention and put the resident finery to shame. There were no bruises on the perfect skin. Later Audrey found Meldrum sitting alone in a corner of the kitchen, still swigging from the bottle. He grabbed her skirt and pulled her down on his lap. She'd thought to be free of him tonight. "What's the matter, your fancy lady run out on you?"

"She's still in there, beautiful and fine as ever. She doesn't swear like you trollops. Plays the piano and reads poetry. I run out on her." He wiped a tear off his cheek with the thumb of the hand that held the bottle and spilled champagne down his vest. "She's too good for me, Audrey."

"Oh yeah, she's a real sweetheart, teaching little girls how to work Pacific Avenue."

"What? You know I can't hear."

"I said she seems to like you a lot, Bob."

"Millie deserves someone fine and young and innocent like she is. Never has any fun, poor girl."

"That poor girl deserves a lot, all right."

"She deserves something like him." Meldrum pointed the bottle at a big kid standing in front of them. The kid had just accepted a puff off a cigar from the man next to him and was coughing up a storm, much to his friend's delight and derision.

"You gotta help me, Audrey."

"I'd like to, Bob, but I have a date in a minute and—"

"Not that." He wiped away another tear and took a swig. "Get him for Millie. Here." He let go of Audrey to reach into his pocket, and dumped her on the floor. He held out a large gold coin. "Where'd you go?"

She reached up and took the coin. "You mean you want me to—"

"Yeah." He nodded and stood to get a better look at the kid. "Yeah, he's just the ticket. Can you do it for me, Audrey?"

"Long as you don't change your mind when you sober up and come after me for it, I can try." She had to repeat it for him and he actually reached a hand down to help her up.

"You shouldn't sit on the floor in that pretty dress. Millie never would." He looked the kid over again and handed her another coin. "You try real hard."

"Sure, Bob, anything you say."

"Then maybe I'll feel like I can even touch her." The drunken eyes misted over, more confused than dangerous now. "I'm counting on you, Audrey," he said, and stumbled out the back door with his bottle.

48

I<small>N</small> Telluride, the revelry was not to last. In Montrose, Judge Stevens of the District Court issued an injunction against the Citizens' Alliance and Troop A restraining them from interfering with the return of the deported miners to their families. In Denver, Big Bill Haywood announced that the strikers would have to be returned to their homes by force because Telluride did not abide by the laws of the land. In Ouray, the miners' union local armed fifty volunteers who offered to escort the exiles back over Imogene Pass.

So Bulkeley Wells and the Citizens' Alliance asked Governor Peabody to return the militia to Telluride. On March 24, Peabody placed San Miguel County once again under martial law and ordered Brigadier General Sherman Bell, commander of the National Guard and adjutant general of the state of Colorado, to Telluride with three hundred troops from the Cripple Creek garrison. Bell had charged San Juan Hill beside Teddy Roosevelt and had been a mine manager in Cripple Creek before the labor wars began. Now he set up headquarters in the lobby of the New Sheridan Hotel. Then he sat back to see what the rednecks proposed to do about it.

Charles Moyer, president of the Western Federation of Miners, was arrested in Ouray on charges of desecrating the flag. He and others had been handing out handbills with slogans printed across the white stripes on "Old Glory." Sheriff Cal Rutan persuaded the sheriff in Ouray to bring Moyer to Telluride and release him, whereupon General Bell arrested him and had him confined to a room in the New Sheridan. Bell then telegraphed to Governor Peabody in Denver, "Take all money on the proposition that the Stars and Stripes are waving over Fort Telluride and there is no one but Moyer in jail."

Bulkeley Wells and the Mine Owners' Association issued a statement to the press, "We do not propose to enter into negotiations of any nature with the Western Federation of Miners. We do not recognize a union in Telluride. There is no strike in Telluride."

Big Bill Haywood persuaded the exiled miners to test Judge Stevens's injunction that would permit them to return home. On April 8, seventy-eight of them boarded the train for Telluride. John O'-Connell was among them.

When John stepped off the train he met absolute silence. The horses of the militia officers seemed turned to stone. Not a dog barked. Even the wind that blew a flag here, a pennant there, the corner of a neck scarf, or the skirt of a greatcoat did so quietly. For a moment John thought he must be dreaming for so many people to be standing so still.

There were over a thousand waiting for John and his friends at the depot and along the tracks and stacked back up into the town: the three hundred men of the National Guard, the sixty men of Wells's Troop A, the proud young boys of the High School Cadets with their empty training rifles, hundreds of nonuniformed citizens with pistols and rifles at the ready, Cal Rutan and his band of deadly deputies.

Brigadier General Sherman Bell nodded his head. The Gatling gun thundered into the silence, echoes ricocheted off the valley walls, horses danced in sudden release from their statue-stance, and

John O'Connell put his arms over his face thinking he was to die. His last thought before he did not die was to wonder at the expressions on faces of friends with whom he'd shared a glass. They regarded him with the same stoniness as did the soldiers, and John marveled that his life could mean so little to them and so much to him. But he lowered his arms to find himself alive, and those who stood with him.

"We have come peacefully and unarmed," Vincent St. John, president of the Telluride Miners' Union, Local 63, announced when the hush fell after the exploding cartridges had ceased their awesome noise but still ricocheted about in John's head. "And by order of Judge Stevens of the Seventh District—"

"Gentlemen," the general interrupted, "your escort." He nodded again. The gold braid and medals on his coat almost hid its true color. Two columns of bayonets formed a narrow path for the strikers to move singly off the station platform and into the town to Redmen's Opera House. The townspeople cheered the bayonets. John searched for the faces of his loved ones.

Callie was running free. It was Ma'am's naptime. Since Callie had paid up the room and board for a while she didn't kowtow to Mrs. Pakka as she had to Mrs. Stollsteimer. She was showing off her plaid dress to Opal Mae in the alley behind the Sheridan when the fusillade from the Gatling gun down at the depot exploded.

Bram was lifting a crate of empty bottles from the floor to a rack. He dropped the crate at the sound, and breaking glass added to the tension. He pounded his forehead against a wooden strut in the warehouse and wondered how long he could stand to ignore the war raging around him, even with Pa ordering it.

Luella awoke from a dream. She and Lilly and brother Joe had been playing fox and hounds instead of tending to the weeds in the garden when their father rounded the woodshed and discovered them at it. His eyes sparked outrage and his arm rose as if he prepared to orate and the crescendo of the Gatling gun emanated from his lips, "Guilty, guilty, guilty, guilty, guilty!"

Captain Wells and General Bell walked among the prisoners being fed a thin soup at Redmen's Opera House while a special train was being prepared. The officers stopped in front of John O'Connell.

"Have you no compassion for those children of yours?" Wells asked him. "Haven't you even considered moving on and establishing a decent home for them?" But he walked off without waiting for an answer. "That man has interesting children, considering their backgrounds. The son is very bright and the daughter very brave. Most of the criminals have stopped returning. Those that persist appear to have families here."

"Sounds as though we have but one recourse, Captain," the general said.

"You are not concerned at the unfavorable editorials we've suffered in the newspapers?" Wells gazed back at John O'Connell with an uncertain frown.

"No, nor should you be. A few socialist newspapermen will make no difference in the course of the history of this great nation. This is still the United States of America. And we have freedom and right on our side."

Bram put on his coat and hat and left the bottling works. He watched the guards marching the prisoners back to the depot until he made sure Pa was one of them. The stiffs were not chained this time. They walked with dragging steps.

Bob Meldrum blocked Bram's way as he moved to step up onto the depot platform. With Bram still on the snow and Meldrum on the platform, the gunman was the taller and Bram about on a level with the man's smile. It was the kind of smile that was looking for trouble, and Bram's stomach tensed. But the smile straightened and Bram watched the flicker of recognition in Meldrum's eyes and then the flash of anger. How would the man know him?

Carefully, Bram opened his coat to show he was unarmed, but Meldrum didn't glance down to note the absence of a gunbelt. He turned his head aside to spit but kept his gaze locked on Bram's. The color that had flushed his face with the anger faded. He moved the chaw around in his mouth, blinked, and seemed to relax. He nodded mysteriously and laid a hand on Bram's shoulder. It was all Bram could do to keep from flinching, keep his gaze steady. His mouth had gone so dry his tongue stuck to his teeth.

"You done real good, boy," Bob Meldrum said even more mysteriously, "real good." He patted Bram's shoulder and turned away. "Just don't do it again."

Bram stood listening to the clink of the gunman's spurs over the sounds of soldiers' sharp commands and the engine's bleeding off steam. He'd gone weak with relief but couldn't imagine what a killer would think he'd been so good at.

Bram rounded the depot to see Pa stumble and a soldier shove him onto one of two cattle cars being loaded with strikers. Bram decided things had gone deep enough. He pushed his hat back on his head, stuck his hands in his pants pockets, and sauntered up to the cattle car.

"You leave that boy be," Bob Meldrum warned the soldier who tried to stop him. He gave the man a stare gone empty of every expression but watchfulness. "Owed you one," the killer explained to Bram when the soldier had stepped back, "and that was it. Don't expect no more."

Bram stepped into the cattle car and sat on the floor next to Pa. "You should be with your Ma'am and sister, not here," Pa whispered, and then hugged him. "But sure and I'm glad to see you. Things is turning out all wrong somewheres."

"You know we're bound to win yet," Vincent St. John said. "We have the opinion of the country in our favor and we've got the right on our side."

And the other side has the army, the governor, and the wealth, Bram thought, and most of the citizens of Telluride. And the strange, tall Cree predicted the union would not win this battle. He'd been horribly accurate thus far. Bram didn't know how the strikers could ignore the odds against them. He did know the next man to shove John O'Connell around would answer for it.

The door of the cattle car slammed shut. The engine hooted its intent to depart. The car jerked, things squeaked and ground, and the floor shook. Their guards sat on barrels, rifles aimed at the ceiling with the butts resting on their thighs. The car smelled of cattle even though the slatted sides provided cold drafts to blow grit into their eyes and strips of light and bandit shadows across the guards' faces. There were seven guards, few of them much older than Bram. One stared at him and Bram read his fear, toyed with the idea of affecting a Bob Meldrum expression, but looked away instead. That boy had the rifle.

There was right and there was wrong. Ma'am had taught him that. And she was good, therefore right. But since his visit to the Pick and Gad, Bram was having trouble with what he knew to be right and what he saw. And what he'd done. "Pa, did you tell Shorty and Sully to take me out on the town?"

"That I did." Pa turned to study Bram. "Don't suppose they explained anything. Just put you in the soup and watched to see if you could swim to the kettle's edge. Did you not enjoy yourself, son?" A soldier lowered his rifle and ordered them silent. Bram was glad he didn't have to answer.

As the train climbed out of Placerville, the drafts grew colder, the shadowed strips darker, the light strips sharper. And when it passed through snowdrift tunnels the car darkened to night. There was coughing and spitting, groaning and creaking of the wooden parts of the car against metal holdings, the clang of metal on metal as the car ahead jerked their car to follow.

The incline steepened and Pa swayed into him. The guards had to set their feet to keep their barrels from sliding. Bram could understand Greek and Latin and the parsing of sentences, could cipher numbers and chart the planes of the earth or of his hand. But books and teachers did not explain these stiffs sitting on the floor with him, nor the soldiers on their barrels, nor the women at the Gold Belt Saloon and Dance Hall and the Pick and Gad.

When the train reached the top of the Dallas Divide it entered long snow tunnels that had been plowed through drifts, and the fumes from the engine seeped through the slats. Even the guards wept and coughed. When they emerged, dusty smoke writhed among the light strips. The train slowed and Bram could hear shouts from the car ahead. A guard rolled back the side door, Bram thought in order to dispel the fumes. The young soldier who'd regarded him with fear looked uncertain now, distressed. But he rose with his fellows and lowered his rifle to aim into the car. His captain turned to the strikers. "On your feet, all of you."

Bram saw a man in the snow through the doorway.

"But we're nowhere near to Ridgway," Vincent St. John shouted.

"Out you go, redneck." The end of a rifle barrel prodded St. John toward the opening, and the captain pushed him out. And then the next man. And another. When they came for John O'-Connell, Bram heard himself roar.

49

"THERE has to be some connection between Aletha and Callie or Aletha and something in Callie's world," Renata said. They'd zapped frozen gourmet dinners in her microwave and stuffed themselves with the salt-laden, gummy fare. Now they sat in the hot tub to soak away the grime of another time and to luxuriate in its decadence. "When you first saw Callie, did you touch her?" she asked Aletha. Having accepted the fact of the impossible, Renata acted like there must be some logic to its explanation. "Did you exchange anything?"

"Not the first time. I touched her hand when she handed Charles to me. I did leave my sketchbook, but I didn't hand it to her."

"I can see where you're headed, Renata, but it doesn't follow," Cree said. "Because what would have made it happen the first time, before any connection was made?" The dark outside turned the window next to them into a flat mirror partially clouded with steam. It made the images reflected patchy.

"And although Aletha always seems to be around somewhere when things happen, Callie often isn't." Cree had his arms over the edge of the tub. Puffs of hair in his armpits looked like dark holes in the distortion of Aletha's black-window mirror. "She wasn't around when we stepped out of that old lady's house into a snowy yesteryear and she wasn't up at Alta when the mine turned into the real thing and I ended up in 1901 for a month."

"But it's always Callie's world or someplace Aletha goes that once had a connection to Callie." Renata sat up and her nipples hardened and contracted in the relatively colder air. "And if we're to believe Aletha, nothing like this ever happened to her until she came into some kind of connection with Callie."

"Telluride and Alta have connections to a lot of people," Cree insisted. "Not just to Callie." A cut and swollen lip made his mouth look off center.

"What if the connection hasn't been made yet?" Renata sat up farther, evidently startled by her own idea, and Aletha could hear the change in Cree's breathing. "These little time warps or whatever," Renata said, "do not always happen in sequence. You go back one time and it's one year and the next time it's before that maybe. So why assume the connection had to be made the first time Callie and Aletha met? Could be the last time they met or one in the middle."

"It may not have happened yet." Cree's eyes were thoughtful on Renata's chest. "Sounds pretty improbable."

"Improbable? The fact these time . . . holes happen at all is preposterous, but given they do anyway, there has to be some kind of explanation."

"I think we should look for a preposterous one," Aletha said.

Cree reached over to muss her hair. "It's the goofy way she reacts to stress. She's been through a lot more of these experiences than you have, Renata."

"Well, if it never happens again, you smug smart-asses," Aletha said, "we'll know little old Aletha figured out the preposterous and did just the right thing. The problem just may no longer exist. I left my pendant at the train depot."

They both watched her, waiting for further revelation. Finally Renata said, "That's it? You left your pendant in the depot?"

"That old souvenir rock?"

"My little piece of Telluride. You said the one constant about all this was me. Well, if I remember right, that little piece of Telluride was hanging around my neck or in my pocket every time except once, and then it was sitting on the TV up against the front door when the fog came up to the crib on Pacific Avenue."

"What the hell is she talking about?"

Cree wiped sweat from his forehead. "Oh, one of those corny quartz fragments on a chain they sell around town," he explained. "Aletha, you don't really think a cheap souvenir could cause all this?"

"We'll find out when I go into town tomorrow to have my tooth capped."

"No way are you going into town tomorrow," Cree said.

"But if it was the pendant, nothing will happen. That'll be the test. Besides, if you think I'm going around looking like this forever, forget it." She summoned the nerve to sit up above the froth. "The pendant leaves a little stained spot on my chest when it gets hot. Right here."

"So, as far as we know, the only things displaced in time were the sketchpad, the sandals, and the cat," Renata continued as if Aletha's interruption and her chest were of no consequence. "And those goons we left in the depot."

"And my pendant."

"And my running shoes," Cree said, "and the boots and clothes I brought back with me."

"And the really mysterious thing is that the sketchbook and my sandals were already here in town and old. Also fairly new when I brought them here with me. They existed then and now both. So my theory is that Callie's dead in Lone Tree Cemetery and alive at the same time right now living her life on the other side of the oval. And for a while there had to be two pairs of sandals and two sketchbooks . . . but I can't figure out how."

"Are you positive she's sane?" Renata asked Cree.

"Well, one of her is. I've never figured out the other one. Of course, we've known each other less than a month, but then, I've lost a month."

"Seems like years," Aletha said unkindly.

Renata climbed to the tiles, exposing the rest of her gorgeous inches. "I'm getting nervous being around either one of you. Turn off the tub when you come up. Both guestrooms are made up but you can make your own arrangements."

"One thing, Renata," Cree fairly sighed at the view, "what did you and Dutch Massey have going?"

"A little coke, a lot of sex. I didn't know he was dealing until after he was dead and it all came out in the papers." She shrugged into a towel and cut off the view. "I've since sworn off both."

"I'll bet," Aletha said when she and Cree were alone. "The coke maybe, but she's dying for you to sneak into the mistress bedroom tonight."

"She'd just close her eyes and pretend I was Bulkeley Wells."

"You underestimate yourself, McCree. Anybody who's remembered at a busy whorehouse two years later can't be all that resistible."

He grinned and grabbed a towel. "There's no way you're going into town tomorrow for that dental appointment, crazy lady, pendant or no."

Aletha's skin felt scoured of lice and dead skin scales and accumulated dirt, that probably hadn't even been there, when she climbed past her father's picture on the stairway. The guestrooms flanked a center hall at the top of the house. She and Cree stood close but indecisive between the two doorways. "What will you do if you find Dutch's stash?"

"Probably get arrested." He slid an arm around her waist under the towel.

"But if you didn't get arrested, would you sell the cocaine to people?"

"I'd take it up in the Cessna and fly over Telluride and heave it out by the handful and everybody'd think it was snowing and they'd be right."

"In that case, I have the damnedest urge to get snuggled." She stretched up to take a nip at his neck.

" 'Course, I'd keep the money."

"Cree!"

"Hell, they took everything but my shirt. What do you expect?"

"Come to think of it, I don't really know you very well, do I?" Aletha pushed away and walked off into the bedroom on the left. But Cree followed her and she got well snuggled anyway.

The sheriff of San Miguel County, Tom Rickard, and his shields and sunglasses showed up the next morning with two federal agents. Renata had left for her office and Cree and Aletha were having breakfast. "I've been telling these gentlemen how you . . . uh left Mr. Duffer, Mr. Bellamy, and Mr. Pheeney way back in history there. And would you believe they do not believe me?"

The agents wanted to ask Cree a few questions. Aletha took her coffee down to the greenhouse area but it was impossible not to overhear most of the discussion up on the kitchen mezzanine, given the openness of Renata's house. "We'd like to know the whereabouts of Mrs. Norman Theil."

"Never heard of her."

"She's the owner of that expensive condominium you've been living in."

"Oh, that Mrs. Theil. I think she's out of the country."

"Mrs. Norman Theil was the mother of your late partner, Dutch Massey. Before her remarriage she was Mrs. Richard Massey. She died in 1941."

"Then you know where she is."

"That condo was the property of Dutch Massey. Tried to hide the fact by putting the name of his mother on the deed. That property is eligible for confiscation and sale by the Internal Revenue Service to pay the estimated back taxes on income derived from the illegal sale of a controlled substance. We also have reason to believe Massey could have hidden drugs and cash in this area when he visited shortly before his death. And that might explain your presence in Telluride, Mackelwain, and that of the three missing men. You've got some talking to do, mister."

Aletha pleaded silently for Cree to hold his temper. He'd been hassled by the law in two different time periods and neither could be blamed for their inability to believe the truth. The voices droned on, with Cree contributing little. Finally the drone turned exasperated and someone suggested Cree be transported into town for further questioning.

"We'll take the girl too," Sheriff Rickard insisted over Cree's objections. "She's involved in this somehow and it's not her first time."

"You'll be sorry," Cree repeated as they filed down the stairs.

"No more stories about holes into history. I've had it with you guys. And don't think I didn't notice you've been in a fight, Mackelwain."

"You don't suppose I could make my eleven-o'clock appointment with the dentist?" Aletha showed her gray incisor to the law and met stares of disbelief.

"Oh yeah, I almost forgot," the sheriff said as they approached the car. He opened the trunk and took out a brown bag. "Got this back from a police lab and another special lab in Gunnison. Guy I know who's into rock and assaying and historical records." He pulled the piece of highgrade ore that his men had found under Callie's cabin out of the bag. "That fellow claims this was mined probably around the turn of the century and probably either out of the tunnels at Alta or the nearby Gold King. But he says it hasn't lain buried in dirt all that time since then. Nor the rag it was wrapped in. Says he never saw anything like this outside of a museum." Tom Rickard watched Aletha and Cree, seemed disappointed in their vacant looks.

Aletha rode in front with the sheriff and Cree in back with the two federal agents.

"I think I should warn you," Sheriff Rickard said, "that I have read a lot about the history of this place. If you're dreaming up another fantastic story, I'm liable to catch you up on your facts." The light from the windshield penetrated his sunglasses to highlight the crinkles at the corner of one eye in sickly green before he turned to face Aletha. "It might pay you to drop this time business and cooperate."

"Then you know all about Willy Selby and the Cosmopolitan," Cree said, "and Eugenio Pangrazia and Cal Rutan and Bob Meldrum."

"Meldrum . . . he was a hired gunman in the old days." Sheriff Rickard sounded pleased with himself. "You mean to tell me you didn't chat with old Bulkeley Wells?"

"Young Bulkeley Wells," Aletha said. "And Callie and Bram O'Connell. But they didn't go down in the history books. They were just people trying to survive in this nutty place. Like me."

"I think you might be interested to know we got the owner of the property up at Alta to blast the mine entrance. Nobody's going in or out of there." He checked the rearview mirror for Cree's reaction and glanced over at Aletha. "If you know what's happened to Duffer, Pheeney, and Bellamy—"

"Pheeney's under a headstone in Lone Tree Cemetery," Aletha told him.

"We haven't had a burial out there in two years." They had entered Telluride and passed the condominium complex at the edge of town when the car began to bounce and then swerve as the sheriff fought the wheel. "What the hell? Where's the road?"

Aletha had her hands over her face for protection by the time they'd jolted to a stop. She kept them there as the sheriff opened his door and got out and the two back doors opened and slammed shut. "You two stay put," Sheriff Rickard shouted in at them and then let loose a string of obscenities.

Aletha lowered her hands. The sheriff's car was up to its axles in snow sitting in somebody's front yard. The eternal mountain peaks were the same but the lower slopes were barren of trees. An old-fashioned train whistle sounded remote, as if it came from a television off in another room. And if she listened carefully, Aletha could hear the mills stamping their rhythms even more remotely.

"Well, there gocs the pendant theory," she said, and bit her lip.

"Jesus, this is the first time you've brought along a whole car," Cree said behind her, and strung together some four-letter words in configurations that made the sheriff sound bland.

Sheriff Rickard wore a leather uniform jacket but the two investigators wore only suit jackets. They soon grew cold and slid back into the car. The sheriff kicked snow away from the tires, turned to stare at the house, turned back to stare suspiciously at Aletha through the windshield.

"I can't figure this one," an agent said from the backseat.

"Some kind of stunt," the other answered. They could all hear the sounds of a steam engine pulling rattling railroad cars into town, beginning to brake. "I didn't know there was track over there."

"There isn't."

Mildred Heisinger wafted between past and present as though passing back and forth through Aletha's oval. Doris Lowell had taken up residence. Dr. Barbara visited frequently and was ready to dash the few blocks over at Doris's telephone call. A few of the ladies belonging to the San Miguel Historical Society brought in food and stayed to chat with Doris and watch the still form in the high four-poster. And word went out that Telluride's oldest living resident was about to leave it.

Renata Winslow had rushed through her office chores, sent out those helpers she'd found jobs for, and hurried over to Mildred's. "I tell you it really happened. I should have looked for information for the historical society but I actually met Bulkeley Wells, Bob Meldrum, and Cal Rutan."

Doris puttered around Mildred's bed. Finally she said, "Every generation has its own way of killing itself. And I realize even salt and sugar are supposed to be dangerous now. I do try to be tolerant. But, Renata, these drugs you young people take nowadays are affecting your minds."

"No drugs, Mrs. Lowell, I swear. Nothing but a couple of glasses of wine with dinner. We just walked out of this house and . . . Nobody's going to believe us, are they? No matter what."

"No, dear, they're not. If I were you I wouldn't be so eager to go around talking this way, either."

* * *

Mildred stood at the door of her house and looked at the girl in the black dress that marked her as one of Mrs. Stollsteimer's girls and wondered how her own life might have been different had she never met this child or her brother.

"Please, ma'am, I have to work and am getting far behind in my lessons. I wondered if you'd have a book I could study since you're a teacher. And I've brought you a book as a deposit to keep until I return the one you lend me. There are wonderful drawings in it you can look at whenever you want."

Mildred took the book of drawings and gave the child nothing in return. "It seems such a petty thing to have done now," she tried to tell Doris Lowell, "but I remember taking great pleasure in it at the time."

Doris just stared across the bed at Renata Winslow and didn't see Mildred watching. Doris and Renata moved their lips but Mildred could hear them no more than they could hear her. Why was she thinking again of that girl and her brother?

Bram had been alternately tender and rough that night at the Pick and Gad. He didn't have Mr. Bulkeley Wells's smooth compelling ways and practiced methods. He told her how he'd thought of her when trapped in a caved-in drift and planning to die. How the peacock greens of the copper had reminded him of the colors she wore and how they paled her eyes even more. How his little sister had warned him he'd pay for carrying Mildred through the mining camp for all to see. How Mildred had figured in his nightmares while he was in the hospital as a vengeful ghost who beckoned him seductively one moment and punished him the next. Mildred was both frightened and excited and quite overwhelmed. This brash young man gorged with anger, youth, lust, and righteousness had been well-nigh irresistible.

50

Bram couldn't be sure when the roaring in his ears ceased to be his own fury and began to be the wind racing by the cattle car. He didn't feel himself pushed from the train but was suddenly tumbling through space. The jolt of landing forced the air from his lungs. Snow clogged his mouth and filled his eyes. Nothing moved, but his body still churned with the remembered vibration of the cattle car and the jarring of impact. His bones, even his jaw, ached from the jolt, his chest screamed for air. Bram fought snow until he realized he was facedown and that a push upward brought the glare of sun.

He spit out the clog and breathed in raw cold. He brought his knees up under him and backed onto his heels, squinted in the glare. The smoke trail of the engine's stack flowed and rippled away behind it as the train left him on the Dallas Divide. An engine, two cattle cars, and a caboose.

"Pa?" His hat was gone. And now the train. An awful silence. The sun burned on the white around him.

Dark things on the blazing white. An outcrop of rock. The top of a telephone pole, its wires not four feet from the snow. A man wallowing, trying to stand, his movements those of a man drunk. "The government in Washington will hear about this." He crawled on toward Bram, blinked. "You seen my hat?"

Bram walked beside his father along the tracks.

"We got 'em now, son. They can't get away with this." John had hurt a leg when the guards pushed him from the train. It supported his weight but he limped, and the jags in his speaking and breathing proved the pain he was in.

Vincent St. John had told them to start on ahead while he and others searched for the lost. "There'll be more injured. You get him down to the trees, Bram. It's a long way yet to Ridgway."

Bram worried about meeting a train. Without snowshoes they had to keep to the tracks. In some places the slushy snow was no more than waist-high on either side of the rails. In others the plow trains had tunneled massive drifts and the rails ran along the bottom of narrow canyons. The blinding white took on a rosy hue and when Bram closed his eyes for a second's rest from it, the color he was seeing became red. Every now and then he'd take both of Pa's arms over his shoulders and hoist him onto his back.

"Can't wait for the country to be hearing of this," John said between gritted teeth. Sweat beaded his face.

"It won't make any difference, Pa. The Owners' Association and the Alliance have all the power."

"They got the power in Telluride and have us outnumbered too, but we have the numbers on the outside of Telluride. There's more stiffs than bosses and when we're organized we'll be having the power."

Bram thought that if the bosses organized they'd still have the power because they had the money. They'd be easier to organize because they were fewer. But he kept his doubts to himself. He couldn't hurt the man who'd raised him, worked until he'd had to be carried home to clear that drift in Alta.

"I can take no more for a bit. Stop and let me rest," John said finally, and they both sat on the tracks. Stopping now with the warm sun on them was fine, but once it grew dark they'd be asking to freeze to death. "If you was to leave me here to wait for the others and go on by yourself, you'd be in Ridgway before night got too deep, big strong lad like you."

"No."

"You could be sending help back for the rest of us."

"No."

"Always was a stubborn kid." They started off again, the sun slipping lower and the world taking on a winter chill. They made it to the trees but couldn't stop for long because of the cold shade they provided. Then Bram was climbing the vertical slush next to the tracks and reaching a hand down to help John. "Train's coming, Pa."

They were in a hollow niche Bram had dug out of the bank when the train passed. An engine, two cattle cars, and a caboose. Returning to Telluride. The side doors were open now. Bram looked down into the eyes of a young soldier, not the same one that watched him on the way here, but the confusion and discomfort were the same. If Bram had had a gun at that moment he'd have tried to kill the man, even knowing the hopeless stupidity of it.

The smoke from the stack hovered above them and they could smell it long after the sound of the engine faded. They started off again but they would not make it to Ridgway before night. The sun continued to withdraw its warmth.

"Remember that story you told us of the man carrying mail to Ophir in the old days? He was caught in a blizzard and built a snow cave on the pass."

"Men was hardier back then, boy. And for every one like him, there's scores that weren't found till snow melt, and some not to this day."

But Bram began scooping with his hands. By the time he'd hollowed out a deep enough cave he was warmed from the effort, but John's teeth rattled and the world had grayed with coming night.

"You appear to have proved the doctors wrong. Have you not thought of going back to the stopes, son?" John asked when they lay inside, Bram curled around him to lend warmth. "Maybe takin' up the hammer and drill after all now?"

But Bram couldn't answer, could barely hear Pa over the thunder of fear in his ears. He could feel the air on his face that passed through the hole to the outside, could fill his lungs at will. Yet being closed up this way brought on the old nightmare with a vengeance, suffocating his reason even while he breathed. How could he ever face the stopes again with this cowardice grown upon him like a boil?

Callie and Ma'am were not shipped out of Telluride on cattle cars as Mildred would remember, but on a passenger coach with families of other strikers who couldn't be discouraged from trying to return. Callie took of their meager belongings what she could stuff into her carpetbag. Mrs. Pakka, as irritated as she'd become with them, had protested on their behalf. "The poor woman's half-demented and I don't know if the girl can handle her. We don't know where the boy is off to."

"Word's being sent to Ridgway for the men to expect the families to arrive there," the sheriff answered. "And the O'Connell boy went on the train with his father."

The passenger coach was packed with crying babies and white-faced ladies. The stove at one end stood empty of fuel or fire. The train sat at the depot for two hours as other cars were loaded. Callie found Ma'am a seat but had to sit on her carpetbag in the aisle. At least Bram was safe with Pa. They'd all be together again soon, away from here. Callie thought that the strange lady, Aletha, had been right. Callie should never have come to Telluride.

Elsie Biggs picked her away down the aisle carrying a little girl. Elsie's coloring hadn't improved. Callie wanted to stand and hug her old friend; instead she sat unmoving and Elsie knelt down in front of her. The little girl was sucking on the chain of a necklace way too long for her. She didn't smell especially good. "What's going to happen to us, Callie?"

"The sheriff says our pas will meet us in Ridgway. Did your mother have another baby?"

"No. I did." Elsie nuzzled the little girl's cheek. "My ma's having a conniption fit up there." She nodded toward the front of the car. "Little Margaret and me had to get away from her."

"I didn't know you had a husband," Callie said. Elsie was still a girl with her hair down.

"I just have Margaret." Elsie blushed nice color into her skin. Margaret smiled a sloppy smile, removed her necklace, and tried to put it around Callie's neck. But it caught in Callie's hair. "She found it on the floor in the depot where they made us wait this morning. Just quartz. Can't think why anyone would want to make a necklace of it. Margaret will probably want it back in a few minutes. It's a game she likes to play with people."

Could someone have left Margaret on Elsie's steps with a note as Bram had been left? Callie untangled the chain from her hair and let the necklace hang down her front to please the little girl. It looked almost like the one Aletha had worn when Callie had supper out at the Senate with the lady of the painting. Could Margaret have anything to do with Elsie's going into a room when the gentleman was present? "Mrs. Stollsteimer dismissed me too. Because of Pa and the union, I guess. Opal Mae says they've hired a new girl and the hotel's filled with soldiers, and Mr. Moyer, the president of the whole union, is a prisoner in a front room on second with his own toilet."

"I don't want them to hurt Margaret," Elsie said when yet another distraught family was shoved aboard. "She's so little and can't help herself. My pa says Margaret's an abomination."

She just smells like one, Callie thought, but she said, "She's very pretty. She must take a great deal of cleaning up after."

"Callie, you haven't introduced me to your friend," Luella said in a perfectly normal voice and startled them. "That is impolite and I've taught you better."

"Yes, Ma'am. This is Elsie Biggs and her little Margaret." Callie peered up anxiously at her mother. "And this is my mother, Mrs. O'Connell."

Luella trembled as would someone very elderly and her face was fever red but she smiled at Elsie and complimented Margaret. When Elsie returned to her own mother and brothers and sister, Luella asked, "Callie, where is my Bible?"

"I didn't have room for it. But Mrs. Pakka promised to send our things as soon as we're settled."

Ma'am squeezed Callie's arm with surprising strength. "You must run back and fetch it, quickly, before the train starts away."

"They won't let anyone off the coach. I saw a lady try to leave and a soldier pushed her back inside."

"They won't *allow* anyone off the coach," Luella corrected and her flush paled to chalk as the whistle blew and the rattling cars began to roll. "All my medicine is in the Bible, between the pages. Without it I shall die."

"Maybe we can buy some in Ridgway."

Luella reached around for Callie's other arm, drew her up against the arm of the seat and off the carpetbag. "You meant to leave it behind. You and Mrs. Pakka planned it this way."

"No, Ma'am, please." All the ladies and infants had stopped wailing to stare at them. "You mustn't behave this way."

Luella released Callie and leaned back in her seat, wrung her hands, muttering words no one could understand. Callie wanted to cry but instead she rubbed her sore arms and prayed Pa and Bram would be at the depot in Ridgway to meet them. The railway spur that serviced Telluride and Pandora met the main line at Vance Junction. The main line led to the Ophir Loop and eventually Durango and the smelter for the ore shipments in one direction and to Placerville, the Dallas Divide, and Ridgway in the other. At Ridgway this narrow-gauge Rio Grande Southern met the standard-gauge tracks and the rest of the nation. Callie's train stopped now at the junction to allow the tracks to clear ahead. The guard at the front of the car allowed several small children with their mothers off to take care of bodily functions and he went with them. The guard at the back of the car didn't seem to notice Luella rise, step past Callie, and follow.

Callie had been caught by surprise too, but she hurried down the crowded aisle after Luella, who seemed to be floating at an unbelievable speed. Callie heard the guard order her to stop but couldn't believe he'd shoot her in the back. She had to get her mother to Ridgway where the rest of the family could help care for her.

As she jumped off the coach steps to the cinders below, Callie couldn't see the women and children led away by the first guard and she couldn't see Ma'am. But she knew her mother would wet herself before she'd stop going back for her medicine. Callie raced down the tracks toward Telluride with the guard still shouting behind her. If he came after her he could help her with Ma'am. If he shot Callie she wouldn't have to worry about this family problem that had grown faster than she had.

51

WORD of the train carrying strikers' families reached Ridgway too late. Most of the fathers and husbands who made it off the Dallas Divide were secreted among various crates, barrels, and supplies loaded on the train bound for Telluride. And this time they were armed. The two trains passed each other at Placerville with the incoming one pulled off on a siding.

Vincent St. John and the others had similarly passed up Bram's snow cave in the night, and when John O'Connell and Bram reached Ridgway the next day, word of the outrage on the divide had spread to angry union men throughout the San Juans and many were filtering into Ridgway. While some joined search parties for those still lost on the divide, others milled around town demanding action. A few, those with families left behind and those hotheaded enough to find and bear weapons against General Sherman Bell and his troops, had formed a disorganized but quiet band bent on revenge. While St. John met with other union leaders to draft protests to the state and federal governments, this quiet band managed to hop a train and be gone with their leaders unaware. And the only sure plan they had was to jump off the train as it slowed for Vance Junction and to take cover, stay hidden until the soldiers had searched and gone on about their business, and then regroup on the road to march together into town. There was even talk of marching on the hotel and saving the union president, Mr. Moyer.

Bram was opposed to the whole thing. His father limped as if one leg were shorter than the other, and should not be jumping off any train. There were bound to be patrols on the road. And even if they made it to town, their anger was no match for the superior numbers that could organize to meet them.

But Bram was on the train headed for Telluride, wedged between crates of eggs and boxes of canned fruit, because John O'Connell was there, because he worried for his sister and ailing mother, and because he had an unreasoning urge to draw blood. These were men he'd be proud to work beside. He wanted to believe their assurances that because they were moving so quickly they would take the town by surprise. Yet a voice as fey as a tommyknocker's patter told him this was suicide.

Callie heard the train departing without her but kept after the figure still moving with that strange floating glide. The tracks were clear but the snow banked high on either side and the ties were either wet or icy. Running made her slide on the ties or slip in the mush between them. So she hopped from one tie to the next, her toes bruising and her ankles turning. Snow and sky soaked up her shouts to her mother. Callie couldn't figure how someone so weak and sick could move with such speed. If the skirts of Luella's coat hadn't whipped about with her steps, Callie would have thought Ma'am on wheels instead of human feet. The figure ahead grew smaller, darker, the bright snowy world grew pink.

This was all unfair. She was too young to control her mother. She'd been too young to be sent out to clean things at the hotel too. Bram should not have gone back into the mine. He'd been warned of the cave-in. Pa should not have had dealings with the union. And Ma'am should be taking care of her child instead of the other way around.

Callie's body pleaded to stop and rest, but guilt drove her on. She'd avoided spending all the time she might have with her mother, had not really listened when Luella talked, had been impatient with her illness. Callie's two petticoats, long dress, and coat fought young leg muscles that could have carried her faster if unhampered. She slipped on ice and came down on her backside, jolting her spine, sending pain the length of it to compound the thumping stamp mill in her head. Cold slush slid up her skirts, weighed them down when she managed to get hopping again.

By the time she reached the depot, Ma'am was nowhere in sight. But one of the guards who'd forced them onto the train was mounting a horse and he took off toward the town. Callie followed, thinking he was chasing Luella, but lost him in the massing of troops on Colorado Avenue. She turned and ran back to the boardinghouse. "I haven't seen her. I told you to keep an eye on her." Mrs. Pakka squinted her disapproval. "Knew you weren't to be trusted."

Callie left Mrs. Pakka's kitchen, which was filled with the yeast-and-cinnamon smells of baking, her stomach muttering but her head high. She stood uncertainly in the middle of a deserted street in Finntown. Over the distant murmur of men and horses up on Colorado Avenue came the clear peal of the school bell across the valley and the squawk of crows startled by it.

Should she run to enlist Aunt Lilly's aid or just begin knocking on doors to find someone who'd seen her mother? In her confused state, Ma'am could be anywhere. Callie started back toward the depot and saw an old man leading a burro out from between the snow banks that bordered Townsend Avenue. "Thin woman? Without her hat?" he asked when Callie questioned him.

"That's her . . . I mean she. Please, where did you see her?"

He pointed back the way he'd come and then called after her. "Needs locking up, that one."

There seemed to be not another soul out except for the soldiers up in the business district. And they were uncannily quiet for so many. A horse-drawn plow had banked the snow high to either side of the west end of Colorado Avenue and home owners had shoveled passageways to the street. The houses here were tall, narrow, stately. Their ornate trim peeked over the snow mounds in bright colors to relieve the unending white of winter.

"Run for your home, child," a lady called from her doorway as Callie hurried from one tunnel to the next. "There's going to be trouble."

"I have no home to go to and I'm looking for my mother." Callie leaned exhausted against the towering snow to the side of the lady's path. "She's thin and has no hat. Have you seen her?" The lady ran down off her porch, slipping on ice patches on the steps, grabbed Callie's hand, and pulled her inside. The house was dark after the sun and snow outdoors. Callie could see only the lady's shape and the light from a doorway at the end of a long hall. "There's no one else to look after her and she's not well."

"You can't be out now. You'll have to wait here until it's over." The lady knelt to unbutton Callie's coat. "You're soaked through. I'll have Dorothy warm you some soup."

Callie's eyes adjusted enough to pick out a staircase rising from one side of the hall and a loaded coat tree at its base. "But I can't leave her out there."

Another shape formed in a doorway across from the staircase. Callie knew the voice but couldn't make out the features of the man. "What is it, Lydia? Has it started?"

"No, Father, a waif in the street looking for her mother. We can't allow her out now."

The man sighed. "You will find your strays, won't you?"

Lydia guided her into a parlor and pushed her into a chair next to a stove. The air was old and stuffed with heat. She unbuttoned Callie's boots and drew them off.

"Until what is over?" Callie asked, but Lydia was gone. Callie blinked until she saw the face of the elderly lawyer who'd accused her father of planning to blow up the railroad to keep the militia out of Telluride. He'd sounded so much more powerful in that room in the courthouse. He sat now and put one foot up on a stool, his hands cupping a goblet with dark drink at its bottom. "I'm not a waif or a stray," Callie told him. "I'm Callie O'Connell."

"I would have thought everyone had been warned by now. Those union devils are marching on the town and no one is safe until they've been . . . O'Connell?" He leaned so close to her she could see the hair in his nose. "You weren't sent off on the train this morning?"

Callie explained about her mother leaving the train as Lydia presented her with a bowl of soup and some tea. If the union was marching into town, would Bram be able to persuade Pa to stay in Ridgway? Did Callie now have to worry about them too? She was too tired to find the strength to decide what to do next. The heat of the room and the food lulled her senses more. Finally she said, "You're Lawyer Barada."

"And you're the spawn of an anarchist," he answered. "But as long as you must be in our midst, you might as well make yourself useful, Callie O'Connell."

"Father, she's little more than a child and distraught over her mother. She—"

"She can help you take the children to the attics, where it's safer. Dorothy and I shall hold the fort down here. Off with you."

Callie swallowed some more of the soup in a tiny attic room with a narrow cot and a washstand. She sat next to a freckled boy and his younger sister. "May I please have my coat and shoes? It's cold up here."

"They're drying behind the kitchen stove." Lydia handed her a blanket and wrapped the children in quilts. Then she stood at the window and shivered. "Finish that soup and hush. We'll find your mother when it's safe to be out."

"My pa is not an anarchist." The soup was cold already but the chill in the air cut through Callie's grogginess. "He's an Irishman."

"What's a pa?" the little girl asked, eyeing Callie with suspicion. She had long sausage curls like Callie once wore.

"She's talking about her father." The boy snickered.

"Your children are rude," Callie told his mother, and slipped off the bed. "I thank you for wanting to help me, but I have a family too."

"Your own manners are not above reproach, miss," Lydia snapped. The planes of her face were so much softer than Ma'am's. Her scent was as delicious as that worn by the fine ladies at the hotel as she knelt and hugged Callie to her. "I'm sorry and I do understand your worry. It's just that desperate men are marching on the town."

Callie pushed away and went to the window. This "fort" provided a clear view of the street above the shoveled paths that could hide her mother if Callie were down there. She could see almost everywhere, but no dark form without a hat scurried below. "Do you have a window this high to look out on the back of your house?"

"There are only paths to the privies out there." But Lydia led her to the door.

"Looking for her maw," the boy explained to his sister, and hooted like Johann Peterson the school troublemaker up at Alta used to do.

But there was another high window in the narrow room across the hall. As Lydia had predicted, paths led only to sheds and privies in backyards as far to either side as Callie could see. All were empty.

"Did you find a maw?" Lydia's daughter asked when they returned. She and her brother stood at the window now, their quilts at their feet. "Is that a maw?"

Callie rushed to look down where the little girl pointed to an oblong object in the front yard. It had a bar of different-colored glass across its top. Its sides opened outward and gentlemen with bare heads and light clothing stepped into the snow.

On Colorado Avenue horses tugged the Gatling gun from the direction of the hotel with the sheriff and his deputies riding to each side and a horde of mounted soldiers behind it and more on foot behind them. Across the street Ma'am darted from a shoveled passageway and turned down Townsend Avenue back toward the depot, her pins gone and her hair flying.

And Callie was flying out of the attic room and down two flights of stairs. The necklace Elsie's little Margaret had insisted she wear flopped so that Callie grabbed onto it to hold it down. The quartz stone on the end of the chain felt hot. She turned at the bottom of the stairs and faced toward the light at the end of the hall, almost colliding with Lawyer Barada as he emerged from the parlor. She'd guessed right. This was the kitchen and a heavy woman sat at a table peeling apples.

"Here, you!" the woman shouted as Callie grabbed her boots and slipped them on without buttoning, yanked her coat from a hook on the wall, and took off back down the hall. This time she did collide with the lawyer. Lydia was there too by now and made a grab for her arm as Callie fought to slide back the bolt on the door. The bolt was well oiled and moved smoothly and Callie managed to slip out of two pairs of hands as if she too were oiled.

52

CAPTAIN Bulkeley Wells had argued with the general about bringing the wonderful Gatling gun on this expedition when word was sent on the telephone wire from the Junction that strikers were headed for Telluride. Moving the weapon was too slow and Wells preferred to meet the rednecks on the road before they made it to the camp. He shivered now in anticipation and frustration riding beside General Bell, behind the lumbering Gatling and Cal Rutan with his unpredictable gunmen. The latters' duty supposedly was to see that any sympathizers in the town did not pick off the Gatling's escort before it could be positioned to fire on the enemy. Actually there was not a man in the lot who would miss out on the bloodletting even with an army to do the job instead.

The sound of the army at his back straightened Wells's spine. But he was stunned when he spied McCree Mackelwain. This was the second time he'd faced this man from horseback over a snowbank, this man who could seemingly disappear as if by sorcery through a door to another world. One of his women was trying to pull the O'Connell girl into an odd contraption—some sort of enclosed vehicle with glass windows. Homer Barada and his daughter watched from the doorway.

"Not here," Wells shouted to the general as the order was given to release the horses from the Gatling and prepare for battle. "We're in the town still."

"No time," the general answered. "The enemy is upon us." The enemy had halted down the street, a ragtag band of ridiculously small numbers.

A man with huge green spectacles and signs sewn on his coat announcing him to be the sheriff of San Miguel County climbed the snowbank out of Barada's front yard. "What the fuck?" he asked in amazement, and sank up to his crotch. "You making a movie or something?" He picked up a handful of snow and tasted it. "This shit's real, man."

Wells's horse, Horatio, began to spin under him and stopped only to rear. By the time he was under control the Gatling's horses were being led away, back through the cavalry already hemmed in by heaped snow to either side and causing an unmilitary fracas as the infantry behind tried to push forward. The Gatling was to be in the forefront always and now could not be easily moved. Conflicting commands shot everywhere as Wells tried to bring his own Troop A to order.

The false sheriff with the foul mouth extricated himself from the snowbank and fell into the street practically under Horatio's hooves. Bob Meldrum appeared, his own horse giving trouble, and Bulkeley ordered him to remove the creature from the path of battle. But General Bell had drawn his sword, shouting at one and all, to either begin the attack or to restore order to the ranks. In the chaos it was impossible to tell which. The general collided with Meldrum and both were unseated. Three men now scrambled on the snow and ice at Horatio's feet. The animal made to leap the bank into Barada's yard. Bulkeley resisted his mount's impulse only by cruel measures and with harrowing danger to himself and those below him but just in time to see the general's horse and that of Meldrum skirt the Gatling and take off toward the enemy.

"Give me your horse, man," General Sherman Bell ordered, and grabbed a stirrup. "Dammit, I'm in command here." Disabused of his need to climb the snowbank, Horatio resumed his spinning and sent the general flying. Wells grew dizzy before he finally found himself thrown off and at the steed's feet with the others.

"He's not actually trained for battle," he explained to General Sherman Bell, and regained his feet in time to see Horatio's amazing leap over the Gatling gun and down the street to join his fellows.

The sheriff in green spectacles asked Wells, "You the director, or what? Where's the cameras?"

The general commandeered another horse by pulling its rider off and raised his sword once more. Wells climbed the bank now to find the enemy advancing again and Simon Doud, the Pinkerton agent, sniffing at the contraption in Barada's yard. Mr. Cree Mackelwain had discovered a hard patch of snow and peered over at the consternation in the street. He was laughing. For a moment Wells saw the humor in this hectic but dangerous situation too and their eyes met in a meeting of minds so profound and unexpected he could almost feel the challenge and questioning beneath the other man's mirth. But Wells had no time for questions and he turned to leap upon the horse offered up to him by one of his officers.

Captain Bulkeley Wells rode his borrowed horse into the fray.

Simon Doud had purposely refused a mount, considering his role as one of observer and investigator. He'd walked among the infantry until it had become disorganized and then had sidestepped the turmoil around the Gatling gun. But sight of the metal object on Barada's lawn through the snow passage shoveled to the lawyer's house had caused Doud to alter his course. Investigating was what he'd been trained to do. There was always someone needed with a clear head to make reports. And everything suspicious at a time like this was worthy of investigation.

Two very tall men wearing tight-fitting suits of gray with no overcoats opened a door on either side and stepped out. One produced a glazed card and flashed it before Doud's eyes, retrieving it before it could be read. "You want to tell us what's going on here?"

Doud liked neither the man's tone nor his bearing. "I would very much like to know what this metal object is, sir." If there was an answer he didn't hear it over the growing confusion in the street and the noisy struggles of a girl being pulled inside the object by a woman in trousers. As Doud moved to the aid of the girl he was physically restrained by one of the tight-suited gentlemen. "What's your name, mister?"

"Simon P. Doud, investigator for the—"

"Hell, join the crowd. What do you think we are?" And with that the man began pushing and pulling Doud around the object. Doud decided they must be instruments of the dreaded union and put up his own struggle. He and his captor were impeded by the snow but eventually Doud found his arms pinned behind his back and himself propelled headfirst into the shiny object. The girl pleaded and fought from an overstuffed seat in front of him.

"Release that child or I'll have the militia off the street and here to see that you do." The other false investigator slipped in and closed the door in front of Doud. He was hemmed in.

"Where's Mackelwain?" one of his captors demanded of the woman, but she ignored him, continued arguing with the girl, and at one point even tried to hug her.

Doud wondered if his voice could carry through the metal and glass over the lamentations of the females in the front seat. And if it did, could it be heard by his allies in the street, who were making plenty of noise of their own? He could see over piled snow—horses rearing, hats flying, and men obviously in sore straits.

"Should I go get Mackelwain?"

"Sheriff's out there. Let him do it."

"I should like you to know," Doud put in, "that the sheriff and I are on very good terms."

"Callie, it's not safe out there," the woman said. "Where did you get that pendant? It should be destroyed or buried or . . . Here, you can't have that." They struggled over something on the seat between them. "It's evidence. Of what I'm not sure. The sheriff—"

"It's highgrade . . ." Callie quieted, leaned away against the glass of the door at her back.

"Well, yes, it's highgrade. Actually it came from under your house in Alta."

"You took Pa's highgrade?"

"It could have been anybody's who lived there in all the years after you moved out. It could—" But before the woman could finish her sentence, Callie had opened the door and slid out and away, carrying a brown paper bag.

Doud was delighted for her and wished he could do the same. One of his captors did open his door and try to grab the woman when she too left the vehicle to give chase to the girl, but he slammed it in Doud's face. The other man drew him back before he could decide which gizmo on the door released the hidden latch.

Cree had left the sheriff's car when the investigators did but hadn't planned to wander far from Aletha. When she went back to the real world he intended to be with her. But the racket in the street drew him farther from the car than he'd intended. He had to get back and he had to warn the sheriff to stay close to Aletha. But the sheriff was gone. Cree found himself staring at Bulkeley Wells over the snowbank instead.

Wells began whirling as if the horse under him were a trick horse at a rodeo. It nearly climbed the bank onto Cree's side. Before Cree could find snow to hold his weight, Wells had disappeared. At first Cree couldn't understand who the uniformed soldiers were fighting. He began to suspect they were two armies in the same uniform fighting each other until he realized they were fighting their horses and the infantry pushing forward too soon, attempting to stay behind the business end of a vintage Gatling gun partially stuck in the snow. The gun's keepers tried to move it forward and aim it in preparation for firing down the street at the same time. The whole business looked staged for a TV sitcom.

Wells appeared on the snowbank without his horse. Cree wished he could get this guy on the right side of time just once. It would be intriguing to share a few thoughts over a few Michelobs. But when he followed Wells's glance down the street he saw what the Gatling was trying to aim for. Cree could even pick out Bram O'-Connell. He should have known.

Cree's job was to get Sheriff Rickard and himself back to Aletha, not to mess in Bram's life or Wells's either. He turned back to the car, determined but gut-sick. It was not his war. He could do nothing but harm. He still couldn't see the sheriff but he did see Bram's sister, Callie, headed for the street with a paper bag. And Aletha was right behind her.

Clyde Duffer saw her too. He and Maynard had been ordered off the streets when they'd walked up to Colorado Avenue to visit one of the more classy gambling joints for a drink and to get Maynard in on the games. They'd decided to develop some more natural talents. When the soldiers ordered them off the street, they obeyed until they were hidden by snowbanks and then angled back toward the edge of town where all the noise was coming from.

They slipped unnoticed back onto Colorado Avenue, toward the west end and around into a shoveled pathway to somebody's house, which gave them a ringside view of the dumb machine gun on wheels these jerks seemed to think was a howitzer. They saw the O'Connell girl dart from the shoveled path across from them, and behind her, Aletha Kingman. When Duffer recognized Cree Mackelwain's head above the snow he touched his broken nose. He decided that if he never got home, neither would Mackelwain. Either way, that man was going to die.

Bob Meldrum hadn't heard Captain Wells's command to arrest the queer man with the badge and green glasses. Hearing a particular command amidst the mayhem was impossible, even though for him the mayhem was muted. Whenever he was in a crowd, a flood of sound came jumbled to his disabled hearing.

He was only partially aware of how his disability affected his actions. It had come upon him gradually and he'd adapted in ways he hadn't realized. Sheriff Cal Rutan had sent him back to question Wells or the general about what the deputies should do, seeing as the Gatling was unhorsed and had become hard to handle on ice and snow. At least that's what Meldrum had interpreted from Rutan's sounds, lips, and gestures.

Now he was without a horse, had lost interest in the fake sheriff of San Miguel County, and was trying to make his way back to the real one when the Gatling finally steadied all its barrels at the enemy and fired.

Even to Bob Meldrum the sound was deafening.

53

ALETHA was covered in blood.

The Gatling gun had roared when she was within inches of grabbing onto Callie's coat. Horses reared, trying to avoid her. One stared at her in terror before its sharp hooves struck her down. Men and horses screamed in pain and confusion. Blood, snow, and ice mixed to a surface so slippery her hands slid out from under her when she tried to rise.

She'd thought the blood to be all her own. Down here she realized the carnage was general. Chaos reigned above her. She made it to her knees. Before she was knocked down again she saw Clyde Duffer leap over a fallen man. No expressionless, mechanical look on his face now, but the killer was still there and he was enraged. Aletha slithered around to see Cree making his way toward her, but Duffer landed on him and both went down out of sight. She could feel no bullets in her flesh, didn't know if she should feel much yet through the shock. But she could feel the numbing cold of the street beneath her, the heated rush of fear in her veins, a soreness in one shoulder where flaying hooves had struck her down. She wiggled past a man with blood spurting from his legs, his arms grabbing at air. She'd never realized blood had such an odd metallic smell to it. Another man, this one in uniform, lifted her to her feet and yelled in her ear, "Ladies shouldn't be out here."

And then he went down too. Whether he was shot or had slipped on the goo, she didn't know, but she dropped back to her knees when a bullet snapped by her nose. Aletha had known war only from films, but Armageddon, instinct told her, was as simple as one death—her own.

Bram O'Connell had blood on his clothes too, but his face was clean of it and the snarl that pulled back his lips. He leapt up to yank Bulkeley Wells from his horse. They struggled silently in the gory sludge. Fury locked Bram's curses inside him as surely as the exertion locked his jaws. He'd surprised Wells and had that advantage and two more: he was clearly the stronger, and Bram alone knew someone must pay for what had happened to Pa. When first he'd caught sight of Wells, he'd known who that someone would be. Throwing down his borrowed rifle, useless in the tight mix of bodies, he'd gone for the man with his hands. Even in the heat of it all a part of Bram reasoned odds. Wells had a couple of advantages too. A pistol—better for close combat, and an officer's uniform to command instant aid from the first soldier to spot his predicament. The captain's advantage was one of time.

Bram determined Wells would not have that time, knowing his own to be limited no matter the outcome. Bram had faced death before, but poorly. This time would be different.

One hand came down on his enemy's throat while the other grabbed the man's wrist to thwart the rise of the pistol. The huge eyes beneath him bulged.

Suddenly Bram was jerked off Wells. He was tumbled and pinned to the street. He stared up at the gunman, Bob Meldrum. The killer's knee came down on his chest and his boot tip in tight to Bram's crotch. The empty eyes lowered so close to Bram's face he could smell the chewing tobacco on the man's breath over the gore and gunsmoke that drenched the air. "She was a virgin, wasn't she, boy?"

"She" and "virgin" had no context in this man's war. But Bram's brain offered up an answer before his emotions could clear. There was but one woman he could answer to for that. Why should anyone care at a time like this? "Miss Heisinger?"

Meldrum read Bram's lips and then shook him. "There was blood on the sheets, wasn't there?"

The kid thought. He looked at Meldrum like he thought he was barmy. Then he shook his head. The kid shook his head no. "No blood."

Bob could feel considerable strength rising in the body beneath him as the kid began thinking of more important things demanding his attention, and he slipped off him before it was too late. Bram O'Connell might not be bright but he looked to be honest. You didn't find many like that in this modern age. Let somebody else kill him. Meldrum had more important things to do too. He walked off and left them all to it. He had a debt to call in.

* * *

Captain Bulkeley Wells watched Meldrum walk away unscathed. The battle seemed to open a path before him as the Red Sea had for Moses.

Wells had barely regained his hold on his pistol before the O'Connell boy faced him again. How could a common laborer have produced such a son? And if all Wells had heard about the mind inside was true as well . . . the trouble with enemies was involvement.

Bulkeley raised his pistol and looked into the face of the man-boy he was about to kill and knew that the military life was not for Bulkeley Wells. He pulled the trigger anyway. There was, after all, such a thing as duty. But the moment Bram O'Connell fell, Wells was on his knees beside him. An enemy is always best unknown.

Cree had wanted to kill Clyde Duffer in the 1904 depot. When Aletha and Renata had dragged him back to sanity and luxury and hot tubs he'd been glad that desire had gone unconsummated. Now he wanted only to drag Aletha back to the sheriff's car, hoping time would switch them to the modern medical attention she obviously needed. Instead he once again faced the nose he'd broken not so long ago. The man had him down so fast Cree didn't feel the fall, only Duffer's weight on his body and hands at his throat. Cree thought about killing again. He also thought about giving it all up. But as his lungs fought for the air Duffer tried to choke off, the rest of Cree bucked and plunged like an animal gone mad at a branding party.

He'd thrown Duffer off before he realized it. The false colors flashing before his eyes gave way to the reality that clashed around them. He'd rolled over to grab his attacker by the shoulders when silence fell on Colorado Avenue. Cree thought he had died. But he could blink. And so could Clyde Duffer.

"Are we going home?" Duffer asked, childlike. He pushed Cree away and struggled to his feet, eyes wandering toward the sky, head turning slowly one way and then the other as one does to listen.

Cree stood warily, ready to pounce on his enemy at the first provocation. He listened too, but all he heard was the labor of their breathing. It was still winter in Telluride, blood still stained the snow, they were still surrounded by men at war. The antique Gatling gun aimed uselessly at a snowbank. Sheriff Cal Rutan, for once without his cigar, sat about an inch above the saddle of a horse swiveling into an unfinished turn. Captain Bulkeley Wells knelt over a prostrate Bram O'Connell, his hand reaching toward the wound at the boy's temple.

All these men, horses, and weapons, the dying, and the unsuspecting with death coming at their backs—all waited. No wind, almost no air. Cree could move, Duffer could move, but their gasps for breath intensified and everyone else, man and beast, seemed stilled to concrete.

Bram's eyes were open, their expression one of arrested surprise. The head wound appeared to be hardly more than a graze, the bleeding slight. Cree knelt opposite Bulkeley Wells and felt Bram's neck for a pulse. The heat of life was there but no movement of blood. There was no pulse in Wells's neck either. Cree couldn't read the captain's expression, but he removed the pistol sagging from the man's hand.

"Hey, Maynard?" Duffer called tentatively into the vacuum.

Maynard Bellamy could move too and he turned to them with a slow-motion smile. Then he stuck his hand into the pocket of the stilled horseman next to him. The horseman had enough braid and metals on his coat to sink the *Titanic*.

Time for once really did stand still. Aletha was on her knees clutching Callie across the body of a fallen man. He had nasty burn scars on the side of his head. His blood was stopped in mid-spurt but it had already stained part of what looked a lot like Sheriff Tom Rickard's hunk of highgrade ore. It stained Callie's hands where she held the highgrade as if she was just setting it down there. It stained one of Aletha's hands where she clasped Callie. Callie wore a chain around her neck and as she was hunched forward it seemed to meld into the rock on her father's chest, as if the highgrade was a giant bauble on the end of the thin chain.

"Is this Renata's connection?" Cree asked the bloody tableau. It was more likely that he was in a dream. If time was really frozen, why wouldn't the fury of sound that had commanded here be drawn out in the unending notes of what had sounded at the second that time stopped? Why the silence? Cree reached for a bullet suspended about four inches from the back of Callie O'Connell's neck and threw it to the snow. If this wasn't a dream, then he was the one messing with history now.

Finger by finger, Cree pried loose Aletha's hold on Callie and gently pushed the girl over. She might be in danger from yet another bullet headed past Aletha. A patch of mist from Callie's breath stayed in the air where her face had been like a cloud or phantom in the forming. Callie's anguish stuck rigidly to her face, her body stayed in the same kneeling posture. She reminded Cree of the frozen burro at the end of Spruce Street in 1901, the night he'd walked the railroad tracks with her brother. But a piece of the highgrade had pulled away with the chain Callie wore and now resembled that quartz pendant of Aletha's. John O'Connell's blood surrounded the hole left in the rock, hovered at its edges, ready to fill it in in red.

The breathable air grew ever thinner. The silence was horrible. Duffer helped Maynard pick pockets now and their soft scurrying, their breathing, was all he could hear. If they and Cree could move, why was Aletha stuck? She felt warm to the touch. Did she have a wound that would be fatal when time resumed? Was that what made her different? Cree picked her up. Her stiffened kneeling position made it awkward, her deadweight strained his air-starved muscles, but he weaved them through hanging bullets, through puffs of white smoke suspended in balloon-billows at the ends of weapons, and through fighting statues. He felt like the only moving piece on a chessboard.

Cree headed for the sheriff's car. He knew Duffer would be right behind him, but he was locked into a nightmare and just had to keep functioning until he woke up.

Cree deposited Aletha on the front seat and turned to face Duffer and Maynard. Duffer, his hands full of loot, was just leaving the snow passage and Maynard just entering it from the street.

One of the investigators crawled out of the back as the screams and shouts and small-arms fire exploded into the vacuum and a dispatcher's voice spurted static on the radio. A man Cree recognized as the Pinkerton agent slipped out of the car and took off toward Duffer. But Clyde Duffer and the snowbank faded into autumn on Colorado Avenue and Simon Doud narrowly missed being hit by a pickup full of split logs and Siberian huskies. The driver honked and yelled suggestions but Doud kept running.

The fed had started after him but stopped now to stare around, nervously jingle the change in his pocket. The sheriff's car sat in front of the same house but on a paved street that passed much closer to it than it had in 1904. As Cree bent inside to see to Aletha, who was trying to sit up, the fed asked, "Where's the sheriff?"

54

CALLIE found herself lying on the ground beside Pa and thought she must have been shot and unconscious because she didn't remember Aletha going away. Pa said something in a voice that gurgled. Then he shuddered and went slack. Callie bent over him staring back at the glazing eyes, willing them to blink for her. She was bumped about by the men jostling around her but she held her place until someone seized her from behind and carried her to where the banked snow opened onto Townsend Avenue up which she'd come looking for her mother, days ago it seemed to her now.

"Are you hurt, girl? You must run from this place." The soldier set her on her feet and glanced over his shoulder. "I have to go back. What on earth are you doing here?"

Callie walked down Townsend Avenue feeling as if she floated like Ma'am had done on the railroad tracks.

"You do have a place to go?" he called after her. "Here, you've lost your necklace."

Callie would never remember by what route she came to the back door of the little crib. She didn't knock. Aunt Lilly sat at her table, her head resting on folded arms. The room smelled of rancid bacon grease and old perfume. Callie stood listening to the snow water drip from the eaves outside and the wind rattles in the soffits. Finally Lilly gave a snort and raised her head. Her face was red and puffy. The dark centers in her eyes almost swallowed up the blue. She wrinkled her forehead as if looking at Callie hurt her eyes

Then she took off Callie's coat and dress, checked to see if any of the blood came from Callie, and wrapped her in a blanket. Aunt Lilly took a long drink from the ladle, doused her face with cold water, and set some to heating to wash Callie. She capped the bottle of whiskey and put it away in a cupboard. "And Bram was there?"

"And I think Pa died. He couldn't live with so much blood out of him." Callie felt as if she'd drunk too much coffee. Her voice sounded like someone else's. "And Ma'am is still out there some-where."

Aunt Lilly cried and sniffed and cut bread and cheese for Callie. "I'll go find out what I can. Promise me you'll stay right here."

Callie pushed the food away and washed herself with the water that hadn't had time to heat. She floated out to use the privy and floated back inside. She had no idea how long Aunt Lilly was gone but she was sitting before the untouched food when her aunt returned. "I have friends out looking for Luella. The wounded have been taken to hospitals and the prisoners to Redmen's. No one would tell me any names. Callie honey, would you do something for me?"

"I'm not hungry."

"Oh, baby, just cry. Please? Just cry."

Callie put on the old black dress from the hotel she'd left here and her aunt sponged stains from her coat and plaid dress. It was dusk and Callie was poking at some stew but seeing Pa and the gore on Colorado Avenue when a big woman with greasy hair brought Ma'am to the door. "Found her in an outhouse halfway to String-town." She had Callie's mother under her arm like a long package. "Her clothes must have been soaked because they're almost frozen to her."

"They're after me. They're trying to keep me from my medicine." Ma'am's voice gurgled like Pa's had and then she began a cough so racking it took them all to hold her up.

Bram stood next to Bulkeley Wells at the undertaking parlor. Wells had cleaned away all signs of fight except for a swelling under one eye, but Bram was smudged and stained. He wore a bandage around his head and rope tied his wrists together in front of him.

"Where do you want the body shipped?"

"Lone Tree Cemetery."

"You know that's not possible. He was deported."

"He's dead."

"He was warned. Deported again and again. I even spoke up for him in court."

"He came back for his family."

"You had good marks in school. In every subject. Why did you quit when you were so close to victory?"

"I wouldn't march with the town against him."

"Ah . . . the cadets. That hadn't occurred to me. What will you do now?"

"Make a home for my sister and mother. Here."

"You know no member of the union will be allowed—"

"I never belonged to the union."

"You marched with them. It's the same."

"I came with him, to protect him."

"You attacked an officer."

"I didn't kill you. And you shot me."

"I want to know what has become of Mr. McCree Mackelwain. He was on Colorado Avenue this afternoon but disappeared again. Who is he?"

"A man who always seems to know what's going to happen. I didn't see him today."

"Did you see your sister? She was there with one of Mackelwain's women. And I have a report from a militiaman who claims he carried a girl from the battle. The girl's description sounds like your sister. She was also seen at the Pakka boardinghouse asking after your mother, who, it seems, left the train sending families out to their deported menfolk in Ridgway. Had you waited in Ridgway you might have found no need to march to this end." Wells gestured toward Pa, who was already stiffening on his pallet. "But no one at the boardinghouse has seen either of them since."

"Callie was there? Did she see what happened to him?"

"It's possible. She was bloodied but could walk. She left this behind." He held a piece of stained rock on a broken chain.

"If they're not at the boardinghouse . . . My sister was bloodied?"

"If it was she," Wells said, "she'll not want reminding of this place."

"We're staying. Every time you see us you'll be reminded of him, and so will the town." Bram watched Pa until the captain turned aside to speak to several men in uniform who had come looking for him. Then Bram bent to lay his cheek against John O'Connell's. When he straightened no one seemed to be looking his way so he slipped around the pallet and broke for the door to the alley.

Callie wiped her mother's face with one of the towels from her aunt's bedside table. Lilly had removed all the pictures of herself from the walls and stuffed them under the bed. Ma'am shook so hard she rattled the iron bedstead, even with Callie sitting beside her, but large drops of moisture on her skin glistened in the candlelight.

The woman who'd found Luella had stayed to help them put her to bed. "She's burning. She'll not last long if that fever don't break. Sounds like pneumonia to me, or what's about to be. And I've seen enough of it to know."

Aunt Lilly started crying again. Callie had never heard of anyone recovering from pneumonia in these high mountains. It was probably the biggest killer of people of all ages in the camps. But she didn't cry. She just kept doing things that needed doing or just sat doing nothing. She didn't particularly care which.

Several candles flickered on the high shelf that bordered the room, and the soft light made Ma'am look pretty again in her sister's ruffled nightdress. Across the room a candle burned between a beer stein and a plate painted with purple grapes. When Callie saw a white cat like Charles, but cleaner and fatter, sitting on the windowsill beneath it she thought it must only be part of this awful dream-day. But her mother sat up suddenly and watched it too. Luella screamed when the cat leapt into the room and disappeared.

Aunt Lilly raced in from the kitchen. Ma'am fell back on her pillow making choking sounds, her eyes rolling back under their lids. Lilly pushed Callie away, turned Luella over, and pounded on her back. She shook Luella by the shoulders. She called her sister's name over and over so loud it was a while before Callie realized she'd been hearing a commotion in the street, men's voices, running footsteps, and then a scuffling on the step.

"Callie girl," Bram called, and there were more scuffling sounds. "Callieee—"

The deadness dropped from Callie with a shock that left her reeling as she rushed for the door. There was enough light left to illuminate Bram's pale hair and the white bandage wrapped in a band around his head. He was trying to shake off two soldiers but his wrists were tied together in front of him.

Callie ducked under his bound hands and wrapped her arms around his chest so the soldiers couldn't untwine them. He smelled of that awful combination of blood and black powder she'd never forget. "I thought they'd killed you too."

Bram stopped swinging his shoulders to shrug off the men and brought his arms down tight to lock her to him, put his face in her hair.

"Pa's dead, Bram."

"I know, I know," he whispered and held to her tighter as the soldiers tried to force them apart.

"Let them be," a deep voice said behind her, and the rough hands stopped tugging at her arms and shoulders.

Bulkeley Wells wondered why he should feel such relief to see Callie whole and unhurt and why he kept thinking of the O'Connell children as children. They looked more like man and woman standing there, haloed by the light from the open door behind them. She had turned her back to her brother and rested her hands on the rope that tied his arms around her. The only resemblance they bore each other was the defiance in their expressions.

"The young man who saved you wanted this returned to you." Wells held out the worthless quartz fragment entwined by its chain. "He'll be happy to know you are safe." The militiaman had accosted Wells while he was still surveying the carnage, trying to rise above the sickening feeling it induced. The soldier had a leg wound but insisted on speaking with Wells before allowing his stretcher to be carried off. "You're of the town, sir," he'd said through his pain. "Could you find her and tell me if she's all right? How could her family have let her out in this?"

Now Callie looked at the stained gewgaw in his palm. "That's Pa's blood on it, Bram."

She ducked out of her brother's hold and took the necklace, held it to her chest.

"Ohthankgod, oh Bram . . ." A disheveled prostitute leaned out of the door and embraced the boy. "I couldn't find out any of the names." And the tart ignored them all to pull him inside. "She's calling for you."

Wells motioned his guards back and followed, but Callie wedged through the doorway beside him. "Why are you in this part of town?"

"She's family," Callie answered simply, and motioned toward the prostitute who stood behind Bram with her hands on his shoulders as he knelt beside the bed. His mother's illness appeared to have progressed beyond recall.

These places all tended to resemble one another. Rarely did one discover originality in a sporting woman. But even so Wells realized at once that he'd had personal business here. The prostitute looked over her shoulder, her tear-smeared face filled with recrimination as if he alone were responsible for the fate of this shattered family, instead of its dead father whose illegal activities had brought such agony down upon his wife and children. Wells was more accustomed to admiration even from these, the least of women, and he turned to the door in anger, prepared to order his men to arrest them all. But the boy choked back a sob behind him and Wells paused on the step, on his way to more important matters demanding his attention. When finally he gave the order it was with great weariness and it was that the O'Connells were to be left alone.

55

ALETHA had no wounds for all the blood on her clothing. She'd come across Callie while trying to crawl out of the conflict, had been pleading with the girl to leave her wounded father and flee, when suddenly she was hearing the static on the car radio instead of gunshots and shouting.

A sheriff's deputy had confiscated her clothes as possible evidence in the disappearance of Sheriff Tom Rickard. Aletha sat now in fresh clothes Tracy had brought up from the crib in a back pew of the empty courtroom with one of the feds. "Well, you can corroborate our story, surely, you were there too."

"All I know is that the three of you left the car at different times and you and Mackelwain came back and the sheriff didn't."

"What about the snow, the horses, the people in old-fashioned clothes—the war?"

"Nobody's going to believe that." He looked at his shoes and shrugged.

"You mean you're not going to tell the whole truth just because it won't be believed? You realize the predicament you're leaving Cree and me in, don't you?"

"I don't have a lot of sympathy for dealers."

"We are not dealers." The clock on the wall was electric now. Aletha kept seeing that flat gravestone in Lone Tree Cemetery and was sure Callie hadn't left the war on Colorado Avenue in time.

"Look, if I told what . . . what I think I saw, what good would it do you if nobody believed it? And it could lose me a job." But he was clearly not comfortable with his decision. "Tell me what you know about Mackelwain and that condo, his association with Massey, the bullet holes in his plane, the whereabouts of Duffer, Pheeney, and Bellamy, and what happened to that highgrade rock of the sheriff's, and I'll see what I can do for you."

So that was why she was sequestered off in this corner with this man. Cree was probably off in another corner with his partner. But Aletha told all of what she knew, the whole truth and nothing but. Like the man said, no one would believe it anyway.

Cree and Aletha were released on their own recognizance and ordered to stay in town for the investigation into the disappearance of the sheriff. The feds must have put in a good word for them.

"There is no case," Cree told her, "just wild stories and a lot of suspicion." They stood on the courthouse steps and he described it as it had been in 1901 with the procession of miners lined up for the burial of those killed in the Smuggler-Union fire. But Aletha stared down Colorado Avenue to Townsend Avenue and the scene of the battle.

The federal investigators stepped out of the door behind them. "We did what we could," the one who'd sequestered her in the courtroom said. He told Cree, "I'm recommending the narcotics investigation be dropped at our level. Doesn't mean it will be. We've promised to come back if the sheriff's body is found. Hell, I don't know what happened either. They're taking the condo. You're going to have to move." He handed Aletha a business card. "If you ever come across that guy who said he was a Pinkerton agent . . . I just want to talk to him so I'll know . . . whatever it was really happened, you know?"

"Do you think it's going to happen again?" Cree asked when they were alone. "Maybe we could get the sheriff home. Then we wouldn't have to stay here. We could get out of town."

"I don't have the pendant."

"You didn't have it last time either, remember?"

"Callie did."

"She still does."

Cree moved into a bed-and-breakfast place, the Oak Street Inn, and applied for a job Renata suggested, helping to create delicacies at MoNika's, the gourmet carry-out place. Before he could start work he was accosted by a well-dressed, well-spoken gentleman with the eyes of a Bob Meldrum but with sharper hearing.

"My guess is Duffer and the boys took the stash and split," Cree told him. "They had Dutch Massey's letter and instructions and found what I couldn't." They stood in front of what had once been Van Atta's and was now a sporting-goods store. Another gentleman sat in a car at the curb watching them. "I know I didn't find it or I'd have been gone too. Hey, honestly now, can you see me taking care of those three?"

The guy looked him over and stood thinking. "You could have had help. I'll keep in touch," he said finally and got into the car with his friend. He rolled down the window. "Mr. Mackelwain, you do realize that should their bodies be found you will be our first visit?"

Times like this, Cree wondered if he wouldn't have been better off if he'd stayed in 1901.

"You can't be the sheriff of San Miguel County, boy, because I am," Cal Rutan said in high good humor. He traced the official shield on Tom Rickard's jacket with the tip of his finger. "But it says here *you* are."

Sheriff Cal Rutan looked over Sheriff Tom Rickard's sunglasses on the table in his office at the courthouse and then the holster and sidearm. "Fancy, fancy, fancy," he pronounced them, and puffed up his cigar to glowing. "And will you look at them boots? You one of them jennymen cowboys from the Wild West Show?"

The crinkles at the edges of Tom Rickard's eyes smoothed out under his pallor. "Listen, I don't understand what's happened but I demand—"

"I do the demanding here. This is my county, friend, no matter what your fancy shields say. Deputy Meldrum, you want to lock this dude up for me?"

"On what charges?" Sheriff Rickard asked, but took another look at the short man standing next to him. Meldrum?

"On the charges that I want you under my thumb, sir," Sheriff Rutan said. "Until such time as I can determine what has become of a certain Mr. Simon P. Doud."

"I'm a Pinkerton man," Simon P. Doud told the couple in front of the tepee several hundred feet above Telluride. He'd never known white men to live in tepees, but these people were more reassuring than what he'd seen of the changed world below.

"No shit? Hey, that's cool, man," said the Man. He was dressed something like a prospector and had a good deal of gray in his beard with not much hair of any color on his pate.

"What's a Pinkerton?" the Woman asked. (That's how they'd introduced themselves. Just, "I'm the Man and this is the Woman.") She handed Doud a metal plate of beans with ground steak and tomatoes mixed in, filled a plate for the Man and one for herself, and settled before the campfire.

"Used to be a detective agency," the Man answered. "You know, like in *Butch Cassidy and the Sundance Kid*."

Aletha read the inscription on the imposing tombstone next to her. *Here rests the body of a dead husband.* THORVALD TORKELSON, *33 years old, who lost his life in Smuggler-Union Mine, Nov. 20, 1901, in trying to save the lives of others. Missed by a loving wife.*

Lone Tree Cemetery held quite a crowd this afternoon. Telluride had turned out to bury its oldest resident.

"Mildred Heisinger must have done something in all those years," the reporter for the Telluride *Times* insisted to Doris Lowell. "The only mention I can find of her in the existing files is a paragraph in the old *Examiner* about her house being broken into by four vagrants in 1904. And it's the same house she died in. That part of town was the red-light district in those days. Could she have been a prostitute? Or a madam?"

"Whatever she was, she wouldn't say when she was alive," Doris said. "Now that she's dead, let her rest, can't you?"

"Hey, Earl, you're about the next oldest native." The reporter cornered a short square man in a baseball cap. "What do you know about the deceased's past?"

"All I can remember is during the Depression us kids used to think she was a witch. Our folks just thought she was batty. Had a black woman living with her." Earl kneaded arthritic hands and looked into the hole awaiting Mildred. "She has to have been one hell of a lot old, I can tell you that."

When the graveside service was over and most everyone but the eternal crows had gone home, Aletha and Cree walked up the hill toward Callie's grave. Aletha knelt to brush dead leaves off the flat stone, wondering again why they'd inscribed only Callie's first name on it.

Up by the fence and to their right, two people sat on the ground, their shoulders hunched in a sorrow no one had exhibited for Mildred Heisinger. They sat before the mounded and raw earth of a double grave. Aletha was about to turn back and leave them to their privacy when she registered that the couple sat on snow and that the woman wore a hat.

"Oh, Callie, you didn't die . . . then." Aletha could detect no hole with a sizzling edge around the newly filled graves and the mourners, but the sun shining on her was not shining on them. The man with blond-white hair had a hat too, but held it on his lap. Tears trickled over prominent cheekbones.

"Our folks are dead, Aletha," Callie said dully. Her eyes were dry.

"Oh, honey, I'm sorry. But I'm so glad you're all right." Aletha started forward onto the snow but Cree pulled her back onto the grass. "Callie, do you know what's become of the sheriff? He didn't come home with us." Callie just gave her a blank look and turned back to her buried parents. "Our sheriff, not yours. I know you have more important things to think about but . . . the pendant, Callie, do you have that piece of quartz still?"

Callie reached into her coat pocket and brought out the pendant and chain. The last sound Aletha heard from Callie's world was the girl saying, "It's got Pa's blood on it."

"Bram," Cree said as the snow and the O'Connells faded. "Tap 'er light, son." And the double graves settled into an unmarked depression of fall-dried grass.

EPILOGUE

T HE union wars were over in Telluride although old hatreds persisted. In 1908 Bulkeley Wells narrowly missed death when a bomb was planted under his bed in the manager's house in Pandora where Arthur Collins had died. For all his charm, his popularity waned when Telluride's own Troop A mobilized to march off to Europe and World War I and Captain Bulkeley Wells refused to lead them. In 1918 Grace Livermore Wells divorced him and took with her their four children and the backing of her wealthy father. He remarried, sired another family, left Colorado, and lost most of the fortunes lent him to invest in the West's mineral wealth. On May 24, 1931, Bulkeley Wells shot off the top of his head in his office in San Francisco.

Audrey Cranston married her painter and moved to the sunny side of Telluride. The nude painting her husband had done of her was to cause her future embarrassment. It found its way to various barrooms, private gambling clubs, sat hidden in the storeroom of a drugstore for years, and eventually became exposed, long after its subject's demise, in a renovated New Sheridan Hotel.

Clyde Duffer and Maynard Bellamy were found with their hands full of the possessions of other men's pockets at a crucial point in Telluride's history. Sheriff Cal Rutan and the powers that were then did not seem to notice their bodies hanging from a tram tower that came down from the Black Bear Mine into Pandora. To this day no one knows the site of their burial.

Bob Meldrum's line of work, extremely specialized, became less necessary as events settled down. He took a job guarding the Smuggler-Union mill at Pandora from feared sniper attacks of rebellious unionists and later did the same up in Savage Basin at the Tomboy Mine. Millie Heisinger would come up to visit his shack and ride in the fantastic scenery in the summer months. But eventually his peacekeeping skills were not properly utilized in San Miguel County and he left for Wyoming, where he and others of his breed protected the cattle interests from the changes brought to the West by the farmer and the sheepman. Although there are many stories, no one knows for sure how or where Bob Meldrum met his end.

Brambaugh O'Connell and his Callie girl moved to the Tomboy Mine in Savage Basin, where Bram was forced to face his nightmare and to prove his mettle in the bowels of the earth with a hammer and drill. And Callie finally achieved her dream of having her brother to herself in a little cabin in the mountains that didn't take long to clean. If only it'd had an indoor toilet.

The *Examiner* made no reference to the vehicle on Lawyer Barada's lawn in its report of the battle because there were no witnesses willing to make fools of themselves who were old enough to be listened to. And it was gone before outside journalists reached the area. Thus it did not make its way into the written history of Telluride.

The highgrade ore was not recognized as such because of its sanguinary coating. A militiaman kicked it to the side of the street during the cleanup on Colorado Avenue. Lawyer Barada's daughter, Lydia, picked up the gruesome reminder of the savagery waged before the eyes of her children and buried it in the snow of the alley behind her house. The spring thaw cleansed it of its coating and it sat with other rocks at the edge of the alley undisturbed because no one looked for gold in an alley. Vegetation grew over it, masked it even as its twin in time sat in as yet uncut rock up at the Alta Mine waiting for John O'Connell to steal it and bury it under his cabin. So that Aletha, wearing the pendant, could switch it in time with Dutch Massey's stash. So the sheriff's deputies could dig it up and the sheriff could bring it back to Colorado Avenue in 1904. So Callie could carry it to her father and complete the circle with his blood in that moment when time stood still.

The pendant, born in that timeless moment, continued to act as the agent of time's misadventures whenever it was not sufficiently covered and either Aletha or Callie came near it. For they too had been bonded in the blood of that moment. Callie would have the chain repaired but it would not age any more than its pendant would lose its bloody stain. The pendant eventually passed down in time to become lost in Callie's effects and surfaced in 1980 when a descendant shipped it along with the rest to the San Miguel Historical Society and the museum. Not considered worthy of display, it was tossed out in the trash, where a little girl found it and took it home. Her mother's boyfriend, a starving-artist-who-liked-to-ski, knew of other artists prostituting themselves making tacky tourist trinkets to survive, and when he came across the pendant one day decided to make more like it to earn needed cash.

He kept the original as a model and inspiration and sold its clones. Eventually he expanded into other worthless gadgets until he had himself a small business which he hated and sold out to a hungry friend some years later. The friend placed the original pendant on the souvenir rack with its fellows in the lobby of the New Sheridan Hotel.

One wonders what might have happened if Aletha or Callie had never come to Telluride. Or if Cree Mackelwain had not messed with history by pushing Callie over in that moment time stood still.

As of this writing, Sheriff Tom Rickard has not been found and the blood on Aletha's clothing has been determined to be too old to be his. Older in fact than he is . . . was. And more mysteriously, older than the clothes it stained. The practical Renata Winslow has stopped talking of her time trip because she has an image to uphold in her small community. Tracy Ledbetter is learning to live with her terrible secret and to trust Aletha to keep it. Charles is the least content of them all because when Aletha took him in for his shots, the local veterinarian insisted she put the Victorian cat on a strict diet.

Aletha and Cree still take a perverse delight in each other's company, but miss the privacy and seven-foot Jacuzzi of the condominium on the second floor of the infamous Pick and Gad. And as the days pass without a recurrence of the frightening incidents, their relationship has had a chance to take a more normal course. In fact, just the other night Cree awoke with the startling idea of feeling her out about making that relationship more permanent. Something he'd sworn never to do again. And that same night, Aletha lay in her lonely bed in the crib and thought about the same thing. The upheaval in her life may have ended at last. Perhaps she could afford to trust this particular man. And perhaps she could dare to look forward to the future and not fear the past.

But of course, on the other side of the threshold, Callie O'Connell still has the pendant. . . .